PRAISE FOR JOHN BROWNLOW

'A fantastic and thrilling new entry into the modern-day spy genre'
Rawson Marshall Thurber, director of *Dodgeball*

'Reads like a winning Amazon Prime Thriller pitch . . . utterly
gripping from get-go'
Irish Independent

'*Agent Seventeen* reinvents the hitman novel. It's a cinematic
rollercoaster, full of authentic emotion and high-octane action. The
tension explodes off the pages; John Brownlow is a master of suspense'
Jeff Abbott, *New York Times* bestselling author of *Traitor's Dance*

'A roller-coaster ride of high-octane action that builds to an
explosive finale'
Sunday Express

'A slick, clever, edge-of-the-seat thriller'
Crime Review

'This is a fresh adrenaline-charged, and snarkily funny spy thriller
with an explosive climax'
The Peterborough Telegraph

'The pace never falters a single inch in this high octane, breathless
thriller. Lean, mean and thoroughly enjoyable'
Crime Time

'The book takes off like a rocket . . . Brownlow is an accomplished
screenwriter, and it shows'
The Financial Times

'Probably the most action-packed spy thriller that fans will read
this year, with short chapters where conspiracies unfold at the rate
of a particularly sharp shooting pistol dispensing bullets'
Irish Examiner

ASSASSIN EIGHTEEN

JOHN BROWNLOW

HODDER

First published in Great Britain in 2023 by Hodder & Stoughton
An Hachette UK company

This paperback edition published in 2024

1

A CIP catalogue record for this title is available from the British Library

Hardback ISBN 978 1 529 38258 7
Paperback ISBN 978 1 529 38262 4

Typeset in Plantin Light by Manipal Technologies Limited

Printed and bound in Great Britain by Clays Ltd, Elcograf S.p.A.

Hodder & Stoughton policy is to use papers that are natural, renewable
and recyclable products and made from wood grown in sustainable forests.
The logging and manufacturing processes are expected to conform to the
environmental regulations of the country of origin.

Hodder & Stoughton Ltd
Carmelite House
50 Victoria Embankment
London EC4Y 0DZ

www.hodder.co.uk

For Heather

"It's hard to go through life without killing someone."
— Richard Ford, *Canada*

PART ONE

I

I am waiting for someone to kill me.

Tonight would be a good night for it. There was a breeze earlier, but the air's almost still now, just a lazy sway in the tops of the trees, nothing that could divert a bullet from its path. The moon is almost full, high enough in the sky for a sniper to slip into position with ease, but not so high that I would be likely to see them. A month ago I'd have been invisible from the knob of the hill opposite, but the leaves have begun to colour and drop, and now the forest canopy provides a clear shot from a mile or more.

The house isn't mine. It belonged to Sixteen, my predecessor, sixteenth in a lineage of professional killers stretching back to the Romanovs. Some started as spies, others as traitors, saboteurs, idealists, policemen and in one case an orphan plucked from the streets of St Petersburg. But all of them ended the same way: elbow-deep in the blood of their fellow men and, sooner or later, their own.

The bearings on which the world turns need grease. We are the grease. We're flies who gorge on and dispose of the world's shit, maggots who clean out its festering wounds. We're the safety valve that stops the boiler exploding, the control rods that prevent another Chernobyl. We're little Dutch boys with our trigger fingers stuffed in the dyke of history.

Or some crap like that anyway.

A number is a vanity plate awarded by acclamation of your peers. It's like being voted Prom Queen or Advertising Executive of the Year (Southern Region), only for killing. In the old days we worked alone, on the tip of a hat or the touch of a nose, rewarded with diamonds sewn into the hems of jackets, suitcases full of used notes, bearer bonds, or that hoary old standby, a numbered account in Zurich. Now? Crypto, wash trades of non-fungible tokens, bogus real-estate transactions, offshore corporations, and the services of professional money launderers.

We also take cash.

Killers like us are the tip of an iceberg of death and betrayal, a perverse riff on the Hollywood star system with its moguls and day-players and marquee names. Top billing brings a hefty payday, but you're only as good as your last job, and there's always some starry-eyed motherfucker clawing their way up towards you on the greasy pole with plans to retire you permanently.

One through Fifteen were all dead by the time I was born. None of them expired in their sleep, or expected to. Sixteen's dead now, too. I didn't kill him, but it wasn't for lack of trying. Once he was dead, I took his place, his routines, his identity.

He was Sixteen.

I am Seventeen.

Somewhere out there is someone who means to become Eighteen .

The road they must travel passes directly through me.

I wish they would hurry up.

2

Officially, I'm retired, at the grand old age of a lot younger than you think. I have no handler, no infrastructure, no protection, no access to the kinds of jobs I used to do, nor any desire to do them.

The old me burned so bright you had to look away. For the best part of a decade he criss-crossed the world with a Welrod VP9 packed into a shoulder holster. It's comforting, solid, Hollywood-quiet *thock* was heard – or rather, wasn't – on all six continents, and beyond the Arctic circle. But that version of Seventeen killed too many people for reasons he didn't understand. He used to say that the first time you kill someone, you kill your old self. You're no longer that person.

He was half right.

Yes, you kill yourself, but not all at once. You annihilate yourself by attrition, until there's nothing left except The Thing That Kills. You're a hunter, tracking prey across a frozen lake, ice thinning as you follow tracks into the rising mist. Then behind you, there's a crack, and you turn to see a fissure in the surface rushing towards you. You run, but every step takes you further from shore until the ice finally splits beneath your feet and plunges you into the darkness.

That's where I am now.

The darkness.

I have no digital footprint.

No internet.

No cellphone.

No credit cards.

No Netflix.

No porn, except for a dog-eared pile of *Shiny Housewives* I found in Sixteen's basement.

I've listened to all his records.

I've watched all his DVDs.

I've tried drinking.

I've tried not drinking.

I've taken up smoking just so I can give it up.

I've grown roses.

I've grown zucchini.

I fucking *hate* zucchini.

I'm nothing.

I'm less than nothing.

A handful of dust. A cipher.

A negative number.

I am the square root of negative fuck all.

The house is sited for defence, an isolated split-level mid-century ranch-style perched on top of a hill, looking down onto the stub of a zero-horse town below. On the far side of the road that meanders down to the gas station, a forest rises up to overlook the big picture windows that stare out over the valley. The eight-foot electrified steel fence surrounding the property, along with buried vibration sensors and armoured steel doors, means any kind of frontal assault would be suicidal. The forest is clearcut a hundred feet back at every kink in the road as it descends, making an attempt at an ambush equally foolhardy. All of which leaves exactly one possibility: a thousand-yard shot from the knob of the hill opposite.

Tricky, but by no means impossible, especially with the light blazing in the wood-panelled room behind me, carefully positioned to ensure I form a perfect silhouette.

My social circle isn't a circle. It's a dot, consisting of one person: Barb, who runs the ramshackle motel on the single road out of town. There used to be two, but the girl with green eyes left six months ago and is never likely to return. I don't have the stomach to say much more, except that she's better off without. Whether the reverse is true is a matter for long nights of staring at the bottle. But she's gone, and our paths are never likely to intersect again.

I still have cable, and I pick up *The New York Times* and *The Washington Post* a couple of times a week. But what I read tells me the world of espionage has changed, moved online. Cryptography, ransomware, chained zero-day malware attacks, bulk collection, keyword analysis, AI pattern recognition, autonomous weapons, remote sensing, side-channel exploits.

I understand the words, know what these things are, but I have no interest in them.

Mine is the world of flesh and blood, and more blood. Of handshakes and hard drinking and bullets in backs. Hotel rooms wired for sound. Silenced weapons and lean muscles and fast cars. Explosions and flesh wounds, zip-tied wrists and beatings in alleyways. False passports and cover stories, blackmail and drunken illicit loveless sex. Nights in police cells, interrogations, escapes. Dead drops and suitcases full of cash. Billionaires and plots, shadowy cabals, private yachts and islands. Dictators in cross-hairs, impossible shots, and falls from high places.

Maybe the world I belong to no longer exists.

Maybe there's no longer a place for someone like me.

Maybe that's a good thing.

Before he died, Sixteen told me why he'd barricaded himself in this shag-piled hermitage. He was afraid, not of some swaggering young pretender coming to snatch his crown, but of the ghosts, the shades of his victims who gathered at his bedside at night to torment him. He kept a pistol in a drawer in the kitchen, a single round chambered, in case the clamour of the spooks ever got too loud.

I've ghosts of my own now, too many to count, and sometimes in the silence of the early hours, I too hear them whispering. Once in a while I open the drawer and stare at the revolver, or pick it up and feel the weight of it in my hand. There have been times I've put it to my head to imagine what it would feel like to simply not exist any more, and how, if at all, that would be different from how I live now.

But then I slip the safety back on and replace it in the drawer.

Because I don't mind dying. Just not like that.

I don't miss it, the life.

I miss it like *hell*.

But I'm done with killing for no reason. That road only ever arcs back to here, to the four walls of a dead man's house, where my only companions are vengeful spirits and a loaded revolver in a drawer.

What I need is a purpose. A *cause*.

And so for a hundred and seventy-four nights in a row, I've stood at the tall picture window with the light blazing behind me, resting my head against the glass, feeling the cool of it on my forehead, holding my breath a minute at a time as if by sheer force of will I could summon a bullet out of the darkness that would call me back to life.

I'm about to turn away for the hundred and seventy-fifth time when I see the muzzle flash.

3

From the top of the hill opposite to the window is a thousand yards. A high-velocity round leaves the muzzle at around two thousand miles per hour, which makes the flight time around a second. Average human reaction time to a visual stimulus is a quarter of that. All of which means I have ample time to literally dodge the bullet.

But I don't.

Because I've made a pact with the universe, kismet, fate, whatever you want to call it.

If the bullet finds its target, fine. Whoever pulls the trigger will become Eighteen and wear the number like flair on a server's uniform – *SMILE if you like HEADSHOTS!!!* Mine will be hung up to fade, the jersey of a forgotten hotshot fluttering from the rafters of an empty arena.

But if the universe lets me live, it will release me from the darkness.

It will mean I still have a place in the world.

And as a result, I will practise not security-by-obscurity, but security-by-being-totally-fucking-out-there. I will drive and most likely wreck monstrously overpowered supercars. I will travel to far-off lands, and perform unlikely stunts of parkour under fire from automatic weapons, eluding the forces of the world's deadliest nation-state intelligence agencies.

I will, on occasion, save the world.

9

There's just one problem.
The shot is fucking *perfect*.

The bullet hits me squarely between the eyes.

4

I am dead.

The end.

5

My vision swims, then slides into focus. Apparently, whatever circle of hell I've been dispatched to has popcorn ceilings and a fan that wobbles in exactly the same rhythm as the one in Sixteen's house. Frankly, I was expecting more from the afterlife.

Either that, or I'm not dead after all.

There's no bullet hole in the window, just a spidering crater on the other side. According to the invoice I found in the basement, the windows are Level 7 bullet-resistant glass-clad polycarbonate, rated to stop five hits from a NATO round.

A professional sniper, some wannabe Eighteen, would have accounted for all of this. They'd have used a .50, a shell that can pierce steel plate armour or six inches of ballistic glass. And they'd have aimed for the body, a guaranteed kill since the shockwave from a bullet that size will turn your viscera into dog food.

But what hit me was smaller, and a headshot. The glass stopped the bullet, and transferred all its kinetic energy to me, like a hammer to the face.

I put my hand to my mouth. It comes away with blood, and a tooth.

I stumble to my feet, still dizzy from the blow, and kill the lights.

Whoever pulled the trigger just gave me my life back.

When I find them, I'm going to thank them, then I'm going to kill them.

Just not in that order.

6

I roar out of the basement on a 4x4, FLIR goggles perched on my head, a Sig Sauer across my back. The shooter must have seen the window shatter, then watched me struggle up. But they didn't try a second shot, so either they chose to retreat or, more likely, figured I would respond by attacking, and needed time to prepare for an open battle.

From the top of the hill there's only one obvious bail route, a rutted forest track that empties onto the highway twelve minutes away. If he goes that way he'll likely escape, and I'll be forced to track him down like a dog, but if his intention is to become Eighteen, he has no choice but to stand his ground and fight to the death.

He, his, him. Why do I think it's a man?

It's not like there aren't women in the profession, but the first amongst them, Bernier, is dead now, chainsawed most of the way in half a year ago by the girl with green eyes, an act which she refused to allow to define her. The second, Osterman's girl, Kovacs, forced me to put a bullet in her in a hotel room in Berlin, with her musk still clinging to my skin. And the third, most dangerous of all to me in every way, has been silent now for almost a decade.

I circle round to where the bush drops down into a hollow hidden from the top of the hill. He'll track me by the engine noise, but this way I'll both remain out of view, and deny him the escape route to the road. Less than a minute later I make the swale, and ditch the ATV.

I pull down the goggles and move silently through the trees. With a year to prepare for this, I know the forest like the contours of my own face. Still hidden by the ridge, I spiral up towards the knob of the hill, using a hidden trail I cleared of brush to keep my footfalls silent.

Every few seconds, I stop and listen. There should be only silence, the forest ambience, and if I'm lucky the snap of a branch or twig under a tactical boot.

But that's not what I hear.

It's breathing. Fast. Panting, almost. And something else. The rustle of leaves under feet. Did whoever it is team up? If so, why are they moving like amateurs? But these aren't the noises of men in tactical gear. They're lighter. *Much* lighter.

I crest the ridge, silent and cautious. Nothing on the goggles. I pull them off to get a better all-round view. And ahead of me something glints in the moonlight.

It's a sniper rifle, a Sako TRG 42. Finnish, high quality. In other circumstances a fine choice. But the Sako is chambered for a .300, and its effective range is maybe 1100 yards. The house was already at the edge of its envelope, and once you factor in the near certainty my windows were ballistic glass, the chances of a kill with it were essentially nil.

There's only one reason anyone skilled enough to find me and brave enough to pull the trigger would use a weapon like this: because the shot was a feint, designed to draw me out.

Well, here I am. So why hasn't he made his move?

The breathing is all around.

It's starting to creep me out.

I pull the goggles back on. Nothing.

And then I see it.

A flash of light. A glow.

Body heat.

Just not a human body.

7

It's a wolf.

And another.

And another.

An entire pack, circling, hunting, maybe drawn here by the crack of the sniper rifle.

Christ, what a way to end.

Here lies Seventeen, eaten by wolves.

And then I realise.

It's not me they're hunting.

It's someone – or something – else.

Their shapes glow green all around me, eyes bright. They're focused on a gnarled old maple, edging forward under the leadership of a full-grown alpha, so intent on their prey they don't notice me circling the trunk to see their intended kill.

I don't know what it was I was expecting to see.

My attacker?

A hunter who disturbed him, whom he killed?

A wounded deer?

Bigfoot?

Whatever it was, it wasn't this.

I have to push up the goggles to make sure it's not an equipment malfunction.

Because pressed up against the tree is a child.

A girl, maybe nine years old, wearing forest camouflage, face painted black.

She's utterly, completely terrified.

The wolf pack chooses that moment to attack.

8

I could hit half of them with the automatic, but the rest of the pack would devour her. So instead I empty my magazine into the trees and stars, shells ripping through foliage, bringing branches and leaves cascading down. The noise splits the night in half, and the wolves hurtle away in panic, tearing through undergrowth into the darkness. I snap the goggles back on and pivot around, hoping they're gone, but instead they regroup in an arc a hundred yards away, hungry and still intent on a kill. But the big alpha is nowhere to be seen.

I quickly click in a fresh magazine. Killing animals who are simply following their instincts gives me no pleasure. But the kid's life is worth more, even one who just tried to kill me.

I turn back to the tree to tell her not to be afraid, that I'll protect her.

But she's gone.

In the corner of the goggles, I see a flash of human body. I spin round. She's running fast, straight towards a group of three wolves, the alpha among them, invisible to her in the dark.

'Stop!' I yell.

She doesn't.

The three animals break into a run towards her. Behind me, the rest of the pack charges, baying. She's caught in a pincer movement, and she still hasn't seen anything.

No matter how I trained, I never broke ten and a half seconds on a hundred-metre sprint. Even that demands Olympic-level dedication, and a body graced with the genetics to achieve it.

I'm currently carrying an automatic rifle, pistol, and ammunition, wearing boots, night vision equipment and body armour, but I swear my pace is under ten as I pound towards her.

I'm *still* too slow.

At the last moment she sees the three wolves, a wall of teeth and fur hurtling towards her. She stops dead and screams, a nine-year-old's scream of abject terror. As the alpha leaps to attack her, jaws wide, I snatch her up with one arm and use the rifle in the other to slam it away.

The huge animal thumps to the ground and scrambles to its feet. The girl writhes and squirms under my arm as I turn to face the wolf, not just hungry, now, but furious at being humiliated. I glance behind me to see the pack creeping closer. I fire into the trees again, but they're used to it now. The alpha lopes forward again, muzzle pulled into a snarl, then breaks into a run.

The kid struggling under my arm makes one-handed aim with the Sig Sauer impossible, so I drop it and pull my pistol, but by the time I have it unholstered the wolf's already airborne, leaping towards us. A moment before it strikes, I nail it between the eyes, and its dead weight slams into me, a hundred and seventy pounds of feral stink that knocks me off my feet.

As I push it off in disgust, the girl slithers out of my grasp. I flip over and grab for her ankle, but her foot slips out of the shoe and sock. I drop the pistol and flail at the bare foot with my other hand, but she bites down hard onto the knuckle, digging at it with tiny, sharp nails. I hold fast, fumble for the pistol with my free hand, and flip back over again to face the wolves. They're edging forward again, but they've forgotten me. It's the alpha they're interested in now, sniffing the still-warm body of their dead king.

I fire a single shot into the air, and they scatter, leaderless and afraid.

I jam the kid under my arm like a football and head back to the 4x4.

9

I have no experience with children. I was barely one myself, dragged from flea-bitten motel to flea-bitten motel by my junkie hooker of a mother, Junebug, who never treated me as a child so much as a friend and partner in crime. I functioned as her lookout, confidant, and banker – I looked after the money she earned, counting it, stuffing it into a battered *Sesame Street* lunchbox and setting aside enough to pay for the motel room and make sure we had enough to eat that week. But I was also her supplier, a go-between who ferried cash to men in sagging cars and dilapidated apartments.

I don't remember a time when Junebug wasn't some version of an addict. There were weeks when she fought it as bravely as I've ever seen anyone battle anything, and others when she gave herself up to it entirely. Her life was a continual struggle to claw her way out of the quicksand of her own history – a childhood desecrated by her religious nut of a father with the silent assent of her mother, an existence she fled at fifteen. But like quicksand, the harder she fought, the deeper she sank.

By the time I was eight or nine, I had an acute sixth sense for cop cars and undercover vice detectives. I knew how to lie to CPS, family court judges, and anyone who asked a question I didn't feel like answering. I watched the ebb and flow of her afflictions. I doubt Junebug was ever diagnosed, but I'm guessing she was what DSM describes as Bipolar II. She'd have periods of sunny optimism, make elaborate plans for our future, save money, buy new clothes, and pull herself together almost entirely. We'd eat healthy food, and she'd read self-help books she shoplifted from the shelves by the grocery store checkouts. She'd lay off the junk, which meant she'd work more than usual, and her clientele would improve. That meant they paid more, and as a result the Big Bird tin under the bed would fill with tens and twenties instead of the usual crumpled fives and singles.

Those were the good days.

But then another day would arrive. I got to know when it was coming because she'd get quiet, and some days instead of working she'd sit on the bed and cry for no reason. And I realise now that she was still fighting, but that she knew inside the battle was already lost, and it was only a matter of time before she surrendered again. She also knew I'd put up a fight, so she'd raid the lunchbox while I was asleep. I knew the signs well enough to hide it, or take most of the money out of it and put it somewhere else, but there are only so many places to conceal contraband in a shithouse motel room, and a junkie knows all of them.

She'd already be high by the time she got back from wherever or whoever it was. I'd wake to find her stumbling back into the motel unit, and at that point the best I could do would be to keep her awake and, if that failed, stop her choking on her own vomit. And the cycle – it varied from a few weeks to a few months – would begin again.

When I was nine years old, a man murdered her in front of me, and after that I was no longer a child in any sense other than the physical.

10

The girl fights me like a wildcat all the way back to the house. I can barely steer the ATV, trying to hold her tight enough that she won't escape without hurting her or breaking any bones.

I make it as far as the front door, but as I close it behind us, she wriggles out of my grasp. I manage to block the exit, but she disappears inside the house. By the time I get the door locked, she's gone. Fifteen minutes of humiliating hide and seek follows, looking under beds and in closets, behind doors and even under the cushions of the sofa. Then as I head down into the walk-out basement, with its gym and armoured cabinets crammed with weapons and explosives, I hear tiny footsteps behind me. I spin around in time to see the bathroom door slam shut, and the sound of the lock.

There's no window, which means she's not going anywhere, so I deposit myself on the top step of the basement stairs, finally with a moment to think.

It was the kid who pulled the trigger, I'm sure of that: I could smell cordite on her as I wrangled her from the ATV to the house. But a nine-year-old girl didn't carry twenty pounds of rifle, scope and ammunition on her shoulder up from the road, choose a firing position, and line up a perfect shot on the window. She wasn't the one who figured out where to find me, but whoever did didn't even bother to tell her she should get the fuck out of Dodge once she'd taken her shot. And something tells me she has no particular ambition to become Eighteen.

So who is she? A proxy? A way of taking a shot at me with no jeopardy?

Who sent her? Why choose a child? Because she didn't understand the risks?

If so, who wants me dead, if it's not to claim the crown?

If not, what the hell was the point of any of it?

More baffling than any of that: what the *fuck* am I supposed to do with a nine-year-old girl?

I need answers. And I know a lot of interrogation techniques. The things you saw in Abu Ghraib – stress positions, waterboarding, electrocutions, dog attacks, sleep deprivation – they were the tame stuff. The real showstoppers were developed out of sight in mediaeval dungeons, Nazi interrogation centres, Syrian prison cells, or the basement of the Kremlin.

But there isn't a single one I am willing to use on a kid.

I listen at the bathroom door for a few seconds. There's a snuffling inside that might be crying. I knock gently on the door, and it stops.

'It's okay,' I say. 'I'm not going to hurt you, I promise. But I need you to open the door.'

I can just make out breathing, fast and shallow and scared.

The bathroom door is flimsy, and I could simply break it open. But to get information, I need the girl to trust me, and that means she has to be the one who opens it.

'I'm just going to sit here,' I tell her through the door. 'Until you're ready to open it.'

I prop my back up against the door, and stay there for an hour. As I listen in silence, the shallow breathing slows and becomes steady, deep even.

After almost ninety minutes, I hear a little snore.

I guess even tiny assassins need their sleep.

There's a tiny hole in the doorknob so that you can open it from outside. I find a screwdriver that fits and, as quietly as I can, turn the lock. I listen for a change in the breathing, but it doesn't come. Gently, I push the door open. In the darkness I can just make out her shape at the other end of the room, huddled between the bathtub and the washbasin. There's something in her hand, but I can't make out what, so without taking my eyes off her I find the light switch with my hand and softly click it on.

Big mistake.

II

The girl snaps upright, and I see what's in her hand.

It's a cut-throat razor.

She backs up against the wall, brandishing it, charcoal face paint streaked with semi-dried tears, glaring at me with a feral intensity that's part defiance and part fear.

My eyes flick over to the still-open bathroom cabinet. The vintage razor was yet another piece of Sixteen's old fart persona. I should have junked it with the rest of his detritus months ago, but I never thought of myself as a long-term resident, and as his guest, even if he was dead, it seemed wrong to throw out his stuff. We had our differences, to say the least, but he was maybe the last person left on earth who could understand what it means to be me.

In some stupid way I felt like this place was a shrine to him.

Well, that's where sentimentality gets you, I guess.

A nine year-old girl is not a major challenge to disarm, but I'm trying to build trust here, so instead I hold up my hands to show that they're empty.

'I'm not going to hurt you,' I tell her again, and move towards her, as slowly and unthreateningly as I know how, palms out.

She doesn't move, her eyes locked on mine.

I'm just six feet away now.

'It's okay, it's okay,' I repeat. 'Just give me the razor.'

I keep coming. She realises she's cornered, because her eyes dart about, and her hand trembles. Maybe it's just her arm

24

getting tired, or maybe it's fear, but it doesn't matter, because as I reach out to take the razor, she suddenly puts it to her own throat.

In her eyes, a look that says, *believe me, I'll do it.*

I put my hands up again, and back off.

The razor doesn't move.

'Please. Just put the razor down,' I say.

The razor doesn't move.

'I just want to know why you tried to kill me.'

The razor doesn't move.

'Can you tell me your name?'

A thought occurs to me.

'Do you understand English? Just nod if you do.'

She doesn't.

Fuck.

I try German, Italian, Spanish, French and Arabic. All I get is a blank stare, but I swear there is a flicker of understanding on the fourth. On a hunch, I try one more time.

'*Tout va bien. Je ne vais pas te faire de mal.*'

Her eyes tell me she understands. The razor barely moves, but I can see that it no longer presses as hard against her skin.

I point to myself. '*Seventeen. Je m'appelle Seventeen. Et toi?*'

Her lips move and she says something but it's so quiet that I can't hear it.

I make to move closer, but I see the razor press into her skin again, so I back off.

'*Ton nom. Tu t'appelles . . . ?*'

'Mireille,' she says. Her voice is tiny, scared.

'Mireille,' I repeat. '*C'est un joli nom. Tu parles Français?*'

She nods.

'*As-tu peur de moi?*'

She nods.

'*Tu n'as pas besoin d'avoir peur. Je te le promets.*'

She lowers the razor a fraction, still unsure.

We stay like that for a moment. I'm at a loss for what to do next, but then it hits me. She must have been out in the forest for hours, waiting to take her shot, but around her there was no sign of any food, no candy wrappers, no canteen, nothing.

'*As-tu faim?*' I say.

She nods.

12

Sixteen, for all his macho bullshit, had strangely childlike tastes, and shoved at the back of his cupboards and freezer is a panoply of junk: Cap'n Crunch™ and Lucky Charms™, Alphaghetti™ and Zoodles™, Twinkies™ and Suzie Qs™, Hot Pockets™ and Pop-Tarts™.

I gather the boxes and packets on the counter, fetch a TV tray from the lounge and set about assembling the unhealthiest smorgasbord on record. As I pour milk into a bowl of dayglo cereal, I glimpse a small face peeping out of the gap in the bathroom door I left ajar. But the moment I look round she darts back out of view.

I take the tray and head over, push the door open. She's back in position, jammed between the bathtub and washbasin, razor still in her hand. But her conviction's gone, and when I put the tray down for her to see what it carries, her eyes widen into childish 'O's of desire.

I retreat, settle with my back against the door, and wait.

She eyes me suspiciously, then slowly approaches the tray, sniffing at it like a cat, the razor all but forgotten. With her free hand she pokes a Hot Pocket, smells it, then puts it down again. She does the same with a couple of the other items, then looks up at me with a question in her eyes.

'It's for you,' I say in French. 'Eat whatever you want.'

The kid's not just hungry, but famished. She works her way through the whole tray with methodical efficiency. First the bowls of cereal, then the pasta and toaster pockets, finishing with the cakes. Her determination is mixed with curiosity, sampling each item as if it was an alien substance, or possibly toxic, then once she's satisfied it's edible, wolfing it down in one go.

There's a feral quality about her to be sure – not least the way she fought me, or threatened to slice her own throat open with the razor. But she doesn't have any of the tells of an abused or discarded child. She doesn't guard her food the way I learned in children's homes. She has no visible scars. Her nails are trimmed and her hair is neatly cut. The fact that North American junk food is new to her suggests a life lived differently, and maybe better.

I spot a pink plastic bobble in her hair.

Whoever she is, however she ended up here, one thing's clear: somebody loves or loved her until very recently. And with the realisation, a wave of déjà vu breaks over me.

She could be me at the same age.

Once Junebug was dead, there was no-one left to protect me from all the horrors that, two decades and an army of corpses later, found me holed up in a dead man's house with only a loaded revolver for company.

I feel no anger. Just a weird, distinctly alien, desire to protect her.

She's still wearing the camouflage jacket, but as she raises a bowl to drain the last trickle of sugary milk, I notice a bump at the front, as if something was stowed there. It's not a weapon – I'd have felt it when I carried her in – so I say in French:

'Mireille, what's in your jacket?'

She looks up, suspicious.

'I'm not going to take it,' I say. 'I just want to see what it is.'

Her only answer is a hearty girlish belch. She pulls her jacket defiantly tighter, and tips her head to the side.

Apparently we're now in a negotiation.

'Do you want something else?' I say in French.

She nods.

'*J'ai soif.*'

I head back to the kitchen. I need leverage if I'm going to find out what's in the jacket, and a glass of water or 2 percent milk isn't going to cut it.

I root around in the fridge until I find something. A bottle of Mexican Coca-Cola. It's connoisseur's stuff, made with cane sugar, not corn syrup, another of Sixteen's boomer indulgences.

I prepare it with the finesse of a mixologist. I drop ice into a glass, pour the Coke over it, then cut off a slice from a lemon on the counter, and twist it into the glass. Finally I find a straw – no, fuck it, *two* straws – and plop them in.

I head back into the bathroom. Mireille's eyes glue themselves to the glass.

Junk food might have been new to her, but the kid knows a Coke when she sees one.

She reaches for it, but I pull it away and nod towards the lump in her jacket.

Show me.

She shakes her head.

I shrug, put my mouth to the straws, as if to drink it myself.

'*Non!*' she says, outraged.

Very cautiously, she unzips the front of her jacket a few inches.

She reaches in and pulls something out.

It's a one-eyed sock monkey, with just a thread where the other eye used to be.

'Can I?' I say in French, and reach for it, but she shakes her head and clings to it.

'It's okay,' I tell her. 'It's yours. I won't take it.'

She goes to stuff him – it looks like a him – back in her jacket.

'Wait,' I say. 'What's his name?'

She says it, and I feel myself go cold.

It's my name.

Not any of the names I use now, not Seventeen, not my sometime alias Jones, but the name my mother gave me. The name I haven't used since the day I blew out the brains of the shiny-faced juvie guard who had abused me for years in the vestry of an evangelical church.

The name that nobody should know.

My dead name.

This just went from bad to deeply fucking creepy.

13

Half an hour later, sleep overwhelms her.

In the harsh overhead light of the bathroom, the skin of her face where tears have washed away the black paint has a certain look to it.

I dampen a face cloth and gingerly wipe the charcoal off. I'm afraid I'll wake her, but she's in that dead, deep sleep of childhood that eludes us as adults. As the cloth does its work, I realise I was right. She's mixed race, part white, part something else. West African, maybe, or African-American, or something else entirely.

I have to sit back as another wave of déjà vu breaks over me. It's not just that she could be me, but something else. Something familiar, like a word on the tip of your tongue, a face you can't place, or one of those scents that instantly takes you back to a time and place, only you can't figure out when or where.

I dab her face dry, then pick her up in my arms and carry her into the still-dark living room. There, I lay her on the couch, cover her with a Navajo blanket, and sink into an armchair to watch her sleep.

It's 3 a.m. now, the moonlight glinting off the fractured window where the bullet hit.

None of it makes any kind of sense.

If someone wanted to become Eighteen by killing me, they'd have done it themselves. Assassination by proxy achieves nothing. So the motive is something else. But I've been out of the game for a year. Whatever secrets I once knew, the details of all my operations, were exposed in the conflagration that ended with both Sixteen and my old manager-cum-agent Handler dead. In short, I no longer represent a threat to anyone, and yet someone was willing to sacrifice a child – a child who somebody evidently cared for – to see me dead.

Mireille stirs in her sleep, turns over slightly, the blanket rising and falling with her breath.

One thing is clear: my cover's blown. Whoever sent Mireille, set her up in the forest with a sniper rifle, aimed it at the window and drew back the bolt, knows who I am and where I live.

If they figured it out, then so can others.

I need to move out, and fast, but I can't leave her here and a single man travelling with a girl-child not his own is going to attract all the wrong kinds of attention.

The alternative is to abandon her, dump her on the doorstep of a random hospital or firehouse, call in her location anonymously, and let CPS figure it out. But the kid is my only clue as to who I'm fighting, let alone why. Besides, bouncing from foster placement to children's home to secure children's home to juvie like I did is something I'm not going to inflict on any child, even one who pulled a trigger on me.

What if that's the point?

What if whoever sent her knows me well enough to know I won't harm her?

What if they know I'm never going to dump a kid – *any* kid – into the same circumstances that produced me? That I'm incapable of simply abandoning her?

What would *that* mean?

I think back to the underpowered sniper rifle, operating at the edge of its capabilities, firing bullets at ballistic glass it could not hope to penetrate, the sock monkey with my own name, the name that nobody should know.

It would mean that my enemy is someone who knows me almost as well as I know myself, and perhaps even better. And it would mean the shot was never meant to kill me, but to draw me out into the open where I'm not just an easy target, but made doubly vulnerable by the baggage of an almost entirely silent, unknown child by my side.

Well, congratulations. It worked.

Bring it on.

14

At first light, I pack the ATV with a low-profile, high-lethality loadout, then go back for the girl. *Mireille*, I remind myself, *that's her name. Mireille.*

She's still asleep on the couch. She doesn't wake as I scoop her up, still wrapped in the blanket, but as I step out of the door, she stirs in the cold night air and throws her arms around my neck, her head unexpectedly heavy on my shoulder.

This must be what it's like to be a father, I find myself thinking, a thought so foreign to me it might as well have flown in from the edge of the galaxy.

The back door of the Jeep is open, and I have to gently peel her arms away as I deposit her in the middle of the rear seat between two kitbags. I support her lolling neck with a rolled-up camouflage net and buckle a seatbelt around her tiny form, padding it out with a jacket so that it snugs tight.

I click the door shut gently so as not to wake her.

Half a mile out of town, a MOTEL sign swings on rusty chains. I pull into the potholed parking lot, then round to the rear, leaving the Jeep out of sight.

The first time I ever drove into this town, the motel snagged my attention. It could have been any one of ten thousand failing motels with empty parking lots and COLOR TV IN EVERY ROOM that line the highways that criss-cross flyover country. But that wasn't what caught my eye. It was the lonely female figure I glimpsed in the lights of the office, her back to me, as I drove past. I couldn't have guessed then how our paths would become entwined, or how it would end, but she's gone now, and our courses are never likely to converge again.

Mireille's still out cold, so I unbuckle the seatbelt, lift her up again and carry her to the rear door of the motel. I hammer on the ribbed glass door as hard as I can without disturbing her. A couple of minutes later, a light comes on, a figure appears, a lock turns, and the door opens to reveal a woman in her late fifties, with bleached Dolly Parton hair in a net, a housecoat wrapped around her and a cigarette clamped to the side of her lips.

She stares at me, with the kid limp as a sack in my arms.

'What the fuck?' says Barb.

'It's a kid,' I say.

'I can see that. Why have you got a kid, and what have you done to her?'

'She tried to kill me, I rescued her from a wolf pack, and I fed her junk food. Her name's Mireille. That's pretty much all I know.'

'Huh,' says Barb, and takes a drag on her cigarette.

It takes a lot more than something like this to knock her off-kilter, which is why I'm here.

'Are you going to let me in?'

'Is there criminal liability involved? Any dead bodies?'

'Not yet,' I say, although I have a feeling this state of affairs is not likely to persist.

15

'Tried to kill you how?' says Barb. She's sitting on the edge of a threadbare chair in the back office of the motel, still smoking. The kid is out cold on an old couch, buried under a blue comforter.

'Pulled the trigger on a sniper rifle someone set up for her in the woods,' I say. 'Whoever it was left her there to do the work and take the consequences.'

'Jesus.' She pauses for a second, takes another drag on her cigarette. 'But you had to know someone was coming eventually.'

Barb might look like a thrift store Tammy Wynette, but she knows the territory. Not least because she got herself tangled up with Sixteen, but also because she led what you might call a full life before she landed here in buttfuck, South Dakota. The amateur tattoos on her upper arm, which only partially disguise her needle scars, tell a tale of their own. I took her hostage once, a mistake I paid for with a full can of bear spray to the face, but we worked through our differences.

I wouldn't say Barb is a friend, exactly, because she correctly regards me and my motivations with deep scepticism, but she's the closest thing to an ally I have within a day's drive, and likely a chunk more than that.

'She talk?'

'Barely. Her name's Mireille. She understands French. But that's all I could get out of her. My guess is she was given orders to stay shtumm.'

'Poor fucking thing,' says Barb. 'You hear about child soldiers, but you don't expect to find them in your own backyard. You got any leads on who she is or who set her up with the shot?'

'That's where you come in.'

'Go on.'

'She's been looked after,' I say. 'No signs of abuse. Nails trimmed. Bobble in her hair. Whoever it was even let her bring a stuffed toy.'

Barb looks over, sees the monkey peeping out from the comforter.

'Which means her handler was someone close to her, or who at least cared for her. Plus, someone who could travel freely with a nine-year-old girl without arousing suspicion.'

'A woman,' says Barb.

'I think so. Probably posing as her mother.'

Barb frowns. 'So they cared enough for her to do her hair and make sure she had a stuffed toy, but they were willing to sacrifice her to kill you? It doesn't make sense.'

She's right. Which means there's something I'm missing.

'Whoever it was, I need to find them,' I say.

'How?'

'If she was travelling with a woman, they needed time to scope out the shot. That means they were overnighting somewhere. Camping out would have been too exposed, and I might have been checking the forest. So what are the possibilities round here?'

'Winnebago in a Walmart parking lot,' says Barb, 'or a motel like this one. Kind of place that takes cash and doesn't ask questions. And preferably no CCTV.'

'Right,' I say. 'Given a choice, I'd go with the Winnebago. But they're not going to get an RV up into the forest, so they'd need a second vehicle. Which means another driver. Which means infrastructure, leakage, a big operation. Too visible, too many moving parts. This doesn't smell like that.'

'So, a motel.'

'I figure running this place you know all of them for fifty miles around.'

Barb nods.

'And I'm guessing there's some kind of phone tree, because if someone's stealing from rooms or dealing or looks like they're human trafficking, you need to know.'

She nods again.

'So here's what we do. We call around and say we had a woman and a kid staying here, and the kid left her monkey. We don't have contact details, but we know they were headed to another motel, and do they have anyone staying there like that?'

'What makes you think they'd still be there?'

'They need to know the outcome,' I say. 'The kid had no cellphone, no way of reporting back. My guess is they're holed up until they know how things broke. That means we have maybe twenty-four hours to find them.'

'Okay,' says Barb. She uses the stub of her cigarette to light another.

'One more question. Why the fuck should I help you?'

16

'I'm not asking you to help me,' I say. 'This is about the kid. You know what her name means in French?'

'Is there some reason I should?'

'It means "Miracle". Somebody gave her that name. Maybe the same person who put a bobble in her hair and made sure her hair was brushed and her nails were clipped. Whoever that was, she was a miracle to them. Maybe she still is.'

Barb grunts, pretending not to care, but I can tell the idea finds its mark.

'This is how we get her back to them,' I say, and, much to my surprise, discover I mean it.

Barb hits the phones. The indie motels all know Barb's husky voice, and if she doesn't get results from the desk clerk, she knows the owners' names by heart.

By now, Mireille is awake, so I find her muffins from the rattling fridge in the motel's excuse for a kitchen, along with a glass of milk, park her in front of a TV and find some show involving grown adults dressed up in foam rubber suits singing songs. This is apparently too babyish for a nine-year-old given the way she rolls her eyes, so I hand her the controller. She flips through the channels expertly until she finds *SpongeBob SquarePants*, and settles back.

Ninety minutes later, we get a hit. Barb waves me over, cigarette in hand, and I listen to the curly-lead handset as she talks.

'Yes, little girl, about nine years old. Looks to be mixed race, and a woman. No, I didn't see her, the night clerk was the one booked them in. I just saw the girl at the ice machine. We found her monkey under the bed. No, a stuffed one. You know, a sock monkey. I just figured she'd be missing it.'

The voice on the other end crackles. Barb covers the mouthpiece.

'She says they checked in three days ago. Still there.'

It crackles again.

'She wants to put me through to the room.'

'Tell her you've got a guest and you'll call back.'

Barb performs perfectly. 'Got it, thanks.' She writes something down, hangs up.

She shows me the pad, a number written on it.

17

I present Barb with a Mossberg pump-action shotgun. 'You know how to use this?'

She takes it, snaps off the safety, squares it to her shoulder.

Anyone who comes looking for Barb is going to find trouble.

Mireille may have tried to kill me, but she's now a potential target. She's the only person who knows who sent her, even if she has no idea why. But she continues to hold out, refusing to answer questions now her belly is full. It's clear that she's afraid, not of me, but something or someone else. Her eyes dart to the windows at the sound of every passing vehicle, clutching the sock monkey tight.

'Take yourself and Mireille down into the basement,' I say. 'Lock up, turn out all the lights but leave them on upstairs. That way, if they come down they make themselves a silhouette, and their eyes won't be dark-adapted. Don't open up for anyone until you hear from me on your cell.'

'What if you don't come back?'

'You know who I am, right?'

'No,' says Barb. 'I know who you used to be. I knew some-one else who used to be, too. He's dead now. So how about you give me a fucking plan instead of bullshitting?'

'Forty-eight hours,' I say. 'If you haven't heard anything, I'm gonna give you a number. Call it, and they'll help you.'

Barb writes it down. 'Who is it?'

'The one person in the world, apart from you, I currently trust.'

'So why haven't you called her already?'

'Because I don't trust her nearly as much as I trust you.'

Barb does that grunting thing again, which I take as a good sign.

As I curl out of the motel parking lot, I get an odd feeling.

I've had it before, in circumstances that have taught me not to ignore it. It's not situational awareness exactly, but a stirring in the air, that restless movement of leaves in a tree that tells you the wind has shifted, an odd quality of light that tells you a storm is on its way, maybe not in an hour, maybe not even today, but soon. And not just a storm, but the kind of storm that uproots forests and changes the course of rivers and wipes away entire towns in mudslides, leaving the landscape so altered that every map you own is useless, a world you must learn to navigate anew.

I glance in the rear-view at the motel sign receding, trying to shake the feeling, but it won't leave me. I think about turning back, but if someone's determined to kill me, all I will do is draw their fire onto two more-or-less innocent people.

The leaves rustle. They're trying to tell me something.

There's only one way to find out what it is.

18

Vermillion is a tiny farming community absurdly dominated by the DakotaDome, the Coyotes' gargantuan stadium, which dwarfs everything else in town. That includes the shabby Travelers Motel, which sits in its shadow.

I drive past at a crawl. It's two storeys high, with a walkway to the second floor. 213, the number Barb has given me, would be the third from the left. Unsurprisingly, the curtains are closed. There are five vehicles in the parking lot, two pick-ups, Dodge and Ford, a cube van, a beige 1990s Corolla, and a late-model Sorento. One of the pick-ups is rusted out and two-wheel drive like the Corolla and the cube van, while the other has graphics of a Sioux City construction firm. The Kia is maybe six months old with the cheap-ass tyres of a rental, and when I drive by for a second time, I spot mud splashes around the wheel arches and a 4x4 logo on the rear. Like the Gladiator ATV, it's riding an inch or two lower in the rear than it has any right to.

Whoever wants me dead is still here, and they're ready for war.

There's an overflow lot for the DakotaDome opposite the motel, so I pull in to wait and watch. It's 11 a.m. now, check-out time, but nobody emerges. A maid pushes a cart along the walkway, cleaning room after room, but when she comes to 213, she passes by. I can't see it because of the railing, but there must be a DO NOT DISTURB sign on the door.

If whoever it is is still in place, they almost certainly don't know the outcome of the hit. It would have been trivial to leave the kid with a radio or burner phone, but there was no sign of either. So either they didn't care about the result – which makes no sense – or they needed to keep so much distance they couldn't even risk a burner phone or a Walmart walkie-talkie.

I pull back out of the overflow lot, past the motel, and curl up out of sight by a mom-and-pop convenience store. I leave the Gladiator running in case everything goes to shit. I'm wearing the lightest body armour I own, and under my jacket is a snubnose automatic and two extra clips, along with a pair of Nammo grenades clipped to the back of my belt.

Motel firefights tend to be nasty, brutish and short, but I'm not taking any chances.

The maid's on the lower level now. I wait for her to disappear into a room, then climb the stairs to the upper floor. I work silently along the walkway to 212, then pause to listen. There's the sound of a TV, some daytime show, playing irritatingly loud. I glance through 212's window, but the TV is off, which means the sound is coming from 213.

Whoever sent Mireille should be in a defensive posture. If the hit failed, they must know I'll hunt them down. But instead, they're watching TV, the sound loud enough to mask the footsteps of someone coming to kill them?

If it's a mistake, I'll take it. But everything so far tells me it isn't.

I pull the automatic, control my breathing, count to three, then pinball off the railing and shoulder into the flimsy motel door. It slams open instantly – no sound of a splintering lock – but I'm already rolling into the room by the time the significance of it hits me.

I spring to my feet, spinning around, trying to locate my target.

But there's no-one here.

Then I see it.

I say it, because whatever it is, it is no longer a person.

19

It's a body, a sack of flesh, a dead thing.

I flick on the light to see better.

It's a woman, her wrists tied to the bed. She's fully clothed, but she's been tortured, her mouth taped shut to mute her screams. She's Black, but her face has been beaten so badly it's hard to make out the features.

I push the door closed. The frame was already shattered by the time I came in, strike plate ripped out of the splintered wood. Whoever got here before me tortured then murdered the woman lying on the bed, using the sound of the TV as partial cover. I prop a chair under the door handle to keep it closed. The last thing I need right now is a maid or manager walking in on me.

Through the door in the bathroom, there are two tooth-brushes. Beside the bed is a pair of holdalls, one large, one small. I pull the smaller open. A girl's clothing, all neatly folded, exactly the right size for Mireille.

There are no devices, no iPhone or iPad or laptop. Whoever killed her must have taken them. But they left something: a topo map. It shows my house, and a line drawn to it from an X, ringed by contour lines showing the sniping point in the forest opposite. There's the exact yardage, and calculations correcting for wind velocity from multiple directions.

I turn back to the bed, and the figure stretched out there, trying not to imagine what she suffered before she died. And then my forehead goes damp. The déjà vu I felt when I watched Mireille is back, but now it's stronger, and with it is a thought running through my head I can't unthink.

It makes no sense, no sense at all, any of it, but I have to know if I'm right.

I find a washcloth in the bathroom, and dampen it. Then I return to the corpse and as gently as I can, even though she can't possibly feel it, peel the duct tape from her mouth. There's another cloth stuffed inside, so I carefully remove it. Her cheeks sink in, making her face much slimmer, and doing nothing to reduce my rising sense of panic.

I wipe away clotted blood from her lips, her nose, her eyes, her forehead, until her real face – swollen and beaten, nose broken, but a face nevertheless – emerges.

I stand back, unable to breathe. She has the same high cheekbones as Mireille, but the resemblance doesn't stop there. The woman on the bed wasn't some amoral handler forcing a child soldier to commit murder by proxy. She trimmed the kid's nails, put a bobble in her hair, folded her clothes, and made sure she had her favourite stuffed toy not because it was her job or because she needed to win the kid's confidence, but because she was her mother.

She took her daughter into the forest at dusk, and left her by the side of a loaded sniper rifle, which she had aimed herself and trained her daughter to use. She told her to wait until she saw my head in the crosshairs of the reticule, to exhale and relax, and then to pull the trigger. Then she said goodbye and left her own child to face off against a man she either dared not confront herself, or had still-unfathomable reasons for not wishing to encounter, or kill.

But that's not why I can't breathe.

I can't breathe because I know who she is. Not just her name, but every curve and crevice of her body. I know the scent of her breath and the musk of her skin. I know the lines of her hands and the way they feel as they press against mine, and her breathing comes quicker and quicker until her entire body tenses, then slowly softens under me.

I can't breathe because I was in love with her, and there were more nights than I can count when I would have sacrificed everything I own and everything I am to see her again.

PART TWO

20

Perched seven thousand feet up at the foot of a mountain, straddling the Nubian and Somali tectonic plates, Addis Ababa likes to think of itself as the political capital of Africa. Bole airport only has a single runway, but it's hard not to feel the sense of occasion as you touch down. Although it's close to the equator, when you step onto the tarmac the air is refreshingly cool, with none of the blast-furnace African heat that assaults you at lower altitudes.

It's a good city. A great city. And for once I wasn't there to kill someone, but to save them.

His name was Suleiman Abdi, and he was a politician, not Ethiopian, but Somali. Abdi was an inspirational leader, both a talented retail politician and a canny statesman. Exiled by death threats from Somalia, he'd spent years building bridges with the neighbouring countries – Eritrea, Kenya, Ethiopia and Sudan. In a month, he was due to speak at a meeting of the African Union, headquartered in Addis Ababa, and the word was he would announce some kind of government in exile. There was even talk of forming a fledgling East African Union, which could be the first step to the long-dreamed-of United States of Africa.

It was vanishingly unlikely that any of this would pan out, but that didn't matter because if Abdi could mobilise the other states behind him, he could potentially return to Somalia as a real power-player, without the stigma of being a puppet of the Great Satan of the USA.

This made a lot of people nervous – not just Somali politicians, Islamist leaders and warlords whose power bases would be threatened, but other regional interests, superpowers who had profited for decades from divide-and-rule in Africa, and the arms dealers and middlemen who profited from every bomb, bullet or anti-tank munition that was fircd in Somalia's bloody internecine conflict.

Which is why someone was being paid a million and a half dollars to kill him, and I was being paid an equal amount to stop them.

That someone was Ali Olusi.

Ali was a tier below me in the hierarchy of death, but he wasn't far below me, and in some ways – at least in Africa, and especially in East Africa – he was more feared.

Ali was my opposite in every way. My trademark was a Molotov cocktail of designer clothes, fast cars, and crazy risks. His was total invisibility. Nobody had the slightest idea what he looked like, or how he slipped invisibly from country to country. He would appear as silently and mysteriously as if he'd coalesced from a vapour, fire a single shot, and evaporate back into nothingness. His targets were killed in hotels, in elevators, in bars, in the street, in their homes. Nowhere was safe. The most anyone ever caught of him was a slender figure, always beautifully dressed, appearing out of the shadows and then disappearing into them again.

He didn't work often, but he never missed. His work was flawless, precise, elegant. Beautiful.

Some claimed Ali was a ghost, or that witchcraft was involved, and profited from selling talismans and potions to rich men who feared they might find themselves in his sights. But I knew he wasn't a ghost. He was just very, very good. His hits were perfect not just because he had flawless technique, but because he took infinite pains. By the time he took his single shot, he knew the position of every CCTV camera within a mile radius and ten or twenty different evacuation routes. He knew the schedules of every bus driver or hotel worker, of every garbage truck and police patrol. He knew exactly where his target would be and when. And he worked entirely alone, which meant there was nobody who could betray him. There was no infrastructure behind him, no handler, no-one booking tickets for him or sending clean-up crews. He booked his own jobs via a seven-deep layer of network proxies, which meant that in addition to everything else he had impressively deep digital chops. He did it all himself.

Ali was, quite simply, the real thing.

By the time I arrived in Addis Ababa I was already a little bit in love with him.

21

Soon the city would be crawling with journalists, diplomats, spooks and NGOs, but if I was to have any chance of spotting Olusi I needed time, so I arrived a fortnight ahead of them. Blending in wasn't my style, and I was still trying to build a brand – *security-by-being-totally-fucking-out-there* – so once I'd had my passport stamped and collected my bags from the carousel, my first order of business was to rent a lime-green Lamborghini, in which I roared up to the entrance of the Hilton. I generously tipped the valet, the busboy, the desk clerk and anyone else who caught my eye, showered, smothered myself in expensive but tasteless cologne, then made a beeline for the bar. There I spent the next six days on a bender of epic proportions, boasting about my connections to a Russian oligarch whose investment fund I now fronted, dropping heavy hints that my interests lay in some combination of money-laundering, arms-dealing, blood diamonds and the trafficking of narcotics and human flesh.

To complete the picture, I paid for and bedded a startling variety of high-class hard-boobed escorts of various ethnicities and nationalities, and lost eye-watering amounts of money in Addis Ababa's premium illegal gambling emporia. I drove drunk, wrecked the Lambo, and paid off the police with bribes that exceeded that month's salary.

By the end of the first week, nobody was in any doubt about who I was. I was *that* guy: an entitled white asshole the hotel staff regarded as a fool, a blowhard, and an easy mark who could be separated from wads of cash by the application of alcohol and/or obliging female company. Everybody knew me, I knew everybody, and they didn't even think about me any more.

The way Ali worked, I was sure now, was to make himself part of the furniture too, but in a radically different way. No-one ever saw him enter or leave a country because he was there long before anyone knew, and he didn't leave until everyone had forgotten him. That meant he'd probably been in Addis Ababa for weeks, if not months, perhaps as a member of staff, a long-term guest, or a daily visitor. He was almost certainly someone I had already encountered. And if he was as good as I thought he was, he would have checked my bona fides, investigated the oligarch's businesses, using all seven layers of proxies so his searches could never be tracked back to him.

My cover was good, verging on perfect. There were Wikipedia entries, corporate websites, corporation numbers, even newspaper articles we'd planted. The problem was perfect might not be good enough. Ali's meticulous preparation and hypersensitivity to potential threats meant it was at least as likely that he would spot me as I would spot him.

I had no idea if his ambitions lay in that direction, but if there was one person on earth who had the potential to become Eighteen, it was Ali.

For the next week, we would be playing hide and seek in plain sight.

Second prize was a bullet.

22

The Ethiopians take coffee very seriously. The centrepiece of this obsession is the coffee ceremony or *jebena buna*, which took place every morning in the atrium of the Hilton. Freshly showered and dressed, but still trailing vapours from the alcohol of the evening before, I would make my way down via the stairs so that I could smell the frankincense that was burned as part of the ceremony.

The host was a young waitress who washed the coffee beans, then roasted them in a skillet over a burner. She was small and slender, but there was a wiry strength in the way she pounded the beans almost to dust using a stone pestle and wooden mortar. Then she'd brew the coffee in the *jebena*, the big coffee pot, and fill tiny mugs which the guests, including me, would cup in our hands. It was sweet, gritty and bitter, and every morning I'd tell her it was the best I'd ever tasted, which was true, and she would smile, which was kind of her because it was the same thing every guest with a hangover told her.

Sometimes she was there for lunch service, too, though I never found myself at one of her tables. On the fourth evening, she appeared behind the bar as I was holding forth in German to a group of Ruhr industrialists in Ethiopia to finalise the purchase of a potash mine. As they got drunker, they revealed their actual business was an elaborate tax evasion scheme in which I expressed interest. We exchanged business cards, and they left around 2 a.m., each with a paid companion.

That left me as the last in the bar, and it was the girl who brought me the chit to sign. I filled out my room number, then pretended to hesitate over the line for the tip, which was blank.

I looked up. She was wearing a name tag.

'Gracious,' I said. 'Is that your name?'

She nodded.

'Your real name?'

She frowned. 'Why wouldn't it be?'

'Oh, some of the girls . . . the girls you see around here. They give themselves new names. Professional names. Those are the names you're supposed to call them by. They get upset if you ask them their real name.'

Her skin was dark, and the light was dim, but I could still see she was blushing.

'I'm not that kind of girl,' she said.

'So what kind of girl are you?'

She was getting nervous now, glancing around. But the barman was nowhere to be seen, because this was the time of night he went out to smoke a reefer before final clean-up.

'I'm sorry,' she said. 'I don't know what you mean. If you could just—'

She gestured at the chit.

'Suppose I wanted to tip you directly, Gracious. How would I do that?'

I smiled. It wasn't a good smile. It wasn't a smile I felt good about, but it was a smile that was necessary, because it was the kind of smile that the person I was pretending to be would smile.

It was a smile that said *I want to fuck you for money.*

Her face changed. Until now it had been the face of a young waitress, maybe a little naive, the kind of girl a young busboy would ask out on a date, secure in the knowledge he could take her home and his parents would approve. But as I smiled, a coldness came over it, a hardness that spoke of a history she'd buried and did not ever want to disinter. A look I recognised because it was the same expression I could feel wash over my own face when people mentioned juvie, or asked about my mother.

'I told you,' she said, her voice changed, 'I'm not that kind of girl.'

'No,' I said. 'Apparently not.' I signed the chit, leaving the space for the tip and the total blank. 'Fill in whatever you want for the tip.'

She pointedly wrote in a fat zero.

The next day it was a different girl who conducted the *jebena buna*. I smiled my best tourist smile and asked her where Gracious was.

'Oh,' she said. 'We swapped shifts. Just for today.'

'And what do you normally do?'

'Housekeeping.'

'Let me guess,' I said. 'Third floor?'

She frowned. 'How did you know?'

23

The housekeeping cart was outside my door. From inside, there was the sound of a vacuum cleaner, but the noise was steady, as if it wasn't moving. Over it, I heard a faint click, like the tabs of a suitcase being closed.

I pulled the pistol from the small of my back where it had nestled ever since I arrived in Addis Ababa and snugged up against the jamb of the door. Thirty seconds later, I heard the vacuum click off. Then there was the sound of the door being unlocked from inside and as the maid came out I jammed the gun into the small of her back, clamped my hand over her mouth, dragged her back inside, and kicked the door shut.

It was Gracious.

With my gun hand, I frisked her, but the maid's uniform was slim enough fitting that I could already tell she wasn't armed.

'I'm going to take my hand off your mouth,' I said, pressing the gun back to her temple. 'You make the slightest sound, I'll kill you.'

I took my hand off her mouth.

'If you kill me, he'll know you're here,' she said.

'Who?'

'I don't know his name.'

I let go of her, and motioned her to the bed, where she sat, shaking and afraid.

'Tell me everything.'

'I can't. He'll kill me.'

'If you don't, I will. And, yes, he'll know I'm here. Which means he'll call off the whole operation, which is what I want. Either way works for me. So talk.'

She started crying. Then she told me everything.

24

It started four weeks earlier. A man she didn't recognise sat on the bus beside her on the way to work. He told her her name, and her address, and that he'd kill her and her entire family if she didn't do exactly as he said. He took her to an open plaza and told her she needed to be his eyes and ears in the hotel. He wanted details of all the guests, especially foreigners, and especially anyone she thought might not be who they seemed.

'What made you think I wasn't who I said?'

'The first day,' she snuffled. 'The day after you arrived. You came to get coffee with the others. You were loud, making sure everyone knew who you were. But you caught my eye, and just for a second you weren't that person. And then you were. He told me to trust my feelings, and if there was anyone I suspected, I should watch them. And if I found anything, he would give me more money.'

'So you did this for money?'

'No. I did it because he said he would kill my family. And the money wasn't for me. It was for my little brother. He's sick. Leukaemia, blood cancer, a very rare kind.'

'What's his name? Your brother?'

'Marvellous.'

'Show me his picture.'

She pulled out her phone and showed me a picture of a teenage boy hooked up to an IV, giving a thumbs up.

'Show me a picture of you with him.'

She scrolled through photographs. There she was, younger, with the same boy, holding hands at the entrance to a zoo.

'Now your Facebook.'

She opened it up. Pictures of her family, mother and father. Grandparents. School pictures.

'All right. Put it away. You've worked here for how long?'

'Two years.'

'The zoo in the pictures, Kano, it's in Nigeria, not Ethiopia.'

'I was born in Nigeria, but we moved here a few years ago.'

'Why?'

'Boko Haram were getting close to our village. They kidnapped schoolgirls only twenty miles away, and murdered their families. My parents had relatives here, so we fled. Two weeks after we left, they came to our village, murdered the men and women, took the girls as wives or prostitutes and the boys as child soldiers. Moving here cost everything we had, and Marvellous was already sick. So when he offered me the money . . .'

She tailed off, wiped snot on the back of her hand.

I found her a Kleenex.

'Does he know about me?'

She nodded.

'How much?'

'Just that I had a feeling.'

'How do you contact him?'

'He just turns up, like he did on the bus. The last time it was while I was in the market buying food. I think he watches me to make sure I'm not being followed.'

'What does he look like?'

She stares at me, blank.

'He's white, black, tall, short, thin, fat, what? Scars? Hair? What does he wear?'

'My height, maybe a little taller. Slim, like you, but you can tell he's strong. He wore something different each time.

Sunglasses, so I didn't see his eyes. A hat over his hair . . . it could have been short or long for all I know.'

'Accent?'

'He spoke English, it's hard for me to tell. From his features, I'd say Kenyan, Somali maybe.'

'Christ's sake, there must be something about him.'

'His teeth,' she said. 'He had bad teeth. Broken. Like someone had once hit him in the mouth with something. The butt of a gun, something like that.'

Then she looked up. 'How did you know I was watching?'

'It wasn't hard,' I said. 'You avoided my table at lunch so you could watch without me noticing you. Then you changed your shift so you could work in the bar and watch me in the evening. That could only mean one of two things. Either you thought you could make money off me, or you were working for Ali.'

'That's his name?'

I nodded. 'That's why I propositioned you. I needed to know which it was. And you told me.'

'You mean if I'd slept with you, you'd never have known?'

I nodded.

She thought about this for a second, then: 'What are you going to do with me?'

'That depends,' I said. 'How good a liar are you?'

She shook her head. 'Not good. My parents were very strict. My mother would beat us with a shoe if we told a lie.'

'Then you tell him the truth. But you leave out everything that happened in this room. You tell him I propositioned you last night, but you turned me down. You searched my room, but you didn't find anything. But you still suspect me. He'll tell you to keep digging, to get close to me. He'll probably tell you to sleep with me. And you'll do exactly what he says.'

'Including sleeping with you?'

It didn't seem like an entirely unpleasant prospect.

'That's entirely up to you.'

'I already told you,' she said. 'I'm not that kind of girl.'

25

That night, I followed her home. She took the bus through the crowded streets to a six-storey apartment block with barred windows and laundry hanging to dry on balconies, kids playing in the streets and dogs running loose. She kept the blinds closed so I couldn't see inside, just her shadow moving about. I waited a couple of hours to see if anyone came or went, but no-one did.

The next day she was back in the atrium preparing coffee. She caught my eye as she served me, but gave no outward indication of anything that had happened the day before. After the ceremony was over, as she was clearing the cups and little bowls of popcorn that she served with it, I said:

'Did he contact you?'

Without meeting my eye, she reached out to take my cup. 'This morning. Early. He was inside my building, waiting by the front door when I left.'

'What did he say?'

'He says I'm to flirt with you. Flatter you. Get you out of the hotel and take a picture if I can. Make you think it's real, that it's you, not your money, I'm interested in. Sleep with you if I have to.'

'So from now on that's exactly how we play it,' I said. 'Right now I'm going to ask you if you want to spend the day with me.'

'Today? I can't. I'm working.'

'Tomorrow, then. Find someone to cover your shift. Here . . .'

I pulled out money. 'Tell them I'm paying you, and you'll split it with them.'

She glanced around, took the bills and folded them into a pocket.

'Now smile. I don't care if it's fake.'

She faked a smile.

Later, in the bar, she wasn't there. I entertained my usual entourage of hangers-on, hookers and hopefuls, but my heart wasn't in it. Later, as I lay in bed, I realised I was nervous about the next day, and not because of Ali Olusi. Yes, he would be watching us – that was the point, to use his curiosity to draw him out into the open – but it wasn't that.

It was because I had a date. And although I'd fucked a lot of people and killed almost as many, a date with a girl was something entirely new to me.

26

When the elevator doors slid open, there she was, standing in the morning sunlight that streamed through the glass doors into the lobby. She wore a white linen dress that hid her shoulders, a straw hat like a schoolgirl's, and black patent-leather shoes.

I walked over to her and kissed her on the cheek. She turned her head away involuntarily.

'Listen to me,' I whispered in her ear. 'Ali isn't going to let you live. He can't afford to have someone who knows what he looks like walking around. He leaves no witnesses, and you're already a witness. The only way you live is if you help me. I'm trying to save your life. Okay? Because if not—'

'It's okay,' she said, and kissed me on the cheek.

Her lips were soft and warm. It almost felt real.

'Where are we going?' I asked.

'Where does it look like?' she said, and stepped back to show me her dress.

The heart of Addis Ababa is *Kidist Selassie*, the Eastern Orthodox cathedral where Ethiopia's war heroes are buried alongside British suffragette Sylvia Pankhurst who, for complicated reasons, spent her last years here as a guest of Emperor Haile Selassie and received a state funeral.

As we passed the angels who guard the entrance and made our way from the sunlight into the cool and darkness of the massive white building, Gracious slipped her hand into mine.

I wasn't fooled that she was doing anything other than playing the part I'd assigned her, but it didn't matter. It was the first time I'd held anyone's hand since my mother held mine as a child.

Inside, it was quiet, empty, and hauntingly beautiful. As we sat together in one of the dark-wood box pews and lowered our heads in apparent prayer, I said:

'Have you seen him yet?'

She shook her head.

'You need to give me a signal if you do.'

'Like what?'

'Something intimate and natural.'

'Like this?'

She picked an invisible piece of thread off my lapel. It brought her so face close to mine I could feel her breath on my neck. She wasn't wearing scent. All I could smell was soap, and fresh-scrubbed skin.

'Just like that.'

After the cathedral, we went sightseeing. As the afternoon wore on, she started to relax, understanding the act, even beginning to play along. Sometimes she would smile, not the shy smile I'd seen before, but a big grin, and once even a hearty laugh that was a bit too loud, and she immediately covered up with her hand.

Around five, we stopped at a bar that looked out onto the street. There she told me stories about growing up in Nigeria, her brother's illness, and how much it cost to get him treatment. But the stories always ended with the arrival of Boko Haram in the neighbouring village, and the way they were forced to flee.

'It's a long way from Nigeria to Ethiopia,' I pointed out. 'Why so far?'

'Oh,' she said. 'My uncle lived here. My mother's brother. He moved here to work for the African Union. He's dead now.'

'And your parents?'

'I'm sorry?' she said.

'Alive or dead?'

For a second, I could swear her eyes filled with tears, but then they caught something behind me, and she picked an invisible piece of thread off my lapel.

27

'He's here?'

She nodded.

'Describe him.'

'On the other side of the street. Five feet eight, maybe nine. He's wearing a suit and pretending to light a cigarette, but the lighter isn't working.'

'Put your sunglasses on.'

'What?'

'If I turn round, he'll know I've made him, and you'll be a dead woman because he'll know it's you who told me. Put them on.'

She reached down for her bag, fumbled to get it open, nerves showing. She pulled out her sunglasses, but as she did one of the legs caught on the strap and she dropped them.

'I'm sorry, I'm sorry,' she said. 'I don't do this kind of thing.'

She scrabbled on the ground for the glasses, found them and put them on.

I stared into my reflection, and behind it the street.

'I don't see him.'

'He's gone. He must have seen – no, there!'

She pointed behind me and to the right. I spun round, but a truck obscured my view.

'Fuck.'

'Aren't you going to chase him?'

I stared at her.

'Was this the plan from the start?'

'What?'

'To get me to chase him? To show myself? You point him out to me, I chase him, and he kills me at his leisure, where he wants, far from the hotel. No commotion, no scandal, nothing to frighten the horses. Then he finishes his hit like he always intended. Is that what's going on here?'

I took her hand like a lover and squeezed it, hard enough to hurt.

'No!' she said. 'No. I – I told you. I don't do this kind of thing. I'm trying my best here. I'm just trying not to get killed and not get my family killed. Please.'

I pulled off her sunglasses to see her eyes better.

There was a tear there, a full one this time.

I let her hand drop.

'I'm sorry,' I said.

'It's okay,' she said.

She picked up a napkin and wiped away the tear.

28

We had dinner in the hotel. She didn't seem to hold the episode earlier against me, and once or twice she even flashed one of those gigawatt smiles. But they faded almost as soon as they arrived, as the reality of what we were doing swept back over her. The only reason she was pretending to like me was that the alternative was a death sentence. Besides, she was much too good for a jackass like me, and she knew it.

Either that or she was a consummate actress, the best I ever met, and the same applied.

We left the restaurant around 10.30 p.m. and headed to the atrium. She turned to say goodbye, but I caught her around the waist. Her face froze because she knew what I was going to say.

'You need to stay the night.'

'I can't.'

'That's good,' I said. 'Keep saying no. If he's watching, he'll realise how much you don't want to. But remember what he'll do if he thinks you had the chance and turned it down.'

'Fuck you,' she said. It was the first time I'd heard her swear.

'No, just kiss me,' I said.

She stared at me, then she leaned forward and did just that.

It was long and slow and tasted of honey and pepper and halfway through it she clamped her teeth down on my bottom lip as hard as she possibly could. Then she pulled away, and as she did I tasted my mouth fill with blood.

And I smiled because it was, without doubt, without any exception at all, the best kiss I had ever had in my life.

I swallowed the blood and spit and held out my hand.

She took it, and we walked into the elevator together.

I took a shower with the door open so I could keep an eye on her, but she never moved from the bed where she sat, nervous and fully clothed, with her hat and shoes on and her bag on her lap, trying not to look as I undressed. I'd frisked her several times during the day, hugging her or putting my hand in the small of her back like a supposed gentleman as she entered a room or took a set of stairs. I handled her bag every hour or so, just to check the weight of it. I'd checked at the beginning of the day, but there was no telling what she might have retrieved from a toilet cistern, or been passed in the street, or removed from under her chair while my attention was diverted.

But she wasn't armed. As far as I could tell she was just a frightened young woman with a kiss that tasted like pepper and honey and blood who had gotten caught up in something she was no part of, and was now trying desperately to save both her life and that of her family.

And as far as I could tell on our brief acquaintance, I was in love with her.

But then, as I showered, I realised something was bothering me.

She'd shown me pictures of her parents in Nigeria – her Facebook was full of them. But there were none after that, after Boko Haram had forced them away. When I asked her if they were alive or dead, she'd tugged at the invisible thread on my lapel, avoiding the question entirely. And the day before, when I asked her to lie, she'd said her parents *were* strict, as if they were dead. The uncle who had moved to Ethiopia to work for the African Union was dead too. The only member of her family she ever spoke of as being alive was her brother, Marvellous.

If her parents were dead, why hide it from me?

Then it hit me: if her parents were dead, she must have lied when she said that Ali had threatened her whole family. And if she'd lied about that, she could be lying about everything.

With the shower still running to cover the noise, I unzipped my washbag as slowly and silently as I could and pulled out the snubnose .38 I kept inside.

Soaking wet and buck naked, I stepped out of the shower.

Too late.

29

Gracious stood in the doorway. She was holding my Welrod in a perfectly balanced grip. She'd kicked off her shoes, her hat was gone, and her feet were apart in an athletic stance. The muzzle I stared down was as steady as I've ever seen, and I've seen enough.

'You don't think I know the sound of a zipper? Drop the gun, turn around, and lie face down on the floor.'

'No.'

She laughed. 'You think I won't kill you?'

'Sure you will. But not yet. A murder in the hotel will blow your cover. Everyone saw us in the restaurant. Elevator CCTV shows you coming up to this floor. Nobody will hear the Welrod, but you have no way to get rid of a body. If it was me, it would be simple. One call, and I can have a clean-up crew here in an hour. But you work alone. No backup, no infrastructure. Which means no clean-up crew. Besides, maybe I took the shells out of the pistol.'

'You think I don't know the weight?'

'Go ahead, then. Fire.'

She didn't.

'The thing is,' I said, 'I'm under no such restrictions.'

I chambered a round and aimed at her.

'I kill you, I'm out of here in five minutes. All anybody knows is that the flashy American jagoff who hung out with hookers and criminals in the bar shot a young woman in his room. The cops will jump to the obvious conclusion, which means they won't give a shit, and the hotel will probably try to pay them off to avoid the bad publicity. If they try to track me down, they'll find I don't exist. By the time I'm back home, the cheque will already have cleared. I won't even need a clean-up crew.'

The Welrod's muzzle didn't waver.

'Go ahead, then,' she said. 'Fire.'

I didn't.

30

Gracious was Ali. Her method was straightforward and beautifully simple. She would slip into the target country on her own passport, posing as a domestic worker, waitress, chambermaid, or cleaner, and use her cover to painstakingly map out every CCTV camera, every bus schedule, every shift, every piece of the target's routine. On the day of the hit, she would bind her breasts, dress in male clothing, usually a suit, with lifts in her shoes to change her height. She'd pull the trigger, and seconds later she'd be back in her regular clothes, the suit torn off and stuffed into a bag or a laundry cart. Then she'd go on with her day as if nothing had happened, perhaps even give a witness statement, making a few helpful errors here and there. She'd stick around long enough for everyone to forget about her, and then she'd move on to another hit.

We stood there, weapons aimed at each other, like some cheap action flick. Then she smiled.

'You can't do it, can you?'

'Sure I can,' I said. 'But maybe I don't want to. Not yet. The only way you kill Suleiman Abdi is if you kill me first, but if you kill me first, you'll blow your operation. Either way, you lose. So killing me gains nothing.'

'You're forgetting one thing,' she said. 'If I kill you, I become Eighteen.'

'No, you'll start a war. If you don't kill Abdi, you tell the world you're unreliable. Which means weak. You'll become a target for every wannabe Eighteen out there. Most of them have backup and infrastructure, which you don't. Yes, you're good at what you do. Maybe better than me. But there's more to the job than killing people. You have to be able to survive with a target on your back and the world's best killers lining up to put a cluster in it. You'd last a few days. Maybe even a few weeks. But you'd be a walking corpse.'

She shrugged. 'Maybe I don't care.'

'That's the funny thing,' I said. 'I think you care very much. I think you're doing all this for a reason, and it's not because you want to step into my shoes. You fooled me because almost everything you told me was true. You're not that kind of girl. Maybe that's why I don't want to kill you. Maybe there's a way we both walk away from this.'

'If you want me to say I won't kill him, I can't.'

'Fair enough,' I say. 'How about this? He'll be here in a week. The day before he comes, either I kill you, or you kill me.'

'And until then?'

I shrugged.

'We hang out.'

31

Maybe it was because we were now freed of all pretence about who we were or what we intended to do to one another. Maybe it was because we were birds of a feather, hired killers who understood and admired each other's work. Maybe it was because we were both lone operators, neither of whom could afford to be trip-wired by an emotional connection. And maybe the whole thing was heightened by the knowledge that it would all end in six days' time, then five, then four, probably badly. But for whatever reason, the six days were not nice, or fun, or relaxed.

They were *enchanted*.

We went on dates. We went to the beach. We roared around in a fresh Lamborghini. We toured nature reserves. We bought dumb tourist stuff in the markets and ate in tiny hole-in-the-wall restaurants. We watched movies. We ate dinner. We drank. We told war stories.

Before we left the hotel room each morning, we frisked each other. At the end of each day, when we went back to the hotel room, we frisked each other again. We drank some more, and then we went to bed.

On the first day, she slept in her dress, on top of the covers.

On the second day, when we frisked each other after returning to the hotel room, we held each other a little longer than was strictly necessary for security purposes.

That night she slept in her clothes, but under the covers.

On the third day, as we crossed a street, she took my hand again. But this time, it was genuine. It was possibly the most erotic thing I have ever experienced.

Go on, roll your eyes. Go ahead. Fuck you. You did this as a teenager. You still remember the first time you held a girl or a boy's hand, that delicious trepidation, the nerves, the feeling of joy and triumph when you felt it slip into yours. That feeling of walking together, head held high, their arm brushing yours. I never had any of that. I spent my teenage years high, drunk, holding up convenience stores, getting beaten in street fights and going back with a baseball bat, thrown in the back of police cars, crashing stolen cars, standing in courts, sitting with probation officers and social workers and detectives and psychologists and court-appointed attorneys and designated adults. There were no boyfriends or girlfriends, there was just fucking and being fucked.

I never did any of that stuff you did.

Not until now.

And neither, it turned out, did Gracious.

On the third night, she took her clothes off and climbed into bed beside my naked self.

She lay there for a moment on her back, and even in the darkness I could tell she was wide awake.

'Are you going to tell me?' I said.

She rolled over onto her side.

'Are you sure you want to know?'

'Your story can't be much worse than mine,' I said.

Boy, was I wrong.

32

Gracious grew up in a village in northern Nigeria, just like she said. She and her younger brother Marvellous were close. When he was eleven and she was fourteen, he started to get fevers and became weak. It took nine months to get a diagnosis: hairy cell leukaemia, a disease so rare in children that nobody had ever seen it before.

The good news was that there was a treatment. The bad news was it cost $3,000 a tablet. The worse news was that just as the family was trying to scrape up the impossible amount of cash, Boko Haram attacked the village.

The soldiers killed everyone over fifteen, and dragged the girls older than ten off to be raped and/or marry one of their soldiers and bear children. Boys who were strong enough would be forced to become child soldiers, while those too young or too weak would be slaughtered on the spot.

The only ones spared were the girls ten and under.

Tall for her age, but skinny and flat-chested, Gracious dressed in her father's clothes and made Marvellous, whose growth had been stunted by the illness, put on a shabby pinafore dress she'd grown out of. She stuffed what money the family had been able to collect into his pocket and told him to pretend he was a ten-year-old girl and she was his brother. Then, as the soldiers broke down the door, she whispered something in his ear and told him never to forget it.

The soldiers murdered their parents, then marched the two of them out into the centre of the village, where they'd gathered the children. The girls were forced into the back of a pick-up truck. The boys her age were already dead – they'd fought alongside their fathers. The younger boys were taken away and shot. That left Gracious and Marvellous.

They stood there holding hands as the leader, a dark-eyed man in his thirties with tribal scars, came up to inspect them. He took in Gracious's clothes, the shirt too big for her, pants rolled up.

'Why didn't you fight?'

'My family didn't own a gun.'

He grinned. His name was Jigo, and his teeth were bad, the detail Gracious had chosen when she described her alter ego to me.

He gestured towards the bodies of teenagers that lay a little way off.

'You were lucky.'

'No,' said Gracious. 'You were the lucky ones. If I'd had a gun I'd have killed you all.'

Jigo turned to the other soldiers.

'This one. He's got balls. Train him.'

Gracious became a child soldier. She was forced to convert to Islam and given a new name – Ali. She secretly bound her breasts as they developed. She knew if the men around her ever discovered the truth, she would be raped, tortured and executed. Her failure to strip off and swim naked in rivers with the others and her insistence on bathing alone all could raise suspicion. The only way to survive was to become the fiercest of them all. So the first time one of the other soldiers mocked her for not wanting to undress in front of the others, she took a knife, slit his throat, and castrated him. Nobody mentioned it after that.

She rose quickly to become Jigo's most trusted lieutenant but was careful never to challenge him, because although she was pretending to be a psychopath, Jigo was the real thing.

There were rumours that he ate the bodies of his enemies, which Gracious discounted as myths, until one day she watched him slice into the corpse of an enemy commander, rip out his heart, and take a bite out of it raw. Blood running down his chin, he offered it around to his men. Nobody moved until he finally reached Gracious. She took it from his hands and took an even greater bite than Jigo had.

She spent the rest of the night vomiting into the latrines.

She'd been with Boko Haram almost two years when she discovered the truth about Jigo. As they were folding up their prayer mats after the *tahajjud* prayer in the middle of the night, Jigo asked her into his quarters.

Many of the other men had taken multiple wives, mostly girls who had been kidnapped and forced into marriage. But Jigo, like Gracious, had not.

Inside his quarters, he stood there looking at her for a moment, then asked:

'Why haven't you taken a wife?'

'I keep myself pure for Allah,' said Gracious, echoing words she'd heard him use.

'The Qur'an teaches that marriage is given so that our desires do not lead us into fornication.'

'I have no desires of that kind,' said Gracious.

'Bullshit,' said Jigo.

He turned away and pulled something from his desk. It was a bottle of Nigerian moonshine they called Crazy Man in a Bottle. He took a slug, then offered it to her.

'Come on,' he said. 'What are you afraid of? I thought you feared nothing.'

'I fear only Allah.'

Jigo roared with laughter, showing his rotten teeth.

'You don't believe in Allah any more than I do. I know your secret. I know why you fight so hard, why you won't undress in front of the other men. I know why you cut that man's balls off when he laughed at you. And I know why you have no desires of that kind. It's because your desires run the other way. You follow me like a puppy because you're as hard for me as I am for you.'

And with that, he thrust his hand between her legs to feel.

Only he didn't feel anything, because there was nothing to feel.

Before he could say anything else, she pulled her knife and cut his throat.

Jigo dropped to his knees, trying to staunch the flow. With his free hand, he lunged for the automatic propped against his bunk, but Gracious kicked it away. He made one last grab for her leg, but she simply stepped backwards. He slumped forward and lay still.

It had all taken maybe thirty seconds, and nobody had heard a thing.

33

She put on Jigo's holster belt, slung a bandolier around her shoulder, picked up his automatic and walked out into the night. The gate guard was the first she killed. Hearing the shot, the other soldiers began running out of the buildings where they slept. She killed them all.

An hour later she led a column of women and children out of the compound. They trekked for two days to a town occupied by government forces. Still presenting as Ali, she told them what she'd done. None of the soldiers believed her, so they took her to the commander's office. He was sitting with a knot of white men in mismatched tactical gear, with ragged beards, shades and bandanas.

They were as sceptical as the sentries. But before she left, Gracious had used Jigo's finger to unlock his phone, then photographed him and the other dead. They handed it around, amazed.

The commander wanted to recruit her there and then. Gracious said she'd think about it, but the truth was she was sick of killing. On the way out, one of the white men gave her a handwritten number on a piece of paper and said if she ever changed her mind and wanted to earn some money – real money, not government soldier money – she should call him.

Gracious found a tin-roofed cafe where they sold internet access. Nobody in her family had had a computer or any kind of smartphone, but at school there was an ancient laptop, and a friend had shown her how to use it to create a free email account.

Before the soldiers took her away, she'd whispered the address in her brother's ear.

She had no idea if Marvellous was alive or dead, and even if he was alive whether he'd managed to remember it, but she pulled up Gmail and entered her password.

She needn't have worried.

Marvellous had emailed her every week for four years. Two hundred emails told how he'd been picked up by government soldiers who'd realised he was a boy and found him a place at an orphanage in the city of Abuja. Once a week, the nuns allowed him to use their only computer to send her an email, never doubting she would one day read them.

His leukaemia, which had been in remission, was back. He was sick, getting sicker, and the soldiers who brought him to the orphanage had stolen the money Gracious gave him. Without treatment, he would die.

Gracious emailed back. She said she was alive and would get him the money.

She went into an electronics store down the street, bought a pay-as-you-go phone, called the number she'd been given and made the white man an offer.

She told him she knew the entire command of Boko Haram in northern Nigeria. She would kill any leader they wanted, for money. She would ask for no payment until the job was done, and the payment would be made to an orphanage in Abuja.

The white man's phone was muted for a minute, then he came back on the line and asked her how much she wanted to kill Jigo's superior, the local area commander.

Gracious named a figure that would pay for Marvellous's treatment for three months.

He agreed.

Ten minutes later, she was wearing a schoolgirl's blouse, a skirt, and patent-leather shoes. In her backpack were her uniform, the phone, and Jigo's pistol. She slung it over her shoulder, and climbed on the bus which would ultimately take her to a hotel room in Addis Ababa, and me.

34

I lay beside her as she talked, and when she'd finished, I asked her:

'What about Marvellous? Did the treatment work?'

In the dim light, I could see her nod.

'Where is he now?'

'I don't know.'

'You lost touch with him?'

'No. I told him, with what I do, it's better if neither of us knows where the other is.'

'He knows you're Ali?'

She nodded again. 'He helps me book my jobs. All that security stuff, VPNs and proxies, I don't understand it, but he does. He's good with computers. The orphanage PC was old and they couldn't afford software, so he taught himself how to write it. He wants to go to school for it, he says. So I send him money for that, and the rest goes to the orphanage and other places that rescue kidnap victims.'

'You don't want to see him?'

'I don't want to put him in danger. I told him, one day, when we've saved enough, and he finishes school, I'll give it all up and we'll live together like a family.'

'Did you mean it?'

Her silence was as good an answer as I needed. A thought struck me.

'Which do you prefer? Being a man or a woman?'

'What does that have to do with anything?'

'Humour me.'

'When I'm a man I like being a man,' she said, 'and when I'm a woman I like being a woman. And if I don't, I change.'

'Is that why you haven't given it up?'

'I don't understand.'

'What you do, nobody knows who you are. You can change from one to the other, and nobody gives a shit. Nobody even *knows*. But if you gave it up, if you went to live with Marvellous, people would expect you to be one thing or another. They'd try to fit you into a box.'

She thought for a moment.

'No,' she said. 'It's nothing like that.

I do it because I like it.'

35

We spent the last day in bed, alternating between eating, drinking, making love, and just lying there. I say making love because it was gentle and tender and sensual and although I helped her come and she me, any time it came close to actual sex, I could feel her freeze. Whether it was fear, or involuntary, or something else, I didn't know, and in any case it didn't matter to me in the least. Because I understood that like me, only in an entirely different way, she'd packed the whole teen romance thing into a week, under the weirdest conditions possible.

She was still a virgin, and so was I in every possible respect except the physical one.

Then, as night fell and the room darkened, and we lay there in silence, I began to wonder how I was going to kill her.

36

Look, let's not pretend.

I know what you think.

I know you think that makes me cold, inhuman, a monster.

I can feel your disdain, your disgust. And probably I deserve it.

But before you dismiss me completely, at least understand something. Yes, I was in love with her, or as in love with her as I ever could be with anyone. And yes, in the last few days I had experienced things, feelings, emotions, as new and alien to me as I guessed they were to her.

But none of that changed a thing.

She was Gracious, but she was also Ali, and Ali had come here to do a job. Gracious might be an innocent young woman with a white dress and a straw hat and a laugh that was sometimes a bit too loud, but Ali was a stone killer. I knew him well enough that if I didn't kill him he was going to kill me. If Ali walked away from a job, it would be a death sentence for him, and if I allowed him his kill, it would paint an indelible target on my own back.

My stomach churned at the thought of what I needed to do, but it was the business we were in, and the business we were in left neither of us the luxury of a choice.

I tried to use my oldest trick, dissociation, separating mind from body. I tried to pretend it wasn't Gracious who lay beside me, but someone else, someone I didn't know, someone whose kisses didn't taste of pepper and honey and blood. Just another job, another meaningless body to dispatch.

If it was anyone else, I tried to tell myself, the obvious thing would be to strangle them. The moment the thought entered my head I had to stifle a physical retch. The .38 would be mercifully quick, but the carnage it would enact on her slender body would be unthinkably worse.

There was only one possibility. The worst, apart from all of the others. The Welrod, the silenced pistol vets used to put down animals, the only gun I'd ever used that was as quiet as they are in the movies.

Nausea surged up, threatening to overwhelm. I pressed it back down below the surface, like I once did to drown a man in a river. There would be blood, and a body, but I could call for a clean-up crew, and the room would be spotless by the time the maids arrived in the morning. I would be on a plane long before anyone noticed that Gracious was missing, if they ever did. The only person who would give a shit was Marvellous. All he would know was that she'd stopped answering his emails.

The logic of it was as inescapable as the savagery of the irony.

Of course the only person I could fall in love with would be another killer.

And *of course* it could only end with one of us killing the other.

But there was one more thing to consider.

If I had thought all of this through, so had Gracious.

37

By now it was dark outside, the hum of the evening traffic starting to diminish. Gracious had been dozing on her side, but then she stirred and rolled onto her back. Her eyes were closed, but I could tell from her breathing that she was awake. Then after ten minutes, she opened them, and I knew what it meant.

'You hungry?' I said.

'No.'

'Want a drink?'

'No.'

Finally I said what we were both thinking.

'What are we going to do?'

'I don't know.'

'I don't want to kill you,' I said. 'But I will if I have to.'

'I know.'

'I don't understand why you can't just disappear.'

'Yes, you do,' said Gracious, and rolled towards me. 'It's the same reason you can't.'

And she was right.

Because the truth is you can't go back from killing. After that, you're a killer, whether you like it or not. When I murdered my rapist, I also murdered the kid who had sat drinking Slurpees under the fluorescent lights of the 7-Eleven with his junkie mother after one of her shifts, listening to her read out the funnies from an abandoned newspaper, believing in the face of all evidence to the contrary that they would both live forever and one day be truly, perfectly happy.

And Gracious did the same thing on the day she killed and castrated the man who laughed at her for not undressing in front of the others. The old Gracious, the innocent village girl who went to church twice on Sundays holding hands with her younger brother, was by now buried under a pile of corpses almost as tall as mine.

There was no going back for either of us.

Then she did something that surprised me.

She took me in her hand and rolled on top of me.

'You sure?' I asked. I didn't know why, except that something told me that this was an act of bravery for her.

'You know I was in love with you before I ever met you,' I said.

'I know,' she said, and slipped me inside her.

'It wouldn't have mattered if you were a man.'

'I am a man,' she said, and grabbed my wrists, pushing my arms over my head. She began to move. 'I'm both. They're both me now. This is who I am.'

And then she fucked me.

We came almost together. I felt her go first, tightening on me, squeezing me like a gentle fist.

I closed my eyes, utterly lost in the sensation of it.

I remember thinking: *maybe this is what it's like to be a woman.*

When I opened my eyes again, I was still inside her, and she was still on top of me, but the Welrod was pointed into my face, pulled from the hiding place behind the headboard where I'd concealed it while she was dozing a day earlier after we'd both drunk too much.

'You thought I wouldn't find it?'

'I knew you would.'

She cocked her head to one side slightly, puzzled.

'It's your choice,' I said. 'I can't make it.'

'You expect me to?'

I nodded.

'What if it's not what you want?'

'It's okay,' I said. 'I'm hardly a positive contribution to the human race.'

She smiled a sad smile.

'That's not what I meant.'

She put the gun to her own head.

'Wait,' I said. I reached under the bed to where I'd put the snubnose .38.

I guess she knew it was there, because she didn't seem surprised.

I put it to my head.

'We go together,' I said. 'Or not at all.'

38

We stayed like that for a long moment, traffic rumbling outside in the dark, a jet whining overhead as it throttled down for final approach, the clatter of pots and pans from the kitchens, and somewhere the beep of a truck reversing.

Then she put the gun down on the sheets. She climbed off me, used a Kleenex from the night table to wipe herself off, dressed silently in the darkness, pulled her shoes on, and walked out of the door without looking back.

I watched it click shut.

And that was the last time I ever saw her alive.

PART THREE

39

As I stare at Gracious's body, it's as if I'm nine years old again, and have just crawled out of the closet where I've been hiding, reading a Spider-Man comic by the sooty light of a failing flashlight as a stranger used my mother for sex, to find her still-warm body lying on the bed.

I didn't understand what was happening at first. I thought Junebug was sleeping, or maybe she'd overdosed. I tried to shake her awake, yelling her name, harder and harder. I'd seen her like this before one time, but I'd managed to wake her, pull her upright, feed her coffee, wipe the vomit away from her mouth, then walk her around the motel parking lot until the sun came up. I knew what to do, because it was the same thing I'd seen her do to another girl a month before.

The one thing I knew not to do, ever, under any circumstances, was call the cops. Drugs meant a violation of her parole, which meant she would go to jail, and I would lose the only person in my life who meant anything to me, and who for all her manifest flaws did her ragged utmost to feed and clothe and love me.

And so when I heard the sirens of cop cars pulling into the motel parking lot and boots hammering up the stairs, I tried to bar the door with my nine-year-old body, and when that didn't work, I fought them, biting one of them so hard it drew blood. Another cop dragged me outside and handcuffed me to the walkway railing. From there, I watched the whole thing play out, alternately hyperventilating and screaming, until someone called homicide, and told a burly female probationer to get the little bastard out of there and see if he saw anything.

It's almost two decades later, but I'm nine again. Only it's no longer my mother's body I'm looking at. It's Gracious, and I'm a thousand miles from being able to process what it means.

Then I notice something I hadn't seen before.

It's a pair of burgundy-coloured passports, both French, piled together on the bedside table by the phone. I pick them up, flip open the first. The photograph shows Gracious, but it's in the name of Grace Okoro, the identity she must have been living under after she disappeared.

She's just as beautiful as I remembered.

I turn to the second. As I do, I hear something outside. It's sirens, lots of them, approaching fast. I know I need to leave, but the rustling is back, and with it the rumble of thunder, that odd greenish hue that seeps into the light, a sharp smell in the air that you think might be ozone.

I find the photo page, and there she is, the girl. I scan the words.

Nom: Okoro
Prénoms: Mireille
Nationalité: Française
Lieu de naissance: Paris

The sirens blare louder, and there's the screech of tyres as cop cars skid into the parking lot below. My brain screams at me to run, but I can't because my eyes are transfixed by the field marked *Date de naissance* on Mireille's passport.

Her date of birth. It's almost exactly nine months from the day that I last saw Gracious alive, the day we slept together, the day that she spared my life and walked away forever.

Which confirms beyond any fragment of a doubt what some part of me already knew.

The girl who tried to kill me is my daughter.

40

Shouts and the clatter of boots on the walkway outside pull me back to reality.

'POLICE!' yells a man's voice. 'COME OUT WITH YOUR HANDS VISIBLE!'

I glance round: there's no window in the bathroom, no door to the adjoining unit, no possible exit but the busted door I came through.

I'm trapped with the corpse of a murdered woman, a woman I loved and didn't kill.

The silhouettes at the window – poorly trained Vermillion cops or Clay County deputies – make them sitting ducks. I could take them all with a single magazine. But a killing spree isn't going to help me find who killed Gracious, or why she would have sent her daughter to kill me.

I shove a chair under the door handle, pull one of the Nammo grenades, stack it with another to double the blast, toss it into the bathroom, duck behind the bed and cover my ears.

'Don't shoot!' I yell back. 'Don't shoot! I'm coming—'

BLAM.

The explosion blows out the front window, filling the tiny motel room with smoke and debris. Head ringing, I lurch into the bathroom where the grenades have blown a ragged hole a foot wide in the exterior wall. Through it, I can make out the mini-mall at the rear of the motel.

I frantically kick the hole bigger. I can hear the cops regrouping outside. It sounds like they're using a battering ram on the door, and they're going to be shooting first and asking questions later once they're in. A final kick takes out a two-foot section of wall. I squeeze myself through and drop out, just as the chair disintegrates under the force of the battering ram.

I land hard and sprint for where I left the Gladiator running, left ankle tweaking. One of the cops looses a couple of rounds at me through the hole in the wall, but they go wide, digging up gouts of asphalt. By the time I make the Jeep, I can already hear prowler engines screaming and tyres squealing out of the motel parking lot, but the jeep is a tank, and I can outdrive all of them and outgun them if I have to.

I jam the jeep into first and floor the gas.

Nothing happens. For some reason, it's no longer running.

When I reach for the ignition to start it, the key is gone.

Flashing light bars appear in the rear-view. I throw open the door to run, but as I do an old-timer in suspenders and a plaid shirt, pants hitched up to his armpits, ambles out from the convenience store, the archetypal pop of mom-and-pop. He dangles the fob in front of me.

'Left your keys in, son. And the engine running. Didn't want you coming back to find her gone.'

I try to smile, and take the keys with a fake cheery 'Hey, thanks!'

Is it even possible he hasn't heard the sirens?

He cups his hand to his ear. 'What's that, now?'

41

I drop the clutch and burn out in a cloud of tyre smoke just ahead of the cop cars, leaving the bemused grandpa to watch the parade stream past.

I have a daughter.

The words make no sense.

I am Seventeen. I'm an asshole, an exemplar of the species. I don't give a fuck about anyone. I kill people. I watched my mother murdered. A man raped me over and over again in a locked cell in juvie. I fought my way through children's homes, beat other kids with iron bars. I smashed my fist into brick walls. I bought a gun and tracked down the man who had raped me. I murdered him in cold blood. Then I tracked down the man who had killed my mother and murdered him too. I taught myself to feel nothing. I trained myself to kill. I found a mentor. I killed one of the best. I studied those who went before me. I killed and killed and killed. I became the best. I became Seventeen.

Seventeen is who I *am*.

Seventeen does not have a daughter.

The highway's north, but I don't need to add state troopers to my list of troubles. So I turn south, towards the only chance I have of not ending in handcuffs trying to explain how I didn't kill the woman in the room.

Vermillion's tiny. We're at the city limits in under a minute. The closest cruiser keeps pushing forward, angling to spin me out or roll me, but I'm guessing he's only ever done this in simulations, so as he draws alongside for the third time, I brake hard and sideswipe him off-road into a scrub lot.

The Gladiator takes air as we cross the bridge over the Vermillion River, back end skittering back and forth as we land. Ahead, the roads fade down to nothing or dead-end where the river sidewinders back. I consider bailing on foot, or taking my chances cross-country, but Vermillion is surrounded by thousands of square miles of canonically featureless fuck all. They've probably already called in the chopper, and I'd be a sitting duck for an airborne search.

And now, up ahead, I see what I'm looking for – a scattered collection of low, white-painted steel buildings behind a chicken-wire fence. It's Harold Davidson Field, the City of Vermillion's one-horse municipal airstrip.

I powerslide into the access road and roar past the admin building. The first couple of cruisers behind me miss the turn and are forced to double back.

There's no security in places like these beyond the locks on the planes and the hangars, and it's a straight shot to the runway. All I need now is a piece of luck. And there it is, in the shape of a sweet yellow Cessna 172, which a burly man in his fifties with a bushy moustache, a beer gut and white Tilley hat is fuelling at a self-serve Texaco gas stand, staring in astonishment at the oncoming convoy.

The Vermillion cops are still too close, so I lead the wailing train of vehicles past him onto the taxi apron. From there, I turn onto the runway, laddering up through the gears to put some distance between me and the closest pair of cruisers. Ahead, a set of orange hazard barriers – RUNWAY CLOSED

– DO NOT ATTEMPT! – has been set up, but it looks clear beyond that, and in any case I don't have a Plan B.

Just short of the barriers, I slew the Gladiator into a hand-brake turn and accelerate back, threading the needle with inches to spare between a deputy's cruiser and a PD prowler. When I check the mirror, I see them both try the same manoeuvre, but they do it in opposite directions and slam into each other sideways. That leaves just one cop in pursuit, and he arcs round to tuck in behind me as I head back towards the Cessna and the gas stand.

As he straightens out, I brake hard, slam the Gladiator into reverse, brace against the headrest and auger into him head-on, but backwards. His airbag explodes, and the front end of the cruiser is destroyed, but the truck frame of the Jeep is tougher, and my airbags are disabled for just this kind of stunt. I roar forward to the Cessna, skid to a halt and jump out, pulling the Sig Sauer.

The burly guy with the moustache drops the fuel line and fumbles for a weapon – evidently he packs while flying. He manages to get a pistol out, but I fire in the air, then level the automatic at him. He drops his weapon and steps backwards, hands in the air.

I jump into the Cessna and hit the ignition. The prop spins right up, engine still warm. By now, the cop I airbagged is out of the car and running towards me, so I slew the Cessna round and aim directly at him. He pulls his side-arm to fire, but before he can he bails to the ground to avoid being chopped to pieces by the prop.

Ahead, the two cars that collided are moving again, accelerating towards me, trying to force me off the runway. Well, if they want a game of chicken, so be it.

I open the throttle all the way and extend the flaps. In still air, the Cessna needs a ground roll of six hundred feet or more, but the windsock shows a stiff 15 mph headwind which will cut that to five. The airspeed indicator inches upwards. Thirty feet from impact, the PD prowler chickens out. Probably has a wife and kids he cares about more than a police funeral. But the deputy means business, aiming his vehicle right at me like a missile. I'm committed to take-off now, so I do the only thing I can think of, which is to pull back on the stick. The Cessna lurches into the air and just clears the cruiser, but I still don't have the airspeed, so it stalls instantly and thumps twenty feet back onto the blacktop.

The deputy's still not done. He peels into a wide 180 and heads after me.

In front of me the orange hazard barriers are closing fast. The runway still looks clear beyond, all the way to the perimeter fence. Whatever construction, resurfacing, or line-painting they've been doing must have been completed. Maybe the paint's still drying. Oh well.

The gap between the barriers is just a couple of inches wider than the Cessna's prop, but I can't afford to lose any more air-speed, so I aim the plane dead centre and close my eyes. The prop just makes it through, but the main gear crashes into the them, sending orange lumber spiralling left and right as I blast through.

I crane out of the window to look behind. The crazy-ass deputy has his gas pedal pinned and is gaining. He'll be abreast of me in seconds.

'Come on, you fucker,' I yell at the Cessna. I'm still short of take-off speed, but then I check the fuel gauge. It's only half full – the man in the Tilley hat hadn't finished fuelling. That means I'm light a hundred pounds at least, so I take a chance and pull back to rotate. The rumble of the wheels stops as the landing gear unsticks, and the Cessna begins to climb, just in time. The deputy passes directly underneath me, then swerves to the right, steering with one hand, window down, his pistol in the other. He's trying to find a shot. I bank right slightly to stay directly over him, still gaining height. He chases me all the way to the end of the runway, slewing left and right with me following, until he finally runs out of runway, and I cross the perimeter fence, still only at a hundred feet or so.

He skids to a halt, jumps out of the cruiser, and empties his weapon after me, but the bullets skim past uselessly.

Which is when I discover why the runway was closed.

42

Maybe it's the sound of the Cessna's engine straining to lift me into the sky, or maybe it was the crack of the shots the deputy fired, but either way, from the field beyond the perimeter, a huge flock of Canada geese, midway through migration, clatters into the air like a swarm of feathery bees, sleek and slow after a summer of eating whatever the hell it is geese eat.

There's no way to avoid them, and moments later I'm in the flock, the birds hurtling past me, left, right, above, below, an airborne minefield of honking Canadiana. I wrestle the Cessna's stick, trying to pilot my way between them, and by some extraordinary miracle I miss them all.

All except one.

It's the biggest, fattest and ugliest of them all, struggling to hoist its overweight ass into the air and join the rest of the flock. Flapping furiously, it rises directly in front of me. I bank hard left, but the goose does the same. I bank right, and it follows suit.

We're on a collision course, and there's absolutely nothing I can do about it.

At the last moment, it sees me. For a fraction of a second, I swear the goose gets an expression of utter surprise on its stupid face, then it augers into the prop. Blood, bone, feathers and goose flesh splatter into the Cessna's windshield, blinding me, as the prop shatters, fragments hurling themselves away into the sky. I'm at a hundred and fifty feet now, with only marginal airspeed. I level out, trying to conserve kinetic energy, and hit the wipers, which smear grease and gore across the glass.

I peer through the ghastly slime, looking for a landing site, but all I can see is a tree line approaching. My choices are to float into the canopy or land short. If I try to float, I'm going to risk another stall, and a nose dive with no chance to pull out. If I sink too far, I'll go head-on into the trees, which isn't much better. So I throw the Cessna into a crab, hard left on the rudder pedals but stick to the right, trying to scrub off enough speed to land. The plane drops satisfyingly quickly, and, at the last moment, I straighten out and pull up, tyres skimming the tops of the grass. But I'm still going too fast, and the Cessna just doesn't want to put herself down.

The trees rush towards me at seventy, maybe eighty knots. If I could just get the fucking wheels on the ground I could use the gear brakes, so I push the stick forward.

This, to say the least, is a mistake.

The geese were camped here for a reason. Below the grass, the field is waterlogged. As soon as the gear hits the ground, it digs in. The nose wheel drives itself into the mulch, and the Cessna catapults into a somersault. Since I never even got close to fastening the four-point harness, my face slams hard into the instrument panel, and for the second time in twenty-four hours, everything goes black.

43

'Where is she?'

The man is yelling, on the cusp of losing it, if he ever had it. A fist slams onto the table on which my head currently rests. 'Open your fucking eyes and tell me where she is!'

I try opening them. This is not a simple task. My face is swollen from the impact with the Cessna's instrument panel, my nose feels like it's broken, and I'm missing another couple of teeth. I manage to get one eye half open and spit out some blood onto the linoleum floor of what appears to be an interview room. Pain spikes through my ribs. Probably the crash cracked a couple of them too, but at least I'm alive, again.

I finally get the other eye open and look up. Deputies swim into view, ranged around the soundproofed walls of the room, wearing the dangerous looks of men and women who would like to kill me, have the means, and are simply waiting for an opportunity to present itself.

They're armed, all of them, but I'd still have a chance if it wasn't for the fact my hands are handcuffed behind the chair back. I look down. They've removed my belt and my shoes for good measure. I'm guessing the door is locked, and probably guarded on the outside too.

The voice comes again. 'I said, where is she?'

I look up and blink my eyes clear enough to take in the man opposite. There's something familiar about him. *The build, the facial hair, the beer gut.* Then it hits me: it's the fat man with the bushy moustache who was fuelling the plane I just crashed. The only thing missing is the Tilley hat.

He's now in uniform, complete with a shiny star. I screw up my eyes to focus on it.

It says 'Sheriff'.

Apparently I just jacked and totalled the Clay County Sheriff's personal plane.

Pro tip: almost never do this.

'I'm gonna give you one more chance,' he says. 'Either you tell us where she is, or things are about to go very fucking badly for you. Very fucking badly indeed.'

His face is getting red, belly struggling to free itself from the constraint of his pants.

'Who?' I manage to spit out.

His answer comes by way of his fist, thudding into my left cheek. He may be out of shape, but he's a big man, and he puts everything into it.

As situations go, this one is bad and getting worse. The fat sheriff may be out of shape, his deputies poorly trained and lousy shots, but law enforcement in small-town America operates in a halo of unaccountability, which means there's no particular limit on how far this assault may go or where it may end if I don't give them answers they like.

As dizziness from the blow subsides, he puts something in front of me.

It's Mireille's passport.

'We know you killed the woman,' he says, massaging his knuckles. 'We already got you on that. That's good for the needle. But you tell us where the girl is, maybe the governor finds it in her heart to grant clemency. That's your one chance.'

Mireille's photograph stares at me, and in her face I suddenly see not Gracious, or myself, but both of us, a memory of that magical, desperate lost week in Addis Ababa made real. Gracious is gone, murdered by some animal for reasons I can't even guess at, but Mireille *exists*.

Yes, you motherfucker, I tell myself. *You have a daughter. And her existence changes everything.*

The sheriff looks round at his deputies. 'Course, you know the boys and girls here, a lot of them have kids of their own. Me too. So we take this kind of shit personally. Could be one of our kids, one of our wives. We're all reasonable people. But we're not going to pussyfoot around when it comes to a paedo who abducts nine-year-old girls. You know where she is. Trust me, you're going to tell us. One way or another, I guarantee it.'

My head hurts, and I'm still reeling from what I've seen and learned. But I need to focus, to consider my options, such as they are.

Option A: I say nothing. But the Jeep is registered in the last name Sixteen was using, at the address of the house on the hill. Which means they already have state cops on the way to search it. Once they get through the armoured door they'll find a trove of unregistered weapons. When they bring in a thermal lance to open up the safe, they'll discover a cornucopia of alternative identities, passports, cash in various currencies, burner phones, and other impedimenta of my profession. They'll call in the Feds and ATF, CIA will get wind of it within hours, and either I will spend the rest of my life in a black site, or more likely be strong-armed into some off-the-books bullshit. House to house searches will take them to the motel within an hour, where they'll find Mireille. They'll sweep her up in beefy law-enforcement arms while Barb is bundled off in handcuffs, trying to explain that the shotgun was to protect the girl, not to keep her prisoner. A stranger will break the news to Mireille that her mother is dead, and then one day when she's old enough she'll learn from a Google search that Gracious was tortured to death by a man, and she'll learn his name, and his name will be mine, because that will be the most convenient truth for everyone concerned.

I can't let that happen.

Option B: I tell them the truth about who I am, what happened, and where Mireille is now. But that just short-circuits to the same result. Either way, I end up a prisoner or a puppet, while Mireille bounces around from foster placement to foster placement, only now with a bizarre and terrifying history attached to her – *the girl sniper, daughter of killers* – and the conviction in her heart that she failed to kill the man who went on to kill her mother.

If the institutions don't destroy her, the knowledge will, just as surely as my own failure to stop a man killing my mother destroyed me.

I can't let that happen, either.

What I need desperately is an Option C. Which means I need time to think.

The sheriff with the bushy moustache is out of his seat now, yelling profanities at me, working himself up to something. A couple of the deputies exchange glances and move away from the wall in anticipation. I wait until his flabby red face is close enough that I can smell the tobacco on his breath, then I hawk up as much blood and snot as I can from my broken nose, and spit it in his face.

Mission accomplished.

His fury overwhelms him. He swings at me, flailing balled fists into my face, nose, mouth, ears, sides. But the beating is exactly what I need, because I've been through this before, and worse, in juvie. And I know how to survive it, dissociating into a kind of fugue state until my mind unmoors from what's happening to my body, like a birthday balloon that slips out of a toddler's grasp and soars away into the summer sky.

I close my eyes.

I'm a balloon.

I float free, and finally I can think.

44

I think about Gracious, her history. How she fought to escape what must have seemed like her destiny, and saved her brother. I think of lying beside her in the long Addis Ababa afternoons, an island of silence amid the noise and heat of the city. Of the bitter-sweetness of a time we both knew had to end, whose shortness made it simultaneously more bitter and more sweet. I think of her preferring to end her own life than mine, and me doing the same.

And then the fact that out of that time came something else.

An innocent to whom Gracious gave the name Mireille because she *was* a fucking miracle. A miracle to end all miracles. The most miraculous, unexpected thing that could possibly have emerged from that place and those people and those circumstances.

I barely know the kid, beyond the few hours I spent with her. And yet she is part of me, and I am part of her, and even though Gracious is dead, a part of her lives on in Mireille. And not just Gracious, a part of Junebug too.

The two people I have loved most in the world, both dead, and both incarnate in her.

Did Gracious try to make it in the ordinary world for the sake of our daughter? Did she try to forget everything she was, everything that had happened, and go back to being the humble village girl in the white dress and the straw hat and the black patent-leather shoes? Did she clean floors, wash dishes, change sheets, and serve coffee like she did in the hotel in Addis Ababa? Did she turn her back on Ali Olusi, on the skills she'd acquired, on her ability to shape-shift between the sexes?

The sniper rifle, topo maps and camo gear I found with Mireille in the woods, the loadout of weapons that weight down the trunk of her rental, all suggest otherwise. And I can't forget what she told me: *maybe I do it because I like it.* Most likely, she floated invisibly in the lower strata of the killing hierarchy, taking jobs that paid enough to live but not enough to draw attention, jobs that barely challenged her – mobsters, corrupt local politicians – but that carried no risk to her or the growing girl-child who now accompanied her everywhere.

While Mireille sat in whatever hotel room or apartment they had rented, watching *SpongeBob*, maybe, Gracious would vanish. She'd do her disappearing act, becoming part of the scenery wherever it was she had decided to make the hit. Then one day she would come home, her backpack or shoulder bag a little heavier than usual, perhaps still with an acrid smell on her fingers that Mireille couldn't know was cordite.

After she had showered, they would go out for dinner some-where that Mireille liked, and Gracious would ask Mireille about her day or Mireille would chatter about childish things, and Gracious would try to listen and forget that earlier that day she had ended another human being's life. And a few weeks later, for reasons Mireille did not understand or par-ticularly care about, they would move on to another city, another country, another job.

Probably Mireille knew nothing about what her mother did until Gracious set her up in the forest with the scope and the face paint and a bobble in her hair, and told her she was going to have to go now and they might not see each other again for a little while.

I can only imagine what each of them felt as Gracious walked back down the forest track towards the rental car, and

Mireille watched her go. No tears streaked Mireille's facial camouflage when I rescued her from the wolves, so she didn't cry, not then. I'm guessing Gracious told her not to, and over the years had impressed on Mireille the importance of doing exactly what she was told, which was why Mireille didn't allow herself to cry until she had locked herself in my bathroom.

I doubt the same was true for Gracious. She must have forced herself not to look back as she rounded the bend to where the car was parked, then backed it down to where she could turn around. She probably made it halfway to the highway before letting the dam burst. God only knows what tortures she went through that night before the physical ones began.

But why?

Why would she do any of this?

Why would she try to kill me?

If she wanted to kill me, why sacrifice Mireille?

Why abandon the one miraculous thing in her life?

None of it makes sense. None of it makes any kind of sense at all.

And finally it hits me.

It doesn't make sense because she didn't do any of those things.

She wasn't trying to kill me.

She was calling me back to life.

She was handing our daughter to me to protect.

Gracious deliberately chose the light Finnish rifle because she knew there was no risk that the shot would penetrate the glass. She knew I'd hurtle out and find Mireille, but that I wouldn't kill a kid, not least because I needed to know who had sent her. And she trusted me to figure out who Mireille was sooner or later.

She must have known that someone was close behind her. She had to protect the girl, which meant she had to take her to a place of safety. It was pure Ali: a triple bank shot, yes, but she'd worked out every angle, considered every eventuality. Once the trigger was pulled, I'd realise my cover was blown. That meant I couldn't stay put. But I wouldn't abandon the girl, so I'd take her with me, and – here's the point – Gracious wouldn't know where.

Which means she wouldn't be able to tell anyone where Mireille was.

Even if she was tortured to death in a motel room in Vermillion.

But why do it that way? If she knew where I lived, why not just roll up the driveway and knock on the door? If she didn't want to talk to me, why not write a letter? Or put a note in Mireille's pocket, or pin something to her jacket? Why not simply tell Mireille she could trust me, talk to me, tell me who she was?

I have no answers, but it tells me one thing: whoever killed Gracious was looking for Mireille as well. They didn't find her. But they did find a map showing the location of my house, which Gracious didn't have a chance to destroy before they caught up with her.

Gracious sacrificed herself to save Mireille, and sent her to me to protect. But now I'm stuck in a locked interview room having the shit kicked out of me by a bunch of redneck cops, and Mireille is hunkered in the motel basement where I abandoned her, with only a sixty-year-old woman to protect her, and a stone killer on the way.

They won't find Mireille in my house, but they'll start going door-to-door, and the motel will be the second place they look. Christ only knows what will happen then.

I need to get to her before he does.

But first I need to get out of this room.

45

Thump. A boot lands in my face. I feel a cheekbone crack.

I'm curled into a foetal ball, hands cuffed behind my back. They've discounted me as a threat by now, which gives me the beginnings of an edge. I snap onto my shoulder and sweep my leg round, taking two of the deputies off their feet, then scramble to my feet, back against the wall. The cops surround me. The sheriff unholsters his weapon, but I shake my head.

'You kill me, you'll never find her.'

He nods to a female deputy, who produces a Taser.

I run right at her, and she hits me with it. Lightning arcs through my body, and I drop like a felled tree. She hits me with it again, and again, and again, and once I finish jerking, I go still, like I'm unconscious, only I'm not.

Whoever put the cuffs on was trained well. They're snug on my wrists, palms out, keyway up, no chance of monkeying with the lock. Maybe you've heard you can dislocate your thumb or some shit like that to get out. Well, try it sometime. I have. It doesn't work.

'Get the motherfucker out of here,' says the sheriff, kicking me in the ribs one more time for his wrecked plane.

So the cuffs are tight. But whatever bureaucrat purchased them cheaped out. They're single locked, not double, which means I could shim them, if I only had a shim. Which I do, because I always do, a sliver of spring steel sewn into the cuff of every shirt I own. Lying there on the floor with the cops standing over me yakking, I slide it out with my fingertips, find the tiny gap where the cuffs ratchet together and slip it in, blind.

'What about the kid?' asks one of the deputies.

'Get an Amber alert out. We have an address yet from the vehicle?'

To get the shim under the pawl, you need to tighten the cuffs. When they're as snug as these, you have one, maybe two chances before you've locked yourself in for good and probably permanently damaged some nerves into the bargain. My hand contorts behind my back, trying to press the cuffs tighter. I groan, trying to cover the noise if the ratchet clicks. One of the deputies kicks me in the groin, and as a result the shim slips and the cuffs snap tighter.

Fuck.

'Some shithole called Milton,' says another voice. 'State troopers on their way.'

I try again, but it's harder now with the cuffs tighter, and my circulation is starting to cut off.

'What are we going to do with this asshole?' asks another.

'Get him in a cell,' says the sheriff. 'Search the vehicle, get him in a jumpsuit, get his clothes to forensics, swab him for gunshot residue, pull DNA, then when he wakes up we go in for round two. Get the troopers to seize any devices and search for porn. Ten to one he's a paedo, a trafficker, or both.'

I hear the door unlock as they prepare to move me out. My hands are going numb. I get the shim back in the gap, but the cuffs are so tight I don't know if there's enough play to free the pawl. I have to use my bodyweight to bear down on the cuffs, forcing them to bite into my flesh.

Through half-open eyes, I see two deputies reach down to pull me up by the armpits. As their thick fingers close on me, the cuffs tighten a sixteenth of a hellish inch, the pawl lifts, and one side slides free.

I let the cops lift me up, then swing my fists together into the temple of the first deputy, using the cuffs as a knuckleduster. He ricochets backwards against the wall and slides down, unconscious. I elbow the second in the stomach, pull the Taser from his belt as he doubles over, and then drive my knee into his face. He drops to his knees, moaning. The sheriff pulls his pistol, but I Tase him before he can use it. He falls to the floor, spasming and foaming at the mouth.

The female deputy goes for her gun, but before she can draw, I have the sheriff's in my hand.

'Call paramedics for this one,' I say. The sheriff's face is going from red to blue behind the porno moustache, and the last thing I need is a tag as a cop-killer as well as a child kidnapper.

'Trust me, the girl's safe,' I tell her, though I wish I knew that was true. 'I'm not going to hurt her. But if I don't get out of here, I can't guarantee anything.'

I guess she believes me, because she nods.

I take Mireille's passport and exit the room. There's a young deputy outside the door. I shove the gun in his face and remove his weapon, then push him into the room and lock the door behind him. He and the other deputy start hammering and yelling, but I'm already running for the exit.

At the front desk, the Gladiator's keys are on the counter, waiting to go into an evidence bag. The duty officer filling out the form, a woman in her forties, raises her hands in surrender. Her handset radio's on the desk beside her, already chattering with appeals for help from the cops in the interview room, so I take that as well and run out of the glass doors into the daylight.

The Jeep's right there, along with four cruisers and the sheriff's truck. I put a shot in a single tyre of each of them, then jump into the Jeep and squeal out of the parking lot in reverse.

Brown uniforms of deputies appear from the front door, chasing me. Evidently the door got opened. Two shoot, but one shell goes wide and the other puts a hole in the top right of the windshield. I return fire out of the window, and they duck behind vehicles for cover. I swing the Gladiator out of the parking lot and onto the road. One deputy chases me on foot for a hundred yards, while a second jumps into a cruiser and attempts to follow. He makes it another two hundred yards before the tyre flaps off the rim. I pull away, back towards the highway this time. The radio squawks by my side, alerting Highway Patrol to the vehicle and licence, but the state dispatcher squawks back that all available units are en route to Milton, where there are reports of shots fired and multiple officers down.

I floor the gas.

46

I make Milton in thirty-five minutes. The radio by my side should still be squawking, but the state trooper channels are now oddly silent. Something is desperately wrong. As I head into town, I see what it is: a column of thick black smoke rising from Sixteen's house. I head up the hill to where the lights of the Highway Patrol cruisers are still flashing. As I pull up, I fish a spare automatic out of the glove compartment. The cruisers are parked at oblique angles, doors still open. One was used to ram the electric gates and is still entangled in the wire and steel. By the side of it, a state patrolman lies slumped, his hand still on his holster.

I lift his head to see a neat 9mm hole in the forehead.

The house is fully on fire. The steel-reinforced door looks like it's been blown open with a breaching charge, not a standard police tactic. Inside, flames are roaring from the living room, licking the ceiling of the kitchen, where two more troopers lie on the linoleum, both dead, with similar head wounds to the one outside.

That's three bodies, but there are four cruisers outside. There has to be another trooper in here somewhere.

Beyond the kitchen, the dining room is full of thick black smoke. I wet a dish towel, wrap it around my face, pull a flash-light from one of the dead troopers and head in. The heat is searing on my hands and face. I scan around with the flash-light. There's a pocket of clear air about a foot high at floor level, but there's no sign of the missing cop. I move further in. Still nothing. Then I see her, the fourth trooper, prone by the stairs to the basement, below the smoke, but with flames from the basement roiling towards her. I go to pull her out, but as I do, an explosion from downstairs knocks me backwards. My armoury is starting to cook off. The whole place could go up at any moment. Eyes screwed up against the intense heat, I grab the trooper's boots and drag her towards me. There's a wound in her thigh, but her body armour saved her from the bullets that have ripped a neat cluster in the tunic over her heart.

I lift her in a fireman's carry, run her out of the smashed front door, and another twenty yards to clear us from a blast, then lay her on the ground. Her pulse is chaotic – the impact on her chest must have sent her into ventricular fibrillation.

I pull off her armour and start CPR. I'm fighting time. I can't stay here long, but I need to get her heart beating. After a couple of minutes of compresses, she suddenly coughs, and I feel a pulse. It will have to be good enough. Inside the house, there are more explosions, so I drag her another ten yards clear for safety. In the distance, there's the faint wail of sirens. Good. They can take over when they get here.

I run back to the still-running Jeep and slalom down the hill and onto the highway, trying not to imagine what might lie ahead of me.

47

It starts to rain, big drops splattering into potholes as I wheel into the parking lot and sprint towards the motel. The lights are still on, just like I told Barb, but the door is hanging half open, window busted. I gently shoulder it fully open, making sure my boots don't crunch on the broken glass, finger on the trigger of the automatic.

I listen for a sound from inside, but there's nothing, just the murmur of rain on the roof.

I step inside, still listening intently.

Nothing.

'Barb?'

Nothing.

'Barb, it's me. It's okay. I'm here now. You can come out.'

Still nothing. But then I see it.

A trail of blood on the floor.

The spatters are shaped like little tadpoles, their tails pointing towards the door, which tells me that whoever bled was leaving, not entering.

'Barb!'

I'm yelling now. From the highway, the sirens doppler as the fire trucks head past.

I follow the blood trail to the back, where it disappears down the basement stairs into darkness.

I take the steps one by one, back sliding along the wall, trying to give my eyes time to adjust.

'Barb?'

I reach the bottom. The darkness is total down here, velvet-black.

'Barb. For Christ's sake. Talk to me.'

Still nothing.

I fumble for a light switch, find it.

'I'm gonna turn the lights on, okay?'

I flick the switch.

The light blinds me for a moment, and then I see her.

It's Barb, slumped against the wall at the bottom of the stairs, crumpled like a doll thrown there by a petulant child. The Mossberg is still cradled in her arms, and there's a cluster of bullet holes in the front of her bloodstained blouse – two close to each other, a classic double tap, one a little further away – and a pool of blood behind her.

'Barb,' I say, even though I know she's gone. A sudden fury wells up and overwhelms me. Gracious had lived by the sword ever since she was a teenager. The cops up in the house, even they knew the risks. But Barb was innocent, protecting an innocent. She didn't have the slightest part in any of this until I put the shotgun in her hand.

Christ, I might as well have pulled the trigger myself.

48

And then she makes a noise.

She's still alive!

I crouch down, lift her head.

'Barb, Barb. It's me. Talk to me.'

Her eyes open. They're glassy and unseeing for a moment, then they snap into focus. To my astonishment, she puts a hand out, tries to lever herself up.

'Don't try to move,' I tell her. 'You've been shot.'

'No shit,' she says, pulling herself upright.

Barb is tough, I knew that. But three shots to the chest should have killed her. I'm still trying to make sense of it when she pushes the Mossberg aside, and reaches into her blood-soaked blouse.

'Stop staring at me like an idiot,' she says. 'Help me get this out.'

Still not understanding, I help her pull it out.

It's a dog-eared, fifteen-year-old, two-inch-thick copy of the *Yellow Pages*, with three bullet holes in it, and behind it an old metal serving platter. I help her pull them out. The shells went right through the phone book, but three dents in the serving platter show that it managed to stop them.

'Are you kidding me? You made your own body armour?'

'You leave me here with a fucking shotgun? I figured if someone came for the girl they'd be a professional and I'd better even up the odds.'

'Where is she? Where's Mireille?'

'He took her,' says Barb. 'I tried to stop him, but the motherfucker took her.'

'Who?'

'How the fuck should I know? He didn't introduce himself. We did just what you said. Came down here and turned the lights off. Two hours later I heard a vehicle pulling in. I showed Mireille a place she could hide in one of the storerooms, and told her not to make a sound, not to come out, whatever happened.'

'She understood you?'

'She did what she was told. Upstairs, there was a knock on the door. Then I heard the glass smash and somebody unlock it from inside. He came down the stairs, silhouetted like you said. But I could see that he was big.'

'Big how?'

'Tall, like six-six, six-eight? Maybe more. He had a gun. I was trying not to breathe, praying Mireille was smart enough not to make a noise . . . I could have shot him there and then, but I was hoping he'd just turn around. Only he didn't. I heard him trying to find the light switch, then he clicked it on. That's when I shot him.'

'You hit him?'

She nods. 'Pretty sure. Knocked him backwards, but he didn't go down.'

'Probably wearing body armour too. And then?'

'I tried to reload, but before I could he shot me twice. Knocked me off my feet, took all the wind out of me. I knew if I moved he'd kill me, so I lay still. Let him think the old bitch was dead. Only then he started walking towards me. I thought I was done, but then Mireille burst out from the room where she'd been hiding and ran past him.'

'I thought you told her to stay put?'

'She was trying to save me, distract him. He kind of lunged for her, but she was too fast. She shot up the stairs and he ran after her. I managed to pick myself up and follow them, but by the time I got to the top of the stairs, he'd got her by the arm. She was fighting him, and I managed to reload, but I was afraid I'd hit her too. So I yelled out to distract him. He spun round and shot me again. Knocked me backwards, and I fell down the stairs. Last I heard was her scream, then the slam of a car door, and he drove off. Then it was lights out. I guess I smacked my head pretty good on the way down.'

She reaches up to where her bleached hair is clotted with blood. 'Guess that's where all the red stuff came from.'

'You're not hurt, apart from that?'

'My chest hurts,' she says, as I help her to her feet. 'I think maybe I cracked a rib.'

'What about Mireille? Did he hurt her?'

'She sounded more angry than hurt. You ask me, she's a survivor.'

A survivor.

That's what Junebug used to call us. 'You and me,' she'd say, 'we're survivors. No matter how bad things get, we survive.'

She was right, all the way up to the moment she wasn't.

49

'You gonna tell me who she is?' says Barb as I help her up the stairs.

'She's my daughter.'

Barb stops, stares at me.

'Your *daughter*? And her mother?'

'She's dead. Killed by the same motherfucker who shot you and took Mireille.'

'Why?'

'I have no idea.'

We make it to the top of the stairs, but Barb has to rest for a moment, and I realise despite her bravado, she's badly shaken up. Her hand hangs on to my arm. 'What are we going to do?'

Outside, more sirens scream past, heading up the hill.

'Tell me something. You said he was big. Anything else? When he turned the light on, did you see his face?'

'Just for a split second.'

'And?'

She thinks for a moment. 'He was weird-looking.'

'Weird how?'

'His face . . . the features were big, like . . . Bigfoot.'

'Bigfoot? You mean . . . Sasquatch?'

'What? Don't be ridiculous. No, the kickboxer, UFC guy. Silva, that's his name.'

The fact that Barb is an MMA fan is the least surprising thing that has happened today.

'They call him Bigfoot,' she says. 'On account he's a giant. It's some glandular thing. Anyway, that's what he looked like.'

She sees my reaction. 'You know who it is?'

I nod. Because I do, and everything suddenly got a lot worse and a lot more complicated.

'Listen to me. He killed three cops, almost killed a fourth. They're going to think it was me, and that I kidnapped Mireille and killed her mother. If they think you're involved, that you know anything about this, about who I am, or who Sixteen was, you're going to be in a world of hurt. And if the man you saw is who I think it is, and finds out you're alive, he'll come back for you. You've a vehicle, right?'

She nods. 'Piece of shit Dodge Caravan, but it runs.'

'Good. What about people? Is there a place you can go?'

'What kind of people?'

'People who won't talk. I mean, I figured . . .'

'Poke-and-stick tats and needle scars, do the math, right?' She laughs. 'Sure, I still have friends in low places. Most of them are dead now, or locked up. But some of them made it. I haven't seen them for a long time, and we didn't always part on the best terms. But if they know I'm in trouble, they'll look after me.'

'You need money?'

She shakes her head. 'I'll take what I need out of the cash. Places my friends live, you don't carry too much, if you know what I mean. People get tempted.'

'Good. I'll give you a burner phone. Turn it on once a week. Nobody has the number but me. If you see there's been a call, call the number back. And I'll tell you if it's safe.'

'What if the call never comes?'

'Then you never come back.'

For a moment she looks like she might object, but then she shrugs.

'Shit, I always hated this place anyway. Nothing left to keep me here. Maybe it's God's way of telling me to move on.'

Five minutes later, Barb's at the wheel of the van with the engine running and the wipers flip-flopping against the rain, still bloodstained and a little unsteady, but a cigarette back between her lips and a look of determination on her face which tells me she's still got some trouble to cause.

'So what are you going to do?'

'I'm going to get her back.'

'And then?'

'I'll figure it out.'

Barb takes a final drag of her cigarette.

'The kid,' she says. 'She didn't deserve this. I don't care what she did, whether she pulled the trigger on you or not, she didn't deserve this. Her mother's dead, which means you're all she's got now. And you aren't much, God knows, but you're something.'

She flicks the stub of the cigarette into a puddle. It sizzles into nothing.

'What I'm saying,' says Barb, shifting the Dodge into Drive with a clunk, 'is you better find her. Because if you don't, I'm gonna find you. And I'm gonna bring friends. Got it?'

'Got it,' I say.

And with that, she pulls away, the bald tyres of the mini-van splashing through the potholes, bouncing on shocks that ceased to function years ago, and turns onto the highway.

I watch her tail-lights disappear, then turn to the hill. Above town, firetrucks and ambulances still strobe, but the fire itself is dying down. Either the firefighters got on top of it, or it simply burned itself out. Then, as I watch, blue and red lights snake down the hill.

Cop cars. They'll have found their dead colleagues and be out for blood. They'll check the gas station first, but they'll be here in minutes. They'll search every house and put road-blocks on the highways. They've already tried and convicted me in their minds for killing Gracious and the abduction of Mireille. Soon they'll add a triple cop slaying.

Something is happening here, something big, something I don't understand that involves forces I can't even begin to identify. My gut tells me they're powerful enough that if I find myself back in custody I'm as good as dead, whether at the hands of the cops or someone else. Even if I survive, every hour I lose makes the chances of finding Mireille increasingly remote.

No time to lose.

I run for the Jeep, but then slow as I see something sticking out of the water pooled in a pothole.

I reach down and pull it out to see what it is.

It's Mireille's one-eyed sock monkey, soaked, heavy with water.

I'm going to give it back to her, if it's the last thing I do.

PART FOUR

50

I'm starting to think maybe the old bastard is dead.

I hammer again on the filthy, anonymous door, set between a shady import/export company and a defunct women's clothing boutique with dust-covered mannequins toppling in the window display. I haven't been here in a decade, but the pattern of knocks I was assigned is burned into my cortex. A battered CCTV camera above the door stares down, but there's no way to tell if it still works.

A dim yellow light goes on somewhere inside. A minute later, the cardboard flap blocking the tiny window in the door lifts, and a pair of eyes peer out through glass obscured by decades of filth. Finally, the door unlatches to reveal a small Chinese man, around eighty years old.

He stares at me for a second, as if trying to work out if it really is me.

'Fuck off,' he says, and tries to close the door, but I jam my foot in.

'Come on, Charlie. Don't be like that.'

'Eleven years.'

'I know.'

'ELEVEN YEARS. And you never call. Not once.'

'I've been a little busy.'

'What do you want?'

'The usual.'

Even Charlie can't hide his interest. 'Show me.'

I grin, revealing my teeth. At one time, they were perfect, like an ad man's dream of pearly whites, thanks to cosmetic dentists in Beverly Hills who put them back together and shined them up every time they needed it. But it's been a year since they've been serviced properly, and recent events haven't done them any favours.

Charlie makes me tip my head back so he can see the upper incisors and molars, then forward so he can peer into the bottom. Then he nods, giving me permission to close my mouth. I can see he's still pissed off with me, but he's more upset about the state of my teeth.

He wags a nicotine-stained finger at me. 'No more bargains for you. Prices gone up.'

51

The stairs lead down to a basement room. The walls are stained, but the equipment is world-class. A lot of it – the X-ray machine, a fancy motorised chair – is new since the last time I was here, which suggests Charlie still does plenty of business. There are black leather couches against two walls, the kind you see for clients in high-end recording studios, and cameras mounted on the walls which feed flatscreen TVs, giving spectators a live view of the patient's mouth.

Charlie motions me into the chair, pulls on a plastic gown and gets to work.

Charlie, just so we're clear, isn't *a* dentist. He's *The* Dentist. Trained in China's top school of dentistry, he found his way to Chicago in the mid-seventies and set up an unlicensed practice using a box of tools he brought with him in his carry-on. He struggled to make ends meet until one day a powerfully built man with tattoos was brought in by two other powerfully built men with tattoos. His front teeth were smashed in, his jaw broken, and it looked like it had been done with a knuckleduster or baseball bat. Charlie knew better than to ask questions, but as he fixed the man's mouth up he gathered from the conversation that they were members of the 14K Triad that originally emerged in Guangzhou as part of the anti-communist resistance.

Charlie's work was good, he kept his mouth shut, and his unlicensed basement was far from prying eyes, so he soon found a regular parade of smash-mouth criminals lining up at his door. It wasn't just Triad members: he became the go-to for every species of domestic and imported Chicago criminal – Italians, Sicilians, Calabrians, Jamaicans, Russians, Puerto Ricans, Haitians, Bloods, Crips, Serbs and all the rest. The one thing he wouldn't touch was the skinheads, the neo-Nazi neanderthals, who wouldn't be seen dead with Chinese hands in their mouths anyway.

Charlie's work expanded beyond simply repairing smashed teeth. Because he was generous with Nonvocaine and gentle with the needle, his clients turned to him for cosmetic dentistry too. Whitening, straightening, implants, and most of all, grillz, because (a) it turned out Charlie had an artistic side, and (b) his grillz didn't rot the teeth like the cowboys who did cut-price work in strip-malls by the projects.

But it wasn't just teeth.

Charlie was never dumb enough to keep a physical Rolodex of his clients, but the one in his head was a *Who's Who* of drug dealers, black-market arms dealers, smugglers, extortionists, car thieves, loan sharks, human traffickers, forgers and every other variety of criminal. His shabby little basement became a kind of crossroads, a windowless Silk Road. Whatever you wanted, Charlie knew someone who could get it. He never charged for his services, but everyone gave him a cut to keep him sweet and because, darn it, people *liked* Charlie. You couldn't not.

Charlie became rich, though he never showed it, and used his wealth to set up a kind of shadow bank. If you owed someone money, you could pay into the Bank of Charlie, and it would get to them. He kept no books, relying on a photographic memory for who paid him what for whom, and operated entirely on trust. Charlie's dark pool of liquidity was so integral to the criminal economy that no-one dared touch him: anyone who tried to roll Charlie would face the wrath of Chicago's entire organised crime community, and sometimes did.

The cops left him alone, courtesy of fat brown paper packets that mysteriously found their way into lockers in the precinct every week. The Feds tried to pop him a couple of times, but the most they ever got him on was unlicensed dentistry, which turns out not to be a felony, or indeed fall under federal jurisdiction.

Moreover, because Charlie's clients were – with one notable exception, meaning me – uniformly criminal, he flew entirely below the radar of the intelligence community. As far as the CIA or NSA or the FBI's anti-terrorism or counter-intelligence branches were concerned, he simply didn't exist.

And all of that is why I'm here. Because once I get my teeth fixed, I'm going to need a lot of shit, but I'm currently wanted for four murders, grand theft Cessna and child abduction, and if anyone can get it for me without bringing any more heat to bear, it's Charlie.

52

Charlie shows me my teeth in a mirror, like he'd just given me a haircut.

'Great,' I say, turning my head left and right to admire them, and they are. But the rest of me looks like shit. 'Listen, Charlie . . .' I say, but that's as far as I get.

'I understand,' he says, the finger wagging again. 'You use me on the way up because I am useful. But when you get to be a big shot, Mr Seventeen, you forget me. You forget all about your friend Charlie Wu who fixed your teeth when you were just a little shit with big head who didn't know nobody or nothing.'

'That's not why I didn't come to see you, Charlie,' I say. Charlie is genuinely pissed off, and I need him to be not-at-all-pissed off right now. 'Okay, you can deal with Chicago cops and blow off the Feds now and then. But you think you can deal with the CIA? NSA? What if the Russians come knocking? Or the North Koreans? Or the Chinese?'

I save the best for last because Charlie isn't afraid of many things, but his association with the K14 Triad – the K stands for Kuomintang, the opposition to the Communists, the 14 for the 14 founders who fought against Mao's army – would put him squarely in the sights of Chinese intelligence if he ever popped up on their radar.

'You don't need that kind of heat, Charlie,' I say. 'That's why I stayed away.'

Charlie shakes his head. 'Bullshit. Back then, you need me because you were on way up. Now you need me because you on way down.'

'Not on the way down, Charlie. Sideways. I'm flying solo now. I need some stuff, and I need to source it from people who have no connections to anyone in that world.'

'And if they trace it back to me?'

'They won't, Charlie. I guarantee it.'

Charlie shakes his head. 'You lie. You can't guarantee nothing.'

I should have known better than to try to bullshit Charlie Wu, so I stand up, clean off, dump my bloody bib in the trash and turn to face him.

'Tell me, Charlie. You have kids?'

He shakes his head, but there's something in the way he does it that tells me there's a story there.

'Had?' I say, on a hunch.

'Daughter, and wife. In China. They die in the great famine. You hear about that?'

I shake my head, not because I don't know, but because I want him to tell it.

His face darkens.

'They called it *dà yuè jìn*, Great Leap Forward. Mao's idea. Organised farms into communes. If they didn't produce enough, leaders would be punished. So leaders lied, made up numbers, said there was more grain than there was. But the grain ran out, and nobody could eat. And anyway, grain was saved for the cities, not farms. In Sichuan, grain stores were full but people – my people, my family, my wife, my daughter – they starved to death because the local leaders were not allowed to open the doors.'

'Where were you, at the University?'

Charlie nods. 'In city, our bellies were full. I had no idea they were starving until it was too late.'

'What would you have done to save your daughter, if you'd known?'

Charlie stares at me. His eyes are a little wet.

'Anything. Anything.'

'I have a daughter now, too,' I tell him. The words still feel strange in my mouth.

He stares at me in justified amazement. 'You?'

'I didn't even know about her until two days ago. Somebody killed her mother, and now they've taken her. I need to find her. That's why I'm here, Charlie. You're the one person in this city I can trust. I'm sorry I blanked you for a decade, but I was protecting you. Please.'

Charlie peers at me over half-moon glasses, as if trying to work out if I'm gaslighting him or not.

'All right, you little shit. What you need?'

His eyes grow wider and wider as I tell him until I start to worry that they might fall out.

'And how you pay for all this?'

'That's the other thing,' I say. 'I'm going to need cash. And lots of it.'

53

Charlie might be old, but the Bank of Charlie has kept up with the times. A simple and untraceable Bitcoin transfer between two anonymous wallets hosted on offshore exchanges, and we're square. Charlie disappears somewhere for twenty minutes and reappears with literal armfuls of cash in used notes, and I realise that in addition to everything else, Charlie is a world-class money launderer.

The first twenty-four hours in a kidnapping – if that's what it is – are the most crucial, and I've already used most of them. But I'm wanted, I'm unarmed, and given the size of the storm that's just enveloped me, I'm going to need every resource I can lay my hands on if I'm going to get Mireille back in one piece.

The alternative is something I don't even know how to contemplate.

Charlie isn't one to be hurried, but I guess the gravity of the situation lights some kind of fire under him because over the next thirty-six hours the basement welcomes a seemingly endless stream of guests, each with a specific knock. By the end of it, I have three new sets of ID, each complete with fully funded bank accounts, biometrically correct passports (US, Canada, Germany) plus credit cards, weapons, ammunition, hand-made tooled leather shoes, a bespoke Ermenegildo Zegna suit in a Prince of Wales *centoquarantamila*, a sharp new haircut which includes a change of colour, five burner phones with two prepaid SIM cards each, and $100,000 in cash.

That night I fall asleep on the black couch, anaesthetised by glasses of *baijiu* supplied gratis by Charlie. As I do, I think about Mireille.

Yes, she's my daughter, but what does that *mean*? You're supposed to love your kids unconditionally, the way that June-bug loved me, like it's a given, like it's something that happens automatically. But I don't even know Mireille, beyond the few short hours I spent with her. Genetics apart, I have no stake in any part of her life. I'm not the one who put pink bobbles in her hair. I never changed a diaper or read her a book or did any of those things that actually make you a parent, as opposed to a high-confidence match on a DNA test. And if I *was* an actual parent I sure as hell wouldn't want any kid of mine hanging around me.

Yet Gracious put her daughter into my hands. She trusted me to protect Mireille, and I failed her. I feel *something* for Mireille, but is it love? Is that what it's called? Am I even capable of it? Do I even have the right? Does any of it matter? And if Mireille is my daughter, did whoever took her know? Is that why she's gone? And if not, why is she so important? What's her significance, and to whom, including me?

The questions tumble through my head like spare change in a dryer until I pass out.

I wake early with a knot in my stomach. There's still one request that Charlie hasn't fulfilled, but the hourglass is empty.

'Charlie, I need to get out of here. They've got a head start on me. If I don't get moving, I'll never find her.'

'What you asked for,' he says, 'it's not easy to find.'

'Well, maybe a substitute. Something easier, cheaper maybe.'

'No, no, no,' says Charlie. 'A few hours, that's all. Did I ever let you down before?'

And it's true, he didn't, so I sink back onto the leather couch and wait.

Ninety minutes later, I feel a low thrumming sound that shakes the floor and rattles the stainless-steel kidney dishes piled on a shelf. Then there's a distinctive knock, and I follow Charlie up the narrow stairs to the front entrance. He flips the cardboard flap to make sure it's the same face he saw on CCTV downstairs, then he opens the door and steps aside so I can take in the sheer unadulterated magnificence of what is now parked in front of the battered grey door.

54

It's a jet-black, impossibly sleek, 6.6 litre, 190 mph Trident Iceni convertible with the track performance upgrade. It is by far *not* the most expensive supercar in the world – hell, you can buy a Mercedes SUV that costs more – but it is the coolest by a country mile, and one of the rarest. British born and made, it oozes sex, the sleek, slim, flowing lines a callback to the Jaguar E-Type. It's powered by, of all things, a heavy-duty diesel engine designed for full-size pick-up trucks but engineered into something wildly different. And because it's a diesel, it gets something between sixty and seventy miles to the gallon, giving it a range of a thousand miles or so – essential when you're trying not to put your face on gas station CCTV any more than is absolutely necessary.

It resembles less a car and more a ballistic missile, with me as the warhead.

The old me would have hated it. He'd have chosen something Italian, in a primary colour, probably with racing stripes. Well, fuck him. 'He didn't have the responsibilities of parenthood.'

I turn to Charlie. 'Holy shit. You actually found one.'

Charlie smiles, which he never does, showing crooked yellow teeth – he refuses to allow anyone to work on them – and holds out a set of keys.

The Trident has, of all things, a trunk, so I load in a few anonymous-looking but remarkably heavy holdalls. Charlie watches from the safety of his armoured metal door. As the lid clunks shut with the kind of expensive click that only mid-six-figures of supercar can give you, I turn to thank him. But all he says is:

'Find your daughter, asshole.'

The grey door closes behind him.

55

It's eight hundred miles to New York City, but the Trident will do it on a single tank.

The rendezvous is already arranged, scheduled using a newly delivered burner as I sat chafing on Charlie's couch waiting for the rest of my loadout to arrive. The number was the same one I wrote down for Barb before I abandoned her and Mireille. I wasn't expecting it to ring, and it didn't. But ten minutes later, my phone buzzed with a different number. Five minutes more and I had an address in Manhattan, along with a time, and a pointed reminder that if I brought company, knowingly or unknowingly, we would all be subject to immediate and permanent cancellation.

I should have been insulted. I've been out of the game, but I've been doing this a long time. I hardly need to be reminded to stay clean from surveillance, or lose it if I pick it up. But it's the fact they thought a reminder was necessary that worries me. It's another rise of the wind that sends horses galloping around the paddock and suggests no matter how dark the sky has grown, the real storm has yet to hit.

I hit the interstate and ladder up through the Trident's impossibly precise six gears, hurtling past everything in sight. By now, with ATF and FBI crawling over the smouldering ruins of Sixteen's house and finding the charred remnants of our combined armoury, I'm undoubtedly a federal fugitive. But the cops are looking for someone who's trying to hide. The last thing they'll be expecting is a jerk with great hair ripping it up in a supercar. They won't even see who it is behind the $900 shades as they write me a ticket, sneer in disgust and move on.

That's the point, of course. Security-by-being-totally-fuck-ing-out-there.

I bare my flawless teeth in a rictus grin to check them in the rear-view. If you discount the bruises I took in Vermillion, now somewhat disguised with foundation, I look pretty good. The clothes Charlie sourced are extravagant, luxurious, utterly on point. The Trident feels like an extension of my own body, a four-wheeled Gundam.

I remind myself: *this is what you wanted. This is what you prayed for all those nights you stood at the window yearning for someone to come at you, to give you an excuse to go back to war.* I should be yelling *It's me! I'm Seventeen, baby! And I'm BACK!* into the slipstream at the top of my voice. But the trappings no longer spark the same kind of joy.

Sometimes the only thing worse than not getting what you want is getting what you want.

Seven hours later, I rumble down into the parking lot of a stunning new glass-and-steel construction in midtown Manhattan. In what I can only assume is an astoundingly tasteless postmod-ern take on New York's iconic and collapsed twin towers, the fifty-storey skyscrapers bend and twist around each other as if entwined in some kind of ambisexual fuck-party. The effect is hardly diminished by the 200-foot bridge suspended between them, harbouring an Olympic-sized swimming pool (residents only, natch). The underside of the pool is made of glass, so you can stare up at the wrinkled crotches and dugs of the rich and famous as they do lengths. I suppose if you had a telephoto lens you could get some decent specialist porn out of it.

But I'm not here for the pool. I'm here for the only person on earth who might know something about what the hell is going on and has no particular motive to kill me on sight.

And I'm not sure about the second part.

56

The valet gives the Trident a look of longing as I burble past, but I may need a quick exit, so I wave at him, find a spot near the elevators and back in. So-called 'combat parking' is a straight tell, one of those things that broadcast either that you're on your guard, which is a mistake, or that you're a poseur who wants them to think you're on your guard, which is worse. But enough shit has happened over the last few days that I can't afford to take chances.

I take the parking elevator up to the lobby, where I give a name to the security desk and tell her what I'm here for. She hands me a perfectly blank, white access card.

'Elevator number seven. Go up and wait.'

I take it and head towards the main elevators.

She calls after me. 'Not those. By the washrooms. Big door, you can't miss it.'

I follow the signs to the men's room and, sure enough, opposite is a wide silver door, like a freight elevator, but with no floor numbers.

I insert the card, and the door slides open.

It's dark inside, but when I step across the threshold, the door closes behind me and a fluorescent light flickers on. It is indeed an elevator, with a second set of doors on the other side, but beside them there are only two buttons. One is marked with a star, for the lobby. The other is unmarked.

That's not the only odd thing about it.

There's a fancy gurney with a pair of oxygen tanks and a portable defibrillator attached.

I hit the blank button. For a second, nothing happens, then the elevator lurches upwards. The way my lunch sinks towards my shoes tells me it's going fast. Twenty seconds later, I feel the weight on the soles of my feet lighten, and my stomach takes a voyage northwards as the elevator slows and stops.

Nothing happens, again.

There's another slot beside the door, so I insert the white card. The doors slide open, and I blink as daylight hits my eyes.

I'm on a lower portion of the roof, open to the air. In front of me is a gentle ramp with concrete walls winding up towards the sky. It's the perfect spot for an ambush, so I slip my pistol out of my concealed holster and chamber a round, then creep up the ramp, my back to the outside wall as it curves upwards.

At the top, I finally see where I am.

It's a helipad, wide and flat, a good twenty feet above the roof proper. Hence the gurney and oxygen tank, for elderly residents who need to be whisked to Mount Sinai *tout suite*. Wind blusters my hair as Manhattan falls away around me. There's no-one here, so I holster my weapon. Two hundred feet away, the second tower gleams in the sunlight, roof equally deserted.

I check my watch. I'm a minute early. Almost exactly sixty seconds later, I hear the clatter of an Airbus H175. It follows the Hudson south, then arcs in towards midtown. But instead of landing, it makes a couple of defensive loops around the twin buildings, spiralling in close enough on the second to see me. I hold out my arms to show that I'm not holding a weapon, but the helo doesn't land. I open my jacket to show the shoulder holster, carefully remove the gun and place it on the ground.

The helicopter still doesn't land.

I remove the magazine from the pistol and lay it on the ground beside it.

It still doesn't land.

I remove the shells from the magazine and line them up.

It still doesn't land.

Somebody is taking absolutely no chances.

I remove the final shell from the chamber and put it with the others. Then I lift my pant legs to show that there are no ankle holsters and the back of my jacket to show there's nothing in the small of my back.

Evidently that's good enough, because the helicopter finally noses forward to land.

The rotor wash nearly knocks me off my feet, blasting dust and grit into my eyes and sending the shells skittering off the edge of the helipad, leaving me completely unarmed as it settles onto the broad concrete apron.

As the rotors spool down, the door opens, and the steps are folded out by someone inside.

The pilot waves at me to approach.

I pick up my gun and the empty magazine and hold them up.

The pilot nods.

I click the mag into place and snug the useless weapon back into my shoulder holster, then hold my jacket together as I head to the door, climb the stairs and step inside. A burly, bald man wearing a dark suit and no expression, a snubnose semi slung over one shoulder, brings the steps up again and closes the door. Above, the rotors continue at idle, ready for take-off at any moment.

The perfectly made-up woman sitting in one of the plush leather seats motions me to sit opposite her.

'*Bonjour*, Seventeen,' she says, watching me try to put some order back into my hair.

'That was quite an entrance,' I say.

'I assure you,' she says, lighting a cigarette, 'it was absolutely necessary.'

57

Nicole Osterman is seventy if she's a day. Tiny, verging on frail, she's one of those women who aged with perfect grace. Her grey hair is bobbed with millimetric precision, her clothes are pure *bon chic bon genre* Parisian elegance, and if her skin hangs looser than it once did, her bone structure still hints at someone who broke hearts on six continents, and probably still could.

Nicole is an old hand. Perhaps the oldest surviving in the world we both inhabit. She predates my deceased and deeply unlamented manager-cum-agent Handler by at least a decade. Nicole came up in the days when the CIA was still effectively a boys' club, still in the thrall of men like Wild Bill Donovan. Disabled by a polio infection as a child – she still walks with a stick – she was never going to pass muster as a case officer, the job that Handler excelled at and allowed him subsequently to build a stable of elite motherfuckers like me.

She arrived at the CIA directly from academia in the last, floridly paranoid, days of the CIA's Chief of Counterintelligence James Jesus Angleton. JJA, as he was known, had become convinced that the CIA had been infiltrated top-to-bottom by the KGB, and that world leaders, including Canada's Pierre Trudeau, Britain's Harold Wilson, Sweden's Olof Palme, Australia's Gough Whitlam and West Germany's Willy Brandt, were all Soviet assets. With her brilliant mind, expertise in linguistics, cryptography, psychology and forensics, and no previous contacts with the intelligence community, she was a natural fit for JJA's paranoia.

For a decade and more, Nicole ran her own shop, beholden to no-one but the CIA Director himself, dedicated solely to identifying and eliminating security risks – not just moles, but potential moles, an early kind of Minority Report. She was the first to use computational linguistics – computer-aided sentiment analysis of letters, reports and transcripts of bugged conversations, along with statistical analysis, as opposed to the flawed human interpretations, of the lie-detector tests that were ubiquitous in the CIA at the time.

But what really made Nicole stand out were her instincts, her memory, her trap-like mind, and her interviewing skills. She could sit at a desk and pore over bank statements, credit card receipts, expense accounts and tax returns, and catch an inconsistency between one item and another she'd seen six months earlier. Her interrogations were unhurried, unfailingly polite, and utterly terrifying. Her subjects buckled, not because she browbeat them, but because it was obvious she already knew and understood everything, and lying to her would only humiliate you further.

JJA's retirement, however, ushered in a new age at the CIA. His paranoia had paralysed the CIA's operations. Defectors from the KGB had been turned away or worse because of the fear that they were so-called 'dangles' being offered up to feed disinformation to the Agency. Now the pendulum swung the other way, and a cowboy phase began – a phase which saw Nicole's office sidelined, and as a result of which traitors like Aldrich Ames, Robert Hanssen and others were able to operate with near impunity for years.

Her office might have been sidelined, but Nicole kept working. In the mid-eighties, she began to suspect that a CIA operation had been compromised by a high-level North Korean asset within the Agency, leading to the deaths of a CIA infiltration team. But when her interim report found its way up the chain of command, a co-worker on her team was killed in a car accident. Nicole became convinced – correctly, as it turned out – that it was an assassination, carried out by the CIA itself, and was smart enough to know that no individual ever goes up against the power of a nation-state intelligence agency and prevails.

She closed the investigation the following day with a recommendation for No Further Action, handed in her resignation and set about independently building her own stable of operatives, not least as an insurance policy in case the Agency decided to terminate her as well.

The man she'd handed the report to was Handler. Eventually, he left too. On the outside, they remained enemies, but by now each had their own stable of killers. Sixteen was Nicole's, and I was Handler's, and when things went sour, I ultimately did her an enormous favour by helping to facilitate Handler's exit from the worldly sphere.

Which is why she's the one remaining contact in the world of perfectly deniable state-funded contract killing and associated espionage shenanigans that I'm even halfway to trusting.

58

'Necessary how?' I say.

'You don't know?'

'I don't know anything. I've been out of the loop for a year.'

'So why are you back now?'

'Because somebody tried to kill me.'

'Well, that's hardly a surprise, is it?' she says, tapping ash. 'It was only a matter of time. Some aspirant Eighteen, I imagine? They've all been looking for you. Quite the scavenger hunt.'

'That's what I thought. But it wasn't. It was a nine-year-old girl.'

Nicole blinks. It takes a lot to surprise her, but that hit the spot.

'Go on.'

'Not only that, but I'm fairly sure she's my daughter.'

'You have a *daughter*?'

I'm going to have to get used to this reaction, which is only fair.

'By whom, if you don't mind me asking?'

'Ali Olusi.'

She blinks again, twice. 'Ali Olusi, as in – forgive me – *the* Ali Olusi?'

'It's a long story,' I say. 'Ali's real name was Gracious, he was actually a woman, and she had a daughter, who turns out to be mine. Someone killed Gracious and kidnapped the girl. I'm in the frame for the murder and a bunch of others, innocent people, not in the game. And I need to find my daughter.'

'I see,' says Nicole, in a tone that implies she doesn't. 'And you think I can help how?'

'Something's going on. Something big. I can feel it. I just need to understand the context. Things that have happened since I've been out. Stuff I've missed. I figured if anyone knew, it'd be you.'

Nicole nods, stubs out her cigarette, lights another. She blows smoke, then looks back at me.

'What's happened,' she says, 'is we're at war.'

'Who's we? And why is there a war?'

'Because of you,' says Nicole, wagging a bony yet perfectly manicured finger at me.

'I don't understand.'

Nicole sighs like she's explaining something to a backward schoolboy, which is not that far off.

'When Handler died, it left a power vacuum. It wasn't just that Handler was gone. So was Sixteen, and so were you. No-one was willing to crown an Eighteen unless they could parade your head on a pole. But nobody could find you.'

'Which meant an impasse.'

She shakes her head. 'Worse. With the three of you gone, there was no-one at the top of the table. No structure, no hierarchy. You know what happens to a pack of wolves when the alpha is killed?'

'The betas fight to the death to become the alpha.'

'Exactly,' says Nicole. 'Which is where we are now. It's not exactly relaxing.'

'And that's why my gun currently has no bullets, in case someone else had hired me. And why we're sitting in a helicopter with the doors closed and the engine running, so there's no chance of sound being picked up or lips being read.'

'I'm glad you understand.'

I think about this for a second. 'Fine. You're at war, I get it. But Handler's been gone for a year. So have I. So has

Sixteen. But this feels urgent. Why is it all suddenly kicking off now?'

'If I had to guess,' says Nicole, 'Deep Threat.'

'Am I supposed to know what that is?'

'Nobody knows what it is. It's a cryptonym. A codeword. We started picking up chatter about six weeks ago. Whispers, nothing concrete. But enough that it had to be real, whatever it was.'

Nicole fiddles with her cigarette. If I didn't know her better, I might think she was scared.

'What aren't you telling me?'

She looks up. 'You're too young to remember. But I came up during the Cold War. We lived under the shadow of the bomb. I was with the Agency for most of it. People don't understand how close we came to Armageddon, to the end of everything. November '83, that was the closest we ever came. A big NATO exercise. The Russians thought it was a ruse to cover for a first strike nuclear attack. So they started prepping a first strike of their own. Which meant *we* started prepping for a first strike. That whole week, nobody went home, nobody slept. We weren't even allowed to say goodbye to our families.'

'Your point?'

'My point is, Deep Threat, whatever it is, people talk about it the way we used to talk about the bomb. There's a phrase that comes up over and over again in the intercepts: "an existential threat to the human race". Everybody's frightened, everybody wants it, but nobody has it, and nobody even *knows* who has it, or exactly what it is.'

'So if Gracious had some information about this so-called Deep Threat—'

'Then she would have made herself a target for every intelligence agency on earth.'

'She was tortured before she died,' I say. 'But whoever it was didn't stop. Which means whatever they were looking for, they didn't find it.'

'So maybe she passed it on to your daughter.'

I nod. 'Which explains why they took her.'

I'm quiet for a moment. Nicole knows what I'm thinking.

'I'm sorry,' she says. 'If it's as big as everyone thinks it is, there's no telling what they'll do to her to get their hands on it.'

The pilot leans into the cabin. 'We should get back in the air, ma'am.'

'You think they'd come for you here?' I say. 'In Manhattan?'

'You don't understand,' says Nicole. 'It's open season. And if people think you might know something about Deep Threat . . .'

'Five minutes more,' I say. 'This thing, you must have some idea what it is. Some clue in the intercepts. I mean, is it nuclear? A bioweapon? Who developed it? Why?'

Nicole sighs. 'The rumour is, it's a zero-day.'

59

In 2009, the Iranian uranium enrichment facility at Natanz, a key component in that country's nuclear weapons programme, began to experience a series of major technical problems. By early 2010 more than a thousand of the centrifuges used to process the uranium appeared to have been destroyed.

The culprit was Stuxnet, an expertly crafted computer worm which targeted the Siemens industrial control systems used by the Iranian enrichment plant. According to *The New York Times*, it was a joint operation by the United States and Israeli intelligence services to disrupt the Iranian nuclear programme. But it also hit infrastructure in North Korea and Russia, and spread to more than 100,000 industrial plants worldwide that used the Siemens systems.

Stuxnet was a zero-day.

A zero-day is a vulnerability, an exploit, a hack, a chink in the armour in the hardware or software of a computer system that nobody else, not even the manufacturer or programmer, knows about. It's called a zero-day because the target of the attack has zero days to come up with a way to protect themselves. They're defenceless, giving an attacker a window of vulnerability to break in and wreak havoc.

A zero-day in and of itself generally has no effect. It's just a way to break into the walled garden of a computer system. What happens then depends on its payload, on how it's been weaponised, and which systems it targets. Stuxnet, for example, combined four separate exploits to get past the layers of security that protected the Iranian facility, and was specifically designed to sabotage the Iranian installation, feeding erroneous control data to the centrifuges that caused them to fail.

Zero-days are one of the most prized assets of nation-state intelligence services. They can be used for something as simple as hacking your iPhone to eavesdrop on your conversations or steal encrypted files. But their potential goes far beyond that. In a world where computers run everything, a fully weaponised zero-day can shut down power grids, railways, banking systems, ports, air traffic control, communications and industrial facilities.

There are many who believe the next global war will be fought in cyberspace, with adversary nations using weaponised zero-days to shut down each other's economies, contaminate water treatment plants, hijack government, military or intelligence systems, send nuclear plants into meltdown, and even retarget or take over weapons systems.

Executive summary: a zero-day can be a frighteningly powerful thing.

But an existential threat to the human race?

Is that even possible?

If so, it's something way beyond anything we've seen before.

And if it's real, Nicole is right to be scared.

60

'Ma'am—' It's the pilot again.

'All right, all right,' says Nicole, then to me: 'You better go.'

The fat man opens the door once more, and I climb out.

As the engines spool up again, I turn back to Nicole.

'Wait,' I say. 'If this is what you say, if it's as serious as it looks, I may need backing. Infrastructure, resources. Right now, I'm on my own. But if you help me with this, I could repay you in kind. Long-term, if you're interested?'

Nicole leans out of the door.

'You mean, coming out of retirement?'

'It didn't suit me.'

She smiles slightly, but there's a sadness in it too.

'I'm flattered,' she says. 'There was a time I'd have jumped at the chance. But I'm too old. I've seen too much shit. I dabble in the shallow end of the pool these days. I don't have the stomach for a fight like this. I took up painting, did you know that? Still life, flowers, that kind of thing. I don't need this. I don't want it. Your daughter, I'm sorry about her. I hope you get her back. But I'm not going to risk everything to help you.'

She's about to close the door, but something isn't sitting right with me. Nicole Osterman is legendary for never turning away from a fight she thought she could win.

'Nicole,' I say.

She turns back.

'Bullshit. Painting fucking *flowers*? You want to tell me the real reason?'

'All right,' she says.

The pilot is throttling up. She has to raise her voice to be heard over the turbines.

'Your daughter. Even if you can get her back, she's always going to be your underbelly, your point of failure. So long as you're Seventeen, the path to becoming Eighteen doesn't go through you any more. It goes through her. I hope you get her back. But things are different for you now. They always will be. The old Seventeen, yes, maybe I'd have taken him on. The new one? I can't take the risk. I'm sorry. I hope you understand.'

And with that, the door closes.

The engine whines up to speed. I protect my eyes as the Airbus unweights and lifts into the air, sliding sideways in the wind, then arcs up and away.

It's just turning east to head back towards the river when I see him.

It's a man on the roof of the other tower. There's something on his shoulder, and I suddenly realise what it is. Instinctively, I pull my pistol, but as I aim it, I remember: no bullets.

The man turns to me for a moment and smiles, then turns back to the helicopter and fires.

61

The RPG streaks across the Manhattan sky and hits the Airbus amidships.

The fuel tank explodes, the tail detaches, and the flaming helicopter spirals drunkenly down into a cross street between Fourth and Fifth Avenue, before striking the side of an office building and dropping into the street below.

62

As I watch the flaming helicopter disappear into the Manhattan canyons, a quiet fury floods into me. Nicole might have run killers, but she was one of the most brilliant and decent human beings I've ever met. The only reason she ended up running her own outfit was that the CIA had become so corrupt that her own life was at risk for revealing it. I'm not dumb enough to believe there was ever a golden age of intelligence, yet there was a genuine *noblesse oblige* about her. As far as anyone I've ever met could be described as incorruptible, it was Nicole.

And now she's gone, just like Gracious, laid to waste for reasons I still don't understand.

But fury isn't going to help me. If the man with the RPG could make it to the roof of the other building, there are others on their way to where I am.

I'm trapped, I'm defenceless, I'm caught in the middle of a war I'm no part of, I still have no idea why my daughter was taken, and my last remaining ally was just incinerated. I sprint down the ramp to the elevator doors, but an arrow shows it's on its way up.

Beside the elevator door, there's a staircase exit, but it can only be opened by the crash bars visible on the inside, and there's probably another killer heading up the stairs to cut me off.

I run back up the ramp, trying to find another exit, but the helipad is built wide, all the way out to the edges of the building. From there, it's a fifty-storey drop to the streets of Manhattan.

Over the rush of the wind, I hear the bing of the elevator, the swish of the doors opening, and the clatter of boots as they pound up the ramp towards me.

I take one last desperate look around then turn to see a head appear at the top of the ramp.

He's older than the last time I saw him by almost a decade, but there's no mistaking the oversized, almost clownish features, the massive skull, the lantern jaw, all of which give him an odd resemblance to Marvel's Thanos, or Boris Karloff in *Frankenstein*.

And the moment I see him, I know who it was who killed Gracious.

PART FIVE

63

Suleiman Abdi flew into Addis Ababa with his entourage, took a few meetings, made a big, well-received speech and flew out again unmolested.

Her scent still clung to me, but Gracious had gone. And in failing to carry out a hit she'd been paid for, she had committed the unforgivable sin of our profession. Whoever had hired her would want revenge, which meant she would now have a price on her own head. She could disappear, sure – invisibility was her superpower – but she would be looking over her shoulder for the rest of her life unless I did something.

What I did was wait.

On the third morning after Abdi left, as I was drinking the gritty coffee prepared by Gracious's replacement in the atrium, I saw him enter. I knew Harkonnen by reputation, not by sight, but with the six-foot-eleven frame and fighter's shoulders that stretched the back of his jacket almost to breaking, he was hard to mistake. Finnish, from the Karelian lakelands and trained as an Arctic sniper, he had served in the Russian special forces for a decade and fought professionally in MMA competitions. His nickname in his native language was *Vasara*, the sledgehammer. His face might have been handsome once, but hundreds of fights had turned large parts of it to scar tissue; that, plus the oversized features common to an acromegalic giant, gave him the look of a deadly Shrek, the heavy jaw and broken nose completing the effect.

There was only one reason he would be here, in this hotel, in this city, at this moment, and that was because he'd been tasked with finding Ali/Gracious, and killing them.

His eyes flicked around as he checked in, dead and calculating. They rested on me for a second, but he had no reason either to know who I was or to expect anyone like me to be in residence. He took back his credit card and headed up to his room carrying his own – single, heavy – bag.

Every killer has a signature. Gracious's was perfect, invisible technique. Mine was audacity. Harkonnen's was brutality. He was a blunt instrument who left a trail of death in his wake. He didn't care about innocence or guilt, and priced collateral damage at zero. Harkonnen was far from an amateur: he got the job done, but the amount of clean-up afterwards meant the upper echelons of middlemen, operators of the calibre of Handler or Nicole Osterman, would have nothing to do with him.

He hadn't made me, which meant it would have been an easy task to kill him. But that would have been a temporary fix – if he died, another would be sent, and another – and I needed a permanent solution.

If I was to save Gracious, I had to find out who had sent him.

64

A plume of smoke from Nicole's wrecked helicopter already disfigures the flawless blue sky as Harkonnen appears from the elevator. The moment he sees me, he opens up. Completely unarmed, all I can do is dodge right, keeping low, and he lifts the gun high over the walls of the ramp, raking fire. Unable to aim properly, his shots go wide, but I'm utterly exposed. There's not a fragment of cover up here and not a single thing I can fight back with.

I'm dead in seconds unless I do something.

All that's left to me is a monstrous gamble, but the alternative is death.

As the bullets skitter and ricochet off the concrete behind me, I sprint as hard as I can to the very edge of the apron and launch myself into the air like a bird.

If I'm lucky, there'll be suicide netting below the edge of the helipad. It'll break my fall, there'll be a way back into the building, and I'll work my way back down to street level and escape.

But there is no suicide netting.

I fall.

65

I saw Harkonnen around the hotel a few more times that day. He made little attempt to hide what he was doing – subtlety was not his style. Money changed hands as he talked to waiters and bellboys and chambermaids, but I could tell he wasn't getting much of any use. Then that night in the bar, he turned up again and took a seat at the bar that gave him a view of the entire room.

I was back in my asshole persona, playing drunk, each arm around a different working girl. But with Gracious gone, I didn't have any appetite for further transactions. I guess by now they were starting to get the message because the one on my left – her professional name was Sabrina, with the fine bone structure of the singer Sade and a degree in Philosophy – politely excused herself and drifted over to the bar, where she positioned herself next to Harkonnen.

Evidently the big man wasn't much for small talk, because ten minutes later they left together. As I watched them go, I turned to the other girl, a feisty Ethiopian twenty-something with a wicked sense of humour who called herself only semi-ironically Roxanne.

'Make sure you check up on her.'

'Why?' said Roxanne. 'You know something about him?'

'No,' I said. 'I just have a weird feeling.'

To keep up appearances, and maintain goodwill, I gave her money to lie about sleeping with me in case anyone asked, then went to bed alone.

The next morning I was woken early by a hammering on the door. It was Roxanne, and the moment I opened the door she started hitting me.

'You knew about him!' she yelled. 'You knew he would do this!'

I pulled her in and tried to calm her down. 'Do what? Did he hurt her?'

'You need to see.'

66

I fall.

67

Roxanne rushed us on a moped through the streets of Addis Ababa to a house arranged around a central courtyard where the girls who worked the luxury hotels all lived, sharing rooms under the watchful eye of a sixty-year-old Ethiopian madam with an eyepatch. A revolver on her hip completed the Rooster Cogburn look and left me in no doubt she was happy to use it on anyone who dared hurt one of her girls or muscle in on her business.

A half-dozen of her charges watched silently, their eyes following me as Roxanne took me to a door on the far side of the courtyard.

The room was dark. Sabrina sat on a mattress, back up against the wall, a pillow clutched in front of her. Roxanne pulled a piece of cloth away from the single high window, and I saw what she had meant. To say Sabrina had taken a beating was an understatement. Roxanne told me Harkonnen had used his fists, but it looked like it had been done with an iron bar. What made it almost worse was it had been done to just one side of her face, leaving the perfect cheekbone and flawless skin on the other side untouched. Her left eye was closed, the left side of her mouth so swollen it had almost ballooned, and the hair on the side of her skull was clotted with blood.

Her open eye stared at me, hostile and frightened.

I squatted down. 'He did this? The big man in the bar?'

Sabrina nodded.

'It hurts her to talk,' said Roxanne. 'But he told her he'll do the same to the other side of her face if she doesn't give him the information he wants. Enat wants to kill him,' she said, by which I assumed she meant the woman with the eyepatch and the pistol, 'but I told her we should talk to you first.'

'You did the right thing,' I told her. 'What does he want to know?'

'The girl who used to serve the coffee. The one you liked. He wants to know everything about her. Where did she live? Where did she come from? Who did she talk to?'

'What did she tell him?'

'Nothing.' It's Sabrina who talks, and I realise the expression in her eye wasn't fear, but anger. 'I told him I'd find out what I could, but only so that the next time I see him I can kill him. Enat says I can use her gun.'

'Listen to me,' I said. 'I know this man. If you try to kill him, he'll kill you. I should have known he'd do this. I can't make it right, but I'll pay for your treatment, surgery, whatever it takes. And more for the pain. But I need you to do something for me, okay? I'm going to write down an address. I want you to give it to him and tell him that this is where she lived. Can you do that?'

Sabrina looked at the address doubtfully, then back up. Except now she was looking past me.

'He needs to suffer,' said a gravelly African voice. I turned to see the madam in the doorway.

'Don't worry,' I said. 'He will.'

68

I fall.

69

I made my way to Gracious's apartment, stopping only to buy supplies from a hardware store. I picked the cheap lock and let myself in, then locked the door again behind me. I didn't need to look around to know that Gracious had sanitised the apartment thoroughly. Harkonnen wasn't going to find anything useful. But he *was* going to find me.

Harkonnen wasn't stupid. He would observe the apartment first, probably bribing someone in one of the apartments opposite to let him check through the window and asking if they'd seen Gracious come and go. I arranged the curtain and blinds so that from his likely vantage point there was a full view of the interior of the apartment, with just a two-foot-wide section of wall to the side of the doorway out of sight.

That's where I stood.

I waited for seven hours, watching the shadows orbit the room. Around six thirty, I saw the glint of a reflection pass across the door beside me, which told me someone was using binoculars that reflected the sun. Thirty minutes later, I heard a noise in the corridor. It was someone heavy trying to be quiet, who wasn't especially good at it. There was a faint noise on the thin wall behind me. I guessed he was using a wall-mounted microphone, sensitive enough to pick up even tiny body movements.

I held myself perfectly still, not even allowing myself to breathe. Two and a half minutes later, with just a few seconds of air left in my lungs, another noise told me he was satisfied the room was empty. The door handle rattled as he tried to turn it, then there was an almighty crash as he kicked the door open, so hard it took it completely off its hinges.

Harkonnen followed, gun drawn, whipping round to cover his flank. But as he did, I brought the crowbar I bought in the hardware store down as hard as I could on his hands, smashing the gun out of them and breaking his fingers. As he staggered, trying to pick it up, I slammed it into the side of his head. He fell sideways, but managed to keep his feet, then rushed at me. I sidestepped and swung the crowbar as hard as I could into the other side of his head. This time he went down.

I kicked his gun to the far side of the room, pulled the duct tape I bought at the hardware store along with the crowbar and other implements out of the bag, and bound him hand and foot. A curious neighbour, hearing the commotion, poked her head in through the door and saw me taping his ankles, but I just shook my head, and she turned away. Two crazy white men fighting was not something she had any interest in getting involved with, and I didn't blame her.

I put the door back in the frame as best I could, then hauled Harkonnen's massive bulk across the floor and propped him up against the wall, his mouth taped.

If it was anyone but Harkonnen, I'd have gotten the information out of him the traditional way, using bolt cutters and welding equipment. But Harkonnen was a tough nut, it would have taken a while, generated a lot of noise and blood, and likely have been fatal. Which, who cares, but if he'd lied to me I'd have no way of going back to him for a second round.

So instead, I fished in his pocket and found an iPhone, used one of his huge, smashed fingers to unlock it and scrolled through the call log. Most of them went to American numbers, and of the two most frequent, one had a Florida code and one California. About seventy-five per cent of the other numbers shared a Florida code, so I tried that one.

A man's voice answered. Older, a smoker. 'Staley.'

Staley could only be one man. Edgar Staley, failson of a billionaire who'd been cut off from his family's money and survived on the largesse of his twin sister, who controlled the family purse strings. Staley was a fuck-up – rumours of addictions to alcohol, sex and gambling bobbed in his wake – and the US Navy had kicked him out after he ran the patrol boat he commanded aground while drunk. He dodged a court-martial by getting his sister to endow a scholarship, and ultimately landed in the world of private intelligence and military contracting the same way a drunk lands in a rose garden by falling out of a tree and hitting every branch on the way down.

It made sense that Harkonnen worked for Staley: no-one more legit would touch him with a bargepole, while having a blunderbuss like Harkonnen in his armoury allowed Staley to punch far above his weight.

'Hark, that you?' he said, hearing only silence.

I whaled the crowbar into Harkonnen's side. He moaned through the duct tape.

'What's that?' I said, and ripped it off his mouth.

'Mother*fucker*,' was all he said, but his face was screwed up in pain.

'What's going on?' said Staley's voice. 'Who is this? What do you want?'

Behind Staley's voice, there was another sound. Men's voices, something in French, then a rattle that slowed and stopped. It took me a moment to place it, but then I realised what it was. It was a roulette wheel. Staley was in a casino. He really was a gambling addict, and from the sound of his voice, the stuff about drinking was on point as well.

'My name' I said, 'is Seventeen. You may have heard of me.'

70

I fall.

71

'What's going on?' said Staley. 'What do you want? Where's Harkonnen?'

I took out one of Harkonnen's knees with the crowbar.

He didn't exactly scream, but it wasn't far off.

'He's here,' I said. 'You want him back alive, it can be arranged. But he needs to learn that beating up innocent women isn't a viable career path.'

Harkonnen rolled over onto his side and began inchworming across the floor to where his gun still lay. I picked up the phone and followed him, the crowbar dangling in my hand.

'How bad is he?'

'He won't be typing much for a while, but he'll live,' I said.

Harkonnen reached for the gun, his wrists still taped, but I jammed the forked end of the crowbar into his broken hand. He moaned in pain.

'Sure,' said Staley, sounding nervous and suspicious. 'I'll take him back.'

'Okay,' I said. 'Now we need to talk quid pro quo.'

'What do you want?'

'I want to know who paid for the hit on Suleiman Abdi.'

'I don't know what you're talking about.'

'Don't fuck with me, Staley,' I said. 'The only reason big boi's here is that the hit didn't happen. Which means it came through you. But you're just the middleman. I want to know who the client is.'

'Why the fuck do you care?'

'I need to talk to them.'

'I'll pass on a message.'

I twisted the crowbar in Harkonnen's hand and pressed down. He made a guttural noise.

'You know,' I say, 'Harkonnen's an animal. But he's good at what he does. You're lucky to have him. Without him, you'd be nothing, just some second-rate wannabe Blackwater. But he also makes enemies easily. I imagine he's made a few on your behalf. Which means without him—'

I leaned on the crowbar as hard as I could. Harkonnen bellowed like a wounded tusker.

'—Without him, you're vulnerable as hell. So, like I said, whoever paid for the hit, I need to parley with them directly. Deal?'

'Deal,' said Staley.

72

I fall.

73

Roxanne and a couple of the other girls helped me carry Harkonnen down the concrete stairs and load him into a battered taxi. On the way down, they dropped him two or three times, which I'm sure was accidental, at least the first time.

The minibus drove us to a private airstrip an hour outside Addis Ababa, where a Gulfstream was waiting with a medical team already on board. They loaded Harkonnen into a wheelchair, still duct-taped, sedated him and put him on board. I gave Roxanne the keycard to my hotel room, told her the combination of the safe and that the money in it – which was plenty – was for Sabrina. Then I got on board and sat opposite Harkonnen, my gun on my lap. He was bound and drugged, but Harkonnen was Harkonnen and the way he stared at me left me in no doubt that he'd return the favours I'd paid him in spades if he ever got the chance.

Twenty-four hours later we landed at another private airstrip in Florida. This one had military trappings, an operational base for Staley's outfit. Harkonnen was unloaded into a Medevac vehicle which roared off to some medical facility to be rebuilt better, stronger, faster.

I stepped down onto the asphalt to find a man in his mid-forties waiting for me. Staley was six feet and change, muscle running to fat, in chinos and a pink polo shirt that stank of aftershave. His mil-spec buzzcut was growing out, and the bags under his eyes told me the previous night had been a long one. There was alcohol on his breath.

'So?' I said.

I talked to the client,' he grunted. 'They've agreed to meet.'

'You going to tell me who they are?'

'You'll find out soon enough,' he said, and gestured to the Sikorsky UH-60 already spooling up on the helipad behind him.

Staley's helicopter took us up through Miami airspace to Palm Beach, where it banked east, out to sea. Ten minutes later, as I saw the vessel ahead of us slide into view, I finally understood who the client was, why they'd chosen to use Edgar Staley as an intermediary, why they'd used Gracious instead of Harkonnen and, above all, why they'd wanted Suleiman Abdi dead in the first place.

74

Between me and the ground, rushing towards me, is the skybridge that links the two towers, with its Olympic-sized swimming pool gleaming blue in the bright sunlight, wealthy inhabitants of the twin towers doing lazy laps up and down the lanes.

That's the good news.

The bad news is I'm going to miss it.

The pool is halfway up the tower, which makes it two hundred and fifty feet below me. That's nearly four seconds in freefall. If I miss it, two seconds later I'll hit the sidewalk at around 100 mph.

I grab the sides of my jacket and hold them out like wings, using my designer rig as a wingsuit. The wind strains against my arms, which tells me it's working, and my trajectory shifts until I'm aimed right for the pool.

That's the good news.

The bad news is that though the pool looks open to the air from underneath, it has not just a glass bottom but a glass roof as well.

The last thing I see before I hit it is the astonished face of an elderly Jewish matron wearing a floral swim cap, who's doing a lazy backstroke as she registers the barely scuffed leather soles of an asshole in nine-hundred-dollar shades and an exceptionally sharp Prince of Wales suit plummeting towards her at north of 70 mph.

75

The name of the superyacht was *La Belle Dame Sans Merci*, and it belonged to Wendy Hipkiss, Edgar Staley's twin, older by an hour, and the woman who bankrolled his operations.

The Staley family were English originally, but they settled in Africa in the 1800s as missionaries, in what became Rhodesia, then Zimbabwe. There, they transmuted into coffee farmers, with a reputation for brutality against their workers, native Africans whose land they expropriated. Following independence, and a brief period of white rule, in 1980 Mugabe took over. The Staley family had done themselves few favours by their treatment of the locals and got out while they could, taking their money with them.

Instead of going back to Britain, they pitched their tent in Florida. Staley senior set up a poultry-processing business, supplying supermarkets and fast-food chains with frozen chicken parts. The business boomed, but he never took it public, which meant that when he died, it all went to the kids. However, by then Staley had already shown his fucked-up colours, so Wendy got the bulk of it, and Staley's relatively paltry share was locked up in a trust fund she administered.

Wendy then married another billionaire – milquetoast octogenarian supermarket magnate Larry Hipkiss, who promptly died and left her one of the richest women in America.

Just another riches-to-riches story. Generational wealth, spo-dee-o-dee. Except for one thing: the Staleys brought their colonial, missionary beliefs with them from Africa, and Wendy inherited it. As she saw it, her family shouldered the white man's burden to bring salvation and civilisation to the savages of the dark continent, only to be driven out of their rightful inheritance by Mugabe and his ilk. This being Florida, it was mashed up with a peculiar perversion of religion which claimed poverty was demonic and that people like her – white, affluent, Christian – were not simply the natural rulers of the world but had a sacred duty to impose their beliefs on everyone else.

Her family's aim had been a white-run Africa. Wendy's was a white-run *planet*.

Wendy's name and holy-roller reputation made her the butt of jokes behind closed doors, but her massive political contributions to both parties gave her enormous clout in DC. To casual observers her bland church-lady niceness entirely disguised her true nature. She avoided electoral politics herself, but her ubiquity in Washington allowed her to sound out fellow travellers, men and women at all levels of government, who turned out to be frighteningly numerous, all drawn towards the heady scent she emitted of access to power and money to burn.

In her Georgetown mansion, instead of dinner parties, she threw church-style potlucks where, over green-bean casserole and potato salad, she triaged her contacts into allies to be cultivated, neutrals to be ignored, and enemies to be destroyed.

The attempted hit on Abdi made perfect sense, since a United States of Africa represented an existential threat to Wendy's vision. If she was now transitioning from politics into operations, that was big news, not least because thanks to her largesse, her brother now ran what was effectively a global private army, with Harkonnen as its nuclear-tipped ICBM.

The UH-60 settled onto the helo deck. The door opened, and armed security relieved me of my weapon. Then I was ushered into a boardroom suite where the woman who wanted to rule the world sat at the end of a long table.

76

I auger into the glass feet first, pivoting sideways to spread the impact from ankles to knees to hips to shoulders. The glass is tempered, tough as shit, but shatters with an astoundingly loud bang, detonating into a billion tiny fragments that shower into the pool like hail in a downdraught.

The glass barely breaks my fall. I slam into the water so hard it feels like being T-boned by a truck. The pool is maybe four feet deep where I impact, and I hit bottom hard.

I rise, spluttering for air, all the wind knocked out of me.

Panicked swimmers scramble for the exits, some screaming, others flailing to pull themselves up onto the pool surround by muscles that haven't seen this much action in years. The water around me is turning red. I look at my hands: they're bleeding. But it's not just my hands: my designer suit has been sliced to ribbons by the glass.

Ragged and bloody, ignoring the screaming that follows me, I claw my way through the water to the shallow end, stagger out and run into the second tower. I pound through the foot bath and women's changing rooms, and out into the carpeted lobby, by the elevators.

Harkonnen saw me jump and must have seen me crash through the roof of the pool. He'll radio for a reception committee on the ground floor, which means if I'm going to survive, I need a weapon.

The man who shot down the helicopter isn't likely to take the elevator – too many witnesses, too many stops – and if he's taking the stairs, gravity got me here first.

I open the door to the stairwell. Above I hear the clatter of feet descending fast.

I tuck myself against the wall. I still have no ammunition, but there's a fire extinguisher on the wall, so I pull it off and wait. As he reaches the mezzanine and turns into my flight, I crash it into his face with all my strength. He goes down hard, dropping the launcher, but struggles to get up. I hit him again, harder, bringing the steel canister down with full force from above my head. He twitches and goes still. Blood dribbles down the concrete stairs like a cheap horror movie.

I stare at the body for a moment. I left the cops in Vermillion alive, which makes him the first person I've killed since I entered my self-imposed purdah a year ago. I have to remind myself that he just killed one of the smartest women I ever met, a woman I owed my life, in cold blood.

So it goes.

I frisk his body and find a pistol and spare magazine. But that's not all. His coat has been adapted to carrying a second mini-RPG. I slot it into the launcher and sling it over my shoulder.

If I'm going down, it won't be without a fight.

77

Hipkiss sat at the end of a long conference table. In her mid-forties, she looked ten years older, with an odd, awkward, angular look to her that reminded me of Dustin Hoffman in *Tootsie*, or a disappointed Midwestern high school principal. She was wearing a white blouse under an ugly purple blazer with shoulder pads, her hair cut in a styleless blob and dyed the colour of cardboard. Nothing about her gave the slightest clue that she was a billionaire. If I had to guess, I'd say she sourced the entire outfit at Filene's Basement.

Hipkiss stared at me for a minute without speaking. There was something odd about it, something unsettling, something in the gaze that I couldn't quite put my finger on. Then a bizarre thought entered my head: *she's mentally undressing me.*

I tried to put the disturbing image out of my mind.

'Well,' she said finally, with a smile so fake and bland you could market it as Velveeta. 'What can I do for you?'

'You ordered the hit on Suleiman Abdi.'

The smile remained bland, giving nothing away.

'You control, what, thirty or forty billion dollars?'

She shrugged. 'Thereabouts.'

'Which means you could have hired anyone to kill Abdi. You could have hired *me*. Except that would have meant going through a third party, Handler in my case. So instead, you kept it in the family, using your brother as the middleman. That way, no-one would know you were in the assassination business. He hired Ali Olusi, which gave you perfect deniability. Only the hit didn't happen, so Harkonnen was dispatched to find out why, and to make sure nobody ever let you down like that again.'

Hipkiss made a note on a pad in front of her with a cheap ballpoint pen. I was reading upside down, so I might have been wrong, but I'm almost certain it included the word 'cute'.

She looked up. 'Supposing any of this were true. Is there something you actually *want*?'

'Sure,' I said. 'I want to make a deal. It's very simple. You take no further action against Ali Olusi.'

'And in return?'

'Nobody finds out who ordered the hit. Because if it ever got out you were ordering up political murders, your political contacts would drop you like a stone. And if the DOJ learned you were leveraging your brother's operational capabilities for political ends, that's the kind of thing that ends with congressional hearings, grand juries, and maybe a lot worse.'

'I see,' she said, and made another note. This one I couldn't make out, but it was longer. Then she looked up again.

'You're bluffing.'

'I don't bluff.'

'Oh, not about telling people. About whether they'll care. The only thing that matters in politics is what people can get from you. You could plaster it over the front page of *The New York Times*, and they'd avoid me in public for a good six months. The money would have to be routed through different channels. But it wouldn't change a thing.'

Her voice was a monotone, as if she'd been subjected to a complete personality bypass.

'So tell me again why I should let Ali off the hook?'

'Because if you don't, I'll personally consider it a declaration of war,' I said.

'Why do you care about Ali Olusi? He's a rival of yours, isn't he? Maybe even a candidate for your successor. I'd have thought you'd be glad to see the back of him.'

I didn't have a good answer. 'I have my reasons.'

She finished a sentence, then jabbed the pad to make a period so hard it went through.

'Do you think I'm stupid? Ali Olusi isn't a he, he's a she. That little tramp of a chambermaid in the hotel who disappeared just before Abdi arrived, and spent the previous week with a flashy young American businessman who I'm told bore a startling resemblance to the man in front of me.'

I shrugged. 'I was paid to stop her, not kill her. I did exactly that.'

'And now you're here trying to protect her. Why?'

'Like I say. I have my reasons.'

She sat back, a smug smile on her face. And I knew what was coming next.

'Does Handler know you're here?'

'This is between you and me. Unless you want the fact you're ordering assassinations to become public.'

'How convenient. Because it would be very bad for you, wouldn't it, if he discovered that you not only couldn't kill her, but had gone behind his back trying to protect her. The legendary Seventeen, sleeping with the enemy and mooning about like a teenager. He'd see that as weakness, don't you think?'

I took a moment to answer. Problem was, she was right. The relationship between a killer like me and a middleman like Handler is a kind of confidence trick. So long as they believe in you, so long as you live up to your own publicity, so long as the winning streak lasts, you're golden. But the moment you lose, or display even a hint of weakness, there's blood in the water. Because if you lose once, you can lose again, and again, and again.

'So,' I said, 'we both have a lot to lose if the truth comes out.'

She finally put the pen down and looked me in the eye.

'Do you want to know why I said yes to this meeting?'

'Because otherwise Harkonnen would have died, and you need him.'

'Harkonnen is nothing,' she said. 'There are always more Harkonnens.'

Her lips parted slightly.

'But there's only one Seventeen.'

I blinked. I swear to God she had flushed slightly, a pink glow spreading down her neck.

'Handler's a snake,' she said. 'You understand that.'

She was right, again. But that was the whole point of him. It was the point of middlemen and salesmen and politicians everywhere. They were *there* to be snakes. Without their forked tongues, the world would grind to a halt in short order. God bless their blackened little souls.

'He'll betray you in the end. He betrays everyone. It's in his nature.'

'Everyone betrays everyone in the end,' I said.

'And yet here you are,' she said, 'pleading for your enemy's life.'

I didn't have an answer for that one.

'How would it feel,' she said, 'to have a patron you knew would never betray you. Who'd repay loyalty with loyalty? And, may I add, make you richer than you could possibly imagine.'

'Are you offering me a *job*?'

'I'm offering you a lot more than that,' she said.

'I'm offering you a *life*.'

78

Ten floors down from the swimming pool, I hear male voices below me approaching: more of Harkonnen's soldiers on their way up to cut me off. At the next landing, I slip out of the door and into the corridor, waiting out of sight until they're past. An older woman in a hijab emerges from one of the apartments to walk a rat-like little dog, which starts yapping frantically. The woman stares at me – I'm covered with blood, soaking wet, my suit's ripped to shreds, and I'm carrying a loaded RPG – but this is New York City, so she simply ignores me and drags the yapping chihuahua away.

I hold my breath in case the dog has attracted the attention of the men on the staircase, but they're still heading up, so I continue back down the stairs, past the lobby, all the way to the parking levels.

At the bottom of the staircase, I ease the glass door open. The Trident sits unmolested, sleek and velvety, just thirty yards away. I run towards it across the concrete, but I'm only halfway there when I hear the scream of engines. Two vehicles screech into the aisle, heading towards me from opposite directions. One's a black Escalade, the other a full-size Toyota pick-up.

It's a pincer movement, and I have no chance of escape.

The pick-up's closer, so I put a cluster of bullets in the driver's-side windshield. The truck swerves and crunches into one of the parking garage's concrete stanchions, fracturing a heating pipe. As clouds of superheated steam envelop the truck, a second figure half climbs, half falls out of the passenger side. He clambers to his feet, raising an Uzi, but I double tap a pair of shots into his torso.

I flick round to see the Escalade accelerating towards me. There are two occupants, but I've maybe one shell left in the pistol, so I drop it and shoulder the RPG.

Harkonnen's riding shotgun. The moment he sees the weapon on my shoulder, he throws open the door and bails. In the same moment, I fire. The grenade hurtles down the aisle, punches into the engine block, and explodes. The Caddy flips and tumbles, grinding and sparking to a halt on its side, wheels towards me, flames spewing out of the underside of the engine compartment. The driver crawls out of the smashed windshield, dragging himself away, still moving but no longer a threat.

But that leaves Harkonnen, who rolls to a stop, ducks behind the wreck of the Escalade and disappears into the thick black smoke pouring out of the SUV.

I've lost him.

I jettison the now-useless launcher and check my magazine.

It's empty.

All I have left is one in the chamber, and I need to make it count.

79

I'll be straight with you. I was tempted by Hipkiss's offer.

I had no particular love for Handler, and with the backing of a billionaire, the possibilities were astounding. Hipkiss was smart enough to know that her brother was an inadequate fuck-up, while Harkonnen was a ticking time bomb with no loyalty to her, her brother, or anyone but himself.

If I took the job, the first casualty would be Harkonnen, whom I would have to kill.

The second would be her brother, whom I would replace. She'd buy him out, leaving him with enough of a fortune to debauch himself to death in whatever way he pleased, and I'd take over. Maybe, after a few years, I'd personally quit the wetwork business altogether, run my own stable of killers, take on Handler at his own game, and beat him.

I could become the kind of person who played golf on the weekend.

Like I say, I was tempted.

But only for about a picosecond.

Humiliating Handler would be glorious, but Hipkiss was a religious nut. I didn't believe in God, and even if he or she existed I strongly suspected we wouldn't see eye to eye. Hipkiss, moreover, was an unrepentant white supremacist, and the pepper and honey and blood of Gracious's kiss was still fresh on my lips. Add to that the odd, almost coquettish way she looked at me which made me think that despite her church-lady vibe her intentions towards me were less than honourable.

I'd rather fuck Handler, who at least had good hair.

And if all that wasn't enough, one simple fact made the whole thing impossible.

I wasn't ever going to be the kind of person who played golf on the weekend.

80

I sprint towards the Trident, keeping low, but Harkonnen bursts out from behind a column and opens up on me. I hurl myself behind a battered white delivery van, hearing shells rip into the panels.

Glancing under the delivery van, I glimpse Harkonnen's shadow, thrown by the burning Escalade. He's approaching, slow and careful. My heart-rate climbs: if I broke cover I could kill him, but I'd be dead myself before he hit the ground.

I glide to the front of the van. The windows are open, maybe because of the stink of cigarette smoke from inside. I peek over the door, checking for keys in the ignition. No luck. Twisting the driver's-side mirror to look through the passenger window, I can just see the rear of the Escalade. Flames from the engine bay have spread back towards its rear, licking around the fuel tank. Harkonnen's maybe ten, fifteen feet in front of it.

Using the mirror like a circus trick-shooter, I line up the barrel with the Escalade's fuel tank, fire, then drop. From under the van, I see Harkonnen's feet pirouette around. A dark river of gasoline spreads towards his feet. He swears in Finnish – '*Vittu!*' – and a moment later I'm rocked by the shockwave as the fuel tank explodes.

Harkonnen staggers into view, enveloped in flames. He drops and rolls, trying to put the flames out. I vault the driver's door into the Trident, fire the engine and floor the gas, fishtailing out of the parking spot and straight towards him.

Harkonnen looks up, still partly-if-not-mostly on fire, and scrambles to the side with inches to spare as I rocket past. I glance in the rear-view to see him clamber to his feet, still smoking, and aim. Behind him, more of his soldiers are running into view.

I figure discretion is the better part of valour and hit the exit ramp so fast the Trident bottoms out. Bullets chitter and whine off the cement walls behind me as I curl up the ramp towards daylight. A moment later, I'm in Manhattan traffic, and somewhere still alive.

81

Hipkiss took my answer badly. Her face became stony – the most emotion I'd seen from her in the entire meeting – and at one moment she bit her lip hard. For a weird second, I thought she might burst into tears. But then she buried herself in a note, underlined something so hard it tore the paper, then, with the look of someone who was eating tinfoil, agreed to my terms.

It can't have been easy, knowing I'd chosen a sexual and cultural shape-shifter like Gracious over a straight white Christian billionaire like herself. In other circumstances, I might even have been able to summon some minuscule fragment of sympathy for her. But then two months later, Suleiman Abdi, his wife and their three young children were killed when the Beechcraft Bonanza they were travelling on crashed on take-off from Kigali airport in Rwanda.

I had a pretty good idea who was behind it, but I was now sworn to silence.

So it goes.

82

Cop cars, ambulances and fire trucks scream past me towards the crash site. I have maybe thirty minutes before the Trident becomes so red hot I have to dump it, but I need time to think.

It was Harkonnen who killed Gracious. Not only did Barb's description match, it was the same brutality I'd seen inflicted on Sabrina a decade earlier, magnified a hundred-fold. The casual cop-killings, the attempted murder of Barb, it was just the kind of vicious collateral damage he specialised in. And above all it was revenge for everything that had happened in Addis Ababa after Gracious left.

I thought I was protecting her, but instead I was signing her death warrant.

Junebug, Gracious, Nicole.

It's as if all the women who have ever been important to me are being eliminated one by one.

Maybe it's me.

Maybe I'm a contaminant, a poison.

Maybe I should have taken the hint of the single bullet left in the chamber of Sixteen's revolver.

Maybe I still should.

Except I'm all out of bullets, and Mireille is still gone.

Harkonnen killing Gracious means the ten-year-old truce with Hipkiss is at an end. The last I heard, she was still a billionaire, and Staley still had his private army. But I no longer have the backing of a Handler or an Osterman. And the scale of what's unfolding means there's no way this is simple retribution for spurning Hipkiss's job offer.

This is about something else. Something dark, and big.

And my mind keeps going back to the phrase Nicole used about Deep Threat.

'An existential threat to the human race.'

I hit the gas.

PART SIX

83

I hate him already.

The cafe is on a corner in Williamsburg, Brooklyn, and it's peak hipster. The name is MOOG, written in block capitals in some retro sans-serif font, and through the plate-glass window, the interior is aggressively mid-century modern, all yellow plastic chairs, Formica tables, bent chromed steel and teardrop lampshades. The girl is alternating between taking orders, ferrying overpriced, probably organic, food to tables, working the till and bussing empty dishes.

There's a grace and rhythm to it that it's hard not to admire. She looks a little older, more self-assured, maybe a tad skinnier. She's dyed her hair blue with a razor-sharp set of bangs that give her a look halfway between Uma Thurman in *Pulp Fiction*, Tokyo from *Money Heist*, and an anime waifu.

She's not pulling coffee, though. That duty is reserved for the bearded dick in a manbun and lumberjack shirt who orders her around and makes small talk with the customers, paying particular attention to the pretty ones. He's tall, with one of those faces so blithely and blandly Ken-doll handsome it's halfway back to ugly. It's clear from the way he flashes his artificial smile or lingers a little too long when he hands a female customer a cup that he's an absolutely first-class creep.

The Trident is stowed in a Brooklyn parking garage. There'll be some fallout from the helicopter crash that killed Nicole, the dive into the pool, and the shootout in the basement, but by the time it reaches the papers, it will have been sanitised to mechanical failure, attempted suicide, and gang-related violence respectively. The intelligence community does not do its laundry in public, which includes stoop-and-scooping the collateral shit of private operators it does business with. There are some things the public doesn't need to know.

I'm still in the bizarre rags of the shredded, bloodstained suit, sitting on the kerb opposite, for all the world just another piece of urban wreckage who got himself into more trouble than he was capable of handling. Which is probably closer to the truth than I would care to admit.

Over the road, there's a lull in the traffic through the cafe door. Screened by the legs of the passers-by, I watch the Ken doll proprietorially slide his arm around the girl's waist. I feel sick. I have to restrain myself from running in there and strangling him with the strings of his unbleached, ethically sourced, artisanal apron. But there's nothing left between her and me that would entitle me to do any such thing, and however satisfying it would be, it would start things off on the wrong foot.

84

Kat's green eyes were the first thing I noticed, but they're the least extraordinary thing about her. Her near-total lack of fear borders on reckless, and her ability to cut through bullshit meant that a professional dissembler like me never stood a chance.

She also happens to be Sixteen's daughter, though neither of us knew it until I barged into her life trying to kill him. The three of us ended up as allies, but she never got to say goodbye to him or, in any fundamental sense, hello. In the chaos of the days that followed, I saved her life, she saved mine, and we ended up tangled together like two fish in a net.

When it was all done, she moved into and ran the gas station at the bottom of the hill below the house out of whose windows I stared nightly.

I'm not sure there's a word for what existed between us for those months. Nobody would ever have mistaken us for boyfriend and girlfriend: it was spikier and more compulsive than that. It was like a marriage on the rocks that had skipped all the earlier parts but whose partners still had their hooks into each other, unable to rip themselves apart.

Sometimes Kat would come up and spend the night, and in the morning I would sanitise the house entirely, removing every trace of evidence that she had ever been there. It was inevitable that someone would come for me eventually, and for all her fearlessness, Kat was still a point of weakness. I carried an indelible target on my back, but I scrubbed hers away every time she left.

Even so, there was no escaping the fact that Kat was her father's daughter. She set up a range in the ramshackle yard behind the gas station where she practised with weapons I supplied, everything from 9mm pistols to squad machine guns. Week on week, the clusters of shots got tighter. One day I went to get gas, found the CLOSED sign hung on the door, went out back unannounced, and found her with a .308 MRAD laid out on the picnic table in pieces. She'd blindfolded herself and was teaching herself to reassemble it, the movements becoming smooth and automatic, until her slender fingers could do it faster and more precisely than mine. I had no idea she knew I was watching her until she clicked the magazine back into place, lifted off the blindfold and smiled at me.

Her given name was Katherine, but Kat suited her better because she had the senses of a cat, not just the physical ones but the essential sixth, the one that told her the moment she laid eyes on me that I was not at all who I said I was, and that attaching herself to me like a burr on a pair of pants would lift her out of the life she'd found herself in to a place more aligned with her spirits.

Kat claimed her interest in weapons was self-defence, given she was now a potential target. I told her in that case she needed to learn how to fight hand-to-hand, at least enough to disable and escape from an attacker. It didn't surprise me when she wanted more. So I taught her what I knew, and though I was stronger and more practised, she was faster and lighter. She also had one advantage: a complete lack of romanticism. I pulled my punches, but she never granted me the same courtesy. Once, when I showed her a brutal head-lock that compressed an artery and was next to impossible to escape, she left me unconscious on the floor for a good five minutes. When I came round, I told her she could have killed me. She looked me straight in the eye and said:

'Don't think it didn't cross my mind.'

85

Kat had Sixteen's genes all right, but she had her mother's too. She spent the empty hours in the gas station waiting for a customer drawing: pen-and-ink stuff, illustrations for a graphic novel about her relationship with her dead mother, which she refused to show me.

I could see she was figuring out who she was, or who she might be, trying to deal with the fact that both her father and her lover were killers and that she herself had killed someone. It was, in short, a lot, and since my input was about the last thing that was likely to help, I tried not to interfere.

Matters came to a head one night when she'd come up to the house on the hill and we'd been drinking. She was chafing at the life she'd ended up with. When her mother ran the motel in town, she'd tried to go to college, but her mother's cancer brought her back. Now her world was this tiny town, her only actual friend Barb, who ran the motel, and like her had been caught in the crossfire between me, Sixteen and Handler.

'I can't do this any more,' she said.

'Do what?'

'This. This bullshit. This so-called relationship. This town. The gas station. Any of it. I didn't choose this life. I didn't choose to be this person. I didn't choose any of it. And I don't want it.'

'So what do you want?'

'I don't understand why we have to stay here. You have money, more than you'll ever need. Why don't we go somewhere? Anywhere, doesn't matter. Somewhere nobody knows us. Somewhere we can actually have a fucking life.'

'There's nowhere we could go I wouldn't be found eventually. And if you were with me, you'd have lost the one thing that protects you, which is deniability. Right now, no-one knows you're anything to do with me. There's not a trace of you in this house. Nobody sees us together. The moment that changes, you're a target.'

'What if I don't care?'

'You may not care. I do. I will not paint a target on your back.'

She was silent for a while, the kind of silence I knew meant trouble.

'What you're saying is, if I want to be with you, I can't be with you?'

'Do you? Want to be with me?'

'I don't even know any more.'

I guess I'd known push would come to shove eventually, because I already had a response prepared.

'So why don't you just go?' I said. 'You're right. I have money. I can wash it nine ways to Sunday. No-one would know it came from me. You could go wherever, do whatever you want. No strings.'

'Fuck you,' she said.

'What?'

'That would be really fucking easy, wouldn't it? You salve your conscience, like I'm your little project, your pet. What am I supposed to do, send you postcards and drawings like some orphan you sponsored in Africa?'

'Listen, you knew what I was when you fucking inserted yourself into my life.'

'*I* inserted *myself*? Nobody asked you to walk into my motel.'

'I guess there's plenty of blame to go around,' I said.

We sat there in silence for a while. I was thinking, and there was a thought rattling around in my head that could not be unthought. I knew I shouldn't say it, but I knew I couldn't not.

'Maybe there is a way.'

She looked up suspiciously, as she usually did when I suggested something.

'You have a lot of potential.'

'Potential for what?'

'Come on, Kat. Don't pretend to be stupid. You shoot as well as I do. You fight like a motherfucker. You've already killed someone, and not just anyone, top tier.'

'Oh, Jesus Christ. You think I want to be like you?'

'No, not like me. And maybe you don't want it. But you're in denial about whose daughter you are. Christ's sake, you can strip and reassemble an MRAD blindfold. You left me unconscious on the mat in the basement when you choked me out. You think any of that was *chance*?'

'So what? You'd be Charlie, and I'd be your Angel? Or more Mr and Mrs Smith?'

She actually snorted with laughter.

'I'm just saying, as a team, we could do a lot of damage.'

'I thought you were done with all that shit.'

'We'd pick and choose.'

'Oh, you mean, like, we'd be killers, but you know, *woke*?'

'Fuck you,' I said. '*All* I'm saying is that you could do the job. And if it's actually important to you to be with me, and you can't take this way of living any more, it's an option.'

She was quiet for a moment, looking at me, and I could see a thought forming.

'You would do this because why? To be with me, or because you're secretly as totally fucking bored as I am? Don't think

I haven't seen you standing at the window, and don't think I don't know why you do it.'

'Because . . .' And I stopped. Because I wasn't entirely sure which of the two it was.

She shook her head. 'You're a piece of work, you know that? Here I am trying to figure out a future that preserves some scrap of life in this emotional desert of alternating screwing and cleaning that we call a relationship. And your answer is, "Hey, I know, why don't you become a murdering fuck like me?"'

'Not *like* me. *With* me.'

For once, she didn't say anything.

'It's the only way to square the circle,' I said. 'And you'd be fucking good at it.'

She sat there for a moment, thinking. Actually thinking. Finally, she looked up and said:

'How about I give you an answer in the morning?'

That night she stayed over.

Some nights when she stayed over we fucked, and some nights we made love, and some nights we did nothing at all. But it wasn't any of those things.

I don't know what it was. It was sweet and bitter and tender and hard and it meant nothing and it meant everything. In amongst it all we managed to finish all the alcohol in the house, and by the end neither of us had anything left to give the other. We just lay there, naked as the day we were born, staring at the ceiling in silence, hand in hand.

I still don't know what it was.

All I know is, when I woke up in the morning I was alone.

86

I cleaned the house. I sanitised the glasses. I changed the sheets and pillowcases for new ones and burned all the old ones in the yard. I vacuumed the cushions in the chair she'd been sitting in. I pulled the bottles out of the trash that she'd handled and wiped them clean. I went over the entire bathroom with bleach, unscrewed the drain from the sink and shower, cleaned out the hair, then put Drano down there just in case. I wiped the security footage that showed her entering and leaving. Then I drove down to the gas station, but in my heart I already knew what I'd find.

A sign in the gas station door said CLOSED PERMAN-ENTLY, THANKS FOR YOUR BUSINESS. FOR LEASE – ENQUIRIES and a number that belonged to Vern, who owned the premises. He told me Kat had called before dawn and left a message saying she'd quit, was leaving town, had taken her deposit from the till and left no forwarding address.

I drove down to the motel, where Barb told me the same story, except she knew where Kat had gone, had no intention whatever of telling me, considered the whole thing for the best, and told me as firmly as she knew how that I should respect Kat's decision.

I drove back up to the house with an odd taste in my mouth. Barb was right: it was the best thing for both of us. Kat had decided who she wanted to be, and it wasn't the Kat who was the daughter of one serial murderer and the lover of another.

She had no interest in forming some fantasy-league Bonnie and Clyde duo. She was going to get on with her life, I would form no part of it, and I would no longer bear the burden of trying to protect her.

In a way, it was a relief. I would be alone again, but I was used to being alone.

When I got back to the house, I threw up in the sink.

I told myself it was the hangover, but it wasn't. That night, I stood at the big windows that looked out onto the valley, watching the day cycle to night as the sun ratcheted below the horizon. Then, once the sky was perfectly black, I did something I'd never done before, but that I did every night afterwards until the evening Mireille pulled the trigger in the forest.

I turned the lights on behind me to make myself a target.

87

The couple at the booth by the window finally pack up and walk out – he's Black and preppy with a flat-top haircut and chequered scarf, she's white and pale in sweats with the angular frailty of a model. They somehow managed to keep one hand knotted with the other's through two macchiatos and a shared avocado and alfalfa burrito. As they head away, leaving the coffee shop empty, I curse them for being so obviously in love, cross the road, wait for Kat to turn her back, then head in and take their place at the booth.

My heart-rate spikes as Kat disengages from the manbun and heads over to clear their plates. She's almost at the table before she sees me, and when she does she stops and stares at me for a full thirty seconds. Whatever's going through her mind, it's plenty and full of variety. Then it's as if she shakes herself free of it all. She picks up the dead plates, mugs and crumpled napkins and goes back to the counter as if I wasn't there at all.

I get up, lock the door, turn the sign to closed and go back to my seat.

Kat pointedly keeps her back to me, but I can see her watching me in the reflection of the milk steamer. Meanwhile, oblivious manbun is dumping more coffee into the espresso maker with one hand while he checks his phone with the other, so I rap loudly on the table with my knuckles to attract his attention.

Manbun glances round, sees me sitting there.

'We don't do table service.'

I rap hard again.

This time he takes in the fact the sign has been changed.

He says something to Kat. She shakes her head, still not looking at me.

Manbun pulls off his apron and heads out from behind the counter, down the aisle towards me. He's nervous, although he's trying not to show it, his stupidly handsome face going a shade lighter as he sees my shredded clothing, the blood-stains, the gashes on my hands.

I can already tell I'm not going to have to hurt him, at least not physically.

'Can I help you?' he says.

'I need to talk to Kat.' I point towards her.

'You mean Kate?'

'I don't care what she calls herself now. I need to speak to her.'

'Does she know you?'

'Hey, Kat,' I say over his shoulder. 'Should I tell him, or do you want to?'

Kat keeps her back to me, but her eyes haven't left my reflection.

'I'm sorry. I'm going to have to ask you to leave.'

'I'm sorry. I'm going to have to say no. Not until I talk to Kat.'

Manbun pulls out his phone.

'You have thirty seconds to get the fuck out of here. Then I'm going to call the police.'

He thumbs in 911, shows it to me.

I pull the RPG guy's pistol from my holster and lay it on the table. 'Go ahead. But you might want to consider what a firefight in here would do for your foot traffic. "Oh, honey, let's go get a coffee at that place, what's it called? MOOG? You know, the one where six cops got killed in a shootout."'

'You're bluffing,' he says, but his voice is shaky.

I rack the slide theatrically. 'Ask her if I do a lot of that.'

'It's okay,' says Kat. Manbun turns to see her right behind him. 'He's a douche, but he won't hurt me.'

'Who the fuck is he? How do you know him?'

'Long story,' says Kat, and slides into the seat opposite me.

Manbun hovers. 'Go grind some beans or something,' I tell him.

He looks to Kat for confirmation.

'How long is this going to take?' she asks me.

'Thirty minutes tops.'

'You've got five.' She sets a timer on her phone, then turns to the manbun. 'Seriously, it's okay.'

He heads away.

She hits START on the timer.

88

'So?' says Kat.

'So,' I say, letting jealousy and bitterness overwhelm me. 'A manbun, huh? Does he want to direct?'

'I'm done here,' she says, and stands up.

'Fuck's sake, give me a chance.'

'I don't owe you a damn thing,' she hisses, but sinks down again. 'What the fuck do you think you're doing here, walking back into my life? Did you think I'd welcome you with open arms? That I'd save myself for you? Is that it?'

'Trust me, I'm under no illusions.'

'Good. Because you of all people have no right to judge me. But sure, let me tell you about him. He's not a killer. People don't die around him.'

'That's a pretty low bar to set for yourself.'

'You still don't clear it.'

'Look,' I say, 'it's your life. Trust me, I wouldn't be here if I had other options.'

She takes in the state of me. 'Let me guess, the helicopter downtown?'

'What are they saying?'

'Engine malfunction. Eight dead, including passengers and crew. Was it you?'

I shake my head. 'Nicole Osterman was on board. She was trying to help me.'

'Help you do what?'

'Find my daughter.'

Kat sits there, dumbfounded. 'You have a—'

She can't even finish the sentence.

'It's a long story,' I say. 'I'll tell it to you, I promise, but that's not why I'm here. You're in danger. They want to kill me, which means they're afraid of me, which means if they can get to me via you, they will.'

'Who wants to kill you? Why?'

'Proximate threat is seven feet of pure distilled sociopathy that calls itself Harkonnen. Who kidnapped my daughter and killed her mother. Last I heard he worked for a man called Staley, whose religious nut of a sister wants to turn the world into some kind of white power Disneyland. It's all wrapped up with some kind of computer malware called Deep Threat that scares everybody shitless. Also, I'm wanted for murder. Correction, murders.'

Kat sits back, almost amused.

'So, pretty straightforward, then. Anything else I should know?'

'They tried to kill Barb.'

'They did *what*?' Her green eyes blaze, which is exactly what I want.

'Harkonnen shot her when he took my daughter.'

'Is she okay?'

'Mostly. But she had to disappear.'

'Barb is good people,' says Kat.

'Yes, she is.'

'She didn't deserve that.'

'No, she didn't,' I say.

Kat's quiet for a moment. Maybe the gravity of the situation is beginning to sink in.

'You understand what I'm saying? They tried to kill her, they tried to kill me, and that makes you a target as well.'

'How?' says Kat, lowering her voice. 'We were *so* fucking careful. That's half the reason I left, because I couldn't take living like that any more. The only way they could know about me and you is if you brought them to my door. Which, by the way, if they're following you, you just fucking did.'

'Nobody followed me. That's not how they know.'

She stares at me. And then it hits her.

'Jesus Christ. You *creeped* me?'

'I needed to know you were okay.'

'Bullshit! You didn't even trust me enough to live my life without you helicopering around like some tiger mom. You're like the analogue monk . . . no internet, no cell-phone, so what? You go to the local library to look me up on Facebook?'

'It wasn't exactly local.'

'My social media is all private.'

'Some of your friends are pretty lax about their security settings,' I say.

Kat shakes her head. 'You're a fucking piece of work, you know that?'

'I've been told.'

'Wait. You did this because you were worried about me? Or because you wanted to know if I was seeing someone? The truth, or I swear I'll call the cops myself.'

'The truth? A bit of both.'

She sits back. 'Christ. Well, I hope you enjoyed the show.'

'Not particularly,' I say, which is the understatement of the decade.

'Good.' Then another thought strikes her. 'But nobody knew where you were. So how would they be able to track from you to me?'

'My guess is they'd been tracking me for a while. Which means they probably know about you.'

Kat's phone squawks an alarm.

'Well, time's up.'

'I haven't finished.'

'Yes, you have. Good chatting. Have a nice life, whatever's left of it.'

She fingers the alarm off, takes the phone and stands.

89

I grab her wrist.

'Get the FUCK off me.'

I let go. 'Have you not been listening to me? You're a target.'

'I know what you're doing,' she says. 'You think if you scare me you'll pull me back in. Well, I'm not scared, so bring it on. Whatever shit it is you've got yourself mixed up in, I'm no part of it. If someone thinks I am, I'll take whatever's coming, and so will they. I made my choices. I'm good with them. I'll live with the consequences.'

'What makes you think they'll stop at you?'

My eyes flick over to manbun, now furiously cleaning the steamer on an espresso machine, throwing us the odd suspicious glance.

'This has nothing to do with him,' says Kat.

'You obviously didn't tell him about me. Does he know who your father was? Or that you literally chainsawed someone in half a year ago?'

'I did it to save your life, you ungrateful fuck.'

'Fine. So let's tell him, right now.'

Her turn to grab my wrist. She sinks down, pulling me with her.

'He doesn't need to know. That part of my life is over.'

'You think that's how it works? That you just walk away? You put yourself in the game the moment you hooked up with me. You knew who I was. You made that choice. You had every chance to extricate yourself, and you chose not to.'

'What the fuck do you think I'm doing here?' she says.

'I've been asking myself the same thing.'

'I'll tell you what I'm doing. I'm trying to make something of my life that doesn't involve killing people. And you can sneer at it, at him, all you like, but trust me, it's a thousand times better than anything you ever offered me.'

'You're in the game,' I tell her. 'And that means he's in the game. Only he doesn't know it because you're afraid to tell him who you really are. He's the innocent party here, not you. If you don't want his blood on your hands, you have two choices. Either you tell him the truth about who you are and who I am and what's happening . . .'

'Or?'

'Or you help me get my daughter back, and finish this.'

Kat looks over to the manbun, now fiddling with a spoon a few tables away as he watches us, eyes full of uncomprehending suspicion.

'Supposing I agree,' says Kat cautiously. 'What exactly do you need?'

'First thing I need,' I say, 'is a place to stay'.

Kat looks down, then glances over at the Ken doll.

'Oh,' I say. 'Oh, no. Oh, you have to be kidding me.'

90

The manbun slides out of his seat and stands awkwardly as I follow her over to him.

'This is Jones,' she says, using the only name she's ever had for me, the meaningless alias I signed into the motel with on the day we met.

'Okay,' he says, nonplussed.

Up close, his resemblance to a Ken doll is almost surreal.

'He's going to be staying with us for a while,' says Kat.

'Hi,' I say, and reach out my hand, still covered with dried blood. 'And you are . . . ?'

'Ken,' he says, shaking my hand as limply as it's possible to imagine.

'No, really,' I say. 'What's your actual name?'

'My actual name,' he says frostily, 'is actually Ken.'

I can tell we are never going to be friends.

91

Actually Ken runs the coffee shop but his ambition is indeed to direct. The apartment above the coffee shop he shares with Kat is filled with storyboards for some kind of slacker horror movie he intends to make once he gets the money for it, which I am reluctant to tell him he actually never will, because he is brim-full of shit.

My view of him is coloured by the fact that it is Actually Ken and not I who currently shares a bed with Kat. Moreover, I am fairly sure they made a point of fucking loud enough for me to hear on the first night I spent on the couch of their apartment.

The pen and ink storyboards themselves are excellent, unlike the concept or the story. It's all Kat's work. She works at the coffee shop days and studies graphics at Community College at night. She's currently revising her graphic novel based on notes from Actually Ken, which I am reluctant to tell her will make it worse, not better.

But I'm not here to tell her how to live her life. I'm here to find my daughter, and if that means listening to Kat and Actually Ken going at it night after night, so be it.

The next morning, point made, Actually Ken heads downstairs to open up the cafe. Kat understandably wants to know everything, so after I raid Ken's closet for clothes that more or less fit, I give it to her as straight as I know how.

Addis Ababa, Ali Olusi, Gracious, how she ended up as Ali, the doomed/enchanted week we spent together, the last night, her disappearance, Harkonnen's arrival, Staley, the meeting with Hipkiss. The bullet hitting the window, the wolves, Mireille, the motel in Vermillion, crashing the Sheriff's plane, escaping from the interview room, the cops' bodies in Sixteen's house, finding Barb shot, The Dentist, Nicole, all of it.

Kat listens intently, green eyes locked on mine. She asks a lot of good questions about Gracious, some of which I can answer and some of which I can't. She's quiet for a while afterwards, some thoughts orbiting through her head I'm not privy to and maybe never will be.

I'm not dumb or naive enough to think she has any desire to go back to the way things were between us, yet it's obvious the news about Gracious, or maybe the fact that I could have that depth of feeling about *anyone*, pulls her up for a moment.

'So, cut to the chase,' she says, shaking herself free of whatever it was. 'Harkonnen works for Hipkiss, which means you think she has Mireille. It's to do with something called Deep Threat, which everybody wants badly enough to torture women in motels and kill cops and shoot down helicopters in Manhattan in broad daylight, and whatever the fuck it is, is to humanity what an asteroid was to the dinosaurs.'

'That's pretty much it.'

'So why hasn't she contacted you? Why kidnap the kid, unless she wanted a ransom?'

'It wasn't about a ransom. They thought Gracious had given Mireille whatever it was they were looking for. But they can't have found it, which is why they came for me. But they missed. Which means now they'll want to negotiate. Which means I need to let them find me.'

I pull one of the burner phones from my pocket. From the other pocket, I pull the battery and a SIM card.

'Which means I need to turn this on.'

Kat's face fills with trouble. 'Can't they trace it? Triangulate your position.'

'It's OK,' I say. 'I had The Dentist set up a forwarding service. To another forwarding service.'

I turn the phone on.

We wait four hours.

It doesn't ring.

Then there's a noise at the door to the apartment. It's Actually Ken, heading up from the cafe below with his phone in his hand, looking exceptionally confused.

'I'm sorry, *who*?' he says.

He holds out the phone to me.

'It's a woman,' he says. 'She wants to talk to someone called "Seventeen".'

'I thought she didn't know you were here,' hisses Kat.

'She didn't,' I say, glaring at Actually Ken. 'But she does now.'

92

'She's pretty,' says Hipkiss. Her voice is older, harder. 'The girl, I mean. Sweet disposition, considering everything she's been through. She's your daughter, no?'

'She's alive?'

'Of course she is.'

'And I'm just supposed to take your word for that?'

'People have called me many things in my life, but nobody has ever accused me of being a liar.'

'You lied to me. The deal was you didn't touch Gracious.'

'Harkonnen wouldn't have touched her if she'd given him what he wanted. Instead, she gave it to the girl. Who no longer has it. Which means either you have it, you know where it is, or you can find it.'

'I don't know what you're talking about.'

'And I think you're lying. But it makes no difference. All you have to do is deliver it to us, and the girl will be released.'

'You killed somebody I loved. And you still think I'm going to play ball?'

'Either you do, or your daughter dies. It's very straight-forward.'

'I didn't even know she existed until a few days ago. Do I strike you as the family type?'

She laughs, a mirthless nasal drone. 'No. I think you're a romantic. That's why you came to me to save her mother all those years ago. And you wouldn't still be talking to me if you didn't care.'

'Let's say I can somehow find what you're looking for. I'm going to need some time. Ten days, at least.'

'Out of the question.'

'For Christ's sake,' I say. 'What do you think I am? Houdini? I'm wanted for four murders and a child abduction. The CIA and FBI are all over my old house right now. They know who I am and that I'm back in action. Now add the shit that went down in Manhattan yesterday, and the fact I don't even know what I'm supposed to be looking for. Either you want me to find it or you don't.'

'Three days,' she says finally. 'For a man of your abilities it should be plenty. I'm going to give you a number to call when you have it. If I don't hear from you, I hand your daughter over to Mr Harkonnen. He has some . . . difficult memories of your time in Africa. I'm sure you understand what I'm saying.'

Static crackles through the silence between us.

'I want you to understand something,' I say, finding my voice. 'If anything happens to her—'

'Oh, please,' she says. 'Handler's dead. Osterman's dead. Sixteen's dead. The girl's mother is dead. You have no meaningful allies and few resources. Whereas I have a great deal of money, my brother's security organisation, and sources at the highest level in the world's most capable intelligence agencies. You'd survive a few weeks, at best.'

'It would be long enough,' I say.

'Perhaps,' says Hipkiss. 'But your daughter would still be dead.'

93

'Let me get this straight,' says Kat. 'The choices are: either you track down and hand over an existential threat to the human race to a religious extremist who wants to see a white planet. Or an innocent nine-year-old girl, who happens to be your daughter, dies.'

'I wish it were that simple,' I say. 'Even if I make the exchange, there's no way Harkonnen lets me live. If he kills me, he becomes Eighteen. That, on top of whatever Deep Threat turns out to be, makes Hipkiss unstoppable.'

'So you rescue Mireille?'

'She's a billionaire with a private army, and I have literally no-one. I have no idea where she's being held, and even if I could find out, they'd be ready for me. Getting myself slaughtered by Harkonnen isn't going to help anyone.'

'What, then?'

'I need information. Right now, I'm still working blind. What *is* Deep Threat? How did Hipkiss find out about it? How did she know Gracious had it? How did Gracious get it? If I could answer some of those questions, maybe I could find some kind of edge.'

'Okay, how about this,' says Kat. She's been Googling something as we talk, turns the laptop round to show me. It's a *New York Times* profile of Staley's company, Whitecastle.

'Third paragraph is where it gets good,' says Kat.

I skim down to it.

A long-time mid-ranking player in the private security and intelligence business, Edgar Staley's Whitecastle has recently expanded into the secretive world of malware and zero-days. Following the acquisition of an elite Israeli hacking outfit, the organisation is now said to be one of the key players in the field.

But purchasing malware is a touchy subject for government agencies like the CIA and FBI. It's one thing to develop exploits in-house, but paying criminal hackers is another matter.

Companies like Mr Staley's provide a firewall against the blowback that would come from paying huge sums to shadowy teams of hackers responsible for ransomware attacks or illegal phone hacking.

The business model is straightforward. Intermediaries like Whitecastle purchase zero-days from hackers at major international security conferences like Black Hat, DEF CON or Ekoparty, then sell them on to intelligence agencies, often with a mark-up of several hundred per cent.

'So that's how Hipkiss got to hear about Deep Threat,' I tell Kat. 'Staley's org picked up the intel and passed it on to Hipkiss. She must have wanted it desperately, but was scared somebody else would pick it up. After all, even she can't outbid a nation-state. So she decided to short-circuit the process.'

'But you still don't know what it is, or even what you're looking for,' says Kat.

'No,' I say. 'But I know someone who will.'

94

Vilmos is a hacker, but the word barely does him justice. His exploits are legendary, not just for their brutal simplicity but for their *enfant terrible* audacity. Whenever you hear of a critical piece of intelligence community infrastructure being compromised, it's Vilmos. In his early days, he hacked the Defense Intelligence Agency email server and attached tentacle porn to every message that passed through it. His later exploits, only marginally less childish, revealed a secret NSA backdoor in an industry-standard cryptography routine and landed him in a Supermax. Now his location is completely unknown, but thankfully the time he served didn't mellow him a jot.

The number I use for him has never changed over the years, but is routed through an ever-shifting chain of relays, VPNs and network proxies. I use one of the burners to call it, but I'm not expecting an answer, just a callback.

For the first time in a decade, the call doesn't go through.

I check Vilmos's Twitter account. It's a wildly anarchic mix of software and hardware hacking, *Star Wars* lore, *Dungeons and Dragons* gossip, computer game speedruns, idealistically cynical political commentary, LGBTQ+ issues, and vegan agitprop. He averages fifty to a hundred tweets a day, going all the way back to 2007, sometimes climbing to two hundred.

But when I try to find it, it's gone.

The website he maintains, also gone.

Vilmos has disappeared. The fact he nuked his account suggests he's not just gone dark but is now on the run. The alarmed comments from his followers all point to him having disappeared a week before this all began.

Vilmos is one of the world's best hackers.

Deep Threat is some cancerous form of malware.

His disappearance cannot possibly be a coincidence.

95

Vilmos's Twitter account is gone, but the Wayback Machine has daily archives of its front page. Kat trawls it for clues, while I hack together a Python script to create a heatmap of how often he posts, at what time of day, and how that varies over the months.

Together we stare at ten thousand random dots on the screen.

'It's cool,' says Kat, 'but I don't see what it tells us.'

'Look at when he *doesn't* post,' I say. 'That probably means he's asleep. In the winter, he stops posting around 8 p.m. Eastern. Let's say the latest he goes to bed is, like 3 a.m. Which means 8 p.m. here is around 3 a.m. for him. That's a seven-hour time difference, which puts him on the same longitude as, say, Hungary.'

'Right,' says Kat. 'But it doesn't tell you how far north or south he is. It doesn't even tell you which hemisphere he's in.'

'Sure it does,' I say. 'In the summer, it's just a couple of hours when there's no activity, around 6–7 p.m. Eastern. That means the nights are much shorter.'

'Which puts him a long way north of the equator. So northern Europe?'

'That'd be my guess,' I say. 'You find anything?'

'Maybe,' says Kat. 'He's pissed off every Western intelligence agency. They'd all love to get their hands on him, but he claims he's in a country with no extradition agreement with the US. If he's in northern Europe, that means it's Russia, Belarus or Ukraine.'

I shake my head. 'I think he's lying.'

'Why?'

'Because Ukraine's a war zone, and the first two are unfriendly to gay people. Being gay is central to who he is. More likely, he's in a country friendly to gays, but close enough that he can hop the border to safety in a hurry.'

'So a state that borders Russia, with decent gay rights. Which means—?'

'Finland. And the tip of Norway.'

Kat sits back, sceptical.

'I feel like we're just making this up.'

'We are,' I say. 'But we don't have a choice. What else do we know?'

'He's permanently online. Which means he wants high-speed internet. Not just high-speed, super high-speed.'

'Anything else?'

'He's Hungarian, from the name. So a place where foreigners would fit in without too many questions being asked,' says Kat.

'So an international community of some sort. A university, maybe, with a tech focus'.

'Helsinki,' says Kat, studying Google Maps. 'It has to be. The University of Technology is two hours from the Russian border.'

I stare at the route she's plotted.

'I don't like it. That border crossing is huge, heavily monitored. Two hours is a long time when you're on the run. By the time he got there, chances are he'd be picked out.'

'I don't see any other big cities with tech hubs any closer,' says Kat.

'What's his focus been recently?'

'Digital anarchism,' says Kat. 'Information wants to be free, that kind of thing. There's this colossal screed about some start-up which put up a network of imaging satellites.'

'Military?'

'No, civilian.' She pulls up the webpage for the company. 'They record the entire surface of the earth, everything from infra-red to UV. You can subscribe to the data, but it's fucking expensive. He says if the data were made freely available, poor farmers would be able to see immediately where crops were failing. Everyone would be able to see troop movements, deforestation, all the shit that's restricted to people like the CIA and NSA right now. It's like a crusade for him to make it available.'

I take this in for a moment. Then it hits me.

'Jesus Christ,' I say. 'I know exactly where he is.'

96

I zoom in on an island, north of the tip of Norway, far beyond the Arctic circle.

'Svalbard. It has to be. Officially, it's part of Norway, but there's a treaty that gives the Russians mining rights. There are two main settlements. Longyearbyen is international – *really* international – and Barentsburg is almost completely Russian. There's even a consulate. No visas necessary to move there and work. It's basically the Wild West. The closest land is a Russian island called Novaya Zemlya.'

'Why do I feel like I've heard of it?'

'The Global Seed Vault is there. Millions of seed samples from around the world, in case we need to reboot the planet. But that's not what he's interested in.'

I zoom in on a network of domes that sits on a plateau above Longyearbyen.

'See that? It's the SvalSat satellite receiver station. It's one of only two that can see satellites in a polar orbit, the kind Vilmos has a hard-on for. NASA, the European Space Agency, they all route data through SvalSat. To get the data off the island they laid an undersea fibre-optic cable, which means it has some of the fastest internet in the world. The satellite feeds are a firehose of the data he thinks should be free. If he could hack into it, his dream would come true. And if things get too hot, it's twenty miles to a Russian consulate, and he doesn't cross a border.'

Kat sits back, sceptical. And I've seen that look before. *Incoming*.

'Okay. Fine,' she says. 'It's all very clever, very neat. But you've no proof for any of it. What if you're wrong? What if you run off to Svalbard, but he's not there? What if he is, but he doesn't know the first thing about Deep Threat? Either way, you're fucked, and by the time you figure it out, it'll be too late. You really think a Hail Mary sidequest into some rando of a neckbeard is the best use of your time right now?'

'Someone I loved is dead, and my daughter's gone because I left her alone with a civilian instead of protecting her myself. Right now I have exactly one lead, one chance at getting her back, and this is it. So unless you have a better idea—'

'That's the other thing,' says Kat. 'You've no proof the kid is yours, you've only spent a few hours with her, you barely even *know* her, but you're willing to risk your life for her, no matter what it takes? It doesn't compute.'

'Because, what, I'm an asshole?'

'That's certainly one word for it.'

'She's . . . part of me,' I say, trying to find the words. 'If it wasn't for me she wouldn't exist, which means what's happening to her now is on me. Poor kid didn't choose any of this. It doesn't matter what I feel.'

'Which is?'

'I don't know. Maybe it doesn't have a name. Maybe it doesn't have to have a name. Feelings aren't going to help her right now. What matters is what I *do*.'

Kat looks at me. For the first time since she walked out of my life, it doesn't look like she's seeing somebody she hates.

'You know,' she says, 'if I didn't know you better, I might imagine that you were developing a *conscience*.'

97

By now, it's almost 2 a.m. The coffee shop closed hours ago, but there's no sign of Actually Ken.

'He's got a meeting,' says Kat, with a defensiveness that sets my antennae twitching. 'Something to do with the movie. He's having drinks with an actor he's thinking of casting.'

Most people, when they want to avoid a subject, will look away. Not Kat. She stares you straight in the eye as if daring you to challenge her. She's staring at me right now.

'Actor or actress?' I say.

Having watched him in the cafe when her back was turned, I have a pretty good idea where this is headed.

'What the fuck do you care?'

'I take it he's done this before. So, you expect him home tonight, or . . . ?'

'Look,' she says. 'You want the truth? It's an open relationship. He's free to screw other people if he wants. So am I.'

'Do you?'

'Maybe I don't want to.'

'Jesus Christ, Kat,' I say. 'You deserve better than this.'

'What, like you?'

'No, not like me. Just . . . better than someone who doesn't even begin to appreciate what you are.'

'Oh, which is what, since you're the expert?'

I shake my head. 'You don't need me to tell you. I may be a killer, all the things you accuse me of, but the day I walked into your motel you saw a door in your life open a crack, and you crashed your way through it. Now you're trying to close it again, and it's killing you. Christ's sake, Kat, sitting in some douchebag's apartment waiting for him to come home after he bones somebody else? Is this what you were made for?'

'Screw you,' she says. 'You just can't stand the fact that I have a life outside of you, one that doesn't involve murdering people, and that there's not a single fucking thing you can do to get me back.'

'Fine,' I say. 'You want me admit it? Yes, I can't stand the thought of you being with somebody else. And no, there wasn't a single day I didn't think about you after you left. But I'm under no illusions that I'm ever going to get you back. It's a lost cause. *I'm* a lost cause. But you're not.'

'Did it ever occur to you that this is what I *want*?'

'Is it?'

She doesn't answer.

'Look,' I say. 'It's no longer any of my business where you go, what you do, who you hook up with. But I can tell when people are lying, even you. So all you have to do is tell me you're okay with this, that this is what you want, that living like this makes you happy, and I promise I will shut the fuck up permanently.'

Kat chews her mouth, and for a second I think she might actually cry, which is not a thing that Kat does. And then, abruptly she stands up.

'It makes me happy, okay? It makes me really, really fucking happy. So happy I could throw up.'

She heads into the bedroom and slams the door.

98

Actually Ken rolls in at about 5.30 a.m. I hear the door unlock, and he tries to sneak past without waking me up, only he's drunk and trips over the edge of the carpet. I hear him open the bedroom door and then close it again.

I listen for sounds of sex from behind the closed bedroom door, but they don't come.

99

I'm wide awake, and sleep's a luxury I can't afford, so I make coffee.

The problem is, Kat's right. I can't afford a mistake. So I go back into Vilmos's Twitter archive. An hour later I find something my previous trawl missed, because it didn't go back far enough. There's an unexplained four-day gap in his tweets three years ago, the only time he ever missed more than twelve hours with a post.

It means something, but I have no idea what.

I flip to Google and pull up news articles about SvalSat from that date range. And on the first page of results, there it is.

I knock softly on the bedroom door. 'Kat! Kat!'

She appears, bleary, a sheet wrapped around her. Dark circles under her eyes. Behind her, Ken is out cold, head back, mouth open, in a drunk's dead sleep.

'I found proof.'

She follows me into the room and sits on the couch next to me. I try to ignore the fact she's mostly naked under the sheet and has trailed the warm, musky scent of sleep in with her.

'Look at this. Three years ago, a Greenland shrimp trawler lost power about five miles off the coast of Svalbard. They're not supposed to drop anchor anywhere near the cable, but if they hadn't, they'd have lost the ship and maybe the crew as well. So they dropped anchor, but it dragged and cut both the cables. Svalbard was cut off from the internet for four and a half days before they could get a cable ship out there and repair the break. Now look at Vilmos's Twitter archive . . .'

I pull it up.

'Those are the exact days he goes dark. The cable is repaired at 4.45 p.m. local time. Literally two minutes later, 4.47 p.m., there's a tweet.'

'Wow,' says Kat.

'You believe me now?'

She nods.

Through the open door to the bedroom, Actually Ken farts and rolls over.

She turns back to me.

'I'm coming with you.'

PART SEVEN

100

Svalbard is stunningly beautiful. This time of year, there are maybe six hours of daylight, but the sun never rises far above the horizon, painting the angular peaks vivid shades of orange and pink before sinking again, plunging the island into a twilight that never quite makes it to night. Twenty-seven hours and three connections out of JFK, we descend through shafts of horizontal sunlight into the blue shadow cast by the snow-covered mountains that ring Longyearbyen.

There are pipelines and construction everywhere, along with abandoned vehicles and long-disused pylons that once were used to ferry coal on overhead lines to freighters waiting in the harbour. On the outskirts of town are warning signs: it's illegal here to go past them without a firearm because of the danger of polar bear attacks.

Above the town, white golf-ball-like structures cover the array of satellite dishes that make up SvalSat. Just below them is the fortress-like entrance to the Global Seed Vault, repurposed from an abandoned coal mine. Another entrance to the same mine leads to the Arctic World Archive, which houses the world's biggest software repository, bits and bytes burned into digital film reels that will last five hundred years or more.

A couple of thousand people live here, a few hundred more up at the satellite station above the town, and that's it. It's a place where everybody knows everybody, and where an eccentric like Vilmos is unlikely to be able to hide for long.

Kat's travelling on her actual passport. Mine claims I'm a Canadian called Jack Sitoski. Longyearbyen is fast evolving into a tourist destination – there's a Radisson Blu and a museum of Arctic exploration – but we needed a more flexible cover. So we've booked the two monastic rooms available at the Svalbard Artists Centre, a former fish-processing factory by the harbour.

A 4x4 Hilux taxi takes us up a narrow gravel road to a low, tin-sided building where the woman who runs the arts centre, Sarah Pybus, greets us with the bounding enthusiasm of a labrador. She's a hearty American divorcee whose enormous, semi-abstract, blue-and-white canvases of the Arctic landscape are scattered around the cavern of the warehouse. By the time we carry our bags in she's already filled us in on the history of the town, its inhabitants, its social life, most of the gossip, and the best places to eat and drink.

When she can get a word in edgewise, Kat lays out our cover story. She's an artist, I'm a writer, and we have an advance from an independent press in upstate New York to co-author a graphic novel about the effects of global warming on the fragile ecosystems of the Arctic. Her spiel is so good, the details simultaneously precise and so vague they're impossible to check (*which* independent press exactly? Who the fuck knows?) that she almost convinces *me*.

'She's nice,' says Kat, as Pybus heads off with a paint-stained wave.

'She's CIA,' I say.

'*What?*'

'You notice how she didn't ask any questions? Only talked about herself?'

'Isn't that the opposite of what a spy would do?'

'No, that's *exactly* what a spy would do,' I say. 'You told her your entire cover story without even being asked. She's checking Google right now.'

'Just because someone likes to talk about themselves doesn't make them a spook.'

'So you checked her bio?'

'Sure,' says Kat. 'She's an artist. Lots of shows, studied at the Corcoran.'

'And her husband?'

'She's divorced.'

'Right. The former Mr Pybus was a diplomat. They spent twenty years in former satellite states. Her thesis in art school was Rodchenko. Lots of visits to Moscow. After she ditched the diplomat, she spent a year painting landscapes in Karelia. Right on the Russian border, close to the crossing where the Brits got Gordievsky out in the trunk of a car after he was rumbled.'

'So why is she running an artists' centre here?'

'Because the Russian nuclear submarine fleet transits through the Barents Sea, and if NATO and Russia face off, this place will be under Russian control in a matter of days. And she's running an artists' centre because it's cover for people like us who want to be able to snoop around with a convenient excuse for drawing diagrams, making notes and taking photographs.'

Kat looks round, suddenly spooked. 'You think this place is bugged?'

'No way,' I say. 'If someone finds a bug, her cover's blown. Right now she thinks we are who we say we are. But she'll file a report tonight and it won't take Langley long to put two and two together. They won't want to deal with the Norwegians, so I figure we have twenty-four hours before they get a team here.'

'You really think she bought the cover story?' she asks.

'You sold the hell out of it.'

She smiles, the first time this trip, and I have to remind myself, not for the first time, that this trip is not about whatever might or might not exist between me and her, but my daughter, and that unless I can bring Hipkiss what she wants, Mireille will die.

IOI

As the day subsides and twilight descends, we sit on the bed to plan our attack. We've gone through Vilmos's Twitter archive to scrape up every morsel of personal information. But he was extraordinarily careful: the only slip he'd made was in a photograph he'd taken of a commercial router he'd reverse-engineered. Reflected in a shiny black computer case, a hand and part of a sleeve were visible. When I threw the jpeg into Photoshop, zoomed in and tweaked the contrast, you could see a crease in the wrist, and sausage-like fingers.

Vilmos referred to his size constantly on Twitter. Fat pride was almost as much a part of his identity as his sexuality. Until I saw the reflection, I wasn't sure it wasn't all just misdirection, part of his elaborate operational security. But, no, he was as heavy as he said.

The clue, however, was the shirt sleeve. Post-processing in Photoshop had distorted the colours, but it was unmistakably a floral pattern with a jaunty seventies vibe.

It's the single clue we have. It has to be enough.

In town, we rent long-track snowmobiles, snowsuits, emergency radios, avalanche markers and bolt-action rifles – the rifles are obligatory on account of the polar bears – from the grizzly bear of a man who runs the outfitters. He's Russian, a former miner at the now-abandoned mining colony of Pyramiden along the coast, and regales us with stories of swapping a dozen bottles of vodka for a Casio wristwatch belonging to a Norwegian miner he met while fishing, or a pair of boots for Norwegian consumer reports magazines which the KGB confiscated as enemy propaganda.

He offers to guide us, but we tell him we're exploring and can look after ourselves.

Fully outfitted, we head out into the night and amuse ourselves for twenty minutes by doing doughnuts on the snowmobiles in the parking lot.

'Where to now?' says Kat at the end, pulling her helmet off, steam rising into the freezing night air from hair damp with sweat.

'Vilmos can't have been here too long. There's a lot of traffic through here . . . engineers, scientists, researchers. But people register a new face. And he isn't exactly inconspicuous. Chances are he showed up somewhere on arrival, even if he's gone to ground now. I figure we go where the locals go.'

Kat grins. 'So, drinks. I can deal with that.'

102

The pub is tiny, decorated with old black-and-white pictures of miners, and packed with locals, some bearded and gruff, others millennial and freshly scrubbed. We find a space at the bar, jammed between a grizzled old-timer with the air of a Wild West gold prospector and a pair of young Germans in white turtlenecks who look like they might be about to drop an epic synthwave mixtape.

'This place, it's wild,' says Kat. 'CIA, Russians, nuclear submarines sailing past. It's like the Cold War never ended.'

'It didn't,' I say. 'The West saw the Berlin Wall come down and got distracted by Iraq and Afghanistan. But the KGB never disbanded. It just rebranded. The FSB took up internal duties while the GRU carried on overseas. The missiles aimed at Washington and Moscow were never retargeted. It's only here that you run up against the sharp end.'

The German synthwave twins are kissing. The old-timer on the other side glances at them and mutters something under his breath.

The bartender, a rangy character with a black knit beanie and lumberjack beard, sees it.

'That's it, Olavi,' he says in English. 'Out.'

Olavi swears at him in Estonian and doesn't move. He's three feet wide with hands like dinner plates. 'Fucking gays,' he says in English. 'They should have their own place.'

'I said out,' says the bartender. But he's built like a twig, and Olavi could snap him one-handed.

One of the best teachers I ever had was an ex-colonel in Estonian intelligence. Along with a dozen other skills, he taught me the rudiments of the language. I tap the big man gently on the shoulder. He looks at me in surprise.

'Olavi,' I say quietly. 'He's small. He can't hurt you. But I can fuck you up so badly you'll never walk again.'

Olavi pivots his enormous chest towards me, sizing up his chances.

I put my hand between his legs and squeeze his balls as hard as I can.

His eyes almost pop out with pain.

'Now how about you do what he asks? Do we have a deal?'

Olavi nods. I release him. He downs what's left of his drink, puts on his cap with majestic slowness, then ambles out of the door with what can only be described as a cowboy gait.

'Thanks,' says the bartender, and pours us another round. 'The old-timers, it's hard for them. In the mining camps, on the Russian side, two men found together could get both of them killed. Now we have Pride parades. First one this summer.'

He gestures at photos pinned on a corkboard behind him, a column of mostly young people, some with handmade rainbow flags or banners, marching through town towards the harbour.

Kat stares at one of the photographs. 'Excuse me. Can I look at it? The photo?'

He pulls it off the corkboard, hands it to her.

'You see something?'

Kat's finger lands on one of the figures in the parade. It's a man with an odd build that makes him look like an apple on two toothpicks. He has thick curly hair down to his shoulders, a black Helly Hansen windbreaker and a pair of oversized Paris Hilton sunglasses.

'That's him,' she says. 'Vilmos. That's him.'

103

'You think because he's in a Pride parade and a little chunky, he's Vilmos?'

'Not that,' says Kat. 'This.'

She pulls out her phone, flips to the camera and zooms in. The windbreaker is unzipped just enough to show a shirt underneath. The pattern is floral, exactly the same as the one we saw in the photograph of the hard drive.

I look over to the bartender.

'My friend thinks she knows this guy. You know where we could find him?'

The bartender takes the photo, glances at it, then hands it back.

'Lots of people pass through in the summer. Probably just a tourist.'

One of the German synthwave duo overhears, leans over.

'We were in the parade too, see, there at the back. Maybe we know him.'

He takes the photo, shows it to his doppelganger. They put their heads together, then he turns back.

'Yes, we remember him. Nobody knew him, but he didn't seem like a tourist.'

'Did he say anything about where he might be staying?'

He shakes his head. 'I can ask around if you want. Who should I say is looking for him?'

'It's OK,' says Kat with a smile. 'We want it to be a surprise.'

He nods and slips off his stool, heads over to another table. Before long, the photo is being passed around, circumnavigating the bar.

Kat swills her cognac thoughtfully.

'There's something I've been meaning to ask you.'

'Okay.'

'Did you love her? Mireille's mother. I mean, were you *in* love with her?'

I look away. 'Does it matter?'

'Yeah,' says Kat. 'Yeah, it kinda does.'

104

For a second, I'm back in Ethiopia, listening to Gracious breathe beside me as the traffic roars outside, wondering if I have the guts to kill her. And then a flash of her body, sprawled on the motel bed, no longer a person, just a thing.

I have to wait for the memory to subside.

'I think so.'

'If you *think* so, you weren't.'

'Okay, yes, I was in love with her. Happy?'

'I guess I didn't know you were capable of it, that's all.'

'Neither did I,' I say, which is true. I had no words for it at the time, but after Junebug died I cut myself off from emotion entirely. It wasn't that I didn't *feel* things, just that no feelings got in, and none came out. I was a human pipe bomb. The pressure would build and build and build until it exploded in some unstoppable paroxysm of violence that inevitably landed me in a worse situation than I'd been in before. In my child's-eye view, the world had done the worst thing it could to me, and I had no choice but to return the favour.

'Why *her*? Why Gracious as opposed to anybody else?'

I have to think for a moment. 'I think I always knew she wasn't just this pure, innocent, virginal girl who dressed in white and took me to a church for a date. There was something inside her that had made her strong and hard. And when I found out who she really was, I didn't have to explain myself. I didn't have to apologise. She'd survived the only way she knew, and so had I.'

'How come you never tried to track her down afterwards?'

'I don't know.'

'I do,' says Kat.

'Care to enlighten me?'

'Sure you want to hear it?'

'I can take it.'

'Okay,' says Kat. 'You never tried to track her down because the whole thing was a fantasy. It was a holiday romance. You'd never had a real relationship before, so you fell hard. Everybody does. It was time-limited and bittersweet like first loves always are, and then it ended. But you never moved on. You idealised her, mythologised her. And now she's dead, she'll always be that ideal to you. Somebody who'd rather kill herself than kill you. Her image can never be tarnished by who she actually was, as opposed to who you imagined her to be.'

'What do you mean, who she actually was?'

'Doesn't it bother you what she did to your daughter? Dragged her around Europe like a spare part? Dressed her up in face paint and camouflage and forced her to pull the trigger on a man she didn't even know was her father? You think being the son of a junkie hooker didn't fuck you up long before your mother died? Now imagine what Mireille went through, what she's *going* through, and what that must be doing to her. Has none of that even occurred to you?'

'My mother loved me,' I say. 'I think Gracious loved Mireille.'

'Love, love, love,' says Kat. 'It's just a word. You were right. Nobody gives a shit what you feel. It's irrelevant. Do you know what matters? What you *do*. Look at what she *did*.'

'She was doing her best for Mireille,' I say. 'Just like Junebug was for me. Maybe their best wasn't great. Maybe it was a lot less than great. But you have to consider the circumstances.'

Kat stirs the O of condensation left by her drink.

261

'Okay,' she says. 'Tell me this. Would you have killed her if she hadn't left?'

'I don't know.'

'But you wouldn't rule it out.'

'Rules are made to be broken. I'm not a big fan of absolutes.'

'So,' says Kat, 'to sum up, you're enough of a romantic to fall in love with someone in a week, but not enough of a romantic to rule out murdering them.'

'It would have been her or me.'

'Even so.'

My turn to swill my glass. 'Okay. You got your answer. Why do you care?'

'Because my answer would be different,' says Kat.

'You'd have let her kill you?'

'No,' says Kat. 'I'd have killed her without a second thought.'

'You're only saying that because you weren't there. It's easy to think about in the abstract. It's not so easy when the person is lying next to you, naked, and you can still smell their scent on you.'

'Maybe,' says Kat. 'Maybe not.'

'So you'd kill me,' I say.

'I'm not in love with you,' says Kat.

'You're avoiding the question.'

'On the contrary,' she says. 'I just answered it.'

105

I'm still trying to figure out what she means when the German in the white turtleneck suddenly appears at my side, still holding the photograph.

'This guy. One person got talking to him. They invited him to a party, but he said he had to get back to Barentsburg.'

'He lives in *Barentsburg*?' I say.

'That's what he said.' He heads off to join his twin.

Kat sees my frown. 'Barentsburg? Why is that so odd?'

'All the housing is owned either by the Russian government or the Russian mining company, Arktikugol. There's literally nowhere to live if you aren't employed by one or the other.'

'So he was lying?'

'Maybe not. The whole coast is dotted with abandoned workings and facilities. He could simply be using Barentsburg to resupply. Which means somebody there knows him.'

'How far is it?'

'Thirty miles, give or take. But there are no roads.'

Kat frowns. 'So how do we get there?'

'Now you know why we rented snowmobiles.'

106

The morning breaks clear, but the forecast is ugly, a front moving in that will bring snow, fog, and genuinely Arctic temperatures for the next week. By the time it passes, the brief window of semi-daylight will be gone, and Svalbard will be in near-perpetual darkness for months.

And, more to the point, Mireille will be dead.

The weather isn't our only worry. If I'm right about Sarah Pybus, there's already a CIA team en route from London or Berlin to take us down. We don't want to telegraph to them how far we're headed or that we may not be back, so we leave our bags and inessentials as a decoy, then suit up and head out with rifles, helmets and radios to the snowmobiles.

We roar out of town, heading up. The route hugs the coast, but the mountains drop precipitously into the fjord, so the fastest route is over the top with only a broad carpet of snowmobile tracks to show the way. Kat surges ahead, burping the engine to send up gouts of snow as she carves left and right, enjoying the power of the machine. Ahead of us, sparse cirrus clouds glow pink, lit from underneath by the submerged sun. But behind, an ominous wall of dark cumulus pursues us across the snowfield.

'Don't get too far ahead,' I warn Kat on the helmet radio. 'We need to keep visual contact. Weather could close in any moment. We lose the trail, we're fucked.'

She slows to let me draw alongside, and we cruise like that, throttles wide open, for another hour. The wind picks up, the storm matching our speed so that snow floats around us as if we're barely moving. Then suddenly the ground falls away in front of us, and sodium lights appear below, glimmering in the snow and the half-light.

We drop down into the town, and find ourselves in one of the strangest places on earth.

107

Barentsburg is a time capsule, a mining colony built during the Soviet era that never caught up with history. The main square is dominated by a massive bust of Lenin, gazing out defiantly over the quay for the bulk carriers that still arrive in summer. Behind him, a massive chute descends from the coal mine entrance in the mountains where, above a five-pointed star, a Hollywood-style sign blares the old Soviet slogan Миру Мир! – *Peace to the World!* – somewhat undermined by the matching slogan on the housing complex below that reminds us *Our Goal is Communism.*

We roll up to the harbour and pull our helmets off. Despite the smokestack plume from the power plant up on the hill, the place is eerily deserted. It has all the charisma of a post-apocalyptic plague town.

'This place is weird,' says Kat. 'I keep expecting zombies. And what the hell is *that*?'

She points to a vehicle rusting away on the jetty. It has the elegant curves of a 1950s automobile, with a cabin half-way between a Volkswagen Beetle and a two-seater airplane. Instead of wheels, it has the keel of a boat, and at the rear a pair of tail fins frame an enormous pusher prop.

I gun the snowmobile to take a closer look. 'Holy shit. It's a Tupolev.'

'A what?'

'Tupolev A-3. They called it the Aerosledge, built to slide over snow or float on water. It's like a flying boat without wings. They used them to deliver post and parcels in Siberia, border patrols in Eastern Europe, medical evacuation, that kind of thing.'

The wind picks up, whipping flakes against our faces. A skein of sea ice has formed on the fjord, chunks lapping up against the shore.

'You were right,' says Kat. 'It's like the Cold War never ended.'

'Maybe it's starting up again.'

I point to a massive bunker-like building set back from the main square. It's modern, curved, red-brick, surrounded by a high wire fence, and adorned with security lights and cameras pointing in all directions. Above it, the tricolour of the Russian Federation snaps in the wind.

'The Russian consulate. See the rear? No windows, massive communication array? That's where the GRU live. Russian military intelligence. There are probably only three or four actual consular officials in there, if that. The rest are spooks with a direct line to Moscow. If the balloon goes up, this place turns into a military installation within days. They probably have people in Longyearbyen too.'

'Like the outfitter.'

'The thought had occurred to me.'

'Meaning our snowmobiles are probably tracked.'

'I wouldn't bet against it.'

'Does it matter? I mean, okay, someone's trying to kill you, but unless the GRU are on the same team, are they a threat?'

'Vilmos went dark for a reason, almost certainly because he knows something about Deep Threat. If the GRU figure out who we're looking for, they'll care very much.'

'So how do we find him without tipping them off?'

'We can't,' I say. 'We just have to get to him before they do.'

108

If Vilmos is resupplying, there's only one place he can go: the town's single grocery store. Inside, it's pure pre-*glasnost* Soviet chic. Linoleum floor, bare painted walls, a sterile wooden counter, and a rectangular absence on the wall where I'm guessing the portrait of Vladimir Ilyich used to hang.

Behind the counter, a middle-aged woman with tight curly hair and a stained apron surveys us, lips pursed in suspicion like a dog's backside. I can tell before we show her the photo she's going to be no help and, worse, will report us the moment we leave. But time is running out, so I do it anyway, and when she claims not to recognise Vilmos, I challenge her in Russian.

'Come on. I know he comes in here. I know you've seen him. Just tell me where he lives.'

'Goran!' she yells, and a big man in his sixties with a broad chest, bald head and biceps like hams emerges from the back wearing a bloodstained white apron and carrying the twelve-inch-long knife he's been using to gut fish. His sleeves are rolled, and under the blood that covers them, his massive forearms carry elaborate tattoos.

'Tell them to go fuck themselves, in English,' she says in Russian.

'Go fuck yourselves,' says Goran in English, thumping the knife on the counter, blade up.

'Look, Goran,' I say, showing him the photo. 'I understand the situation. He pays you to not talk about him to anyone who asks, right? Which includes the bastards up on the hill.'

Goran glances out of the window towards the lights of the consulate. Under Putin, the real power of the Russian state is vested not in the oligarchs or the military but in the hated *silovarchs*, the security forces who report directly to him.

'And I'm guessing they'd be upset if they found out you've been taking money to not report things to them. You being Serbian and not Russian, that could make things difficult, no?'

Goran leans on the counter too, his head coming close to mine. The tattoos on his arms are crudely drawn tigers and below them the letters СДГ.

'Who says we didn't tell them?' says Goran.

'Did you also tell them what you did in Vukovar?' I say.

Goran stares at me in astonishment, his eyes filled with a combination of hatred and fear.

'I don't know what you're talking about.'

'Yes, you do. Does your wife? Do the men in the consulate? What about the investigators at The Hague? Shall we find out?'

Goran's hand shoots out to grab my snowsuit, and he presses the knife to my throat.

'Let him go,' says Kat, from behind me.

Goran looks up to see her rifle levelled at him, safety off, finger at first pressure on the trigger.

He slowly releases me. His wife doesn't move, watching the whole thing with her arms folded as if it was on TV.

'They call him *tolstyy otshel'nik*, the fat hermit,' says Goran. 'He comes into town once every few weeks.'

'From which direction?'

'From the west.'

'What's to the west?'

'Nothing.'

'There has to be something.'

269

'What do they want?' asks his wife, in Russian.

'They want to know where the fat hermit comes from,' says Goran. 'I told them, there's nothing that way.'

'Yes, there is,' she says. 'The old mine.'

'That's to the east.'

'No, not the old mine,' she says. 'The *old*, old mine.'

109

'What the hell was all that about?' asks Kat as we head towards the snowmobiles.

'He's a war criminal,' I tell her. ''90, '91, after Yugoslavia fell apart. The Tigers were a Serbian paramilitary unit. They massacred hundreds of people. The International Criminal Tribunal indicted the leader, Arkan, but he was assassinated before he could be tried. The rest of them fled, tried to disappear into the woodwork. With the amount of blood on his hands, if Interpol got hold of him, he'd be looking at forty years in prison, if he made it that far.'

'You knew all that from the tattoos?'

'And the initials. SDG, Serbian Defence Group.'

'What if I hadn't been there with the rifle?'

I turn to her. 'I knew you were.'

'You trusted me?'

'You'd have killed him, right?'

She nods.

'I do now.'

I spread out a topo map on the seat of the snowmobile and I use my finger to follow the coast west. There it is, a cluster of buildings in an inlet about six miles away.

'How are we going to find it if there's no trail?'

'We hug the coast.'

'What if we can't *see* the coast?'

I look up at the lowering clouds. The storm is closing fast, wind whipping up snow devils. But then I notice something: a line of transmission towers trailing up and away from the red-and-white smokestacks of the power plant. I go back to the map. A thin black dotted line.

'There's a powerline.'

'You think it goes all the way?'

Behind Kat, a figure emerges from the grocery store. It's Goran's wife, bent against the wind, scuttling across the town square towards the hulk of the consulate to inform on us.

'We need to go,' I say. 'Whether it takes us all the way or not.'

110

The trip from Longyearbyen was smooth, the trail compacted by other machines, but this is virgin snow, drifted several feet deep in places. An hour out of Barentsburg, the powerline takes a near vertical route up a steep chute. We try blasting up, but there's no way we can make it, so we detour round to the side instead. But in the lee of the hillside, the snow is soft and deep, and as she turns back up the shallower backside of the rise, Kat's machine gets stuck.

'Fuck! Fuck!' I hear her yelling. She guns the engine over and over again, jamming the machine into reverse, then forward, but the long track digs in deeper with every throttle burst.

I climb off and try to move the snowmobile with my hands, but it's bedded in. In the cargo box behind my seat, I find a tow rope and hook it to the front of Kat's sled. But as I take the strain, I feel my own sled starting to sink.

'It's no good,' I yell. 'I can't pull you out. We have to abandon it.'

Kat hesitates, then grumpily wades through the hip-deep powder towards me, climbs on the back, and wraps her arms tight around me.

In my earpiece I hear her voice.

'Don't get any ideas.'

'Too late,' I say, and twist the throttle.

What's left of the light has been obliterated by the storm. I peer ahead, trying to spot the next pole in the snowmobile's headlight. The gas gauge is dangerously low. We're long past the point of no return, and maybe thirty minutes from the fuel giving out, at which point we will most assuredly freeze to death.

And then I feel the engine ease up. Ahead, the ground begins to slope away in front of us, each pole lower than the last. I kill the headlight to let my eyes adjust to the darkness. In front of us, at the foot of a steep slope, dim and flickering as a candle, is the yellow light of some kind of human habitation.

'Hang on,' I tell Kat, and she wraps her arms around me again.

We slalom down the chute like a skier on a double black until we finally bottom out on a narrow plateau. In the lee of the hill, the blizzard thins out to reveal a ghost town, the rotting shell of a long-abandoned mining camp. Ugly, square buildings with broken windows and smashed-in asbestos roofs, some tumbling down the hillside to what is presumably the sea below. The biggest of the buildings, constructed around the mine entrance, stands on a slope so steep that the front of it is supported by pillars. But that's not where the light's coming from. Instead, it comes from a warehouse a few hundred yards away.

'So what,' says Kat over the helmet intercom, 'we just go and knock on his door?'

'Unless you've got a better idea.'

She doesn't, so I throttle up once more to make the last couple of hundred yards to the building. But we don't need to knock. As we approach, the door of the building flies open, and a wild figure bursts out with a pump-action Remington already shouldered. Obese and wild-haired, he's wearing the same flowered shirt as in the photograph, a pair of purple Y-fronts with white trimming and an antique, oversized pair of white Sorel snow boots.

I pull off my helmet to yell 'Vilmos!', but before I can get the words out, he starts shooting.

III

Shotgun pellets ping off the bodywork and windshield as Kat and I dive behind the snowmobile.

'Vilmos!' I yell over the wind. 'It's me! Seventeen!'

'Fuck off!' he yells back, and looses another shot.

I stand up, hands in the air.

'I just want to talk! I'm not here to hurt you!'

'Who's that with you?' he yells back.

'Pull your helmet off,' I tell Kat. 'Let him see you.'

She does, stands up beside me, snow whipping into her face, hands raised.

'Her name's Kat,' I yell. 'She's okay. She's with me.'

'Put your weapons down,' he yells. 'No guns.'

'Okay, okay!' I yell back. I unsling the rifle from my back.

'You sure about this?' says Kat, quietly enough that he can't hear.

'It's okay,' I say. 'He's harmless. Just do it.'

She unslings her rifle too. We dump them into the snow, raise our hands again.

'Come on, Vilmos,' I yell. 'We've come a long fucking way.'

'Nobody asked you,' he yells back. 'Go away.'

'We're out of gas,' I yell. 'We couldn't leave even if we wanted to.'

'Not my problem,' he yells back.

It's too much for Kat, who strides forward, furious, dumping her helmet in the snow.

'Listen to me, you asshole,' she yells. 'Maybe you think you're some super-fucking-cool hacker hiding behind VPNs and proxies and shit, but you know how long it took to find you? Two days. And why? Because you're addicted to Twitter and own exactly one shirt.'

'Screw you,' says Vilmos, offended, looking at a sleeve. 'It's a great shirt.'

I join her in front of the snowmobile. 'She's right, Vilmos. If we can find you, so can somebody else. The only way to protect yourself is to help us.'

He's freezing now, his bare white legs shaking with cold.

'To do what?'

'Get my daughter back. She's nine years old, and whoever took her killed her mother, a bunch of other people, and is trying to kill me.'

'Boo hoo,' says Vilmos. 'And this has *what* to do with me?'

'Deep Threat,' I say. 'It's connected.'

'I have no idea what you're talking about.'

I shake my head. 'Don't bullshit me, Vilmos. If it's malware, you know about it. You went dark the moment this started to go down. And you're so scared right now you came out to take pot shots in your underwear before you even knew who we were.'

He yells back over the howling wind, 'If this is about Deep Threat, I need a lot better reason to help you than some sob story about your mythical lost spawn.'

'Like what?'

He considers a moment, snow whirling around his head.

'I need you to destroy it.'

112

Vilmos slams the door behind us and bars it.

As he pulls on a pair of bell-bottomed yellow corduroy pants, and plops a kettle on the stove for coffee, I look around in amazement. The warehouse has been gutted, roof and walls reinforced with steel beams. This end is set up as Vilmos's living quarters and workshop. His personal belongings are minimal – a camp bed, an open suitcase, a kitchen area strewn with open cans and empty frozen pizza boxes. Opposite is his workshop, piled high with computer and communications equipment, mainly in pieces, while above the door we entered screens show an array of security cameras, switched to infra-red night vision.

Further along, UV lamps hang over tiered hydroponics, promoting an eye-watering amount of weed and a healthy crop of vegetables. Beyond that, a massive rack of exotic GPUs is cooled by a giant barn fan – presumably Vilmos's legendary Bitcoin mining rig. There are persistent rumours that Vilmos is Satoshi Nakamoto, the pseudonymous inventor of Bitcoin, who vanished in 2010. He's always denied it, but whatever the truth, he's a Bitcoin multi-millionaire.

None of this compares to what lies further down the hall. It's a gigantic satellite dish array, some balanced on massive gimbals controlled by hydraulics and powerful motors. Thick cables run to a power distribution panel that could power a small town. At the very far end, swathed in darkness, I can make out a broad pair of double doors like an aircraft hangar, but not much else.

Vilmos turns from the stove. We've corresponded for years, but this is the first time I've seen him in the flesh. He has a shambling, eccentric, avuncular presence, halfway between Apple co-founder Steve Wozniak and a beardless Hagrid, but underpinned by a revolutionary seriousness of purpose. It's not hard to imagine that he ended up in a Supermax, and might again.

He eyes Kat warily. 'Who is she? What's she doing here?'

'I'm here because this asshole's life needs saving now and then,' says Kat, not entirely inaccurately.

'It's OK, Vilmos. She's OK. I vouch for her.'

'So you two are—'

He pokes his index finger into an O formed by his other hand.

'Not currently,' I say.

Kat gives me an evil look.

'Or likely to be at any time in the future,' I add, and quickly nod at the gimbals and dish array. 'So you're hacking the satellite station, right?'

'Not the station,' says Vilmos. 'The network is massively secure. Besides, the bandwidth you'd suck up getting the traffic out would trigger the network tripwires in milliseconds.'

'So instead . . . ?'

'The satellites are tiny, and the processors inside them are slow. But they have to beam a firehose of data down each time they pass. Which means most of it is sent with only basic encryption, because encryption takes computing power. But they don't care, because who the fuck would be stupid enough to set up a *second* satellite station in a place like Svalbard? And even if they did, how would they keep it secret?'

He grins, gesturing at the dishes. 'Ta-da!'

'You're pirating satellite TV,' I say, 'on the grandest possible scale.'

'Exactly,' says Vilmos.

'But how are you going to get the data out?'

The kettle whistles. As Vilmos makes coffee, he pokes a medium-sized cardboard box with his foot. 'You know how many cheap-ass one-terabyte hard drives that holds? Five hundred. Let's say I give it to a man on a boat, and it takes twelve hours to get to Norway. What's the bandwidth?'

'Eleven gigs per second,' says Kat, not skipping a beat. Apparently mental math is her thing. *Huh.*

'Right,' says Vilmos. 'Eighty times the fastest domestic internet in the USA. By helicopter, seven *hundred* times faster. And any time you want to double the speed . . .'

'You just give him another box,' I say.

'Right,' says Vilmos. He brings coffee over. Outside, the storm is ramping up, wind howling in the powerline and snow hammering the side of the building so hard it sounds like hail.

'So,' says Vilmos. 'I have your promise? You have a chance, you have the *slightest* chance to destroy Deep Threat, you'll do it?'

I nod.

Vilmos leans forward. 'You know what a zero-day is?'

'Sure. Malware that exploits a previously unknown vulnerability in a computer system, meaning they can take control of your entire network, maybe your entire infrastructure. You don't know about it so you can't protect against it.'

'And what does every piece of malware have in common?'

'A mistake. A bug, or a vulnerability in the code that can be exploited.'

'Right,' says Vilmos. 'Find the mistake in your code, fix it, update your systems, and you've protected yourself. But what if you look at the code and there's no mistake? What if there *is* no bug, no vulnerability? How do you protect against *that*?'

I frown. 'That makes no sense. How can there be a bug if there's no bug?'

'Because you're looking for it in the wrong place,' says Vilmos. 'What happens to your code between you writing it and it actually doing something?'

'It gets compiled,' says Kat. 'Turned into actual computer instructions, by a compiler.'

The math nerd in Kat is new to me, but I'll take it.

'Right,' says Vilmos. 'But the compiler is just another program. So the code you're looking at could be perfect, but if the *compiler* has been compromised, you'd know nothing about it.'

'Can't you just look at the code for the compiler?'

Vilmos turns back to me. 'Sure. But what if you don't find a bug there either?'

My head is starting to hurt.

'Then . . . maybe the compiler that compiled the compiler was compromised?'

I'm not even sure if what I'm saying makes sense. But Vilmos nods.

'Maybe,' says Vilmos. 'Or the one before that. Or the one before *that*. Do you have any idea how many generations there are, going all the way back to the sixties? Almost every major computer system on earth traces its lineage back to one of those early tools. If one of those was compromised, it would be like a genetic flaw that's passed down from generation to generation. To the power grid, banking, internet, the whole internet-of-things . . . your car, your microwaves. Trains, planes, navigation systems, manufacturing, communications, weaponry. *Everything* would be vulnerable.'

'And that's Deep Threat?' I say.

'No,' says Vilmos. 'Deep Threat is *worse*.'

113

'How could it be worse than *that*?' asks Kat.

'Nukes,' says Vilmos. 'Every nuclear nation has its own command and control systems. They're insanely hardened, built using proprietary tools, and the code is audited. But the entire infrastructure is ultimately descended from a few compilers created in the sixties. So if you find a vulnerability . . .'

'The entire nuclear arsenal worldwide is vulnerable to attack,' says Kat.

'Not just attack,' says Vilmos. 'Control. And the beauty of it is, you don't need to control all of them. You just need to control one. Let's say you hijack a launch system in China, targeting the US. The moment it launches, the US begins a retaliatory strike. But you route the attack through a Russian military intelligence network centre you also compromised. China knows it didn't launch the missile and blames Russia. But Russia figures out the network centre was compromised from an IP in San Diego. Presto! We're in the middle of nuclear Armageddon.'

'And that's Deep Threat?'

'*That's* Deep Threat,' says Vilmos. 'A weaponised computer vulnerability that allows you to start the global nuclear war of your choosing, at will.'

'Jesus Christ,' I say. 'Who came up with this? You?'

Vilmos stares at me, horrified. 'What? No. Fuck, no. I mean, I was aware of the possibility. As an intellectual challenge, it was interesting. But to actually do it? No way.'

'But you know who did?'

Vilmos nods. 'His hacker name was Alveolus. Not his real name, obviously. We only ever communicated by a secure messaging app, except once. He knew my reputation, wanted my advice. I got the impression he was young but brilliant. He'd come across an old research paper that talked about the possibility and started digging into legacy code, mapping out the bloodlines of all the different systems. He traced almost all of them back to one program. He started looking for vulnerabilities, he found one, and then he weaponised it.'

'Did he understand what he'd created?'

'Sure. He wanted to sell it, to get rich. But word had gotten out in the malware community he might have something. He started to get paranoid, thought he was being followed. That's when he reached out to me. He knew I'd been through some bad shit. He was scared and wanted to protect himself.'

'And what did you tell him?'

'I told him to publish it.'

'You told him *what*? So *anyone* could start a nuclear war?'

Vilmos shakes his head. 'Publishing is how you neutralise an exploit. It's like UV light to bacteria. Once everyone knows what the exploit is, they can protect against it. Your secret attack isn't secret any more. They can just patch their systems and move on.'

'But why not *destroy* destroy it,' says Kat. 'Delete the files, scrub everything?'

'It doesn't fix the problem,' says Vilmos. 'If this kid found it, so can someone else.'

'So what did he say?'

'He refused. That's when I managed to talk to him. Just a single voice call on an encrypted line. He was crying some of the time. He said he needed money, and there was something about a family situation I didn't understand. His sister was in a bad situation, something like that. He wasn't making a lot of sense.'

A sudden, weird thought strikes me.

'Did he have an accent?'

'We spoke English. I can't tell accents. I don't think he was a native speaker, though.'

I grab a pen and pizza box from Vilmos's fantastically cluttered desk.

'What about his screen name? Alveolus, right?'

'That's what he called himself,' says Vilmos. 'But his screen name had "mister" in front of it.'

I hand him the pizza box. 'Write it down for me.'

Vilmos gives me an odd look, but obliges.

Kat takes up the slack. 'What did you tell him about how to protect himself?'

'I told him he needed to go to a two-key system. Like one of those safes that need two keys to open it. You hold one, somebody else has the other, and neither of you can open it on your own.'

'How does that work for software?'

'A file is just a string of bits, ones and zeroes. So you split it in half. First bit goes into one file, second bit goes into the other. Third into the first, fourth the second, and so on. Like the teeth of a zipper. Separately they're meaningless, but zip them back together and you have the original. I told him to keep one half and give the other half to someone he trusted. Once they were sure a deal had been done and he was safe, they would hand the two halves over. If anyone came for him, all they would get was his half, which was useless on its own.'

'And that's what he did?'

'I have no idea,' says Vilmos. 'The next message was from his partner. They called themselves Raevan. They told me they'd come home to find their place ransacked, and Alveolus had disappeared. There was blood. His computer gear was missing, along with everything to do with Deep Threat.'

'And that's when you went dark?' I say.

'If he'd managed to split the malware, I was the obvious person to send it to. If whoever killed him only got his half, they'd come looking for the rest. And they wouldn't stop until they found it. Only he didn't send it to me.'

'No,' I say. 'But I know who he *did* send it to.'

I hold up the pizza box, where Vilmos's spidery hand has written *@MrAlveolus*.

Underneath, using the pen, I've rearranged the letters into a familiar name.

114

Marvellous.

115

Vilmos stares at the pizza box. 'Who the fuck is Marvellous?'

'Gracious's brother,' I say. 'Everything fits. He's young, probably a native Hausa speaker so English isn't his first language, and Gracious told me he was good with computers. He must have been working on Deep Threat, but Hipkiss got wind of it. She sent Harkonnen to get it from Marvellous, but he only got one half. Harkonnen probably tortured him to find out who had the other half, which was Gracious. Gracious ran, but she had Mireille with her. She set up the hit on me so Mireille would escape, and I'd be forced to protect her.'

Vilmos shakes his head. 'That makes no sense. Maybe you're right, maybe it was her brother, but why not just tell you what she was doing and ask you to help?'

'I don't know,' I say. 'I've tried to figure it out over and over again, and I always come up blank. She could have easily told me, written me some kind of note, anything. Maybe she didn't have time. Maybe she was afraid I wouldn't believe her. Or maybe she just thought I might say no.'

I can tell from the silence that neither of them is convinced. And neither am I.

'Bullshit,' says Kat, after a moment.

'Excuse me?'

'Vilmos is right. None of that makes sense. But I'll tell you what does. She didn't tell you because she knew damn well that if you knew Harkonnen was trying to kill her, you'd try to save *her*. And that would put Mireille at risk. She wanted all your attention on the kid, not her.'

'You think I'd risk my own daughter to save her?'

'I think you have a Messiah complex and an inflated idea of your own abilities. Plus, you were still in love with her. Or the idea of her. And she knew it, because you couldn't kill her even to save your own life. She couldn't risk you putting on your Sir Galahad armour and coming to save her. *That's* why she didn't tell you. And she was right, wasn't she?'

I have no answer to any of this because it's all true.

'No wonder she was able to find you,' says Vilmos, filling the silence. 'If her brother was good enough to create Deep Threat, he was easily good enough to track you.'

'Why didn't she just destroy the file herself?' says Kat.

'Because it was a ticket out, just like Marvellous intended,' I say. 'My guess is she'd been doing low-key wetwork for a decade with a kid in tow. Deep Threat was a way to give Mireille a proper life. She could sell her half to Google or barter it to the CIA for a new identity. But she had to get clear of Harkonnen first, and he was closing fast. So she gave it to Mireille. Or maybe she planned to draw Harkonnen's fire, make sure that Mireille got away with something valuable, something that could give her a future. An inheritance, almost.'

'Wait,' says Vilmos. 'I thought you said Harkonnen didn't find it on the kid?'

'He didn't.'

'So if Gracious didn't have it, and Mireille didn't have it, and you don't have it,' says Kat, 'where the hell *is* it?'

'I never said I didn't have it,' I say. 'I just wasn't sure until now.'

Out of my snowsuit I pull the one-eyed sock monkey that bears my name.

116

Vilmos sacrifices the monkey to science. Inside is nothing but stuffing, which leaves its single button eye. He takes it to his workbench and puts it under an illuminated magnifier, turning it over and over with a pair of tweezers.

'It's been cut in half and epoxied. I don't know if I can get it open without destroying it.'

'We have to try.'

Vilmos finds a dirty glass, fills it with a clear liquid.

'Isopropyl,' he says. 'Sometimes it works on epoxy, enough to soften it, anyway.'

He drops the button in. We stare at it.

'How long is this going to take?' I ask, as casually as I can.

Vilmos picks it up, swivels round on his stool. 'Does it matter?'

'I think we're safe until the storm blows through,' I say, 'but—'

'Wait,' says Vilmos. 'You *think* we're safe?'

I glance at Kat. *Don't tell him.*

'We had to ask about you in Barentsburg,' she says. 'The woman in the grocery store tipped off the GRU in the consulate. They know we headed west. It won't take much to figure out where we are.'

'You led them to my fucking *door*?'

'Come on, Vilmos,' I say. 'If I'd told you, we'd be polar bear food by now. Besides, Kat was right. If we could find you, so could they, and so could Harkonnen. It was only a matter of time.'

Vilmos grabs a hammer, furious, aims it at the glass. 'I should just fucking—'

But at that moment, the button in the glass pops open like a corn kernel in a pan.

Vilmos extracts a tiny black-and-gold plastic chip with the tweezers. 'It's an nCard,' he says. 'Same form factor as the nano-SIM in your cellphone, but way more storage.'

'Can you read it?'

Vilmos finds an Android smartphone, snaps out the SIM and inserts the card. He hooks the phone up to a battered laptop plastered with stickers of comic-book conventions. The screen fills with hieroglyphics.

'Binary data,' says Vilmos.

Kat pulls close and peers at the screen. 'Is it what we think?'

'No way to tell without the other half.'

'But if it is,' I say, 'what's it worth? Dollar value.'

Vilmos extracts the card from the phone.

'Combine it with the other half, and you can start a nuclear war. What's that worth? A billion dollars? Two? Ten? A hundred? You tell me.'

Vilmos slips it into a Ziploc and holds it out.

'But you promised to publish it, remember?'

'I remember,' I say, and take it.

Which is when we hear it.

The sound of a snowmobile, distant, but closing fast.

Then another, and another, and another.

PART EIGHT

117

In the FLIR camera above the door, pale against the blackness of the freezing night, figures appear, bodies grey and engines white-hot, shapes of weapons slung over their backs. I count them. Nine, ten . . . a round dozen.

'GRU,' I say. 'I guess they decided not to wait out the storm.'

Our hunting rifles are all lying in the snow outside, where Vilmos forced us to drop them. But even if we had them, with ten shells total, we'd be no match for an entire squad carrying automatics.

'You have weapons?' asks Kat. 'Beside the shotgun?'

'Just a rifle, same as you,' says Vilmos. 'A few shells, because it's the law.'

'If we stay here, we're dead,' I say. 'How do you get to Barentsburg? Snowmobile?'

He nods. 'Sometimes.'

'Even if we could get the three of us on a snowmobile, we'd never outrun them,' says Kat.

'There's another option,' he says. 'Follow me.'

He grabs the pump-action and a box of shells and hurries past the satellite array into the rear of the building. Kat and I follow. I glance back at the CCTV. The snowmobiles are pulling into a group, men dismounting, spreading out to form a perimeter.

'Vilmos, if we're not out of here in thirty seconds—'

Bzzzzt! Electricity arcs as he throws a knife switch that looks like it came out of a horror movie. Dazzling overhead lights flick on, revealing a workshop full of sheet-metal fabrication tools, automotive repair equipment, and aircraft parts. A snowmobile against one wall, sidelined. And in the middle is not Frankenstein's monster, but something almost as astonishing.

It's a Tupolev Aerosledge. But unlike the relic rusting away in Barentsburg, this one is in near-perfect condition. The fuselage is polished silver, with black and red go-faster stripes curving nose to tail and three powerful spotlight headlamps. Each rudder has a red five-pointed star and a gold hammer and sickle, while the massive eight-cylinder rotary engine has two six-foot counter-rotating propellers. The open gull-wing doors give it the impression of a bird about to take flight.

It is gobsmackingly, astoundingly, beautiful.

'You restored it?'

Vilmos nods.

'And it drives? Everything works?'

Vilmos holds out a set of keys.

'You're not coming with us?'

'Ninety per cent chance they catch you and kill you,' says Vilmos. 'This way, you draw their fire, and I go in the other direction. But remember what you promised. Worst case, you destroy it before they get their hands on it. If by some miracle you get the whole thing, forget what it's worth. You publish. Okay?'

I reach for the keys. He pulls them away. '*Okay?*'

'Okay,' I say. I take the keys and climb in.

The controls are straightforward. Brake, gas, lights, radio, steering yoke. I hit the contact and ignition button. A compressed-air system whirls the prop, and the massive rotary engine sputters into life. Ahead of us, Vilmos throws another switch. An overhead motor spools chain, and the big hangar door slides open, snow whirling in from the darkness.

I open the throttle, and the Tupolev slides forward, Duralumin rails grating on the floor, the entire craft vibrating. As we pass Vilmos, he unexpectedly throws the Remington and the box of ammo to Kat, who manages to catch them.

We pull the gull-wing doors closed and roar into the storm.

118

The Russians hear the roar of the airplane engine as we skim out onto the snow. In the side-mirror I glimpse them running back to their machines, then converging onto our six in pursuit.

The sound in the cockpit of the Tupolev is deafening, and the ride isn't much better, bucking and bouncing over the frozen ground. But as it accelerates, the nose lifts, like a speedboat going on plane, and the ride smooths out.

Kat loads the shotgun, cranes round. 'They're gaining.'

I glance in the mirror again. A couple have abandoned their own sleds and are riding pillion as tail-gunners.

'Max speed of this thing is seventy-five,' I yell. 'Those things behind us will do ninety, a hundred, maybe more.'

Behind us, one of the pillion riders opens up with an automatic. I hear bullets ping off the body. If they snag an oil line or shatter a prop, this will be over before it's even begun.

'So what's our plan?' she yells back.

'Hold them off until I think of one.'

Kat gives me a look and unlatches the gull-wing hatch.

The storm is brutal now, the wipers on the Tupolev barely keeping up, and the headlights reveal only a vortex of snow hurtling towards us. Kat flips up the door and braces herself against the fuselage, half in, half out, the slipstream whipping hair and ice into her face.

She opens fire. The closest sleds drop back, but at this distance the chances of her hitting any of them are remote.

Blinded by the snow, I have only a vague sense of where we are or where we're going. If we could get back up to the powerline, I could follow it to Barentsburg, but the GRU would radio ahead and there'd be a welcoming party. Besides, every time I point the Aerosledge uphill, it slows, the props straining to push our weight against both wind and gravity.

Which leaves precisely one alternative.

Another couple of snowmobiles pull forward for an attack, and Kat blasts away, forcing them back. But the six shells in her magazine are soon gone, and she drops back into her seat to reload, pulling the door shut.

Her hair is already half frozen, cheeks going white from the beginnings of frostbite, hands so numb they can barely fit the next set of shells into the magazine. If the Tupolev has a heater, I can't find it, although there's a radio and a box in the cargo area behind us with EMERGENCY written in Russian.

Behind us, a pair of the Russian machines fanned out, trying to outflank as Kat reloads.

'Kat,' I say, but she's fumbling to reload the Remington and doesn't hear. 'KAT.'

She looks up.

'How much longer can you hold them off?'

'Not long,' she says. Her teeth are chattering so hard she can barely get the words out.

'One more time, okay? Whatever you do, don't let them overtake us.'

She nods. 'And then?'

'Close the door and hang on for your life.'

She gets the last of the shells into the Remington, opens the door again and stands. The sled on her side is coming up fast, much closer than before. Driving one-handed, he pulls up an automatic to fire, but Kat gets her shot in first. He jerks backwards, and the snowmobile rockets up a slope, blasts through a corniche and flies twisting through the air and out of sight into the storm. The last I see of the rider is his body tumbling to a halt in the snow behind it.

Kat swivels to aim at the rider on the other side, but the gull-wing door blocks her view. To get a clear shot, she climbs up out of the cockpit onto the sill, hanging on with one hand as the Tupolev lurches over the snowfield.

'Kat, no,' I yell.

'Slow down,' she yells back.

I ease off. The rider on my side swoops into view, raking us lengthwise with bullets that slam into the metal hull. Kat fires, using the roof as a rest, but the bucking of the Tupolev spoils her aim. The rider pulls back, then heads in for another pass. Kat follows him, and this time she hits him. His body cart-wheels away, but his snowmobile takes on a mind of its own, veers across our wake and brutally T-bones a third machine, taking out both its pilot and the tail-gunner behind him.

But at that moment, the Tupolev ploughs into a drift, and Kat slips off the sill of the door. Holding on by one hand, the shotgun still clutched in the other, she struggles desperately to get herself back inside. I lean over and hold out my hand for her to grab, wrestling the yoke with the other. But she's determined not to drop the shotgun.

'Lose the gun,' I yell. 'LOSE IT!'

Instead, she lets go with the other hand and lunges for mine. Our hands connect, but only just. I strain to haul her in, but I can feel her ice-cold palm slipping away.

If either of us lets go, she's dead.

But then she throws the shotgun into the footwell and uses her free hand to pull herself forward. Together, we drag her back into the cockpit, and she pulls the door shut.

'What the fuck was that?' I yell at her, trying to get the Tupolev back under control.

'You're welcome,' says Kat, but she can barely get the words out, arms wrapped around herself, her hair still caked with ice.

'Fine,' I say. 'You're a hero. Now hold tight.'

I haul the yoke left. The Tupolev slews sideways, then begins to pick up speed.

'What are you doing?'

'We can't outrun them on the flat. But if we use gravity . . .'

A tsunami of snow plasters the windshield, the storm buffeting us left and right like a small plane in a crosswind. There are still seven snowmobiles behind us, but we're accelerating now, taking air as we hurdle over drifts.

'But it goes down to the sea,' she yells.

'That's the idea,' I yell. 'We're amphibious. They're not. They can't follow us on water.'

Kat stares at me. 'What if it doesn't float? What if—'

She doesn't finish, because at that moment, the Tupolev takes air. Kat has to hold onto the dash to stop her head slamming into the ceiling, and when we crunch down, the pitch is suddenly much steeper.

'No choice now,' I yell. 'I couldn't stop if I tried.'

The Tupolev is a missile. Behind us, the GRU are barely visible, appearing only intermittently from curtains of snow. And we're still gathering speed, taking air, every leap trying to pin us to the headliner and every landing thumping us back down onto the hard Russian seats. The steering no longer does anything, our momentum so great that the Tupolev just skews left or right, like a car sliding on ice.

And then, suddenly, all vibration stops and I feel myself go light.

I turn to see Kat floating out of her seat, weightless as an astronaut.

119

We plummet in freefall for a second and a half, the Tupolev nosing forward into a dive.

'BRACE,' I yell, and Kat does, grabbing the seat with one hand and a strap with another. I cross my arms on the yoke and push my forehead against it. For a split second through the driving snow, I see the ground rushing towards us, brutal and unstoppable.

There's no way we survive this.

Except that we do. The bone-shaking impact isn't into rock or frozen earth, but sea ice. It shatters the windshields and freezing seawater floods in, submerging us in darkness until the Tupolev's buoyancy chambers pop us up again into the half-light like a battered aluminium cork, the wind slewing us around to face shore.

I gasp for air from the shock of the cold and see that Kat's doubled over, head between her knees. I grab her hand, but she coughs out seawater and manages to say, 'I'm okay, I'm okay.'

Behind us, the engine stutters and fails, the props subsiding into stillness. Around us, the storm still roars, and with the windows gone, gale-driven ice hammers into our faces, needle-sharp and blinding. I shield my eyes enough to see the remaining Russian snowmobiles circling down to the shore from the hills above, avoiding the sheer drop we found.

We're still alive, but the situation is dire. We're soaked and chilled, there's a foot of water in the Tupolev, and with the wind ripping through the cabin it won't be long before we're hypothermic. We're an easy target now, turned so the Tupolev's engine no longer protects us.

A hundred yards away, the snowmobiles converge. The squad confer with their leader, then start unslinging weapons.

'Try to keep them back,' I yell to Kat, as I try to restart the engine.

Kat fumbles with the shotgun, scooping up shells that spilled out from the box into the footwell seawater. Her hands are so cold she can barely get them into the magazine tube, but somehow she manages. She pokes the shotgun through the remnants of the windshield and fires, sending the Russians scrambling for cover.

I hit the starter. The engine turns, coughs, but doesn't fire. It's designed to operate in cold regions where batteries would fail, so it's started by compressed air from a tank instead. I have no idea how many attempts we have until it's empty, or if the engine is even capable of running, but it's our only chance.

On shore, the Russians return fire, using sleds as cover. We huddle behind the instrument panel as Kat reloads, and I try again. This time the engine catches, but then coughs, and stops. I can tell the pressure in the tank is getting low.

Kat fishes around in the icy footwell water for more ammunition, comes up short.

'Four shells. If there are more, my hands are so numb I can't feel them.'

'Do your best. Make them count.'

For a moment, our hands grip together. Then she rises up again. The shore is further away now – the wind is pushing us out to sea. As she fires, I hit the starter. Again, it catches, then subsides.

Kat sinks again as the Russians return fire. But I was right: the wind is drifting us out of range. Onshore, the GRU commander realises he's losing the initiative. He yells at one of his men, who mounts his snowmobile, circles back, then throttles up to full power. He roars across the snowy shore, then into the sea, skimming across the surface, using the snowmobile as a Sea-Doo. He raises his gun to fire, but Kat looses off a round, and he curls away back to shore.

Emboldened, two more of the Russians crank their snowmobiles back and round, then full throttle across the frigid water towards us. Kat fires again, one-kerchunk-two, and they wheel away, but this time both manage shots that ding into the hull.

Kat collapses back into the seat. 'That's it. I'm out of ammo.'

Onshore, four of the Russians circle back and make a run for the sea ice. They've got the hang of it now, backing up as far as they can, using the slope that feeds down to the shore as a ramp to give them speed, then standing and leaning back on the snowmobiles as they auger into the slush, keeping the noses up in a kind of snowmobile wheelie.

They're heading towards us and there's nothing to stop them.

120

I try the engine one more time. There's barely any pressure left in the pneumatic starter, and the props turn sluggishly, with just the odd cough and stutter. Two of the oncoming riders open fire. One-handed, and trying not to sink into the freezing water, their aim is poor, but slugs thud and chink into the metal hull. Kat drops into the footwell, and I make myself small, holding the starter button down this time instead of trying to conserve pressure, using the last drop of air in the compression tank.

That must have been what was missing, because the engine coughs into life, maybe of the eight cylinders. But the prop blast is enough for the rudders to steer, so I swivel the Tupolev round, feathering the throttle to keep the pistons firing. Then the next cylinder catches, and the next, and suddenly the big rotary engine spools up. I thin out the mixture, and the Aero-sledge surges away from shore and into the blizzard, blasting a rooster tail of ice and salt spray at the quartet behind us. One of them loses momentum and founders, his snowmobile sinking. Another turns to help him, but loses speed and starts to sink too. The third arcs round, abandoning the chase and retreats to the shore.

The fourth pursues us, emptying his magazine, but finally realises it's a lost cause, and turns back as well, his shape dissolving into the fog layer that clings to the ice.

We're free of the GRU, but we're in a bad way. The shore is now lost in the freezing mist, the wind's blasting through the wrecked windshield, and the swell is getting heavier as the water deepens. I try to ease off the throttle, but the Tupolev isn't built for anything but flat water, and if I don't keep the nose up we'll be swamped or capsize. Our soaked clothes are literally freezing, ice crystals growing on seams and folds as the fabric stiffens into boards. My feet are numb from sitting in the water, and the Tupolev is starting to list. I'm guessing the impact into the ice took out a buoyancy compartment, or the gunfire, or both.

'What are we going to do?' asks Kat. She's almost blue, shuddering with cold, arms wrapped around her knees to lift her feet out of the water.

'We can't go back to shore,' I say. 'They can't see us, but they can hear us. There's still three of four of them, they've probably called for backup, and we're defenceless. We can't stay still, because they know our rough position, and they've probably called for a boat. We have to try to make it to Longyearbyen somehow.'

Kat stares at the storm still swirling around us. 'How do you know which direction?'

I reach into my suit, pull out the phone, thumb to Google Maps, hand it to her.

'GPS working?'

'Looks like it, but no cell service.'

'I cached a map before we left. Can you see Longyearbyen?'

Kat zooms out using her frozen fingers. 'Yeah.'

'Can you figure out a bearing?'

'I think so,' says Kat.

'You need to be quick. The battery says thirty per cent, but in this cold it's going to die in minutes, if that.'

'Okay,' says Kat. 'We're heading north-west. We need to be going east.'

I steer round.

'A bit more. More. Okay, too much. There. That's our bearing.'

She clicks the phone off to save battery, resumes her position, face tucked into her knees.

We cruise in silence for fifteen minutes, my forearm shielding my face against the snow and spray. Behind us, the engine is starting to misfire. First one cylinder, then another. I work the mixture, trying to keep it running as evenly as I can.

Kat looks up at the misfires, face full of concern.

'It's okay,' I tell her. 'Just try to keep yourself small, and don't go to sleep. We should be there in an hour, two max.'

She drops her head back into her knees.

The problem is, I'm lying.

Even though we have a bearing, and even though I'm trying to correct for the wind knocking us sideways, we're fucked. If we're not capsized by the heaving sea, and the engine holds out, and we don't run out of fuel, and we don't succumb to hypothermia before we get there, we still have almost no chance of locating Longyearbyen in what's now a thick sea fog. The phone will be long dead before we get there, and finding the port by dead reckoning in near-darkness and zero-visibility isn't like trying to find a needle in a haystack. It's trying to find a pebble on the moon.

I'm still wondering how to summon the courage to tell her when it happens.

A massive, deafening foghorn blast splits the air.

And if it sounds like it's just yards away, it's because it is.

Out of the fog bursts the bow of a ship, headed directly towards us. It's moving fast, twenty or thirty knots. There's no time for us to do anything. It slams into us, rolling us over and driving us down under its keel and into the inky, icy blackness of the ocean.

121

We tumble in the darkness, the giant keel tumbling us over and over and over in the freezing water. Completely blind, all I can hear is the roar of the propellor and the grinding and clanking of the Tupolev's bodywork on the ship's hull. I grab the yoke and fumble for Kat with my free hand, but I can't find her. The prop noise rises to a climax as the stern closes on us, then the ship's propellor tear into the bottom of the Tupolev, flipping us again, and spewing us out into the wake.

As the rumble of the props recedes, I claw to the surface and take a massive gulp of air. The stern of the ship – some kind of trawler, with no lights showing – is already disappearing into the fog. I look around for Kat, but she's nowhere to be seen.

Then I look down.

The lights of the Tupolev are still working somehow. It's sinking, nose up as the weight of the great rotary engine drags it down, overwhelming the wrecked buoyancy chambers.

And I realise: *Kat's still in there.*

I suck in a massive breath and dive into the blackness, kicking down towards the lights. In the ambient seawater glow, I can make out the cockpit of the Tupolev and a shape that must be her. I pull myself in through the smashed windshield. She's trapped, one arm jammed under a gull-wing door.

I try to pull her free, but the door is stuck, crumpled by the impact. My lungs are ready to explode, my muscles weakened by the cold. I swivel my hips to bring my legs to the seat, hook my hands under the lip of the door either side of Kat's arm and use the power of my thighs and back to try to ease it up. At first there's nothing, but then I feel it give an inch, and Kat's arm slides loose.

I hook my arms under Kat's, pull her back out through the windshield and haul her to the surface with me, the lights of the Tupolev disappearing into the oblivion below. We burst out together, and I take another enormous lungful of air. But Kat doesn't.

She isn't breathing.

Treading water, I knot my hands together over her sternum, and start compressing, hard, twice a second. Over and over and over I squeeze, legs kicking to keep us both afloat. But I've lost all feeling now from the cold. I'm exhausted, spent, nothing left. And what's the point, anyway? There's no sign of the trawler. Even if I can bring Kat back to life, all that's left for us is to drown together. Maybe it's kinder to let her go, to let the world go on without us, to sink back into the embrace of the ocean together. My mind starts to drift until I'm barely aware that I'm still doing the compressions. And then suddenly she coughs and spews up a lungful of water, then another. She gasps for air, alive.

'It's okay, I've got you,' I pant. 'Breathe. Just breathe.'

A moment later, out of the fog, lights appear. It's the trawler, circling back, engines now throttled down, a fisherman in a red immersion suit using a million-candlepower searchlight to scan the surface. But before they can find us, I sink into unconsciousness.

122

Kat and I glide downwards through the water, warm, my arms around her. Around us, the ocean fills with light and she turns to me, green eyes wide open and sparkling, hair floating round her like seaweed. She kisses me, and we dissolve into each other, deeper and deeper. For a moment, it's as if we're one person, or two people who had gotten mixed up in each other like the silvery shoals of fish that merge around us, glinting in shafts of sunlight that spear down from above. And I suddenly feel a deep peace, a calm that I've never experienced before. It's as if I've been made whole, as if all the wounds that life had ever dealt me, all the way back to the motel room in Stockton, and maybe even before, have been healed.

And I think to myself: *so this is what it means to be happy.*

But then Kat slips out of my arms. Whether she pushes me away, or I lose my grip, I can't tell, but when I reach for her, my hand closes on seawater. She floats up towards the surface, a mermaid haloed with light, but I sink down, down, down into blackness. And now I'm cold again, freezing, but simultaneously racked with brutal pain as if my limbs were being roasted over an open fire. I try to scream but find myself coughing, struggling against unknown hands holding me down.

And then I'm not underwater any more, but on a table, staring into a fluorescent light fixture in some kind of industrial room, and a man is leaning over me, checking my pupils.

'Who the fuck are you?' I manage to splutter out.

'Sigrid Olafsson,' says the man. 'And you?'

His English is good, the consonants soft and Icelandic.

'Jones,' I lie.

'Is that your first or last name?'

'Yes.'

'What year is it?'

'It's twenty fuck you.'

'Okay. Let him go,' says Sigrid.

The burly, bearded men who have been holding me down let go. Sigrid nods at them to leave. I struggle to sit up and find I'm wearing only a red blanket. I pull it around me. I look around and realise I'm in the trawler's mess room, the dining table serving as a hospital bed.

'We pulled you out of the water two hours ago,' says Sigrid. 'You were hypothermic. Your core temperature was down to thirty degrees. Eighty-five in American. You're lucky to be alive. We had to warm you up in the shower. You'd breathed in a lot of seawater too. When you finally came round, you started having fits. I had to get the deck hands to hold you down. Here.'

He throws me clothes that aren't mine. Work pants, T-shirt, thick sweater. I pull them on.

'You're the medic, what?'

He laughs. 'On a boat this size? No. I'm the captain. But hypothermia's an occupational hazard. We know how to deal with it better than the doctors.'

He hands me a mug.

'Coffee. Lots of sugar.'

I take it. Then it hits me. Panicked: 'What about the girl? Did you pull a girl out as well?'

'Kat? Yes, she's fine. She's in my quarters. She's tough, yes?'

'She was under for a while,' I say. 'She wasn't breathing.'

Sigrid nods. 'If it wasn't for the cold, she could have had brain damage. But freezing water does strange things. People get pulled out after half an hour under, more even, and they're fine. Children, small-boned people. They chill fast and warm up fast.'

I suck down the sweet coffee, feeling myself become human again.

'And now,' he says, 'do you want to tell me what the fuck you were doing in a Russian tin can floating in the fjord in the middle of a storm?'

'Not particularly,' I say.

'We have to land you somewhere, you understand, and report you to the authorities. A collision at sea, there are rules we have to follow.'

This is maybe the last thing I need.

'Sigrid, right? So, this boat's Icelandic? Out of, where, Reykjavik?'

'Sure. So what?'

'You were running at night, in fog, without your main lights. Which suggests to me you were trying not to be seen. Which probably also means your transponder was switched off. Which tells me you were fishing in Norwegian waters illegally.'

Sigrid laughs. 'I can assure you Icelandic boats are permitted to fish in the Svalbard Zone.'

'So are the Europeans and the Greenlanders. But only four at a time, total, right? What's the betting you were number five, sneaking in under cover of the storm to poach a few cod.'

'Shrimp,' says Sigrid, and he looks like he just tasted a bad one.

'What would the fine for that be? Or do they just confiscate the boat?'

He doesn't grace me with a reply.

'Look. Here's what I propose. You return to Reykjavik with your catch. We walk off as part of your crew. As far as anyone else is concerned, none of this ever happened. Kat and I drowned. You were nowhere near Svalbard when you made your weight.'

'Or I could just throw you back, you ungrateful little fuck, and the girl as well,' says Sigrid. 'That way, I save myself a whole lot of trouble. You think I had to turn back to pick you up?'

Something tells me he isn't bluffing.

'Okay,' I say. 'Let's say I match the value of the catch. Every man on board goes home with twice what they were expecting.'

'How do I know you won't cheat me? You walk off the boat, I never see you again?'

'Once we're in Reykjavik, there'll be cell service. I'll do the transfer in Bitcoin onboard. No taxes, nothing. It's up to you what you tell the crew, how much you give them, how much you keep for yourself. You only let us off the boat if I come through.'

Sigrid strokes his beard. Finally: 'Deal.'

I stand. My legs are shaky. 'Can I see her? The girl?'

123

On the way to Sigrid's cabin, I ask about my clothes. He takes me to the ship's engine room, where they're drying. I check my pockets for the Ziploc, but it's gone. I have a sudden horrible vision of my only piece of leverage falling out as I struggled to rescue Kat, disappearing into the blackness just as I dreamed I did. But then, over the hammer of the ship's engines, Sigrid says: 'This what you're looking for?' and I turn to see him holding it up.

I hold out my hand, but he doesn't give it to me.

'Something tells me whatever we make by landing you in Reykjavik is nothing compared to what this could be worth.'

Behind him, a heavy-set engineer watches. He can't hear what we're saying over the clatter of the diesels, but he senses a problem, and in his hand is a monkey wrench as long as my forearm.

'You have a family?' I ask.

'Sure.'

'Sons? Daughters?'

'One of each.'

'You care about them?'

'Of course I care about them.'

I nod. 'You're right. It's worth more. To the right person, that is. But to the wrong person? It's worth your life, mine, the life of everyone on this boat, and everyone you've ever cared about, including your son and your daughter. So unless you feel real confident about knowing which is which, my advice to you is give me the fucking bag.'

'Or maybe I should just throw it overboard.'

'Sure,' I say. 'And then you can explain to the crew how you cheated them out of their share of what I was planning to pay you. I'm sure they'll understand.'

Sigrid glances round. The engineer glares, wrench in hand.

'Everything all right, boss?' he yells over the din of the mechanicals.

'Sure,' says Sigrid. 'Everything's fine.'

He hands me the Ziploc.

'One more thing,' I say. 'I'm gonna need a satellite phone.'

124

Sigrid's quarters are barely less squalid than the crew's mess, but at least he has a proper cot and a desk with an ancient Dell, maps and charts pinned up on the wall alongside outdated tables of allowable sizes for shrimp.

Kat sits on the bed in men's clothes that hang oddly on her. She looks pale, hands still cupped around a mug that probably went cold half an hour ago.

'Can we—?' I say, indicating the door.

Sigrid gives me a sour look, then exits.

Kat stares at me in silence as I count to thirty for Sigrid to get clear.

'How are you?'

She shrugs, but I can tell something's wrong.

'Want to talk about it?'

'Want to tell me what happened?'

'We got run over by a ship. Boat. Whatever the fuck this thing is. Shrimp trawler.'

'I know that,' she says. 'I mean afterwards.'

'The Tupolev sank.'

'To *me*,' she says.

There's something haunting in the way her green eyes lock on mine.

'You went down with it. Your arm was trapped under one of the doors.'

'How did I get out?'

'I pulled you out.'

'Was I breathing?'

'You were underwater.'

'Just answer the fucking question, will you? *Was I breathing?*'

'No.'

'Had my heart stopped?'

'I don't know. Maybe. When I got you to the surface, I gave you chest compressions, best I could. That's when you started breathing again.'

She rests her chin on the cold coffee cup, wrapped up in some thought I can't decode.

'What's this all about, Kat? Did you see something? While you were – I mean, lights. An out-of-body experience? What? What's got you so fucked up?'

I'm just considering telling her about my own hallucination, sinking with her into the light, then seeing her ripped away, when she looks up.

'Nothing. It's nothing. It's just dumb. So you saved my life?'

'I've lost too many people because of things I've done. I wasn't going to lose you.'

She smiles a little ruefully. 'I guess this means we're even.'

'We're not done yet.'

Her smile fades. 'So what now?'

There's a knock on the door.

It's Sigrid, with an Iridium satellite phone.

I take it, but Sigrid doesn't leave.

'This is my boat,' he says. 'I need to know what's going on.'

'I refer you to our previous conversation. The less you know, the better. For everyone.'

He grunts, but then he turns and closes the door behind him.

I dial the number Hipkiss gave me.

125

Hipkiss is all business.

The deal is straightforward enough. She gives me the name of a city. There, I will deliver the card in person to Hipkiss's representative, who will validate it using an MD5 hash, a digital fingerprint of the file itself that guarantees it is what it says it is. If the hash matches, Mireille will be released to a third party of my choosing. I will take her place as a hostage, and the file's contents will be combined with half of the malware they already have.

If it all checks out, I will be released.

'I'm going to need proof of life,' I say.

'I have a video call open with the girl now. I can ask her anything you want.'

I think for a moment.

'Ask her the name of her sock monkey.'

The line is muted for a moment. When it comes back, Hipkiss tells me my name.

Mireille is still alive.

'One more thing,' says Hipkiss. 'A little bird in a three-letter agency tells me you turned up in, where was it, Svalbard? Now there's chatter about a GRU operation up there. An amphibious vehicle, some kind of pursuit. I take it that was you.'

'What if it was?'

'The reports are that there were *two* passengers on board. One was the girl, yes? From Brooklyn?'

There's an edge to her voice, the first time her business-mask has slipped.

'Maybe.'

'Is she still with you?'

I glance over at Kat. 'No.'

Kat frowns. *What?*

'So where is she?' snaps Hipkiss. 'I don't like loose ends.'

'We were T-boned by a trawler. I was almost dead by the time they picked me out of the water. They didn't find her. Maybe she was chopped up by the prop, maybe she went down with the Tupolev, or maybe they just couldn't find her in the dark and the fog. Either way, she's gone.'

There's a momentary silence on the other end. Then Hipkiss's voice comes again.

'Was she important to you? A lover, perhaps?'

That creepy huskiness is back in her voice again.

'Once upon a time,' I say.

'I'm sorry for your loss,' says Hipkiss.

'You don't have to be,' I say, with a glance at Kat. 'She'd outlived her usefulness.'

126

Kat knows I'm lying. It still doesn't make her happy, but she manages to swallow it.

'So? You make the deal, right? It's your daughter's life.'

I hold up the Ziploc. 'If I hand over the power to start a nuclear war to a woman like Hipkiss, what kind of a world is Mireille going to be living in?'

'Hipkiss will just sell it on to the highest bidder, won't she?'

'She's a billionaire. She doesn't need money. The way she's going after Deep Threat, this is about something more. I don't think she's rational. Handing it to her . . . Jesus, I can't even imagine what that would mean. Or what she wants to do with it.'

'It's a binary choice,' says Kat. 'Heads or tails. You have to do one or the other.'

I'm silent for a good five minutes, thinking, trying to grab the ragged ends of the problem and stitch them together. *There has to be a way.* And then it comes to me. I look up.

'What if it *isn't* a binary choice?'

'Don't get it,' says Kat.

'When you flip a coin, what are the possibilities?'

'Fifty, fifty. I'm always wrong, by the way.'

'What if it lands on its edge?'

'What are the chances?'

'Of landing a coin on its edge? About one in six thousand.'

Kat considers this. 'What are you saying?'

'Maybe there's a way to square the circle. Free Mireille *and* neutralise Deep Threat. We flip the coin, and if everything goes just right, we land it on its edge.'

'And if we don't?'

'Chances are neither of us makes it out alive.'

Kat's silent. It's an odd silence, like some gorilla of emotion has wrapped her in its fist. She turns away, pretending to study one of the fishing charts. And she's the hardest person to read I ever met, but it doesn't take a psychic to know what she's thinking.

'It's OK. I get it. There is no "us". This isn't your fight. You almost died back there, and we'd both be dead now if you hadn't shot up the GRU. I had no right to ask anything else of you. I'm lucky you came this far. I can do this next part alone.'

'No,' says Kat, turning back. 'You don't understand. I didn't tell you the truth.'

'The truth? About what?'

'Being dead. I said it was nothing. But it wasn't nothing.'

'What do you mean?'

She takes a deep breath.

'I was underwater. But I wasn't in the Tupolev. It was . . . deep, like the Mariana Trench or something. And it wasn't dark, it was light, and warm, and there was sunlight streaming down past us.'

I fight the oddest feeling I've ever felt.

'Past *us*?'

She nods. 'You had your arms around me and I had mine around you and we were just floating there together. And then—'

She stops.

'And then what?'

Kat hesitates, then stands up and walks over to me. She takes my face in both hands and kisses me on the mouth.

A long, good kiss. Maybe the best kiss I've ever had since one that tasted of pepper and honey and blood.

Or maybe just the best I've ever had.

Then she lets go and steps back.

'It was like we were one person, like we'd gotten tangled up in each other like seaweed. Like I couldn't tell where you ended and I began.'

She smiles, but then her face changes. 'Then you were ripped away from me. And I was going up to the surface, and you were going down, and I knew I was never going to see you again. And it was like a part of me had gone, and I was never going to get it back.'

She turns back. She isn't crying, but it takes everything she's got.

'I know, I know, it all sounds fucking stupid,' she says. 'I mean, I was hypoxic, my brain was making shit up. But I was *dying*. I was *dead*. It has to mean something.'

And I almost don't tell her, because it sounds so crazy, but I know that if I don't there may never be another moment like it. So I say:

'I had the same dream.'

She stares at me.

'Don't say that. Do not fuck with me. This is too important to be fucking with me.'

'Everything you saw, I saw. Everything you felt, I felt.'

'No', she says. 'It makes no sense. It's not even possible. It's a coincidence.'

'I don't believe in coincidences'.

'Neither do I', says Kat.

We stand there in silence for a moment. And neither of us says anything, because neither of us has to. Then she puts her hand on my chest, over my heart, as if to feel it beat.

'But your plan, if you try to do it alone . . . it only ends one way, right?'

'If it's between me and Mireille, she's the one who gets to live.'

Kat shakes her head. 'All I can think about is how I felt when you were ripped away from me. I never want to feel that again.'

'Meaning?'

'This thing, this you and me, this *us*, whatever the fuck it is, whatever it takes . . . from now on we follow it to the end, okay? To the very end.'

'To the very end, I say.

And then I kiss her again.

PART NINE

127

I disembark alone, wearing a deck hand's clothes. Sigrid watches me go from the bridge of the trawler, tens of thousands of dollars richer. Once clear of the docks, I make my way into central Reykjavik, where I begin a three-hour dry-cleaning run to shake any potential tail, starting at the massive mid-century cathedral that towers above the city and ending at the Penis Museum. There, I stare in awe at the genitalia of walruses, bulls, the entire Icelandic handball team, an elf, a sperm whale and, I kid you not, the Invisible Man.

From there, I make my way to Laugardalslaug, the geothermal swimming complex where all of Iceland seems to congregate on holiday weekends. Amid the smell of chlorine and Icelandic grannies padding past me, I retrieve a backpack I left three years ago on a mission, the kind of opportunistic cache that has gotten me out of more tight situations than I can remember.

In it is a change of clothes, an American passport in a fresh name, cash in dollars, a credit card, a burner phone and a bag of toiletries. There's no weapon, nothing to suggest that it's anything but luggage dropped by an American tourist. In the changing rooms, I swap not just my clothes but my hair, using bleach powder and peroxide from the toiletry bag.

Back in town, I buy two expensive suitcases, the clothes to fill them, and change into business attire. I take a limo to the airport at Keflavik. From there, I'm ticketed all the way through in business class. A Finnair A320 to Heathrow, a British Airways 380 to Miami, and from there an American Airways 787.

Thirty hours later, I'm in the back seat of an Uber Premium driven by a garrulous middle-aged woman named, inevitably, Eva, watching the gated communities of Ezeiza Partido scroll by through the smoked glass, headed directly towards the jaws of the trap that awaits me.

128

I check into an apartment hotel in Buenos Aires' renovated docks area, a dazzling waterfront full of swing-for-the-fences modern architecture and wealthy young Argentinians. The hotel is independent, low-key and relatively private, unlike the swanky affairs that cluster around Dock 1, but more importantly the balcony gives me a panoramic view of the Rio de la Plata, from the container port to the north to the sprawling nature reserve to the south.

Through a pair of binoculars I bought in Duty-Free, I inventory the inner harbour. I count three Argentinian naval vessels, two massive cruise liners, a square-rigged three-masted sailing ship, numerous tugs and pilot boats, a couple of maxi-yachts – the kind of thing you settle for when you can't afford an actual megayacht – and an orange-painted Arctic exploration vessel, presumably bound for the South Atlantic.

None of these interests me at all, so I wait. In three days' time, I'm to call the same number as before, and I'll be given a time, place and further instructions. If all goes well, Mireille will be released and I will be taken prisoner.

I have no particular expectations that I will survive.

But between now and then a lot of things can happen.

A day later, with the southern hemisphere's spring sun glinting off its polished steel sides, *La Belle Dame Sans Merci II* slides into the outer harbour. Its predecessor, the vessel I met Hipkiss on, was an ageing run-of-the-mill superyacht, now decommissioned and sold for scrap. The replacement is something else. One of the most expensive megayachts ever built, it's intended to resemble a weapon of war, as if a nuclear warhead had been designed by Philippe Starck. In reality, its four hundred feet of gleaming stainless steel make it look like nothing more than a gigantic seagoing dildo.

The new *Belle Dame* has, it's rumoured, anti-paparazzi shields, underwater threat detection, an impregnable citadel in its bowels, a missile defence system and a deployable mini-submersible. It has supplies to stay at sea for months, and the ability to ice-break its way into and out of the Arctic. A second boat follows in its wake, a mini-me supply tender – *La Jolie Fille Sans Merci* – featuring a helo deck on which sits a military-spec Bell 525 helicopter.

With all its defences and a heavily armed security team headed by Harkonnen, a one-man assault on the yacht would be both suicidal and pointless. Hipkiss is far too smart to have Mireille on board: a single call to the Argentinian authorities alleging human trafficking could end with the megayacht impounded, a search team on board, and the beginnings of a gruesome international incident. Mireille, I'm sure, is being held in a remote location by a separate team. Until she's free, I have no choice but to play ball, or at least appear to.

La Belle Dame doesn't berth, anchoring off-shore while the tender heads to the quay for supplies. A couple of hours later, it heads back, and through the binoculars I watch a smaller tender, a butt-plug to the megayacht's dildo, emerge from automated sea doors at the rear and head to the support boat. A male figure in black climbs aboard and heads to the helicopter. It's Edgar Staley, ten years greyer and ten years heavier, but otherwise much the same. The Bell lifts off, wheels round, inclines towards downtown Buenos Aires, then disappears behind the residential towers that line the waterfront.

I pull up a flight-tracking website on my phone, zoomed into the harbour and downtown core, showing real-time positions of all air traffic. I filter it to rotary craft. Most show tail markings, but one's simply a blob, vectoring out from the harbour in a cloak of anonymity. Over the next twelve minutes, I watch it track across Buenos Aires, past suburbs and low-rise distribution centres and rail terminals, to the liminal region where the city fades into countryside.

There, it begins to circle. The altitude drops, and then it disappears from the tracker, which means the transponder was turned off.

When I pull up Google Maps' satellite view, there's nothing but an empty field.

129

For reasons nobody can quite put their finger on, Argentina has produced some of the best hackers in the world. The overt sign of this is the annual Ekoparty Security Conference, an international gathering of black- and white-hat code-monkeys and cyberpunks who swarm into Buenos Aires to take part in hacking competitions, announce new hardware and software exploits, or be recruited by the world's leading security companies and intelligence agencies.

All of this takes place amid a wild party atmosphere including bars, nightclub areas and even a dating service for nerds who want to hook up. But Ekoparty is serious business. If you want to sell your malware to the highest bidder, this is the place to do it. None of this takes place in the official venues, but in hotel rooms, private suites and – now we get to the point – Starckian dildos moored in the River of Silver. Hipkiss's choice of the city is no coincidence: *La Belle Dame* is here on business, so Staley can hoover up zero-days, or broker deals between malware authors and nation-state intelligence agencies.

The nerve centre of Ekoparty is the Ciudad Cultural Konex, a former industrial building in the hip Balvanera district. A stolen pass identifies me as a PhD candidate from the Universidad de la República in Uruguay and gets me inside. The place is vast and dark, a quarter of a city block, with multiple auditoriums and breakout rooms. Throngs of young people crowd around laptops, monitors and Arduino boards. Almost everyone is in jeans and T-shirts, but there are a couple of girls in anime cosplay with bobbed blue hair and sailor suits, and even a couple of furries.

It's mid-afternoon, practically the early hours of the morning for this crowd, but a team of refugees from Kyiv are planning to announce a vulnerability in Apple's end-point authentication later. An exploit built off this could be worth seven figures, making it the biggest draw of the entire conference.

This year there are more than three thousand registered participants and, if I'm right, most of them are already in this building. But I'm looking for just one. I don't know their name, their sex, their age, their nationality or anything else about them apart from the screen name Vilmos told me: Raevan. Most likely, given how protective hackers are of their identities, few people here know who they are either, and asking around is going to out me as a spook or journalist, both deeply *persona non grata*.

But Raevan was close to Gracious's brother. Given the sophistication of the malware he developed and the hermetic closeness of the hacking community, they're probably also highly skilled. Which means there's a possibility they're not simply an attendee but a presenter.

I go through the programme to check the names. There are papers on avoiding law enforcement, bug bounties, physical penetration testing of facilities, hardware hacking, cyber-finance, lock picking, radio experimentation, telecoms, mobile hacking, and more, but nothing leaps out. I wander the floor until my feet ache, trying to read faces and will the needle out of the haystack. I'm about to give up hope when a man in a Disco Elysium T-shirt pushes something into my hand.

It's a flyer, listing unofficial presentations that either didn't make it through the Ekoparty committee's screening process or chose to keep a lower profile. A lot of it is abstruse or conspiratorial, but something catches my eye. The subject is *Implementation of a Turing-complete compiler in a Xerox copier using the state machine in a proprietary font format*. It's the world 'compiler' that jumps out at me, but then I read the name.

Dr Rachel van Werden.

Raevan.

130

The presentation is in a lecture theatre in the mathematics department, three and a half miles away, but it's about to end. I run out into the sunlight. Buenos Aires' traffic is at a stand-still. I could jack a scooter or bike, but the last thing I need is cop trouble, so instead I run.

I make it in twenty-two minutes, soaked with sweat and gasping for air. A puzzled co-ed points me to the lecture theatre where young people with Ekoparty passes are streaming away.

I push past them and through a swing door into the lecture theatre.

It's empty.

Fuck.

I head out into the corridor again. It's almost empty now, except for a knot of three people. I say people, but only two of them are actual people. The third figure is a tall blue fox with a bushy tail, holding a laptop. I move closer. The furry is explaining something about font formats.

'Rachel?' I say.

The fox turns to me.

'Can I help you?' she says. The soft consonants of a Dutch speaker.

'You're Raevan, right?'

I can't see her face, but I sense her anxiety spiking.

'I have no idea what you're talking about,' she says, and turns back to the boy and girl.

'Vilmos told me everything,' I say.

She stops again. 'Excuse me,' she says to the couple. 'A student problem. I need to deal with this.'

They nod, and head away together.

She turns back to me. 'Who the fuck are you?'

'Can we talk without the—'

I indicate her fox-head.

She looks around. 'Not here.'

131

Rachel's apartment is a converted loft, with few concessions to comfort but a wild variety of laptops, ancient PCs, and a DEC PDP-1 mini-computer that must be sixty years old. She reappears from the bathroom in jeans and a white T-shirt, hair wet, and hangs the fur-suit on a garment rail alongside several others. In her early fifties, out of the fur she has a kind of Gen X rock star chic, like Aimee Mann with a side of Patti Smith.

'It's OpSec, right? The fur-suit,' I say, as she makes us coffee.

'What makes you think that?'

I shrug. 'Makes you invisible to facial recognition, probably fucks up gait analysis too.'

She smiles. 'That's a bonus. For me, it's a way of escaping biology. Until I took the head off, you didn't know how old I was, whether I was beautiful or ugly, Black or white. It's operational security on a human level. We bleed information to each other through our faces and voices and bodies. This is a way of taking that back. And if people stare, so what? All they see is the suit.'

Then the smile fades. 'Now tell me who you are, and what the fuck you want.'

I tell her the whole story.

At the end, she says simply: 'How can I help?'

'Tell me about him. Marvellous.'

'He didn't call himself that here. I thought his name was Luis until I looked him up on the student database.'

'So he was your student?'

'Initially. But it was soon obvious that though he was self-taught, he knew more than I did, or anyone else in the faculty. So he dropped out. Which was when—'

She stops.

'I know what you're thinking. The older woman, a kid from Nigeria half her age. But he wasn't a kid. He was twenty-six, old enough to know what he was doing. And, I know it's a cliché, but he was an old soul, and not just the smartest, but the kindest person I ever met.'

'You loved him.'

She nods, fighting tears. 'And he loved me.'

'What was he like?'

'Here,' she says, finding a photograph. 'This is the one I gave to the police.'

The photograph shows a young man with a round face, smiling broadly into the camera. He's wearing a vintage Atari T-shirt that's a bit too small for him.

Rachel smiles sadly. 'That shirt . . . he'd had it since he was a kid. He refused to get rid of it or buy a bigger one.'

'His face looks a little puffy. Was that from steroids?'

She nods. 'He'd been in remission for years, but a few months ago the cancer came back. I tried to reassure him, but he was afraid he wouldn't beat it this time. I think that's why he worked so hard.'

'He felt he was running out of time?'

Rachel nods.

'So did you know what he was working on?'

'I showed him the Ken Thompson paper from '84, the Turing Award lecture on trusting trust, and it was like he saw the whole thing right there and then. From that point on, it was just a matter of finding the vulnerability and working out the details. I used to tease him by calling him Amadeus, because the code just flowed out of him the way music flowed out of Mozart. It never occurred to him how

336

dangerous it would turn out to be. When I tried to warn him, he called me Salieri. But I told him he shouldn't sell it, that he should publish it, get it out there so the world could defend itself.'

'Why didn't he? Greed?'

She shakes her head, amused. 'He had no interest in money, at least not for itself. That old T-shirt was the tip of the iceberg. I had to force him to buy new shoes once because he wore holes in the soles of the old ones.'

'What, then?'

'Family. He'd seen them murdered. All he had left was his sister, and her child. She'd saved his life by sacrificing her own future, becoming a child soldier, pretending to be a man, and he had this dream of saving her, of being reunited, and making sure her daughter didn't have the kind of life they'd both had. *That* was what the money was for. The way he talked about it was, that he'd found this thing, like a man stumbling over a diamond in the dirt, and he wasn't going to give it away. He said it was Mireille's inheritance.'

'You didn't think about having kids yourself?'

'He wanted it more than anything. At my age, it would have taken IVF, maybe for years, and the risks would have been huge. But when we got tested, it was he who was infertile. The cancer treatment, they said, probably. After that, all he ever talked about was Gracious and Mireille. Let me show you something.'

She leads me over to a chest of drawers and opens one up.

It's filled with a girl's clothing, all new, neatly folded.

'The plan was for them to come and live with us,' says Rachel, lifting out a T-shirt, then gently folding it and putting it back. 'Every time he went out he'd come back with clothes for her. I used to tell him, by the time she gets here she'll have grown out of them, but it went in one ear and out the other.'

She closes the drawer, gently and sadly.

'Do you know what happened to him? Vilmos said you only found blood.'

Her face crumples a little. 'They found a body in the river a few days ago. The head and hands had been cut off to make identification harder. It had been stuffed into a suitcase with bricks to make it sink, but it came open, and he floated up.'

'You identified him?'

She nods, touches her side. 'He had a scar in his side where they'd put a stent in at one point. It was him. The police said it was probably some gang thing. But I knew it wasn't.'

She stops to think. 'You really think it was these people?'

I nod. 'Most likely it was Harkonnen. He's a bastard. A killer.'

'Are you? A killer?'

'Only when necessary.'

She nods.

'So what is it you want me to do?'

132

Rachel listens, but at the end she shakes her head.

'You don't understand. I'm not a hacker. I'm an academic. The stuff I do, it's theoretical. I wouldn't know where to begin.'

'But you know people,' I say. 'The hacker world, it's a community. You walk into Ekoparty, you can feel it. If they found out that one of their own had been murdered, they might help take revenge. But the suggestion would have to come from someone they trust.'

'They already know,' she says. 'Some of them. That he was murdered, and why. Just not by who.'

'And?'

'Everyone's paranoid they'll be next. They're kids, most of them. The nearest they've ever got to actual violence is playing video games. Some are from the street, but they're the ones who got out, not the ones who fought with the cops or ran round with gangs. Most of them have never seen blood, never been in a fight. So, yes, they're angry. But they're more scared than angry. I don't know what I could tell them.'

'Tell them if they help me, they'll have their revenge,' I say. 'Once the world sees what it looks like, no-one will ever dare to come after them again. And if it all goes wrong, I'll be the one who's blamed, not them.'

'I don't know if that's enough.'

'So tell them about Deep Threat. If anyone can understand what it would mean for the world, it's them.'

She nods. 'Okay.'

'There's just one other thing,' I say.

'What's that?'

'We only have three days.'

And that's when she smiles, a wry crooked smile that makes me instantly understand why a kid like Marvellous would fall for a fifty-something woman in a fur-suit.

'Three days? That makes it easier, not harder.'

'How come?'

'Because it makes it a game. And they always win.'

133

Every day since I arrived, I leave the apartment at 10 a.m. and make my way to the brutalist Museo de Arte Latinoamericano. I spend an hour in the cafeteria drinking coffee and reading *La Nación*, pay my bill and leave.

Finally, the day after *La Belle Dame* glides into port, a woman I don't recognise slips into the seat opposite me. She has striking, shoulder-length copper-red hair and bright red lipstick. She's carrying boutiquey paper bags from three of the most expensive clothing stores in Buenos Aires and wearing the kind of polka-dot sundress you imagine clinging to Audrey Hepburn. Her nails are manicured, and when she finally removes her Dua Lipa shades, her eyes are sapphire blue.

It takes me a moment to find my voice.

'Holy shit,' is what I say eventually.

'Security-by-being-totally-fucking-out-there,' says Kat, with a smile. 'You're right. It works.'

134

Sitting there in the sunlight of the terrace, she fills me in. I left her on the trawler in Reykjavik. A day later, Sigrid landed her on a deserted beach on the Scottish island of Orkney. She hiked the ten miles to Orkney's tiny capital, Stromness, and took a windswept ferry to Thurso, on the northern tip of Scotland. A bone-jarring series of train journeys took her to Edinburgh, then Manchester. There she caught a flight to Montreal under her own identity, trusting correctly that if Pybus had flagged her to CIA, they would not have shared the information with the British or Canadians.

In Montreal she rented a car and crossed back into upstate Vermont at one of those mom-and-pop crossings where they barely check passports if the face is friendly and white. From there, she drove to Chicago, where The Dentist provided her with a new passport and credit cards. She used the twenty-four-hour delay to figure out a new persona ('trust fund Barbie with an edge') and enlisted the help of a personal shopper at Neiman Marcus to execute it. From Chicago, a flight to Dallas and a connection to Buenos Aires.

And I guess I should have lost the ability to be surprised by Kat long ago, but now here she is, transformed so completely into somebody else that I'm not sure even I would have recognised her if she hadn't sat down at my table.

'You look—' I say, but that's as far as I get because I am genuinely lost for words.

'I know,' she says. 'Don't get used to it. Are they here?'

I nod. 'Came in yesterday, currently at anchor. Helo departed yesterday around 1830. I tracked the flight, but where it landed . . . it's weird, there's nothing. Nothing on Google satellite, at least.'

'Sonny boy on board?'

I nod. 'Made the return leg four hours later.'

'There has to be something there,' says Kat.

I nod. 'Let's find out.'

135

We buzz out across Buenos Aires on a rented scooter, sunlight streaming through the jacaranda trees that line the boulevards, like any other pair of young lovers. Kat rides pillion, arms tight around me, red hair in a headscarf. Eventually, the suburbs thin out to farmland, and the route Google has mapped out for us takes us down a dirt road lined with rotting barns, signs announcing land for sale, and the odd new build, the first signs of the city bleeding outwards.

Finally, we arrive at the spot where the helicopter transponder was turned off. At first, I think there's nothing – a screen of trees hiding whatever it is from view – but as we approach, the dirt road is deeply rutted from construction trucks turning, and a tall wrought-iron electric gate slides into view. I stop short, out of view of any security cameras, but close enough to see what lies beyond.

It's a vast McMansion, the grounds still being landscaped, but there's a broad swathe of half-dead turf laid to the left, and a drooping windsock. The house itself has a grand entrance with steps and colonnades, along with two wings, each an asymmetrical mess of gables and mismatched windows.

'That's why it wasn't on Google Maps,' I say. 'New construction. Satellite pics are three years old.'

'Is it what we hoped?'

'I think so. But you're the one who's going to have to find out.'

'When?'

'The exchange is in two days. You need to be on board by then, which means tomorrow night.'

'What if we don't have what we need by then?'

'Then we're fucked,' I say.

'If you exchange yourself for Mireille, they'll kill you.'

'I know.'

'I don't want you to die,' she says, and pulls her arms tighter around me.

And there's a part of me that wants to just ride away like that, the two of us, and disappear. Free Mireille, let Hipkiss have what she wants and damn the consequences. It's not our fault the world is fucked up: why should we be the ones to pay the price?

Except the world doesn't give a fuck what you or I or anybody else deserves. When the bill comes due, the universe doesn't ask if you can pay the vig. It just slips on the knuckle-dusters and gets to work.

I twist the throttle, and we wheel around, back towards the city.

136

I drop Kat three blocks from the Hilton, where she's booked a suite. I watch her walk away, head held high, and it strikes me: despite everything, she's enjoying this.

Back on my balcony, I watch *La Belle Dame* through the binoculars. Around 9 p.m., the same routine unfolds: the tender takes Edgar to the support vessel, the helicopter departs, and I track it on my phone to the same location as before. There, the transponder switches off. Last night, the flight tracker showed it returning around 2.30 a.m. Tonight, it's 3 a.m.

Half an hour later, I'm trying to sleep but thinking about Kat when my phone lights up and thrums by the bedside. I sit up. It's a message from Rachel, a single word: *come*.

A cab takes me through deserted night streets to her loft. When the rickety freight elevator opens, I'm greeted with an extraordinary sight. Thirty or more people are working on laptops, surrounded by routers, printers and networking equipment. Every tabletop and chair is occupied. A team of five are working on the bed, more in the kitchen, and a group of twelve or so cross-legged on the floor. Everywhere there are pizza boxes and cans of Red Bull, plus beer, wine and sushi.

Rachel's wearing the same clothes I left her in. It doesn't look like she slept, or anyone else.

'You were right,' she says. 'We had so many volunteers we had to turn people away. There are two other apartments working in parallel.'

'You found something already?'

She smiles and motions to a Chinese kid, short and sturdy, one of the group sitting on the floor. He gets up and heads over, laptop in one hand. He's maybe nineteen.

'This is Wen,' she says. 'Wen, this is—'

She stops, realising. 'I don't even know your name.'

'Seventeen.'

'That a screen name?' says Wen. His English is good, a tinge of California.

'Something like that. What do you have?'

Wen props the laptop on a kitchen counter, brings up a webpage.

'OK,' he says. 'Superyachts, megayachts, it's a huge business in terms of money. But it's a small world in terms of the numbers of yachts, and even smaller when you look at who builds them. When you get down to the subsystems – security, automation, access control, that's even more specialised. One company in particular does the hyper-high-end stuff. They design the software and hardware, install it, monitor it and maintain it. They're good. The systems are beyond military spec. Hardened, firewalled, encrypted, digital tripwires everywhere. Nothing we can hack in three days.'

'But?'

'These things are designed to be floating fortresses,' says Wen. 'To stay at sea for weeks if necessary. But what if a system goes down? You're an oligarch on a sanctions list, two weeks away from a port where you won't get arrested, and suddenly the automatic doors don't function, or the alarm won't stop screaming. You have a tech on board, but they don't have the skills to fix it. So there *has* to be a way to do it remotely.'

'So even at sea, the guys who design and install the system still have access.'

'Right. They can log in remotely, patch software, change settings, and fix stuff.'

'So, what, you crack the password and—'

Wen looks at me as if I was a child. 'It's all on a VPN, encrypted, relayed via a private communication satellite. I told you, they're good. It never touches public infrastructure.'

'What, then?'

'We hacked into the control centre.'

'The security company?'

Wen nods. 'We had two zero-days on hand. Stuff they couldn't know about. Probably worth seven, eight figures on the open market, but fuck that. We chained them together, and that got us in.'

'And from there you have direct access to the yacht?'

Wen smiles like something's deeply funny.

'No,' he says. 'We have access to *all* the yachts.'

137

It's light by the time Kat arrives. By now, it's just Rachel, Wen and me: the rest of the team have been sent home, ostensibly to get some sleep, but mostly because we need complete privacy for what we're about to discuss.

'So, we have access to the yacht's CCTV,' says Kat. 'What else?'

'Main security systems,' says Wen. 'That means we can disable electronic door locks, trigger the fogging system . . .'

'What's that?'

'It pumps chemical fog into critical areas, like the VIP deck, the owner's suites and so on,' I say. 'It's meant to disorient hijackers, thieves, any kind of onboard physical threat, long enough for any high-value targets to make it to the citadel.'

'The citadel?'

'It's a safe room below decks. Armoured, lockable from the inside, and self-contained. Has its own power, air supply, food, everything. Also, some overrides of the yacht's systems.'

'Our exploit doesn't touch it,' says Wen. 'Once they're in there, we have no control or visibility.'

'Above the citadel is the crew deck, accommodation, kitchen, messes,' I say, pointing them out on the blueprints. 'Next is the guest deck. Above that are the two owner's suites. Those and the guest decks are VIP areas, fully access-controlled. The crew areas are more porous.'

'So,' says Rachel. 'You know our capabilities. You know the layout and how access is controlled. How about you tell us what the actual plan is?'

'Yeah,' I say. 'I was just coming to that.'

138

Kat knows the outline, but she listens intently as I explain the operational details to Rachel and Wen. In essence, it's simple enough. We have one half of Deep Threat and Hipkiss has the other. If we give her our half, she can combine them to reconstruct the malware. But if we can get hold of *her* half, we can do the same thing. And once we have our hands on Deep Threat, we can publish it, which means the vulnerabilities in the world's nuclear arsenals can be fixed.

Once that happens, Deep Threat is worthless, a relic. And the world is safe.

The broad strokes are simple. But the details are anything but, and I see Wen and Rachel swapping sceptical looks as I get into the weeds of it.

At the end, Rachel sits back and says, 'There's no way this can work.'

I look to Wen. 'It's technically feasible, yes?'

'Yes, but—'

'So what's the problem? Kat and I will be the ones taking the risks. Nobody else goes anywhere near the line of fire.'

'Maybe not,' says Rachel. 'But we're part of this, whether you like it or not. Marvellous is already dead. So is Gracious. If this goes to shit we're going to be looking over our shoulders for the rest of our lives. Maybe you two are used to that kind of thing. But we don't live like that.'

'I understand,' I say. 'But ask yourself this: if Marvellous were here, if he knew what we planned, if he knew what they'd

351

done to Gracious and what they planned to do to Mireille and the kind of thing Hipkiss might do with Deep Threat, what would he say?'

Rachel's silent for a long moment. She looks over to Wen.

'Come on, Rachel,' says Wen. 'You know fucking well what he'd say.'

'Think about it this way,' says Kat. 'What are the alternatives? Either Mireille dies, or Hipkiss gets the keys to the nuclear kingdom. Maybe you don't want our deaths on your conscience, but could you live with either of those?'

'No,' says Rachel. 'You're right. There's no other choice. We have to do it.'

Wen leans forward, studying printed out plans. 'How do you know where the malware will be stored? Plus, if it's secured, there'll be a keycard, a combination, biometrics, something like that. How do we get that?'

'Hipkiss is crazy, but she's not stupid,' I say. 'It's her prize asset, so she'll keep it close. The blueprints show a safe in her suite. That's where it'll be. A keycard can be stolen, and biometrics can be spoofed. So she'll use a combination. When I deliver *our* half of Deep Threat, she has to open up the safe to get *her* half so they can combine them. Your team uses CCTV to eavesdrop the combination visually. You think they can do that?'

'They're good,' says Wen. 'If anyone can, they can.'

'I understand how you get on board,' says Rachel. 'What I don't understand is how Kat's supposed to get on board.'

'*La Belle Dame* is here for Ekoparty,' I say, 'not just Mireille. Staley's in the market for malware. Kat needs to offer him something he can't refuse and which can only be demonstrated on board.'

'Wait,' says Wen, 'you expect us to find *another* exploit in the next twelve hours?'

'No need,' I say. 'We're already looking at it.'

At that moment, there's a buzz on the intercom. It's a courier I ordered bringing a package from Big Shop, Buenos Aires' biggest toy store. I head down in the elevator and return with a large box, covered in wrapping paper.

'Okay,' says Rachel, 'but Kat still needs an introduction.'

'That's what this is for,' I say, and tear the paper off to reveal the contents.

The rest of the day is spent frantically ironing out details. Wen pulls his visual team back in to go through the CCTV system, including recordings from the previous twenty-four hours, while Kat and I memorise the layout of *La Belle Dame* from the blueprints until each of us can verbally walk the other through the ship with our eyes closed. We spend the rest of the afternoon sitting on the floor, playing with the contents of the box. We go through permutation after permutation, eventuality after eventuality, until our eyeballs feel like pinballs. Kat takes notes to begin with but soon realises there's no point: she will have to rely on memory for this.

Halfway through, a white limo pulls up outside, driven by a chauffeur who accepts two months' wages in cash, leaves his uniform, and heads off to spend his loot in a local bar.

At 6 p.m., Kat figures she's as ready as she'll ever be, so we head back to my hotel and Kat retreats into the bedroom to change. She reappears forty-five minutes later, transformed again, wearing a sleeveless cross-backed black mini-dress, a choker of pearls, and a pair of low-heeled boots. With her copper hair and red lipstick, it's impossible to tell if she's a tech CEO, a high-class hooker, or an international assassin.

'What do you think?' she says.

'I'm not sure if I'm supposed to pitch you, fuck you or take a bullet in the head.'

'Thanks,' says Kat, 'I think. So, what now?'

'Now we wait.'

139

I monitor *La Belle Dame Sans Merci* from the balcony, Kat beside me. She's quiet, but I can tell from the way she chain-smokes half a pack, using the last to light the next, that she's nervous. I'm beginning to think we've struck out when light spills out from the yacht as the rear sea doors open and the tender emerges, crossing to the supply boat. Moments later, the lights of the Bell flick on, and a pilot enters to begin final checks.

'I think this is it,' I tell Kat, pulling on my chauffeur's cap.

'You think I can pull this off?' says Kat.

I can't help smiling. 'I think you could pull it off in your sleep.'

Her face becomes serious.

'How far am I supposed to go?'

From across the harbour, I hear the Bell's turbines starting, the rotors spooling up.

I swallow the taste of bile, trying to suppress the images that come to mind. What am I supposed to say? *Sure, fuck him, if that's what it takes for us to save Mireille and stop Deep Threat!* But who the hell am I to tell her anything? It's not like I haven't done the same myself, a hundred times or more.

And yet and yet and yet, this is Kat, and the thought of it makes me want to vomit.

I finally find my voice. 'I'm the wrong person to ask.'

'You want me to tell you?' says Kat. 'You know, if—'

I shake my head. 'Just tell me what I need to know. The rest . . . it's your choice.'

I turn back to the harbour, feeling unclean. Kat leans her head on my shoulder for a moment, and her hand sneaks into mine. But then the Bell's engines whine up, and it unsticks, the tender lifting slightly in the water as it does. It angles away, its lights reflecting in the glass of the buildings that face the ocean.

I check my phone. The flight path is the same as the night before.

I turn to Kat.

'Here we go.'

140

I watch Kat in the mirror as I drive through the darkened city. She sits in the back, staring out, face reflecting in the glass. Yes, she's fearless, but fearlessness is often the daughter of ignorance, of not understanding the true dangers that lie ahead, or deliberately blocking them out.

What she has to do next requires something else: bravery.

I turn off the highway and bump down the dirt road to the gates of the McMansion. It's lit up now, and beyond the wrought iron, expensive vehicles are parked everywhere: Lamborghinis, jacked Bentleys, a Maserati saloon, a couple of vintage Porsches and a top-end G-Wagon.

Two massive bouncers with shaved heads flank the car as I pull up at the gate. Both are carrying short-barrelled AR-15s slung over their tuxedos. The ape on my side taps my window. I roll it down.

'And the back,' he grunts in Spanish.

I roll down Kat's window. The Gorilla surveys her appreciatively then turns to me.

'*Para quién es la puta?*'

'I'm sorry?'

'*La puta.* The hooker,' he says in English, picking up my accent. 'Who is she for?'

Behind me, Kat's eyes blaze.

I stare at him.

'Did you just call Señor Staley's business associate a prostitute?'

The Gorilla goes pale.

'Señora, my apologies, I didn't mean—'

Kat leans forward, pure alpha bitch. 'It's Señorita, moron. I suggest you let us through the fucking gate if you want to keep your job.'

'Absolutely, Señorita.' He backs away, simultaneously bowing and yelling commands at his partner by the controls.

The electric gate slides open.

I crunch the limo up the drive and stop at the entrance, then get out and open Kat's door. She passes close to me as she exits.

'Wish me luck,' she says quietly in my ear.

'It's not too late to change your mind,' I say, admiring the curve of her neck.

'Have you even met me?' she whispers, then heads up the stairs and through the half-open door without looking back.

I shut the door and climb back into the limo. As I negotiate the turnaround, I can see two figures in *La Belle Dame*'s helicopter. One is the pilot, the other a familiar, hulking tall shape.

It's Harkonnen.

I weigh my options. Other limos are parked here, but the drivers are out of their seats and standing off to the side of the house, smoking and chatting. If I stop here, I can keep an eye on Harkonnen and potentially protect Kat if anything goes wrong. But if I stay in the limo, I'll stick out and draw his attention, and trying to blend in with the other drivers will be even worse.

So I head back down the drive and out through the gates, then turn down the dirt road until it bends a couple of hundred yards further on. There I pull up and, through the wire fence and a line of scrubby, parched cedars, settle down to watch the entrance through binoculars.

As I do, the sick feeling I had sitting on the balcony returns. It's not just the thought of what Staley might do, or want to do, but the fact that Kat's in there unarmed, with only the most vestigial intelligence about what's inside, attempting to execute a triple bank-shot of a plan she's had barely any opportunity to plan or train for.

I've built a career out of doing just that, but Kat's new to it, and it's all on her.

As I watch and wait, I make a promise to myself.

The chances of us both getting out alive are slim to none.

But if only one of us does, it's going to be her.

PART TEN

141

Kat takes deep breaths, trying to calm the acid gnawing at her stomach. She's spent her life avoiding unwanted male attention, but now she's about to be the centre of it.

She hesitates at the foot of the steps leading up to the portico. It all feels so unreal. For a moment, she wishes she was back in Williamsburg, but then she remembers the sick feeling of betrayal the first time Actually Ken failed to come home, and the contempt she felt when he delivered the first of his chumbucket of lame excuses. She should have decked him on the spot, but she was still pretending to be someone who hadn't recently cut another human being in half with a chainsaw.

Kat and her mother were never particularly close, but her mom had a saying, even when she was dying of cancer: *if something scares you, run towards it.* That, the green eyes, and the ability to draw are about the only things she inherited, but maybe it's enough.

She heads up the steps to the half-open door. As she reaches it, it opens fully, courtesy of a short Chinese man with no neck and a head like a thumb, bulging out of another regulation tuxedo, the lump of a shoulder holster by his left arm.

Inside, the atrium is well lit, decorated with flamboyant gangster chic. Lots of gold, a few poorly painted pictures of semi-naked women. A couple of girls awaiting clients sit together on a red chaise longue, eyeing up potential competition. Kat gives them a smile that she hopes signals both solidarity and zero threat to their livelihood.

Through a pair of glass doors to the right she can make out a bar. A hostess emerges with a tray of drinks and crosses to the doors opposite, which open long enough for Kat to glimpse inside.

She feels a millimetric easing of tension. It's what they thought.

'Señorita?'

It's the man with a thumb for a head. Kat lifts the clutch purse she's brought with her and produces a J.P. Morgan Reserve credit card, courtesy of The Dentist. It's clear the thumb recognises the significance of it – *invitation-only, $10m in assets under management* – because he nods behind her, where a petite older Chinese woman sits behind an armoured window.

Kat heads over to the wicket and places the card in the gap at the bottom.

'*Cien mil, por favor.*'

The old woman nods, takes the card. '*Pesos?*'

'*Dólares.*'

The old woman pushes the card back.

'*No es posible.*'

Kat pushes the card back at her. '*Cien mil. Dólares.*'

The old woman pushes a button under the counter. There's the sound of a code being entered into a lock, a beep, and a door behind her opens to admit a Hispanic man with slicked-back hair, in a sharp business suit. He could be any hotel manager but for a long scar that descends from one temple to the corner of his mouth, pulling it into a twisted kind of smirk.

The Chinese woman whispers to him, gesturing at the card, and Kat. 'I'm sorry, Señorita,' he says in English. 'The amount you request is impossible. Those amounts are reserved for regular clients. I can offer you ten thousand dollars only.'

Kat frowns. 'Señor Staley said it wouldn't be a problem.'

The man in the suit blinks, then smiles. 'My apologies. A friend of the Señor. In that case—' He whispers something to the old woman and disappears back through the door. The teller counts out a hundred thousand dollars in chips and places them in a black velvet drawstring bag. Kat takes it and turns back to the atrium.

She takes a deep breath. *This is it.* And heads through the double doors, trying to act as if gatecrashing an illegal Triad casino with a hundred thousand dollars in her hand was no big deal.

142

The room is hazy with smoke. The croupiers and pit bosses are Chinese, many with tattoos, and about half the clientele are some variety of Asian, but Kat also catches snatches of Spanish, Portuguese, Russian and Arabic.

The gamblers are almost all men, many with much younger women leaning on their shoulders. Some of the faces are mashed in, broken, guys who fought their way up from the streets. Others are businessmen, quiet and reserved, while still others are barely more than kids, with the nervous energy and bling of chancers who made it good, maybe in sports, or music, or crypto.

There's every kind of game in progress. Craps, poker, baccarat, *pia gow*, *sic bo*, and in the centre, a single-zero roulette wheel. That's what Kat prepared for, but her heart sinks as she scans the gamblers seated around the wheel for the face she's studied in photographs.

He isn't there.

But then she spots him, a little older and heavier than the pictures, heading in from the bathroom. He's in the ex-military uniform of polo shirt and chinos, with a belly jutting out over a webbing belt, and thinning hair cut close, and greying at the temples. His face is jowly and flushed, and by the way he walks and the tumbler of scotch ready for him by his seat, he's been drinking steadily for a while. Back at his place, he relights a cigar and continues playing.

There's no vacant seat, but then one of the other gamblers, a chubby Filipino, loses the last of his chips on red. He swears, rises, and stalks away, allowing Kat to take his place.

'*Haga sus apuestas,*' says the croupier.

Staley looks up and sees Kat. His gaze lingers on her for a moment, as if undressing her. Kat meets his eye, giving nothing away. He smiles, but she doesn't smile back. He shrugs, then pushes a pile of chips onto red.

Follow the plan, that's all you have to do, she reminds herself. She takes five thousand dollars of her chips, and pushes them onto black. Staley glances up again. She's matching him, but taking the other side of the bet. Deliberate, or coincidence?

Kat smiles blandly.

'*No más apuestas.*'

The croupier shoots the ball. It rattles to a near halt on 12, then hops into the next slot.

'*Treinta y cinco. Negro.*'

35, black. He sweeps Staley's chips over to Kat along with hers.

'*Haga sus apuestas.*'

This time Staley watches to see what Kat will do. She sits tight. He waits until the ball's in play, whirling round the outer rim, then dumps another five thousand onto even. Kat matches him on odd.

The ball drops down. Clatter, clatter, clatter, *clunk*.

23, odd.

The croupier returns Kat's chips, and adds Staley's to them.

Kat glances at Staley. He's trying not to show he's angry. She knows it's just beginner's luck and it can't continue, but it couldn't have been a better start.

143

Parked out behind the screen of trees, watching the mute door through binoculars, I know nothing of this yet. But I know the plan because Kat and I gamed it out the day before using the plastic roulette wheel the courier brought us and a Wikipedia article on roulette bets. I was worried we wouldn't have time, but Kat's maths brain made short work of the system.

Staley was a gambling addict. It had always been the rumour, and his flying out to an illegal casino on his first night in Argentina confirmed it. Roulette was his game – it's what I'd heard in the background the first time I ever spoke to him – but his motivation remained a mystery. Gambling addiction is as physical as it is mental: the adrenaline rush of risk, the endorphin spike of a win. But winning or losing six or even seven figures meant nothing to Staley. The risk or reward, relative to his fortune, was zero. The buzz he got from the skitter of the ball on the diamonds had to come from something else.

It wasn't too hard to see what it might be.

Staley lived in his sister's shadow. They presented a united front, but she was the alpha, and Staley was the beta. In the casino, however, Staley's wealth made *him* the alpha. His indifference to losses meant he could humiliate gamblers who couldn't keep up with him, and indulge in massive, reckless bets. He didn't care if they failed because what he craved was the admiration of spectators who watched in awe. Ten insane bets that cratered were worth one that paid off and humiliated the man opposite, or brought those watching to their feet, applauding.

In any regular casino, this kind of behaviour would make you a prime mark for professional gamblers. But Staley's world was illegal casinos, places where pros wouldn't set foot. The men he humiliated or impressed were dangerous, but that was the point. They were all fully aware that if they ever lifted a finger against him, they would meet a swift and painful end at the hands of Harkonnen, who was never far away.

Hence our theory, that if you wanted to beat Staley, you simply played the opposite strategy. One time out of ten, his winnings would head to the stratosphere and bring him the endorphin rush of a mighty, obliterating win, but the other nine times you'd come out modestly ahead. That would goad him into riskier and riskier bets, while your losses would remain sustainable.

Our aim wasn't to beat him, or humiliate him. It was simply to get his attention.

There was a good chance we'd end up doing both.

But there was also a non-zero chance that Kat would end up dead.

144

After his initial fifty-fifty bets on black or red, odd or even, high or low, Staley now understands the game being played between him and Kat. *Whatever bet he makes, she takes the other side of it.*

But the bets in roulette extend far beyond the simple binaries. There are the table bets – columns, dozens, streets, lines, corners and a few others, signalled by the placement of chips on the green baize. Staley runs through them all, testing Kat on her knowledge of the game. She matches him, play for play. Nobody wins at roulette in the long run – the zero on the wheel ensures the house has an edge – but Staley's bets are increasingly risky, his wins and losses greater and greater, while Kat's pot remains relatively steady. Once or twice she gets close to her limit, with just ten or twenty thousand in chips left in front of her, but each time Staley does her a favour with a risky bet that fails and puts her back in the game.

The table bets exhausted, Staley moves to the called bets – complex combinations of numbers and regions of the wheel that have no equivalent on the table, signalled by simply naming them to the croupier. *Voisins du zéro*, for example, bets on all the numbers around zero on the wheel. Or *Le tiers du cylindre*, bets on a certain combination of numbers that makes up a third of the wheel. There are many more. Kat has them memorised, but that's not enough. For each bet that Staley calls, she has to mentally calculate the combination of *other* bets needed to win. Staley's been drinking steadily, and his eyes are glassy, but he's still smart enough to wait until the ball's in motion before calling each bet, putting Kat under as much pressure as he can.

Other gamblers have started to notice the strange game they're playing. The cream of Buenos Aires' underworld gathers around, enjoying the stress Kat's under and applauding when she manages to reel off an answering bet to Staley's.

'*Haga sus apuestas*,' says the croupier. No-one else is betting now, and he knows the routine, so he spins the ball. Staley waits, then calls '*Orphelins*,' pushing $20,000 over to the croupier.

Kat closes her eyes, trying to visualise the notes she wrote on the floor of Rachel's loft.

A 5-way bet, $4,000 on 1, and $4,000 on each of the pairs 6–9, 14–17, 17–20 and 31–34.

She opens them again. '*Voisins du zéro, tiers du cylindre*,' she says, covering all the other numbers, moments before the ball drops down from the outer rim. She watches it bounce over the brass diamonds, then her heart sinks as it rolls into 17. A big win for Staley. The crowd's sympathy is with her – it's obvious who the big player is here and who's the underdog – and there are disappointed exhales and 'ooh's. But then the last dribble of momentum tips the ball out of 17 and into the next pocket, 25.

There are a couple of cheers, and some applause.

Staley pulls a face. Kat watches him. We were right. It's not the money. It's dominance he's after. His face is flushed, and there's sweat beading on his forehead now, his collar wet where it meets his thick neck.

'*Haga sus apuestas*,' says the croupier. He's about to spin when Staley holds up his hand.

He pushes a vast mound of chips over to the croupier, almost everything he's got.

'Twenty-three, full complete.'

'Señor—' says the croupier, taken aback.

'You heard what I said,' says Staley.

It's the great-grandaddy of all roulette wagers, the nuclear option, a crazy twelve-way split involving every possible combination of table bets with a particular number, in this case, 23.

At the table limit of $10,000, Staley has just wagered $400,000.

If his number hits, the payout is enormous, almost $4,000,000.

If any number around it – between 19 and 27 – hits, Staley wins, not as much, but he walks away ahead. Anything else, he loses the entire stake.

The crowd presses forward. The man in the suit from the teller's cage heads in almost at a run, signalled by a pit boss. The croupier looks over to the suit. A panicked look – *do we honour it?* The suit looks around at the crowd, pressing forward. Kat can almost hear the calculation in his head – *however much it costs, you can't buy this kind of buzz.* He nods to the croupier.

'Twenty-three, full complete,' confirms the croupier. 'Madame?'

Kat smiles. She can't resist giving the crowd some theatre. She nods. *Spin it.*

The croupier spins the wheel, then sends the ball in the opposite direction.

The crowd cranes in, muttering to each other. *There's no way she can answer a $400,000 bet, so what will she do?*

'Thanks,' says Kat. 'I'm out.'

She returns her chips to the black velvet bag and stands.

'*No más apuestas!*' says the croupier.

The crowd parts for her as she walks away, not looking back. Her heart pounds, but she's determined not to show it.

As she reaches the door, she hears the ball spin, clatter down to the wheel and bounce a few times. She pauses, listening as it settles.

The croupier announces. '*Seis, negro.*'

Six, black. Staley just lost.

And then there's the oddest sound.

Laughter.

She doesn't speak Spanish, but it doesn't matter – she can tell what they're saying to Staley as they clap him on the back. *Too bad, bro, she played you!*

She heads back out to the atrium and returns her chips to the wicket. The Chinese woman puts her winnings back on the card and returns it.

She turns back to the lobby, expecting to see Staley. But there's no sign of him.

Fuck.

A group of gamblers head out from the gaming floor. She glances through the door, but the roulette table is now empty. No sign of Staley there either.

Did she just blow the whole thing by humiliating him?

Trust the plan.

She heads for the exit. The man with the shoulder holster and thumb head holds the door open for her as she passes, with a little smile that tells her he enjoyed Staley's humiliation as much as anyone else.

She pauses for a moment at the top of the steps, letting the cool night air wash over her, the stink of cigarette and cigar smoke still clinging to her.

'What the *fuck* was that?' says a voice.

It's Staley, at the bottom of the steps, smoking.

145

Kat descends the steps more confidently than she feels.

'Is there a problem?'

'The problem is you just cost me the best part of half a million dollars.'

'So I take it I have your attention now?'

Staley chuckles. He's not taking it as badly as he pretends. He nods at her dress. 'You had it before you made a single bet.'

'Maybe I needed you to start thinking with your head instead of your dick.'

Staley's face darkens. 'Who the fuck are you?'

'I'm someone who has something you want,' says Kat.

He drops his cigarette and stubs it out on the gravel dismissively. 'Jesus. Is that all this is? A fucking *pitch*? You know how many times I hear that line a day?' He shakes his head. '*Buenos noches*, whoever the fuck you are. Enjoy your winnings.'

He turns and walks towards the helicopter.

Her last chance. She agreed not to use it unless she had to, but the moment's slipping away.

'That watch you're wearing. The Vacheron Constantin. You leave it on your right-hand bedside table every evening. It's the first thing you look at when you wake up, before you put on your orange-and-black Fendi slippers.'

Staley stops and turns, astonished.

'You really want to know who I am and what I have,' says Kat, 'you send a car to the Hilton, 10 a.m. tomorrow morning. Once I'm on board *La Belle Dame*, I'll tell you everything.'

She can see he's shaken, but he's trying to hide it.

'So you played me in there. So you have some inside information from some bitch I slept with. So what? You think that entitles you to an invitation? Fuck you.'

Kat smiles. 'At 8 a.m., a female steward brings you a *café con leche*. You ogle her ass when she walks out. Do I need to tell you what you do afterwards in the shower?'

Staley stares at her, silent.

'10 a.m.,' says Kat, and walks away, down the drive towards the gate.

146

I see all this play out in dumb show from the limousine.

I try to read the body language as they talk: Staley intrigued, then dismissive, then startled. It looks like Kat unloaded the motherlode on him. She walks away, head held high, towards the gate.

He watches for a moment, then heads back towards the helicopter, still shrouded in darkness. The blades are starting to turn, but only the pilot is visible now.

I lose Staley in the shadows for a couple of seconds longer than I should, then pick him up again, silhouetted in the interior lights of the Bell as he climbs up the steps.

Then it hits me: there's no sign of Harkonnen.

He must have been waiting in the shadows as Staley approached, and said something to him. Which means – *oh, fuck.*

I whip-pan the binoculars over to Kat, but as I do, I pick up a figure vectoring in from the left. Kat hasn't seen him, and he's moving fast.

It's Harkonnen, and everything just went to shit.

147

The giant with the burned face slams into her hard, almost taking Kat off her feet. He jams a pistol to the side of her head with one massive hand, wraps the other around her mouth, then drags her towards the helicopter. She tries to pry his hand away and aims a few useless kicks at him, but Harkonnen is massively stronger than she is.

Kat knows other ways of fighting back, but she doesn't need anybody to think of her as a physical threat right now.

Harkonnen manhandles her in through the helicopter door. Staley's already there. He pulls the door closed behind them, barks 'Go' at the pilot, and the helicopter lifts off, rising above the trees, then tilting forward and banking back towards the city.

Staley nods at Harkonnen, who finally removes his massive paw from Kat's face.

The raking shadows of the harsh cabin light show the left side of his face as horrifically burned. The eye is half closed, and his left hand is still swathed in bandages.

'The fuck?' she says, looking away, wiping her mouth with the back of her arm.

'You think you can drop that kind of shit on me and just walk out?' says Staley.

'You just fucking kidnapped me.'

'You wanted a negotiation,' says Staley. 'Now you have one.'

148

Twenty minutes later, the helicopter settles on the support boat, *La Jolie Fille,* and the tender takes them to the yacht. *La Belle Dame* towers above them as they approach, gunmetal sides gleaming and reflecting the submerged running lights.

As giant sea doors close behind them, claustrophobia tightens around Kat's chest. Until now, she could almost pretend this wasn't happening, that it was some kind of role-playing fantasy. But here, amid the hum of marine generators and the smell of diesel and the clang of metal, with blinding floodlights glaring down from above, Harkonnen hovering, and two men in black tactical gear with automatic rifles dimly visible in the shadows – here, it's all suddenly real.

Staley disappears up a staircase, but before she's allowed to the upper decks, Kat's subjected to an alarmingly intimate search, carried out by an unsmiling female crew member wearing obligatory blue nitrile gloves. Her phone is taken away. Then Harkonnen takes her up to the VIP area.

The interior of *La Belle Dame* combines a kind of Death Star chic with the overdesigned flash of an LA boutique hotel trying to justify its rates. Kat's expecting to have to deal with Staley again, but instead Harkonnen shows her to an aggressively luxurious cabin on the guest deck. Once she's inside, Harkonnen closes the door, and she hears a beep as the lock sets.

She waits a minute, then tries to open it, but she can't.

She sits on the bed.

The sheets are thousand thread-count Egyptian cotton percale, but she's a prisoner now.

149

The helicopter's over the horizon by the time I get the limo turned around. As I roar past the gorillas at the gate, I'm already on the phone to Rachel, giving her details of the helicopter. She tracks it on her laptop, updating me live as I career through the streets of Buenos Aires back to downtown.

Meanwhile, one of Wen's team gets on a scooter and races to the quayside, where she watches the helicopter land on *La Jolie Fille*, using the zoom on her phone to film the tender as it crosses to the mothership.

I make it to the harbour ten frantic minutes later. I watch the video three times, trying to read Kat's body language. Harkonnen stays close to her, but his gun's holstered. Kat looks more obstinate than afraid, which is peak Kat, but it could just be bravado. Staley keeps his distance, but he can't take his eyes off her, and that worries me.

There's nothing more I can do, so I drive back to Rachel's. She suggests reaccessing the CCTV feed, but Wen's paranoid the abnormal network traffic will trigger a tripwire in the system. He's already made two exceptions – one to capture the images from Staley's suite that Kat described to him, and the second for the visual team who will snoop the code for the safe in Hipkiss's suite. There are two cameras in the main cabin, both aimed away from the safe by design, but the first has waste pixels outside the frame that can be accessed with a hack, while the second captures a reflection in the window opposite. Since both are hi-def 4K cameras, the team thinks they have a chance of capturing what's entered.

It's three in the morning. We sit around the kitchen table. Rachel and Wen's faces are drawn. They're freaked out, and so am I, but I do my best to hide my feelings.

'We didn't anticipate this,' I say, 'but it could still work. The plan was that Kat would be picked up and taken on board tomorrow morning. We're just ahead of schedule.'

'They fucking kidnapped her,' says Rachel. 'You know what they did to Marvellous. You're not afraid they'll do the same to her if they find out who she is?'

'I trust her,' is all I can say. 'What she needs from us is that we stick with the plan, not start panicking. Okay? If anyone can pull this off, she can.'

I'm so sincere I almost convince myself.

150

Kat's not expecting to sleep, but she does, exhaustion taking over as the tension of the night's events recedes. The cotton sheets don't hurt. At 8.30 a.m. the following morning, she's woken by a polite knock, followed by the beep of the door unlocking. A white-gloved female steward brings in a tray of coffee and orange juice, along with a copy of *The New York Times*, and invites her – *at your convenience, Madame* – to join Staley for breakfast.

As she leaves, the steward opens the door to the cabin's closet slightly, giving Kat a look that's clearly meant to be meaningful.

Kat devours the coffee and realises that despite the nagging anxiety in the pit of her stomach, she's actually hungry. Ever since she was small, people have told her that she's fearless, so many times that it irritates her, not because it isn't true but because it isn't the whole truth. It's more that she's never done what people have wanted, and fear is just another thing trying to stop her from doing what she pleases.

Well, fuck you, fear, she thinks to herself. *I'm hungry.*

She stares at herself in the mirror, make-up gone, trying to figure out how to make the bitch/hooker/killer dress she wore the previous evening look less ridiculous in daylight. The way Staley stared at her gave her the shudders, and she has no intention of giving him further encouragement. Then she remembers the steward opening the closet door. She opens it fully and sees there are dresses, gowns and swimwear hung up, all of it designer stuff, and in various sizes.

Another shudder. *This is the cabin he uses for all his women.*

She goes through the hangers, finds a couple of things in her size, and chooses a plain white sundress that she hopes makes her look virginal enough to keep Staley at bay.

There's a balcony by the stairs to the owner's deck, the doors opening to form a breezeway. As she's about to ascend, she hears faint voices from the balcony above. A man and a woman are arguing, trying to keep their voices low. One voice is Staley. The other must be Hipkiss.

'Who is she?' says the woman.

'She's nobody,' says Staley. 'Just a girl I met.'

'You know I don't like surprises. Is she staying tonight?'

'That remains to be seen. Why?'

'I have some business to see to. I'll need Harkonnen for the evening.'

Kat hears her footsteps recede and a door close. She gives it thirty seconds, then heads up the stairs to the owner's deck. An armed guard at the top moves aside to let her through, and indicates the door to Edgar's suite.

It's as overdesigned as everywhere else, with white leather couches and a massive round bed. But it's dominated by hunting trophies, including a stuffed ibex, several other deer, a mountain lion and what looks like a snow leopard, all positioned amidst a diorama of fake rocks. But pride of place goes to the head of a white rhino, staring balefully out from above a massive desk, flanked by two enormous elephant tusks vertically floor-mounted on heavy wooden plinths. The effect is rounded off by various antique hunting rifles and Masai spears, with the *pièce de résistance* a massive broadsword mounted above the bed.

It is, Kat concludes, not the cabin of a man entirely secure in his masculinity.

A door from the cabin leads out to the balcony where Edgar stands, smoking, looking out to sea. Seeing Kat emerge, he flicks the cigarette overboard and motions to a table set for breakfast – croissants, scrambled eggs, yoghurt, more coffee.

'No,' says Kat. 'First, I want to make something clear. I'm not negotiating with a gun to my head. You bring me here at gunpoint, lock me in my cabin, and expect me to make a *deal* with you? Either I'm a guest, in which case maybe we have something to talk about. Or I'm a prisoner, and we don't. Which is it?'

Staley shrugs. 'Fine. You can leave any time you want,' he says. 'Or you can have breakfast with me like a human being, and tell me who you are, what you have, and what the hell possessed you to play it this way.'

151

'The Nigerian boy,' says Kat.

'I don't know what you're talking about,' says Staley, and it occurs to Kat that Staley may genuinely not know about Deep Threat, or his sister's pursuit of it.

'The hacker who disappeared,' says Kat. 'Maybe it wasn't you who had him killed, but somebody did. Now everyone's running scared because they're afraid if they start shopping a major exploit around, it puts a target on their back. But I'm just a broker. You kill me, you get nothing. I don't even know who I represent. I'm just here to tell you what they have and give you the chance to make a pre-emptive offer.'

'Say I buy that. What is it you have?'

'A zero-day.'

'Obviously. That gives you access to our onboard CCTV. That's it?'

Kat shakes her head. 'Not even close. We're offering direct access to the network infrastructure not just of this yacht, but all yachts that use the same system. That includes full, live, remote CCTV access, and visibility into their network traffic, security and communications. The biggest megayachts on the planet. Oligarchs, heads of state, narco-terrorists, Stephen Spielberg. You get to eavesdrop on their conversations, disable their security, and track them wherever they go. And they never know a thing.'

'Okay,' says Staley eventually. 'Let's say I'm interested. What's the ask?'

'A hundred million. US dollar equivalent in crypto.'

Staley tips his head back and laughs. 'Keep dreaming.'

'Fine,' says Kat. 'But my instructions are this is a one-time offer. My partners have set a deadline of noon tomorrow. If they don't hear about a deal by then, it goes on the open market. You'll be excluded from the bidding. Which means, whoever buys it, you'll likely be one of the first targets.'

Staley's face goes stony-cold. 'Whoever the fuck you are, you should have done your research better. If you had, you'd know I don't respond well to threats.' He stands and dumps his linen napkin into his eggs. 'I'll have the tender take you back to shore.'

He's already halfway out the door when Kat stands up and says after him:

'There is another reason you might want it.'

He turns. 'And what would that be?'

'To spy on your *own* yacht,' says Kat.

152

'Why the fuck would I want to do that?' says Staley. But he's keeping his voice low.

'The same reason you lied to your sister about who I am and why I'm here,' says Kat. 'Because it's not your yacht, it's hers. You're a pragmatist, not a true believer. You go along with her ideas because you like having access to billions. You like the power and swagger of running your own private army. You like having a megayacht and being able to fuck who you want whenever you want and never having to worry about the consequences. But you're not stupid. You don't think you're one of God's chosen. In your heart, you know what she's capable of. Probably you think of yourself as a moderating influence. That you could stop her from doing anything really stupid. But you're not sure because she doesn't trust you, not enough to tell you what she's actually thinking. And if you did try to stop her, what would she have Harkonnen do to you? This way, you could know what's in her head, what she's planning, and defend yourself.'

'You're suggesting I buy your product myself and not tell her?'

'I think that was your plan all along,' says Kat. 'And, by the way, once you have it, you can also erase any records of this conversation, or any other conversations you might have had or have in the future. Having your religious big sister as the unseen guest at every encounter can't be easy for a man like you.'

Edgar thinks for a long minute. 'You're prepared to demonstrate the exploit?'

'Of course,' says Kat. 'Real-time demo on a live target.'

'The target being?'

Kat gestures around her. 'Why do you think I wanted an invite?'

'You want to hack my own yacht? You're insane.'

'No freebies,' says Kat. 'You want to hack another yacht, you pay. This way, you get to explore all the capabilities risk-free before you commit.'

Edgar eyes her, calculating.

'Say we were to set this up. How does it work?'

Finally. Kat resists the urge to smile.

'I'm going to need my phone.'

153

None of us can sleep until we know what's happening with Kat. But there's nothing we can do but sit around a table and stare at a burner phone, waiting for it to ring.

Hers is a burner, too, with a single number programmed in. Staley undoubtedly has access to tools that could triangulate it, but a member of Rachel's team is currently moving around central Buenos Aires carrying two more burners, one to receive messages from Kat and another to retransmit them to our *fourth* burner. Currently, our mule is in a massive twenty-four-hour nightclub, and in the morning he'll move to the crowded streets and shopping malls, just be one of hundreds of people, with no way to distinguish him from anyone else.

Our only hope is that Kat manages to get access to her phone. But if *La Belle Dame* leaves port, it will be out of cell-phone range within an hour, maybe less. At which point, our plan falls apart completely.

To distract herself, Rachel takes the now zero-eyed sock monkey and sews a single button eye back onto it. Out of all of us, it's Rachel who thinks most about Mireille, about what she's been through, about how to break the news of her mother's death to her, and how the events of the few days and weeks might resonate down through her life as she grows up.

As I watch her sew, and think of the drawers full of clothes that Marvellous bought, a thought forms in my mind that refuses to be unthought, so around 4.30 a.m. I take Rachel aside and tell her I have two proposals for her, but she has to accept both.

She listens as I explain the first and accepts almost before I finish.

'Of course,' she says, wiping half a tear away from the corner of an eye. 'What on earth made you think I wouldn't?'

'The second part,' I say. 'Don't agree until you've heard it all.'

She listens in silence, her face becoming grave.

'You can't be serious,' Rachel says, finally.

'I don't see any other way, do you?'

'Does Kat know?'

'If I'd told her, she'd never have agreed.'

She's almost angry now. 'What makes you think *I* will?'

'Because this is how Mireille has a life that doesn't involve looking over her shoulder forever. Think about the start she's had in life. Abandoned by her mother and forced to pull the trigger on a man she didn't even know was her father, then dragged off by a psychopath. God only knows what she's been through since then. If there's even a sliver of a chance that she could live some kind of normal existence after all that, don't you think she deserves it?'

Rachel shakes her head. 'I'm not sure I can do this.'

'Then we can't do any of it. I can't put Mireille at risk like that. I'll find someone else.'

Finally, she looks up.

'All right. I'll do it. For her, I'll do it.'

154

At first light, one of Rachel's team goes out with a pair of binoculars to the Playa Reserva, where there's a view of the outer harbour. She reports seeing Staley with a red-haired woman in a white dress, having breakfast on *La Belle Dame*'s owner's balcony.

Kat's still alive, but that's all we know.

It's 11.30 a.m. when the phone on the table finally buzzes with a relayed message.

Demonstration authorised. Please confirm.

The room erupts in cheers, and I feel myself sag with relief. But we need to keep Kat on the yacht until I trade the malware for Mireille, so I text back a delaying tactic.

Network topology changed. Need to reconfigure proxies. Suggest 12 noon tomorrow for demo. Will confirm in a few hours.

We hold our breaths. Forty-five seconds later, a text comes back.

Standing by.

We're on.

The swap is scheduled for 8 p.m., but there's still an issue unresolved.

The world of malware is full of stories of exploits being reported and ignored. Even if we manage to get our hands on Deep Threat, making it public achieves nothing unless governments realise the significance and act on it immediately.

'We need clout,' says Wen. 'Someone serious. Someone high profile, who's done gnarly shit, and has a track record. Someone nobody is ever going to accuse of being a bullshitter.'

'Huh,' I say. 'I sure wish I knew somebody like that.'

At that moment, the doors to the elevator clang open and a familiar shirt appears.

155

The rendezvous is a set of GPS coordinates, which resolve to a location in the Rio Santiago shipyards, an hour to the south. Rachel drives me there in her ancient Fiat 500. It's almost dark, the feeble headlights barely lighting up the road. On my lap is a tiny mil-spec Nanuk case, and inside it the card with half of the malware that could bring about Armageddon. Perched on the dashboard, the sock monkey regards us with its restored eye. Behind us, in a bag on the back seat, are a selection of the clothes that Marvellous bought, for Mireille to change into.

Something tells me my daughter will be in good hands.

The coordinates take us to a long straight road that runs along one of the docks, and ends in a low brick warehouse surrounded by a rusted wire fence. Two armed guards stand at the entrance and wave us to a stop. They wand us down with both magnetic and RF detectors, then search us with painstaking thoroughness, checking behind our ears, our hair, and sparing no blushes for either of us, between our legs. They take Rachel's phone, keys, and wallet and put them back in the Fiat, then have us remove our belts, shoes and socks, and check the soles of our feet.

They are taking absolutely no chances.

One tries to take the monkey, but Rachel refuses.

'It's for the girl,' she says.

He squeezes it all over, then hands it back with a nod and points us to a door by the loading bay where another guard stands at a regulation low ready. We head through the gates and across cracked asphalt, avoiding broken glass in our bare feet.

As we approach, the third guard says something into a radio and opens the door.

Inside, it's dark, but the moment we enter, a light blazes on. As my eyes adjust, I make out four more armed men stationed around the walls, while in front of us, in what appears to be a disused meat-packing facility, a trestle table has been set up. A laptop sits on it, and behind it a young woman with red lipstick and bangs. Beside her, almost directly under the blinding light, stands Harkonnen and, with him, Mireille.

She's ash-grey, her face tired, her thin frame pathetic among all the men and guns.

'Let her go,' I say, voice echoing off the rusted steel walls and high gantried roof.

'Card first,' says Harkonnen.

'Let her at least come to me,' says Rachel. She takes a few steps forward. Harkonnen's clawed hand pushes Mireille forward, but she resists, afraid.

'The monkey,' I say quietly.

Rachel squats down. She holds the monkey in front of her. 'Look who I brought.'

Mireille stares for a moment, then – the first time I've ever seen it – her face cracks into most of a smile, and she runs over and grabs the monkey, hugging it to her so tightly it practically forces the stuffing out of the stitches.

Harkonnen signals to me to bring the case over. The muzzles of four automatics follow me.

'Stop,' he says, as I'm halfway there. 'Open the case.'

I do, showing everyone the contents.

'Take the card out and put the case on the floor.'

I follow his orders.

'Now bring it over and put it on the table.'

I step forward a few paces, put the card on the table, then step back. As I do, I feel a gun in my back. It's the guard who let us in. He pulls my hands behind me and zip-ties them.

The girl with the red lips and bangs takes the card and inserts it into a reader. A few keyboard strokes, a couple of seconds, then she looks up.

'The MD5 hash matches.'

'That means it's real,' says Rachel, her hands on Mireille's shoulders in front of her. 'You can let him go.'

Harkonnen pulls an automatic pistol. He walks over to Rachel, places the muzzle in the centre of her forehead, then slowly runs it down her face and neck and chest and stomach to Mireille's head instead.

'Maybe you'd prefer it if we took the girl back?'

'Rachel, it's OK,' I say. 'It's what we agreed.'

Rachel looks Harkonnen in the eye.

'I hope the other half of you burns in hell too.'

The guard behind me opens the door to let Rachel and Mireille out. As Mireille exits, hand in hand with Rachel, still clutching the monkey, she turns back, and I realise it may be the last time I'll ever see her. For a split second, I imagine her growing up, trying to picture the young woman she might become. But then the door closes behind her, and I turn back to see Harkonnen in front of me.

'Let's take a ride,' says Harkonnen.

'I thought you'd never ask.'

He punches me in the gut so hard I drop to my knees. Two of the guards pick me up and haul me after him and the girl with the bangs, who are already heading out through loading doors at the far end, through which I can see the blades of *La Belle Dame*'s helicopter rotating.

PART ELEVEN

156

Kat worries that stalling Staley will annoy him, but he's delighted she'll be forced to remain another night on the yacht, and invites her to have dinner with him in his suite. He takes her phone back, but promises to relay any messages. She spends the rest of the day avoiding him, reclining on the guest balcony pretending to soak up the sun as a flunky ferries spring water and pomegranate juice to her on the half-hour.

Around 4.30 p.m, three and a half hours before the exchange is due to take place, she hears the chopper spool into life.

It's happening, she thinks. *It's actually happening.*

Staley suggested 8 p.m., but she leaves it as long as she can, and it's 8.45 p.m. by the time she opens the door to his suite. There are drinks waiting, but by the red of his face, he's a few ahead. He's donned black tie for the occasion, with a purple cummerbund struggling to corset his belly.

He offers her one of two drinks.

She takes one, waits for him to drink his first.

'If you think I'm about to slip you a roofie, you got me all wrong,' he says. 'I don't need that shit.'

'Let me guess,' she says. 'You let the money do the talking.'

Staley shrugs. 'You're the one asking for a hundred million. What's your cut? Ten per cent, fifteen?'

'That's between me and my clients,' says Kat.

She mimes taking another sip of her drink. The door to the balcony is open, and through it she hears a noise, growing louder. It's *La Belle Dame*'s helicopter returning.

'So, ten to twenty million dollars,' says Staley. 'What do you plan to do with it?'

'Found an orphanage,' says Kat.

'I could help you found ten "orphanages". A hundred,' says Edgar.

Kat has no intention of spending the rest of the evening fighting him off, and he's already on the hook, so decides to go on the offensive.

'I guess when you're as rich as fuck, you think anything can be bought.'

'In my experience, everyone has a price.'

'Or maybe it's just that shit attracts flies. When you have money, the only people you ever encounter are people who want to separate you from it.'

'You're a cynic.'

'Tell me the truth. When was the last time you met someone who was interested in you, and not just your sister's money? Can you even remember what it feels like to have a relationship that isn't some kind of transaction? You've probably spent a lot of money to have people pretend they liked you, or were in love with you. But you're a smart person. I bet you never fooled yourself for a second.'

Edgar swallows a bitter taste, unable to find a response.

'So how about,' says Kat, 'you stop trying to fucking *buy* me, and instead we attempt to have an actual conversation?'

For a second, she thinks she may have pushed him too far, but then he just says:

'Deal.'

157

Before they load me into the helicopter, they zip-tie my ankles, slip black goggles on me, and a black hood which tightens around my neck.

Twenty minutes later, the chopper lands. There's the stink of aviation fuel and exhaust as hands drag me down the steps to the tender, which takes us to the yacht. From there, the hands lift me by the armpits and hustle me down into the bowels of *La Belle Dame*.

Under the hood and goggles I'm blind, but both Kat and I have memorised the yacht's layout. A right turn and a set of stairs tell me we're headed to the tank deck, and what's labelled 'Secure Storage A' on the blueprints. It's secure, windowless, lockable, and right by the engines, so nothing can be heard over the roar of the diesel.

The guards toss me in like a sack of garbage, still zip-tied. My head slams hard into the metal floor. I black out, then drift in and out of consciousness until I hear the beep of the lock and the electric bolt sliding open. Hands haul me upright, and pull off the hood and goggles.

I blink at bright fluorescent light. Harkonnen stands in the doorway.

'You want the good news or the bad news or the good news?'

I choose not to grace him with a reply.

'The good news is the card's genuine. The bad news is I'm not supposed to kill you. The good news is I'm going to do it anyway.'

'Go ahead,' I say.

He comes over, squats and jams his gun under my chin.

'The problem is,' I tell him, 'you can't. First, you don't want the rest of the crew to hear a shot, let alone anyone else in the harbour. Second, you won't kill me until we're in international waters because otherwise the Argentinians have jurisdiction, and that gets messy. And third, there's a man with a bucket and sponge behind you, which means your boss has asked to see me, and doesn't like it when you get blood all over the VIP area.'

Harkonnen presses the gun harder under my chin, finger on the trigger. He'd love to prove me wrong. But I'm right. He turns to a deck hand.

'Clean the motherfucker up.'

158

Someone finds a crewman's shirt to replace the bloodstained one I'm wearing. Harkonnen has the zip ties round my ankles cut, drapes a fresh hood on my head and leads me at gunpoint up three sets of crew stairs to the upper deck. The smell and sound change as we exit the spartan crew area into the plush, soundproofed VIP area. I'm hustled into a room billed as the library on the blueprints and pushed into a chair.

'Remove his hood,' says a familiar, honking voice, and they do.

The room is not a library, but a high-tech situation room, with multiple speakerphone hubs, flatscreens, videoconferencing, and motorised metal shutters over the windows, currently closed, that make it impervious to eavesdropping.

Hipkiss sits at the other end of a long, leather-covered table. Ten years on, she looks the same but different. Before, she wore no make-up, but today she's liberally powdered, with lipstick that bleeds into the filigree of fine lines above her upper lip. Her hair is frizzed in a tight, weird perm that reminds me of Ma from *The Golden Girls*. The blazer is now green, with shoulder pads last seen in *Dallas*. She still can't be more than fifty-five, but everything conspires to make her seem a decade older. The weirdest part of it is, I have the distinct impression the ensemble was carefully chosen.

She smiles blandly, but there's a brittleness to it that suggests there's more riding on this interview than even I anticipated.

'Do I have your word you're not going to do anything stupid, Mr – may I call you something other than Seventeen? It's so impersonal.'

I shrug. 'Sometimes people call me Jones.'

'Your word, Mr Jones?'

I nod.

'Well, then,' she says to Harkonnen. 'You may go.'

'Ma'am, I—' says Harkonnen, but before he can finish she snaps at him.

'I said you can go.'

Harkonnen leaves, with a look to me that says *we're not finished*.

The door closes with a heavy thump. Like the room, it's soundproof.

'So,' she says. 'Here we are. Would you like some coffee?'

There's a carafe on the table with a couple of plain white cups on a tray, the kind of thing you'd find in a Holiday Inn Express. I indicate the zip-tied wrists behind my back.

'Ah, of course,' she says. 'Water, then.'

She takes a bottle from the tray, unscrews the top, then walks over to me. She's thin, angular even, but with broad hips that give her a slight waddle.

'Open wide.'

She sits on the desk, smooths out her skirt, and gently pours water into my mouth. She's so close I can smell her scent, which is cloyingly sweet and probably called something like Ashes of Roses. But there's a hint of something else, something musky I can't quite place until I realise with a shock that it's her breath.

'Now swallow,' she says, and I do. 'You want some more?'

I nod, and she pours more in, then uses a paper napkin to wipe my mouth.

'There, that's better,' she says.

For one off-the-charts-fucking-weird second, I think she might plant a less-than-matronly kiss on me, but instead she heads back to her end of the table, where she has a notepad and a cheap ball-point pen which, I kid you not, has a furry purple troll on the end.

'I'll get to the point. I assume you know what's on the card you exchanged for the girl?'

'I have a pretty good idea,' I say.

'Do you know what I'm going to do with it?'

The truth is, I couldn't give a shit what she plans to do with it, but as long as I'm here, I'm safe from Harkonnen. The final act of the plan relies on me being alive, so I play for time.

'I couldn't begin to imagine.'

'Do you know the story of Noah?'

'My childhood didn't involve a lot of Sunday school,' I say, which is an understatement since on any given Sunday I was likely hidden in a motel room closet trying not to listen to my mother fuck strangers to buy drugs.

'Well,' she says. 'I'll simplify. God gave Adam and Eve dominion over the earth. But their descendants filled it with corruption and violence. The flood was God's way of hitting the undo button. Forty days and forty nights of rain. In some versions, each raindrop passed through the fires of hell and scalded the sinners before killing them. Noah and his wife were the only survivors. Together they repopulated the earth.'

'Okay,' I say, although frankly the whole scenario seems unlikely.

'So the question is this,' she continues. 'If the burning rain were to fall again, would you rather be on the Ark or off it?'

'That depends,' I say.

'On what?'

'On who else is on it with me.'

159

I'm imagining Kat as I say it, of her shape beside me in the darkness of the Ark's wooden cabin, the great ship heaving beneath us on a massive ocean swell, rain drumming endlessly on the deck above. The smell of straw and animals, the snore of the dogs sleeping at our feet. Then a dove returning to us with an olive branch in its beak, signalling the receding waters. The pair of us making landfall on a mountain top as the waters subside, stepping out as naked as the day we were born, the only man and woman left on earth.

It wouldn't be so bad.

160

But it's not Kat smiling back at me. It's Hipkiss, and I swear, under the powder, a flush just spread from her cheeks down to her neck.

'History has gone wrong,' she says. 'God had a plan. He gave us an entire country, a virgin land for the faithful. We became the most powerful country on earth because he wanted us to have dominion over the entire planet. And because there is evil in the world, he gave us a tool to overcome it. Do you know what I'm talking about, Mr Jones?'

'Nuclear weapons. The bomb.'

She smiles, that bland smile. 'Exactly. But we became terrified of the power God had placed in our hands, too terrified to use it. We lost our nerve. God gave us a gift, an extraordinary gift, a gift that could usher in his reign on earth, and we threw it back in his face like spoiled children. But when I heard about Deep Threat, I understood what it meant. It was God's way of giving us another chance, just as he did to Noah. That's why I had to have it.'

'To do what exactly?'

'To create Heaven on earth.'

She smiles again, not bland this time, but proud.

It is easily the most unsettling smile I have ever seen on another human being.

'Let me guess,' I say. 'Your plan is to use Deep Threat to provoke a nuclear exchange between the superpowers, and once they have obliterated themselves, step into the breach.

You ride out the critical period here on *La Belle Dame*. Then, when the smoke clears, courtesy of your brother, you'll hit the ground running with bases of operation in surviving non-nuclear states, plus an army, tame politicians, and an intelligence operation. A hundred million people will be dead from blast effects and fallout. But that will be your flood. You'll have rolled back creation, just as God did for Noah.'

'I'm so glad you understand,' she says. 'My generation is lost. Yours too. But our children will inherit a new world. We'll teach them to love God and obey his laws. They'll grow up among ruins, but the ruins will crumble away, and the grass will grow over them, and the earth will be as it was always meant to be, under the dominion of God's people. And our children's children will be kings of the earth.'

'What about the others? The ones who believe in other gods, or none at all?'

'There won't *be* any others,' she says firmly. 'That's the whole point.'

161

Hipkiss's plan sounds absurd, and it is. But the Nazis dead-enders who fled to South America to escape Nuremberg had almost the same fever dream: rebuild a power base by leveraging their relationships with the plentiful supply of dictators available locally, provoke a conflict between the USA and USSR, and build a Fourth Reich in the wreckage.

My conclusion: she is (a) absolutely fucking nuts and (b) entirely serious.

That's the thing about being a multi-billionaire. You can be both.

'And you're telling me this because . . . ?' I say.

'My brother is weak,' says Hipkiss. 'He doesn't have the stomach for a real fight. He's too *involved* in the world as it is to be able to see what it might be. And Mr Harkonnen has many qualities, but loyalty is not one of them.'

'So, what are you proposing?'

'That you come and work for me. Kill Harkonnen if you must. I don't care. The only thing I ask is your absolute and permanent loyalty.'

'And in return?'

She smiles, and suddenly the smile is much less bland.

It is, and I am horrified to discover I cannot find another word, *coquettish*.

'Oh, dear,' she says. 'Do I have to say it out loud?'

I stay silent for a moment because it suddenly hits me what she intends.

She wants me to be Noah's wife.

162

It takes me a few seconds to find my voice. 'Doesn't it bother you that I don't believe in God?'

'You'll be doing God's work,' she beams. 'The rest will come in time.'

'You'd be killing a hundred million people,' I point out. 'Maybe two hundred million.'

'How many people have you killed?' she says. 'Tens? Hundreds? Thousands?'

'I never killed anyone who didn't knowingly put themselves in the line of fire.'

'We're all in the line of God's fire,' she says, 'whether we like it or not.'

I'm suddenly struck by Hannah Arendt's line about the banality of evil. Arendt was referring to Eichmann, the so-called architect of the Final Solution. But Hipkiss fits the bill perfectly.

'Is this the bit where you tell me "we're not so different, you and I"?' I say. 'Because if it is . . .'

'What?'

'I'd rather burn in hell.'

She blinks in surprise. For a fraction of a second, I think she's going to cry.

'Well,' she says, 'that's your choice. I'm sorry. I think—'

She stops for a second, and under the powder, a slight blush comes to her cheeks. She rises and passes me, close enough that I can smell her scent, then stands behind me and gently slips the hood over my head. She pulls the drawstring tight, then rests her hands on my shoulders. Through the borrowed T-shirt, her fingers feel cold.

'I think,' she says softly, her mouth close to my ear, 'we could have been good for each other.'

She presses down for a moment, then releases me.

There's the beep of the door, the whirr of the electronic lock, and then her voice.

'Mr Harkonnen? He's all yours.'

163

The dinner is world-class, courtesy of *La Belle Dame*'s Michelin-starred chef, but Kat barely tastes it. She has a biography prepared, but Staley prefers to talk about himself, dropping names of Saudi princes and Central European oligarchs, deposed world leaders, and billionaires. He drinks steadily, sometimes losing the thread of whatever it is he's rambling on about as his increasingly glassy eyes wander over her.

It doesn't take a genius to guess what he's planning later.

Kat's phone remains face down on the desk under the white rhino. As one self-absorbed anecdote T-bones into another, she says a prayer to any god who cares to listen for the final text from Rachel's team, giving her the last piece of information she needs, to rescue her.

Then, around 11 p.m., she feels a vibration beneath her feet and senses motion. She heads over to the panoramic window to see the lights of Buenos Aires gracefully rotating around them.

La Belle Dame is turning out to sea.

'What's happening?' she says. 'Where are we going?'

'What's the problem?' says Staley. 'Does the shit you're trying to sell me only work if we're in port? Is that why we're the target?'

'It works fine,' says Kat, which is true. But the plan doesn't. They could be out of range of cell service in less than an hour. And without the text, everything falls apart.

Behind her, reflected in the glass, she sees Staley approach.

'Come on,' he says, slurring his words slightly, close enough for her to feel his breath on her neck. 'Lighten up. How about we discuss those orphanages?'

She feels his hand on her waist.

She turns, pushing it away, but his arms wrap round her, and pull her towards him. She gets her elbows up between them, keeping his face and booze-soaked breath away. She knows that plenty of women in the business have leveraged their flesh to honeytrap men like Staley, but she can't understand how anyone could dissociate brain and body like that.

Though he's heavier and taller, she knows enough martial arts to put him on the floor with ease. But then she risks blowing the whole fucking operation.

They struggle like that for a second, but then her phone buzzes on the table.

Staley grudgingly releases her so she can pick up the phone. He stares at the screen in confusion.

'What the hell does this mean?'

'Let me see,' says Kat.

The text is from the same number as before, but this time it's just a code.

79855(3/2/1/0)

'It's good news,' says Kat.

'Good news how?'

'It means I don't have to fuck you.'

And with that, she knees him squarely in the balls.

164

Staley doubles over, then drops to his knees, wheezing with pain.

As he does, there's a mighty *whoosh* as fans blast cloaking chemical fog into the room, a dense cloud of aerosolised Glycol that renders the air opaque.

Staley gasps for air and grabs at Kat's leg, pulling himself up. 'Fucking bitch!'

She takes his head in both hands and slams his face down onto her knee, feeling the cartilage crunch as his nose breaks. He drops back to the floor again, blood pouring from between his hands.

Kat steps back, out of his reach. Staley rises, bellowing with rage and pain, and stumbles forward to attack again. Without taking her eyes off him, Kat feels behind her for one of the ivory tusks that bracket the desk. It's much heavier than she expected, but using it as a club, she lifts it up and swings it round with all her force.

The wooden plinth slams into Staley's temple, and he drops like a sack of flour. Through the thickening fog, she can see blood pooling from a head wound. He moans, then goes still.

That's for the white rhino, she thinks to herself.

The yacht's security alarms are blaring, but she can hear another sound above the wail. One by one – *beep, schick, beep, schick, beep, schick* – the ship's electronic doors are unlocking.

165

I'm back in the secure store, zip-tied at the wrists and ankles and Tasered a few times for good measure, when I hear the alarms, the whoosh of the fog, and doors unlocking.

Harkonnen's posted a guard outside with orders to shoot to kill if I escape, and I hear him shouting for help. Even with the fog, he'll be ready for me.

Harkonnen's priority will be to get Hipkiss to the ship's safe room, the citadel, which is on the same deck as me. Inside the citadel are manual overrides for the fogging and other security systems, which means Kat has maybe five minutes before the advantage of invisibility dissipates.

In the meantime, my job is to cause the biggest distraction I can.

But first, I need to get out of the zip ties. If they were in front of me it would be trivial, but my hands are behind me, and the ties are worryingly thick. I lean forward on my knees, raise my hands behind my back, then slam them down with all my force on my hips, trying to force my wrists apart and snap the ties. But instead, the plastic bites into the flesh of my wrists. I try again and again, ignoring the excruciating pain, until my wrists are bloody. But it's no good.

Fuck.

My arms aren't strong enough, which means the only alternative is bodyweight. My ankles are still bound, but I struggle to my feet, take a deep breath and launch myself upwards and backwards. I slam down hard on the steel floor, my full bodyweight driving my hips into my wrists. There's a loud snap, and for a second the pain in my wrists makes me think I broke them, but then I realise they're free.

I struggle to my knees and yank the door open.

Blinded by the fog, the guard outside immediately opens fire. But he's aiming where he expects me to be, not where I am. Staying low, I lunge forward, tackling him hard at the waist. The Sig Sauer blazes, bullets ricocheting off the metal walls and gangway, as I bring him down, but I manage to grab it and slam the stock into his forehead.

He stops moving.

From the deck above, there are shouts. They've heard the gunfire. Good.

My ankles are still bound, but I sledgehammer the butt of the Sig Sauer down on the zip ties, and they snap. I'm free.

The fog is completely opaque now. Down the corridor what sounds like a pair of guards hurries down from the crew deck. I press myself against the bulkhead, tracking the sounds of their boots. I let them get halfway down the corridor before I fire. They go down with a single burst, leaving my magazine empty.

I loot two magazines from their weapons. It isn't much, but it has to be enough.

166

Kat fumbles her way through the fog to the door of Staley's suite, trailing one hand against the wall, phone in the other. She stops for a second as she hears gunfire from below. *It's OK*, she tells herself. *We planned for this. It means he's here. It means this is working.*

She feels her way out into the gangway, then presses herself against the wall as she hears the muffled stamp of boots on the crew stairs. The door bangs open, and what sounds like three pairs of feet run out.

'Get Staley! I'll handle Hipkiss!' yells an accent she recognises. *Harkonnen.*

A man runs past her, so close she feels the air move, into the cabin she just left. From inside, she hears him shouting for Staley, but there's no response.

She holds her breath. *Please don't let him find the body.*

From Hipkiss's suite, the woman's voice.

'What happening?' Her voice is annoyed but edged with fear.

'He's free,' says Harkonnen. 'Seventeen.'

'You let him *go*?'

'The security systems have been compromised. We need to get you to the citadel NOW.'

'Where's Edgar?'

'No sign of him,' says the guard, emerging from behind Kat.

'He must have already gone down,' says Harkonnen. 'Now, *please*, ma'am—'

The crew door closes behind them as they ferry her down to the lower decks.

It will take them forty-five seconds to get to the citadel. A minute to operate the override, and maybe two minutes for the fog to clear.

She has four minutes and counting.

167

From above, I can hear voices getting closer. It's Harkonnen and a couple of men, bringing Hipkiss down to the citadel. But I don't hear Staley, which means he's still above deck, and maybe still a threat. Meanwhile, more of Harkonnen's men clatter down from the deck above and run past me towards the store room I just escaped.

Ahead, I hear the citadel door open and close. Harkonnen's voice orders two men inside as bodyguards, then he too runs past to where the others have found the wounded. Now another arrives with a million-candlepower flashlight which penetrates a few feet into the fog, and Harkonnen orders them to use it to clear the deck.

The beam blazes towards me, but I slip inside the stairwell as it flashes past, holding the door open a crack to stop it from clicking.

'Deck's clear,' says the man with the flashlight.

'Find the motherfucker,' yells Harkonnen. 'Staley's missing, and so is the girl. Start on the owner's deck, then work down.'

The owner's deck is where Kat is. *Shit.*

I need to get there before they do.

I sprint up the stairs, my footfalls soft, releasing the door. It self-closes with a loud click, and from below, I hear Harkonnen's voice.

'That's him. Go, go, go!'

168

Kat feels her way into Hipkiss's suite.

She knows where the safe is from the blueprints. The number Rachel texted – *79855(3/2/1/0)* – is the combination, picked up by Wen's visual team. The slashes at the end mean the last number could be 3, 2, 1 or 0, a code they arranged in case the team couldn't read the whole thing.

She trails her hand along the wall to where the safe should be, but can feel nothing.

She subdues a moment of panic.

All it means is that the panel concealing it must be flush-mounted.

She clicks on the flashlight on her phone. The fog's so thick that she has to put her face six inches from the surface to see anything. Wen's team told her there was a mural, but nothing has prepared her for what she sees.

It's a floor-to-ceiling reproduction of Leonardo da Vinci's *The Last Supper*, accurate in every detail but one. To the right of Jesus, the figure of John the Apostle has been replaced by an airbrushed version of Hipkiss herself, with flowing blond hair and a loose blouse falling open to reveal a deep cleavage that, Kat is reasonably sure, Hipkiss does not possess in real life.

Boy, lady, do you have issues, she thinks to herself, then runs her hands over the surface more carefully. There is a panel in the wall for the safe, disguised by the busy lines of the mural.

There must be some way to open it, but where's the control? The blueprints didn't show it, so Wen's team were supposed to text her with the information after the code.

She pulls out her phone and sees the problem.

No signal.

They're already out of range of cell service.

She's going to have to find it herself.

On the far side of the mural, she finds a desk and feels for a button, but there's nothing there. Beyond that is a bookcase. She feels under shelves, frantically pulls books out.

Still nothing.

For a moment, she thinks she hears a noise behind her. She stops dead still, holding her breath, to listen. But there's only the hiss of the fans still blowing fog into the room, muted shouts and the clatter of feet from below.

Nerves, she tells herself. *You're imagining things. Focus!*

If the control isn't in the desk and it isn't in the bookcase, it has to be part of the mural. But the thing is massive. Twenty feet wide, maybe eight high, and in the fog she can only see a tiny portion of it at a time.

Be smart, she tells herself. *Where would she put it?*

Kat's the opposite of religious, but *The Last Supper* was an assignment at community college. The figures on the far left are bit players. Same thing on the right. To Christ's immediate left are Thomas, James and Philip. But the left signifies lower status. To his right, there's the John/Hipkiss character. And then there's Peter, but he's hidden by Judas Iscariot. The man who would betray Christ for thirty pieces of silver, clutched in a bag in his right hand.

Thirty pieces of silver.

Money.

The kind of thing you keep in a safe.

She feels the surface. It's smooth. But there's a sudden click as a touch sensor operates and a panel lifts out and away from the wall on hinged arms.

She shines the phone's light into the cavity.

The safe glints back.

169

I pound up the port stairwell. There are men behind me and others including Harkonnen paralleling me in the staircase opposite. I loose a couple of shots behind me to keep my pursuers back, but there's nothing I can do about the others.

Just as I make the guest deck, the ship's whooping alarm abruptly stops, and the fans blowing fog whirr down and stop. The overrides in the citadel have been activated. Kat now has maybe two minutes before she's totally exposed.

Above me I think I hear boots descending, so I exit into the VIP area. The fog is already beginning to clear. To my left is the lounge and, dimly visible, the grand curving staircase that leads to the owner's suites.

I'm hopelessly outgunned and can't afford a firefight here. But that doesn't mean I can't even the odds. I fire at the door to the port stairs, put a couple of shells into the starboard version, then run towards the curving staircase.

Still half blinded by the fog, both sides open fire at each assuming their target is me. A man cries out in pain, taking a hit. It takes more shots, confused yells and swearing before they figure out it's friendly fire.

I'm almost at the grand staircase when I hear footsteps behind me. A hulking shape looms out of the fog. It's Harkonnen. He fires and a shell rips into my side. I blast back, hitting him in the chest. He falls backwards, but then struggles up, saved by body armour.

The pain tears into me as I stumble up the stairs, firing backwards, using up precious ammunition to keep Harkonnen at bay. As I make the top, I hear him below, splitting his squad into three – one for each stairwell and one to follow me up the staircase.

I can already feel myself going into shock, but I'll be trapped if I don't move, so I retreat to a bulkhead wall. Around me the fog is thinning fast. I'm outnumbered, outflanked, almost out of ammunition, and I can't cover all three staircases simultaneously.

I shake my head clear and remind myself: my objective isn't to survive. It's to buy Kat enough time to open the safe.

I loose a couple of final shots, then run for Hipkiss's door.

170

Around her, the fog is clearing, the gunfire steadily closer and more intense, punctuated by shouts and the odd cry of pain. Kat tries to shut it all out and focus on the safe.

Ballistic steel, steel deadbolts. A five-spoked metal handle. And, according to the manual, a number pad which allows three tries before it shrills an alarm and dumps into failsafe mode for an hour.

She checks the numbers on her phone. 7-9-8-5-5 then one of 3, 2, 1 or 0. Four possibilities, but only three guesses.

She taps in C to clear the memory, then 7-9-8-5-5, a beep for each keypress.

She hesitates, then – *here goes* – hits 3 as the last digit, then # to enter.

The lock responds with four beeps.

Wrong.

She wipes sweat off her palms and tries again.

C-7-9-8-5-5. This time she hits 2 – then #.

Four beeps. *Wrong.*

Fuck fuck fuck.

She thinks she hears another noise, but it's hard to tell with the gunfire.

One more attempt left. Everything depends on this.

She hits the familiar combination again. *Beep beep beep beep beep beep.*

The last digit has to be either 0 or 1.

A binary choice.

Fifty, fifty.

Just fucking choose, she yells silently at herself. *It doesn't matter.*

She hits 0, but as her finger touches the # button something stops her.

You were always bad at fifty-fifty choices, says a voice in her head. *Coin flips, if you said tails, it was heads. Heads, it was tails. Every time, your whole life, you always chose wrong.*

Quickly, she hits C to cancel, then 7-9-8-5-5-1. She hesitates again, the gunfire is closer now. She's running out of time.

Just do it.

She hits #. The locks squawks three times. Inside, a click as something moves.

It worked!

She spins the handle, and pulls the heavy door open, illuminating the contents with her phone. Inside are two shelves. On the lower shelf are legal documents, passports, a money pouch, and a bag that looks like it might hold precious stones. Several phones, including two boxed brand-new flip phones, three bare hard drives, several bottles of pills, a tattered family Bible, and a bundle of letters and photographs held together with a rubber band.

The upper shelf is almost bare, but for a small orange waterproof case. She's just reaching for it when she hears a voice behind her.

'Find what you were looking for?'

171

Staley staggers out of the translucent fog, covered in blood, a deep wound in the side of his head, breath bubbling through his broken nose. He looks like a figure from a nightmare, but that's not the worst part.

Lofted above his head is the broadsword that hung above his bed.

Before she can react, Staley lets out a huge roar and charges towards her, bringing the blade down with all his force. Kat throws herself sideways, feeling the wind of the sword as it slashes past her cheek and clangs off the heavy door of the safe.

As she picks herself up, Staley turns and charges again. This time, she dodges the other way, and the broadsword smashes a Cocobolo desk to tinder.

Kat could easily outrun him – he's old, injured, and tiring – but she still doesn't have the card, and Staley stands between her and the safe.

They're bull and matador now. Seeing her hesitate, Staley hurls himself towards her once more, but this time she's ready for him. As he whirls the broadsword like a mace, she uses a judo throw to send him sprawling across the cabin.

As he picks himself up, she runs for the safe. Staley's tiring fast, his breath coming in great gasps, but somehow he manages to hoist the broadsword once more, and charges.

Kat reaches into the top shelf of the safe, then glances back to see him thundering towards her, bloody face straining with effort, the broadsword high.

At the last moment Kat's hand finds what it was looking for.

Not the orange case, but the tiny 9mm Ruger, Hipkiss's personal protection weapon that was hidden behind it. She has no time to check if it's loaded, but in a single fluid movement – the kind of thing she practised over and over again in the improvised range behind the gas station – she flicks off the safety, racks the slide and pulls the trigger.

The shot hits Staley in the centre of his forehead. He tumbles forward, dead before he hits the ground, and his hands release the broadsword. It arcs through the air towards her, but Kat steps aside and it impales itself instead in his sister's vanity portrait of herself, standing beside Jesus.

'Nice shooting,' I say.

172

Kat lowers the gun, seeing the blood and the hole ripped into my T-shirt. The safe is open. Edgar's body lies on the floor, a neat bullet hole in his forehead. Behind Kat, a broadsword is impaled, still vibrating, in a gigantic and fantastically tacky portrait of Hipkiss. I try to guess the sequence of events that led up to this scenario and fail.

'You're wounded,' she says.

'I'm okay,' I lie. 'You have the cards?'

She pulls the orange box out of the safe, opens it, then shows me two nCards – the one Hipkiss had, and the one I swapped for Mireille – nestled together in anti-static foam.

Outside, there are boots on the staircase. I have ten rounds left, or maybe nine. I rotate out of the door and use three of them. Returning fire slams into the metal bulkhead as I duck back in.

'Go,' I say. 'Use the balcony. I'll hold them off as long as I can.'

'We're out of cell range,' says Kat. 'I don't know if—'

I cut her off with another burst of three out of the door.

'If you know of another way we get off this piece of junk alive,' I yell, 'be sure to let me know.'

I blast another round out of the door. Two or three left. I'm using it too fast, but Kat needs to get clear, and this is the only way.

She wraps the strap of the orange box around her wrist. But she's still hesitating.

And I know why. Because she's thinking the same thing I am.

It's the last time either of us may ever see the other.

There are about a hundred things I need to say to her, and a thousand I want to, but there isn't time for any of them, so instead I yell:

'GO!'

She grins, unfolds her middle finger, and blows a kiss from it.

173

Kat runs onto Edgar's balcony. The night is dark, moonless, stars obscured by a layer of high cirrus. She scans the horizon, but there's no sign of any other vessel apart from *La Jolie Fille*.

From inside, there's yet more gunfire.

He'll be OK, she lies to herself. *He always is. He's a survivor.*

She retrieves a lifejacket from one of the hatches in the hull, then kicks off her shoes and pulls off the dress. The seawater temperature around Buenos Aires hovers around 70°F this time of year, cold but survivable, and she needs freedom of movement more than any insulation a dress picked out by a horny fifty-something is going to give her.

She slips on the lifejacket, cold against her skin, and buckles it up.

Here goes.

She climbs the rail, balances there for a moment.

From somewhere, she hears her mother's voice.

If something scares you, run towards it.

She grips the orange box tightly, and launches herself into the dark.

174

I fire my last two shells. *Click.* I'm out of bullets now.

I could run inside and follow Kat off the balcony, but I'd be drawing fire onto her. And as much as I'm desperate for her to live, it's not just her I'm thinking about.

Mireille is free now. She's been through enough. I'm not going to let her grow up in a world where a lunatic like Hipkiss has the power to launch a nuclear strike.

If that means I die here, so be it.

175

It's forty feet to the ocean surface. The slam of the water is brutal, and knocks all the wind out of Kat. The water's cold, but thankfully nothing like what she experienced in Svalbard. The lifejacket pops her up quickly, but as Kat gasps for air, she sees its saltwater-activated light strobing out powerful white flashes in groups of three.

Kat shakes the hair out of her eyes and tries to cover it with her hand, but it's too late. On board, a man's voice yells out, 'I have her! Overboard, port side, four o'clock!'

La Belle Dame is still under power, moving away from her, but Kat can make out a figure on the deck, pointing. Two more figures join him and start firing, using the glow of the flash through her fingers as the target.

Bullets zip into the water. She has no choice. She unbuckles the lifejacket, tosses it as far as she can, takes a huge breath, and dives under the waves.

176

I consign whatever remains of my soul to the hereafter, close my eyes and am about to burst out of the door into a hail of bullets when a crewman's voice yells, 'The girl's in the water! She's in the water!'

The distraction gives me a chance to glance around the door. One of Harkonnen's men appears from Edgar's suite. 'No sign of Mr Staley, but there's blood everywhere.'

'Fuck!' screams Harkonnen. He yells at his men, splitting them into three teams – one to the rear deck, one to hold me here, and the third to launch the tender.

'Shoot to kill,' he tells them, his voice receding back down below. 'Whatever happens, don't let the bitch get away.'

Fuck.

Hipkiss's suite looks aft, a wall of windows giving a panoramic view of the floodlit decks below. A couple of guards are already at the rail, and more are joining them. Most carry snubnose semis, useless at range, but a moment later Harkonnen joins them carrying an H-S Heavy Tactical Rifle with a thermal scope.

It's one of the most accurate rifles on the planet.

He yells at his grunts to stand aside and settles the rifle on the rail.

The night is dark, but Kat's body heat against the cold of the water will light her up like a signal flare. She can't be more than a few hundred yards away. In his day, Harkonnen was one of the best shots in the world, and the calibre of the rifle makes an instant kill.

Kat will be dead in a few seconds if I don't do something.

I drop my gun, sprint out onto the balcony, leap up onto the rail and launch myself into the air. The muscles in my side, shredded by Harkonnen's bullet, spasm, but I blank the pain. Twenty feet below, I hit the deck hard, roll forward and catapult myself towards Harkonnen.

One of his men sees me, yells and starts firing, but I'm moving too fast and his bullets skitter off the deck behind me. Harkonnen's massive head flicks round to see me hurtling towards him, and he spins round to fire, but he's too late.

I hit him with full force, grab the rifle with both hands and ram it hard and up into his chin. The force of the impact drives him backwards over the rail, and takes me with him. We tumble through the air for a second, flailing and struggling, then slam into the inky ocean.

Still locked in battle, but weighed down by the rifle and Harkonnen's loadout, we sink.

177

Kat's still underwater, swimming as hard as she can as bullets spear into the ocean around her, the dull thud in her water-logged ears growing more distant as the guards continue to fire at the strobing lifejacket.

Finally, unable to hold her breath any longer, she breaks the surface to suck down air. Ahead of her is the dark shape of *La Jolie Fille*. If she could just make it behind the support vessel, it would block any shots from the yacht. But she's tiring in the cold of the ocean, with no lifejacket to keep her up, and even if she survives the bullets she'll be left in open water, too far from shore to have any hope of making it to dry land.

She's trying to figure out if it's better to drown, or try to make it to *La Jolie Fille* and hide, when she hears the sound of a marine engine.

Her hopes spike, and are immediately dashed. It's *La Belle Dame*'s tender, roaring out from the stern, bow lifted high, two armed guards scanning the surface as a third operates a powerful searchlight. Kat ducks her head back under-water, knowing her pale skin will give her away the moment the floodlight flashes across it. But one of the guards is wearing goggles, which she knows will show her body heat.

The orange case is still strapped to her wrist. She could open it, let it sink, but there's no guarantee Hipkiss hasn't already made a copy of the malware, and if by some miracle Kat survives, they'll be left with no way to publish the exploit and eviscerate the threat.

But then, behind her, there's the muffled roar of another engine – an outboard, this time, and much closer than the tender. Kat pops her head up above water again to see a Zodiac inflatable surging towards her from behind the support vessel, where it was hiding. A flashlight momentarily blinds her as it picks her out, and then suddenly the boat's beside her, throttling down, and hands are hauling her out of the water.

The moment she's on board, the Zodiac wheels round, throttles up and accelerates away.

'Get down! Get down!' says a woman's voice.

It's Rachel hunkered beside her, sheltering from the shells that zip over their heads, steering with one hand as a heavyset man behind them fires back, using the rear seat as a rest.

'You okay?' says Rachel.

Kat nods, coughing out water she swallowed.

'Keep going,' says the man in the back. Something in his voice is familiar, but Kat can't place it. 'We're too fast for them, but we need to get clear.'

He exchanges fire with them for another minute, the gunfire from the other boat becoming steadily quieter, until it finally stops.

'They're turning back,' he says. 'We're safe.'

Kat levers herself up, shivering, as her adrenaline fades and the cold hits her. As Rachel throws a blanket around her shoulders, Kat looks back to see who it was the voice belonged to, and has to wipe saltwater out of her eyes to make sure she isn't seeing things.

'Vilmos,' she says. 'Is that *you*?'

178

I can feel the pressure squeezing me as we sink. Around us, the blackness is total. All I know is what I can feel. The giant Finn struggles, trying to wrestle the sniper rifle round to aim at me. Water will stop a bullet dead within a few feet, but a shot at this range will kill me. He's taller, stronger, and I'm wounded, and manages to get the muzzle by my head, but desperation gives me strength to keep it an inch away.

He pulls the trigger anyway.

The crack of the bullet, carried by the water into my ears, is like a tank going off. Pain spears into my skull as my eardrums rupture, but somehow I stop myself from screaming, because the air in my lungs is all that's keeping me alive.

Instead, I release the rifle and grab for his face, clawing my thumbs into his eyeballs. Air bubbles up against my face, and I realise it's *him* screaming. One of his hands grips my shirt. I try to pry it off, but as I do I feel a dull pain in my uninjured side, as if he'd hit me with a hammer. Then another. And another. And I know what it is, because I've felt it before.

It's a knife. He's stabbing me in the side.

I grab it, feel the razor-sharp blade slice my palm, and slide it up to the hilt, trying to force it away. But as I do, the fist of his other hand smashes into the side of my face.

I can't last much longer. I'm losing this fight, and my body is screaming at me to breathe, but breathing is instant death. No matter what happens, I'll be dead in less than a minute unless I can think of something.

Then I remember: he's wearing body armour. That's ten pounds at least, plus boots, clothes, ammunition, and whatever else he's carrying. All of that means he's going to sink, not float. And if he's stabbing me with one hand and punching me with the other, that means he's no longer holding on to me.

In a fast, single movement, I grab his right shoulder with both hands, spin him round, clasp my hands under his sternum, and jerk backwards and upwards with all my strength.

I'm giving him the Heimlich Manoeuvre, forcing what's left of the air out of his lungs. It's meant to save a life, to force out a piece of food that's choking someone. But I'm using it to kill him.

As I release my grip, his chest expands, sucking water into his lungs. He panics, frantically scrabbling for a hold on me, but I push his shoulders down and kick them off with my feet towards the surface.

He sinks like a stone.

Then at the last moment, I feel a hand wrap around my ankle.

He's going to pull me down with him.

179

Vilmos turns and grins. 'Svalbard was too fucking cold anyway. The climate here's much better.'

He looses off another couple of shots at the retreating tender. One takes out the searchlight.

'Fancy shooting,' says Rachel.

'Call of duty,' says Vilmos. 'All those hours paid off.'

Rachel reaches under the Zodiac's wheel, and pulls something out.

'Here,' she says, handing it to Kat. 'Drink this. It'll keep you warm. It'll take us an hour at least to make it back.'

Kat unscrews the top. The sweet smell of hot chocolate, overtones of rum.

'You have the cards?' asks Vilmos, stowing his rifle and moving forward.

Kat pulls off the wrist strap securing the orange case, and hands it to him. Then:

'Wait,' she says. 'What about Jones. Seventeen?'

Rachel and Vilmos swap a look. They knew this was coming.

'What about him?' says Rachel.

'The plan was, while they're looking for me, he jumps off the other side, and we circle back to pick him up.'

'No, honey,' says Rachel. 'That's not the plan.'

'That's what he told me,' insists Kat.

'That's what he *told* you was the plan,' says Rachel. 'But it was never the plan.'

180

Harkonnen's massive hands are wrapped around my ankles. I tear at them with my fingers, but I can't get them loose.

Down, down we go.

This is it, I tell myself. *This is what you dreamed before, in Svalbard.*

This is how it ends.

And then I feel his grip relax, his hands slip away as he loses consciousness. The Heimlich did the trick, emptying out the air from his lungs so he blacked out before me.

I kick for the surface, the air I kept in my lungs buoying me upwards.

I surface, sucking huge, whooping gusts of air, trying to shake my head clear.

A half-mile away, *La Belle Dame*'s tender is turning back towards its mothership, its searchlight illuminating the receding Zodiac momentarily as it pulls away from them.

That means Kat made it. Rachel and Vilmos found her. She's going to be okay.

I'm going to die here in the water, but it doesn't matter, because we won.

But then I see it.

The mil-spec Bell sits on the pad of *La Jolie Fille*.

The cockpit is lit up, the pilot on board, blades already turning.

That's why the tender is heading back. Not because they've given up, but because they're going to use the helicopter to follow the Zodiac.

It'll be a turkey shoot.

My stab wounds are deep.

There's a bullet hole in my other side.

I'm losing blood, and fast.

My head's light.

I'm exhausted.

But I'm not done yet.

Digging down for the last of my strength, I strike out for *La Jolie Fille*, racing the tender to the sea-dock.

I make it with maybe twenty seconds to spare, pull myself up the ladder and stumble, bleeding, up the stairs to the flight deck. Behind me, the guards on the tender see me and open fire. Bullets chink and whine off the metal, but I make it to the helipad.

The helo door is still open, the pilot focused on his pre-flight checks, and he doesn't see me until the last minute. I crash a fist into his face, then throw him out. He lands heavily, then runs, limping to where the guards are already heading up the stairs.

I need a moment to breathe, but there's no time. I should apply pressure to the wound, try to staunch the flow of blood. But it takes two hands to fly a helicopter, so I raise the collective, getting the Bell light on the skids, then throttle up hard to maximum power.

The chopper unsticks quickly – with just me and a full tank of fuel on board, the big bird is riding light. I push forward and right on the cyclic, accelerating forward and arcing away from *La Belle Dame*, gaining height and speed as I go.

181

Rachel eases off on the throttle to conserve fuel. The last thing they need to do is run out before they make sure. But as the engine note falls, Kat hears the chatter of *La Belle Dame*'s helicopter and turns to see the Bell arcing towards them.

She turns to Rachel in alarm. 'Go! Go! They're coming for us. We're sitting ducks.'

But now the sound of the rotors changes, dopplering down.

Kat looks back. The helicopter is no longer heading towards them. It arcs round, noses down to gain speed, and vectors directly towards *La Belle Dame*.

Rachel idles the engine and swings the Zodiac around to watch.

Kat stares at her in confusion. 'What the fuck are you doing?'

Rachel shakes her head, her face suddenly severe and sad. 'It's not coming for us.'

'What do you mean?' says Kat, but her insides churn, because she already knows.

182

I think back to that first day, lifting Mireille off the couch as she slept, and carrying her to the Gladiator wrapped in a Navajo blanket, without a single clue that she was my daughter but with an unearthly sense that something had changed in my life.

I think back to the few hours I spent feeding her Cheerios and Pop-Tarts, trying to get a look at the sock monkey that had my name, and wondering about the significance of the tiny, lethal, stranger who had erupted into my life.

Those are the only things she will remember me by. She'll never know that I was her father, or that the name she called the one-eyed monkey by was my own. She'll never know how much blood was on the hands that lifted her out of the Gladiator and carried her into the motel, or the battles I fought to save her from the life my and her mother's combined histories consigned her to.

I'll never get to see her grow up, not because I don't want to, but because she needs a future that's severed from her past, transplanted like a seedling into fresh, fertile earth that will allow her to grow into who she always should have been.

In three or four years, she'll be a teenager, and a few short years beyond that, a woman.

If she has anything of Gracious's brains and courage, she'll be a force to reckon with.

If she has anything of me, let it be not what I am, but what I might have been before my own future was destroyed by seeing Junebug die. And if there is anything of Junebug in her, let it be the person I loved and who loved me, the person she might have been before that future was annulled by what her father did to her.

I say a silent prayer to the universe: *may the circle of violence be broken here.*

I shove the cyclic forward.

183

The Bell's avionics scream at me: *SINK RATE! SINK RATE! PULL UP! PULL UP!*

La Belle Dame Sans Merci is directly in front of me. The fuel tanks are amidships, right at the waterline, and I'm aimed at the weakest point: the invisible join the blueprints revealed between the metal plates that form her hull.

By now my airspeed is a hundred and fifty knots and climbing. It finally sinks in to the crew what I'm about to do, because some run, while others open fire from the rail. Two hundred yards out, the first bullets hit, chinking into the fuselage, then shattering the side window.

Then the weirdest thing happens.

It's as if time slows, and I'm no longer the pilot of a helicopter, but an astronaut alone in his ship, piloting through an asteroid field. And my ship is accelerating, faster and faster, and the asteroids are getting thicker and thicker. And then suddenly it's a video game, and I'm slewing left and right to avoid the asteroids, only the asteroids are bullets now and—

—I shake my head clear. The blood loss is taking its toll. But I only need to keep the helicopter straight for a second or two longer.

A hundred yards out, a burst of automatic fire crawls across the windshield. The external glass layer fractures. Fragments of acrylic spear into my face. I throw up my hands to protect myself, and the first bullet rips into my left arm, then the second into my shoulder. By the time the third hits, I'm no longer even partially in control.

The Bell begins to spin madly, a whirling, ballistic missile.

Payload: a ton of aviation fuel.

And me.

184

Kat shoots upright in the Zodiac as the helicopter spins wildly out of control.

'NO!' she yells. But there's nothing she can do.

A moment later, it smashes into the side of *La Belle Dame*, rotors buckling and hurling themselves into the air. As its full fuel tank bursts, the Bell explodes into a searing fireball that mushrooms upwards, the twisted wreckage settling into the water as flaming debris rains down.

But that's not the end of it.

The impact rips a hole in the side of the hull, exactly where *La Belle Dame*'s diesel tanks are located. The tanks rupture, brim-full after refuelling in port, and diesel oil gushes out, only to be vaporised by the inferno that is now the Bell. A second explosion tears through the megayacht, then another, then another, as the fuel compartments ignite in succession, an unstoppable chain reaction.

The Zodiac is a mile away, and it's five seconds before they feel the shockwaves. Its hull split wide open at the waterline by the explosions, *La Belle Dame* is already taking on water and beginning to list. Oil burns fiercely on the surface, painting the hull of the megayacht orange as it continues to spill out, while inside is an inferno.

Above decks, some crew are already pulling on life jackets and launching themselves from the high side of the ship into the water, while others attempted to get the yacht's high-tech life-capsules launched. The tender, which raced away from the initial explosions, circles back cautiously, but the continuing explosions keep it at bay.

'We should go back,' says Kat. 'He could be in there. He could be alive.'

'Sorry, honey,' says Rachel. Her voice isn't quite steady. 'There's no way anybody could have survived that.'

'You don't know that. You *can't* know that,' says Kat.

She scrambles forward to pull Rachel away from the wheel but suddenly finds herself on the wrong end of Vilmos's rifle.

'The fuck?'

'We can't risk it,' says Vilmos. 'There's nothing we can do, and we need to get this shit uploaded.'

'Don't you understand?' says Rachel. 'This was what he *wanted*. This was the plan all along.'

Vilmos's gun doesn't waver. Kat sinks back down.

Rachel throttles up, wheels round, and they surge towards the lights of Buenos Aires glimmering on the horizon.

Kat stares back at *La Belle Dame,* now on its side. From it, a pillar of flame reaches up into the night sky, the stern beginning to loft into the air as the bow sinks.

But all she can hear are words repeating in her head as the unbearable reality of it sinks in:

He's gone. He's gone. He's gone.

PART TWELVE

185

It feels like the end of the world, and in some ways, it is.

She's been travelling for days, with little sleep. Buenos Aires to São Paulo, São Paolo to Heathrow, a six-hour layover, then another plane to Glasgow. Four hours on a bus to a rainswept ferry terminal, little more than a parking apron and a few rusting Portacabins. A heaving ferry through a vomit-inducing Atlantic swell to a tiny island fishing community. Another, much shorter trip on a tiny rustbucket ferry to the neighbouring island, then a twenty-mile drive along the coast in a cramped Hebridean taxi with a silent Scot at the wheel and a single working windshield wiper. She thought it would take her all the way, but the road has slowly decomposed from a single lane of blacktop, to cracked asphalt and grass, to a dirt track which the driver refuses to attempt.

Seeing Kat's face, the driver offers to take her back to the ferry for half price. But Kat figures she's come this far, so she steps out into the wind and the rain and watches the taxi do a nineteen-point turn, then fade back down the winding road and vanish into the mist and the sky and the hills.

The four miles down the rutted dirt track take her an hour and a half, stumbling and slipping as the daylight fails, wind whipping her hair into her face. Her coat was warm enough when it was dry, but she's soaked to the skin in ten minutes. The taxi driver, in one of her few utterances, told her it was a lazy wind – it couldn't be bothered to go round you, so it went straight through you.

The countryside here is both bleak and beautiful when it appears through the curtains of rain. Up on the hillside, deer graze in the downpour, one big stag watching her pass with cautious interest.

Kat's phone died an hour ago – the charger in the taxi didn't work – and she's starting to wonder if she's somehow taken the wrong road, when she finally sees it appear through the mist and rain. A solid, white, ancient stone-built house with a slate roof, nestled in the hillside overlooking the strait to the mainland. It's flanked by a pair of fieldstone barns, one with the roof half collapsed, revealing the timbers. Inside, to the right of the red-painted front door, there's a single light burning, but a faded yellow curtain decorated with flowers is drawn across, so she can't see who, if anyone, is inside.

It takes her a moment to summon the courage to knock on the door, but she does.

If something scares you, run towards it.

186

For the first twenty-four hours, they left her alone. At first, Rachel tried to talk to her, but she had no wish to be comforted and pulled away from her touch. She sat alone in the bedroom, knees pulled up to her chin on the bed, watching TV reports of the sinking of *La Belle Dame*, the unexplained helicopter crash, the race to find survivors, and then to recover bodies.

The first footage was from the early hours of the morning, the megayacht still burning as she sank. By sunrise, she was gone, settling on the bottom in a hundred feet of water. Later that day, divers were sent down. One of the first bodies they recovered was Staley's, but the citadel, where Hipkiss was thought to have been taken, remained secured from inside. Teams of demolition divers were eventually pulled in from offshore gas platforms and used underwater thermal lances to cut through the four-inch steel. Inside they found two bodies, both men, but no sign of Hipkiss.

The internet immediately began to buzz with wild rumours that she'd been raptured or would miraculously appear after three days like Christ himself. After studying the blueprints, Wen came up with a more likely explanation: some kind of one- or two-person submersible either retrofitted or kept off the plans that allowed her to escape. But with limited range, and most likely damaged in the explosions, the chances were that she was at the bottom now too.

Kat used the DVR to rewind the footage of survivors being rescued, pulled out of the water by helicopters, or hauling themselves onto the support boat or the fishing boats and coastguard vessels that came to help. She watched it over and over again, for any fragment of evidence that I might have survived. But there was none.

The second night, Rachel brought her *locro* soup, and Kat agreed to ingest something other than the bottle of rum that hadn't been out of her hand since they made it back. Rachel told her Vilmos had combined the two halves of Deep Threat and sent copies to major intelligence agencies, tech giants like Apple and Google, and selected other parties. The whole thing would be made public shortly. The danger of the world being hacked into WWIII was receding.

It didn't make Kat feel any better.

Through the door, she could see Vilmos squatting on the floor, playing with Mireille and teaching her English phrases. He was a natural with kids, she could see that, but Mireille was quiet, now dressed in some of the clothes that Marvellous had bought for her, a pink bobble back in her hair, the one-eyed sock monkey comfortably ensconced in a chair watching them.

Rachel and Mireille had bonded almost immediately, partly because of the sock monkey but mostly because Rachel knew Marvellous, the uncle whom Mireille had heard about from stories her mother had told her. The one thing Rachel had been dreading most was telling Mireille that Gracious was dead, but Harkonnen, in his unspeakable cruelty, had gotten there before her.

'The man with the burned face told me *Maman* was dead,' she said in French. 'He said he killed her.'

Rachel told Kat she showed almost no emotion as she said it, and Kat couldn't help thinking back to what I had told her about my own mother's death, about how I chose to feel nothing, but how the feelings later exploded into violence and madness.

When she told Rachel, all Rachel could do was shrug. 'We'll show her love,' she said. 'That's all we can do, and hope that when the dam bursts, we're there to catch the deluge.'

By 'we', she meant herself and Vilmos, who had chosen to stay. His disclosure of Deep Threat had at least somewhat erased the memory of his previous transgressions in the eyes of the world's Three Letter Agencies. He would never be seen as a white hat, but at least the threat of deportation had receded. There were adoption papers for Rachel on their way, courtesy of The Dentist. If what it took to square the circle was a marriage of convenience between the two of them, well, as Rachel pointed out, it would be a hell of a party, and she would help Vilmos pick out a furry.

'Look,' said Rachel, watching Kat poke at the soup. 'He's gone. I get it. You feel like shit. Maybe you loved him, I don't know. I think he loved you, as much as he could ever love anyone. Yes, it's sad. But he did it because it was worth it. I know it's sad, but—'

Kat couldn't take it any more. Still half drunk from the rum, she hurled the bowl of soup against the wall. Chunks of pumpkin, sausage, beans and corn slid down.

'I'm not *sad*,' she yelled. 'I'm *fucking* furious. How dare he do this to me? Lie to me, use me as a tool, then kill himself because he thinks that's the only way to save the fucking world! All because of some ridiculous messiah complex, like I'm such a stupid fucking girl that he can't tell me what's going on. Fuck him, and fuck you too for playing along.'

'Okay,' said Rachel. She picked up the pieces of the bowl and walked out, then paused at the door. 'You can stay as long as you like, you know,' she said. 'But only if you can clean that shit off the wall.'

Three weeks later, the postcard arrived.

187

At first, there's nothing, but then she sees a shadow move across the curtain. Then there's the sound of someone moving inside, slow, with the thump of a stick.

The postcard had no message and nothing written on it but an address in handwriting she didn't recognise, along with a smeared postmark over a Scottish stamp. Rachel didn't even bother to show it to Kat, assuming it was meant for a previous tenant who had died or moved out. But the moment Kat found it, discarded on a table, she was gripped by a feeling that it meant something.

On the front was a photograph which showed a spectacular vista of low mountains, blue sky and frigid water. The photograph looked like it had been taken in the seventies, with the faded colours of Kodachrome. When she flipped the card over, the caption read simply *SCOTLAND*. The only visible human habitation was a single white house in the bottom left corner, half hidden behind a hillside. It was barely there at all, but it was there.

It took her a day of searching on Google Earth before she figured out the location: a remote island in Scotland's Hebrides archipelago. She found the house and zoomed in as far as she could, then sat there staring at it for an hour. The next day, early in the morning, while the others were still asleep, she left without saying goodbye or leaving any clue where she was going.

The last thing she did was look in on Mireille, fast asleep in the half-light, the one-eyed monkey still clutched to her. Standing in the doorway, she wondered momentarily what it would be like to be a mother. But she's sure now she never will be. She's killed two people, and the fact her conscience doesn't bother her has convinced her that she's inherited her father's killer genes. It's a curse she does not intend to pass on to anyone else. She's never bought my line that the first time you kill someone, you kill the version of yourself that never killed anyone. She doesn't feel any different at all. Maybe it's more like becoming President. It doesn't *change* who you are, it *reveals* who you are.

And now here she is, standing at the door, revealed, waiting for someone inside to shuffle from the kitchen and answer it. As she waits, rain pelting her back and drumming on the windows, her heart sinks steadily: it sounds like an old woman.

Maybe she got the whole thing wrong.

It wouldn't be the first time.

The door opens.

188

Kat stands there, drenched, hair plastered over her face, head down, hands stuffed into her coat. She looks like she slipped and fell a couple of times on the farm track because there's mud all up one side of her. Her face is white, as much from anger as the cold.

But when she sees me, her anger fades.

'I thought you were dead,' is all she says.

'I was,' I say, still wheezing from the exertion of making it to the front door.

She helps me back inside.

We sit at the rickety kitchen table. Just getting to and from the door has exhausted me. It takes a minute to get my breath. Kat stares round, taking in the farmhouse. There's no heating, no phone, no electricity except that provided by a generator. The stove is wood-fired, water heated by a propane tank. I tell her where the tea is stored, and she uses the kettle that sits there boiling to make some for us. There's a bottle of Islay whisky on the table, which I add to both mugs.

'I didn't know if you'd come,' I say.

'I didn't know either,' says Kat, hands cupped around the tea. The doors to the ancient stove are open now, and steam's rising off her into the cold air. 'But I had to know one way or another. Are you going to tell me what happened?'

I shrug. 'I'm not even sure myself. All I know is I got shot
to pieces, but some lizard part of my brain must have managed to bail me out of the chopper just before it hit. I have a
vague memory of being pulled onto a boat. Turns out it was
an Argentinian coastguard vessel . . . the yacht put out a May-
day the moment the emergency systems were triggered. A
chopper airlifted me to Buenos Aires. Multiple bullet wounds,
one hit my left lung, and one took out a piece of my liver.
One smashed my tibia to pieces. Burns, a skull fracture, brain
bleed. They lost me twice in the helicopter. Then six hours on
an operating table. The only ID they had for me was the tag
on the crewman's shirt I was wearing, so that's the name they
gave me. But it was only a matter of time before they figured
out the truth. So I discharged myself.'

'You were that badly fucked up, and you walked out?'

'There's a doc in the Hospital General who'll be retiring
early. He gave me a month's supply of morphine, antibiotics,
all the rest of the shit. Then he signed a death certificate. By
the time the Argentinian cops figured out I must have been
the guy flying the helicopter, the body had been cremated.
It just wasn't *my* body. Besides, it suited everyone for me to
be dead. The attack on the yacht, solved. The killing spree in
South Dakota, solved. Child abduction, solved. All that shit
that went down in New York, solved. The humiliation of the
GRU in Svalbard, solved. No awkward questions. Everything
tied up neatly with a big red bow.'

'And from there to here?'

'A soy-bean freighter to Grangemouth that didn't ask
too many questions. I spent most of it either delirious from
infections or high on morphine. But they had satellite
internet, which is how I found this place. I found the postcard
in the town where the ferry docks. I got the clerk in the post
office to write the address. I didn't know if I should send it. I
didn't know if you'd get it. I didn't know if you'd figure it out.

I didn't know, even if you figured it out, whether you'd come. But here you are.'

'Why the hell didn't you tell me what you were going to do?' she says.

'Because if you'd known I was going to be killed, you'd never have gone along with it.'

'I still don't understand why you thought you had to die.'

'If I hadn't taken the helicopter, they'd have caught up with you in minutes. But even if you got away, Hipkiss still had Deep Threat. There was always going to be a window of vulnerability before it got fixed. If she'd managed to deploy it, we'd have failed. And even if none of that was true . . .'

I have to pause for breath. My leg feels infected, and the antibiotics the doctor gave me ran out days ago. I wipe sweat away from my forehead with my sleeve.

'Even if none of that was true, *what*?'

'I had to do it for Mireille. So long as I was alive, she would always be my underbelly. The way people would get to me. So long as Seventeen was alive, the road to becoming Eighteen ran straight through her.'

'So you decided to kill him.'

I nod.

'Except you failed.'

'Ironic, isn't it?' I say. 'Number one hitman on the planet. The one person he can't kill is himself.'

Kat's hungry, so she pokes around in the mildewed cupboards, then looks over.

'You're out of food.'

'I know.'

She picks up the medicine bottles I've lined up on the shelf over the sink. They're all empty too.

'How do you get supplies?' she asks.

'I don't,' I say. 'No phone. No cell service, and I don't have one anyway. There's a bicycle, apparently, but I'm not in any state.'

'So what was your plan,' she says, 'if I didn't show up?'

'You heard of Corryvreckan?'

'Should I have?'

'It's a whirlpool, where two tides meet. George Orwell wrote *1984* near here, and nearly drowned there in a boat. It sounded as good a way to go as any.'

'You're serious?'

'If you weren't coming, I figured I might as well finish the job.'

'Holy shit,' she says. 'You sad fuck.'

It hurts to laugh, but I don't care because it's the first time I've laughed in a long time.

'Do you have even the slightest idea how angry I am with you?'

'I can guess.'

'The only reason I haven't punched you yet is it would be like kicking a puppy. The moment you recover halfway, I'm going to fuck you up.'

'I'm depending on it,' I say.

And I make it sound like a joke, but it isn't, not at all.

189

Kat sleeps next to me on the mattress in the downstairs bedroom. Piled under blankets with the stove door open for warmth, we listen to the rain hurtling down on the slate roof and the wind rattling the barn doors and windows.

The next day she sets off on the old boneshaker of a bicycle down the muddy track. Hours later, she returns with a basket and backpack full of supplies. She loads the stove full of wood, and we roast and consume an entire chicken, grease dripping down our chins as we eat the drumsticks with our fingers. She brings fresh bandages and helps me change dressings that haven't been changed in a week.

The next couple of days are unseasonably warm. The deer come close to the house, unafraid, while golden eagles wheel about riding thermals over the hills beyond.

'We could just stay like this forever,' says Kat, lying on her back in the grass, watching the clouds slide by. And I don't want to say it, but I can't stay silent.

'No,' I say. 'No, we can't.'

She sits up. 'What do you mean?'

'There are still too many loose ends. The doctor in Buenos Aires. The freighter. The postcard. The woman who wrote the address. The taxi that brought me here. The taxi that brought *you* here. It's enough.'

'Enough for what?'

'Enough for someone motivated enough to figure out that I'm alive. And that Mireille is how they draw me out.'

'Like who?'

'Anyone who wants to take my place. All the obvious candidates are dead now. That makes it an open field. All it takes is one. And this time, I'll have no idea who they are.'

'What are you saying?'

I hesitate, then pull the 9mm I bought from the freighter's first mate from my jacket.

I hand it to her by the squat barrel.

'When they find me, they'll search the house and find a letter explaining who I am and how I got here. This time there really will be no loose ends. Mireille will be safe, and you can get on with your life as if I never existed.'

Kat stares at the gun in her hand.

'You want me to *kill* you? Isn't it enough I watched you die once already? You send me a postcard, make me think you might be alive, drag me halfway across the fucking world and ask me to do it again for real because, why? You're too shit-scared to do it yourself? You're scared you'd fuck it up again? Or just to fucking torture me some more?'

'I needed to see if you'd come.'

'What for? Some macho power trip? Trying to prove you still have some hold over me? What?'

'You could have ignored the postcard,' I say. 'You could have thrown it away. You could have gone back to your life, to that asshole in Brooklyn, or wherever. You didn't have to come. But you did. Which means I have to give you the choice.'

'What the fuck are you talking about?'

'I said all the obvious candidates are dead. They're not.'

She's silent for a moment, reading me, trying to work out if I mean what she thinks.

'I asked you once before, remember? You said you'd give me an answer in the morning. But instead, you ran away.'

'Did it not occur to you that *was* my answer?'

'So how come you're here?' I say. 'How come you came with me to Svalbard? How come you didn't throw away the postcard? How come Staley's dead?'

'You think I want to be like *you*?'

'You're nothing like me. I killed people for reasons I didn't understand, or for money, or to lie about how big my dick was. That's not you. If it hadn't been for you, right now a religious lunatic would have her finger on the nuclear button. I'd be dead, most likely Mireille as well. And maybe a hell of a lot of other people. You didn't come here because of me. You came because it's who you are. Your whole life, you've been an arrow in flight, looking for a target. I'm just saying, maybe this is it.'

'And if I just walk away?'

'Then I'll do it myself.'

'And what if I don't do any of it? What if I just stay here with you?'

'Then one day you'll wake up before dawn and find I'm not in bed. And you'll think to yourself, it's okay, he's just gone to the bathroom. But then you'll hear the shot from the barn, and you'll know you were wrong.'

'Maybe I'll take your gun.'

'There's always Corryvreckan.'

She looks down. 'So all that stuff on the boat, things we saw in the water, all of that meant nothing at all?'

'Of course it did. But you don't love me, Kat. You told me as much in Svalbard. I think you recognised something in me that was already in you, but you didn't even know it was there. Or maybe you did and just didn't have a name for it.'

'And what about you?'

'I told you. It doesn't matter what I feel. All that matters now is what I do.'

Kat looks down at the gun. And I realise: *she's actually considering it.*

Then she looks up.

'When I said I was going to fuck you up, I didn't mean like this.'

'I know.'

'Although it's not like I haven't thought about it.'

'I know.'

We're simultaneously both laughing and both crying.

Then, abruptly and with perfect seriousness, she raises the gun and aims at my head.

The silence is intense. Just the soughing of the wind through the bracken and bog-cotton, the soft sigh of sea on shingle a mile away, the odd caw of a rook.

Her finger goes to the trigger. I see the hammer move backwards.

Her gaze is steady. I meet it.

Her green eyes were the first thing I noticed, and they will be the last thing I see on earth.

I'll take it.

190

The world of intelligence is abuzz.

Everybody wants to know who she is.

The girl with the red hair and blue eyes – or is it blue hair and green eyes? – who busked her way into an underworld casino on the outskirts of Buenos Aires, proceeded to take billionaire Edgar Staley to the cleaners at the roulette table, conned her way onto his megayacht, gathered an elite team to hack its security systems, killed him with a single shot to the forehead, broke into his sister's safe, stole the most valuable malware on earth, escaped with it, and then published it to save the world.

Rumour is, it's the same girl who a year ago bisected that alpha motherfucker Bernier with a chainsaw.

Rumour is, it's the same girl who tracked down one of the world's most elite hackers, confronted a Serbian war criminal, then escaped from an elite GRU unit by snowmobile in Svalbard, killing three of them in the process.

Rumour is, she's Sixteen's daughter.

Rumour is, that sucker Seventeen was so head-over-heels for her, he kamikazed a helicopter into the side of a ship just so she could get away.

Rumour is, she tracked him down to some spiderhole of a Scottish island where he fled to lick his wounds, and delivered the *coup de grâce* in person.

Nobody knows who she is.

But they all know what to call her.

Eighteen.

ACKNOWLEDGEMENTS

Assassin Eighteen is hardly a documentary, and I am entirely responsible for any errors, but many of the stories, places and incidents in the book are informed by real events and reporting.

In telling the story of Gracious and her escape from Boko Haram I used information sources including the US State Department, the Global Terrorism Index (maintained by the Institute for Economics and Peace), Amnesty International, the *Washington Post*, BBC News, NPR, Aljazeera and the Daily Beast.

I was also helped enormously by two non-fiction books: *A Gift From Darkness*, by the journalist Andrea Claudia Hoffmann and Boko Haram survivor Patience Ibrahim, which tells the story of a pregnant young Nigerian woman who endures horrors to save her unborn child after she is kidnapped by Boko Haram; and *A Different Kind of Daughter*, by Maria Toorpakai and Katherine Holstein, which tells the story of a girl from tribal Pakistan who cross-dresses as a boy in the frontier city of Peshawar to evade the Taliban (and rises to become the number one squash player in Pakistan!).

Deep Threat, the so-called zero-day exploit at the centre of the book, is my own invention and some of the technology has been simplified to make it more digestible to a general reader. However, much of the background, including the existential threat from malware and the back-room trade in exploits is drawn from NTY reporter Nicole Perlroth's astounding book *This Is How They Tell Me The World Ends*, along with the many computer security specialists I follow on Twitter. These include former high-end exploit broker and security researcher @thegrugq and grey-hat hacktivist @th3j35t3r, whose laptop now resides in the International Spy Museum in Washington, DC.

The paper Deep Threat is inspired by is real; *Reflections on Trusting Trust* was a Turing Award Lecture by one of the fathers of computer programming and a pioneer of computer science, Kenneth Thompson, who received the award – the so-called 'Nobel Prize of Computing' – in 1983, along with Dennis Ritchie. The backdoor attack described in the paper is known as the 'Ken Thompson Hack' or 'trusting trust attack' and the paper is considered a seminal work in computer security.

The descriptions of Longyearbyen and its environs are directly inspired by the wonderful photography of painter and photographer Elizabeth Bourne, the Director of the Spitsbergen Artists Center, who makes her home in Longyearbyen and has spent the last few years documenting the effects of climate change and the industrial truth of the high Arctic.

My thanks as always also goes to the amazing editorial team at Hodder and Stoughton, including but not limited to Jo Dickinson and Phoebe Morgan, along with my agent Oli Munson, whose input at the first draft stage was, as usual, enormously helpful and clarifying.

Finally, none of this would be possible without the continued, unstinting support of my family, including my wife Heather to whom this book is dedicated, and my three sons, all of whom patiently endured multiple telling's of this story as I slowly tried to untangle and re-tangle it.

Check out John Brownlow's first book . . .

AGENT SEVENTEEN

Call me Seventeen. I have no other name, not anymore.
Sixteen killers have done this job before me. Officially, I
don't exist, but every government uses me. I'm the most
feared hitman in the world.
But nobody gets to do this job for long. Because to be the
best, you must beat the best, and there are rivals on my tail.
**My days are numbered. But until then, it's one hell
of a ride.**